Crown of the Alchemist

THE MAN IN RED

B.G. LYRAX

TABLE OF CONTENTS

PROLOGUE

A WOLF, A LION, AND A HUMAN

I was not meant to be alive. Not like this, that is.

The lonely thoughts of a solemn warrior echoed louder than the cacophony of noise behind him as he planted one foot in front of the other, willing his body to carry him away from his fears and deeper into the night.

Tyrus Abbisard was a species known to the world of Tevus as a zoa: powerful beings enhanced by alchemy, born into this world with a bestial form and transmuted to become humanoid, forced to acclimate within the societal structure of mankind.

However, when men create a new type of being, they will always view themselves as superior to it.

Cobblestones turned to soft grasses underfoot as Tyrus distanced himself further, the physiology of his lupine heritage granting him speed and silence as he vanished into the woods that lined the kingdom he called home.

Tyrus was a wolf zoa in his young thirties, with long silver-gray hair and piercing amber eyes. Pointed ears swiveled atop his head as Tyrus drank in his surroundings, only slowing his pace once the noise behind him had finally subsided.

I seem to have lost my pursuant. Tyrus thought, satisfied.

In the wake of the wolf-man's footsteps, the Kingdom of Zenluve stood proud as the heart of the Deepwood. After the creation of zoa, mankind's oppression and cruelty towards these new second-rate citizens became the catalyst for a secret booming society of zoa, nestled in the only corner of Tevus that man could not reach and left only to fairytales.

A kingdom where zoa could be anything: a guildmaster, a king, or a humble warrior. Many consider such a place to be a safe haven, a blessing from the Deepwood itself.

Unfortunately, even a land governed by zoa cannot escape the shackles of society. These fetters that clasped invisibly around Tyrus' limbs bound him to a world that he had never resigned himself to live as a part of. A world of laws, duties, and oppression. A world that will never know the true depths of natural life. A world without freedom.

No man has ever asked an animal if they want to become like them. To men, it would be foolish to even think that a beast would want to live as anything other than human.

Tyrus took a deep breath, the comforting scents of the forest igniting his lungs. Taking in his surroundings, the wolf-man found himself in the center of a small clearing in the woods, marked by a single small boulder in the middle. This place was a common spot for Tyrus to find solace within, oftentimes bringing a whetstone to hone his sword while sitting atop that very boulder and enjoying the forest's welcoming arms.

My true home is here, alone. I never asked for any of this.

"Tyrus Abbisard, Sievtet of the Zengarde. What are you doing out here in a place like this? Don't you have duties within the

The Man in Red

castle?" A sudden voice jostled the wolf from his thoughts.

Looking up at the source of the comment, Tyrus locked eyes with a young lion zoa as she crouched on a branch above his head. The lioness jumped down, landing gracefully on her feet with a flick of her tail.

The young woman looked to be in her twenties, donning leather armor with white furs and a deep blue cloak. She had a thick mane of honey blonde hair and cold blue eyes. A large bow was slung over her shoulder, the bow's elegant gold plating revealing her high status.

Tyrus' eyes widened in recognition at her approach.

I-I didn't even sense her before she made herself known. My Seventh Sense should have noticed her ages ago. Is erasing her presence like this the ability of the legendary hunter herself?

Tyrus opened his mouth to explain himself, searching for an excuse as to why he had abandoned his duties as a Zengarde.

Every soul within the kingdom knew of the mighty Zengarde: Zenluve's ten strongest fighters who were sworn to protect each generation of royals for the last thousand years.

"Edelein von Luvemann," the woman introduced herself before he could speak, "Zenluve's best monster hunter. No more, no less. Though, I'm sure you need no introduction of me."

Right.

"You know, if you wear Zengarde colors out in the woods, someone is bound to recognize you," Edelein continued.

Tyrus looked down at his uniform, the deep green and gold hues betraying his status. His decorated armor was indicative of that of a high-ranked soldier, confirming Edelein's point.

"I do believe that Her Majesty the Queen was hosting a gala tonight in King Alderis' honor. Were you and the other Zengarde not stationed there?" Edelein asked, looking up at Tyrus as she stood close to him.

Even alone in the woods like this, Edelein has a powerful aura, Tyrus thought to himself, stepping away from her.

"May I ask what you are doing out here, then?" Tyrus choked out, trying to maintain a professional demeanor.

"Patrolling."

"Alone?"

"Jealous, are you?" Edelein laughed, shrugging her shoulder as she readjusted her bow.

"Being alone in the woods is dangerous," Tyrus warned.

She most likely knows these lands better than anyone else. Why am I telling her that? Tyrus realized in embarrassment.

"Says the man who is also alone in the woods. Sievtet Tyrus, we are not even outside of Zenluve's walls yet. The danger lurks in the Deepwood, not here," Edelein retorted. "Should I be reporting you to Ehret Zander for shirking your duties?"

"That would be unwise for both of us. Miss Edelein, I do find shame in leaving and I plan to return. I just needed some time away from the nobility."

Edelein grunted in agreement, sitting down with a huff on the large stone in the center of the clearing. "I hear that trade has been a popular subject within the zoa clans, lately."

"The guildmasters want to open our borders beyond our sparse allies, but the zoa clanheads are more apprehensive. Our population is growing, and we need to trade with more kingdoms throughout Avalstice if we want to have enough revenue to keep up with the growth," Tyrus commented, feeling exhausted from just thinking about such topics.

"King Alderis' gala, ruined by the ever-hungrier mouths of the everyman," Edelein sighed. "I don't blame you for stepping out. Do you want to sneak outside of the walls with me and kill a monster or two?"

"Quite," Tyrus agreed, helping Edelein up from the stone

she was sitting on.

One of Edelein's ears flicked backwards. Tyrus turned towards the same direction as the sound of footfall grew louder. The approaching steps were heavy and Tyrus' face dropped as soon as he recognized the pattern.

My pursuant appears to have finally caught up with me.

A human emerged from the underbrush, seeming a bit worse for wear as he put his hands on his knees and heaved for air. The young man had soft blonde hair collected in a small ponytail and he shut his silvery-blue eyes tightly as he tried to catch his breath.

"Tyrus... you damn zoa are too fast..." The man panted, standing up straighter and meeting Edelein's curious gaze with a look of surprise. "W-wait, are you–"

"The huntress, Edelein," Tyrus explained bluntly, interrupting the human.

"You are Aktet Cyzen," Edelein mused. "It seems several Zengarde have chosen to forsake their responsibilities at the gala this evening, then."

Cyzen was one of the only people that Tyrus would call a friend; a quiet warmth in the wolf zoa's life that reminded him of the first ray of sunlight after a cold winter storm. Ranked as the seventh and eighth members of the Zengarde, Tyrus and Cyzen spent much of their time paired together for duties.

Zenluve was a kingdom of zoa that found pride in welcoming all those who were outcast from the rest of the world. Thus, it was not uncommon for human, elf, fellborn, or other races to make their home within Zenluve's walls.

Cyzen, one of such humans, was a kind and approachable man, born and raised alongside his zoa friends. He was one of only two human Zengarde who, alongside one elf and one fellborn, made up the minority of the group. The other six members of the Zengarde were all zoa, a fairly common occurrence in their kingdom and throughout their history.

"I-I was trying to get Tyrus to come back!" Cyzen waved his hands in denial. "He just outran me, that's all. We will be heading back now–"

"We're hunting, Cyzen," Tyrus demanded. "Come."

The Aktet of the Zengarde sighed, defeated.

"Are you pulling rank?" The human asked.

"He is not. Let's say that I am," Edelein replied, laughing. "Come, Aktet Cyzen. The company of two Zengarde will be welcomed, although your uniforms make me look more like a royal rather than a hunter, and I must admit that I would not want to be mistaken as such."

"Right. Just… one moment, please. A word, Tyrus?" Cyzen pleaded, pulling his partner aside. "Tyrus, what the hell is going on here? What are you two doing?"

"Miss Edelein was out here on a hunt, and invited me to join. There's nothing unusual going on. We are going to head outside of the walls, take down a beast, and come back before anyone knows we're missing."

"Don't give me that, Sievtet Tyrus! Don't tell me that there's nothing unusual about this. I know her, and–"

"Surely your history with her won't be a problem, right?" Tyrus clapped a hand on his friend's shoulder.

Cyzen paused, letting out an unsteady breath as he nodded.

"Great," Tyrus confirmed, turning back to Edelein.

I understand Cyzen's concerns, to be honest. Everyone in the kingdom knows who that woman is, and the extensive history she carries. In a setting like this, she's the most wild and unpredictable of us all. After all, Edelein von Luvemann is–

Tyrus' thoughts were cut short by a sudden loud explosion resonating from the trees ahead. Hand flying to unsheathe his sword, he scanned the area for threats.

"What was that?" Tyrus growled.

"We aren't even outside of Zenluve yet. There shouldn't be anything within the walls," Edelein cautioned, reaching for her bow.

"It's probably just Alett testing some new technology." Cyzen laughed uneasily, Tyrus sparing a quick glance in his direction.

Alett, a horned owl zoa of the Zengarde, was known for tinkering with inventions that were often combustible in nature, so Cyzen's theory could hold truth to it.

Tyrus' ears perked up, facing directly forward as his senses registered a sudden, imminent danger ahead. In front of him, Edelein's ears had mimicked his own.

"Get down!" Tyrus and Edelein screamed in unison.

Tyrus strafed sideways to tackle Cyzen to the ground. Edelein dove into the dirt on her own with not even a moment to spare as a violet beam of energy shot out towards them from the woods.

"I don't think that's Alett!" Tyrus warned with an alarmed growl, helping Cyzen up while the two stayed low to the ground, ready to move.

Ahead of them, a colossal beast emerged from the shadows beyond the clearing where Tyrus' boulder sat. It stood bipedal, but hunched over with hulking muscles coated in an inky black skin that seemed to swirl like shadows. A grey head broke through its midnight flesh, purple eyes glowing as it stared down at them. The creature had a large mouth twisted into a cruel grin, mouth filled with long and sharp teeth. It dug large black claws into the ground beneath it and the purple eye on its chest began to glow brightly.

"Another blast incoming!" A new voice called out.

A tall elven man darted out from the shadows, long platinum hair flowing behind him as he bashed the beast across its face with the petrified ironwood hilt of his sword.

The elf was wearing dark blue armor with a deep violet cloak, the colors of a Zenluvian patrolman. These patrols were designated hunters that contained the local population of Deepwood beasts, deterring them from Zenluve's walls.

As his sword struck the monster, the next beam fired off aimlessly into the night sky. The inky black beast roared horrifically, pulling its claws from the ground and baring them, head swiveling in search of a target. It turned around, trying to locate the elf who had expertly vanished into the shadows of the woods.

I recognize that elf. He is Thanis Wakeleaf, one of the patrol captains. We worked together briefly before I joined the Zengarde. If he's here, his patrol must be nearby as well. Tyrus stepped in front of Edelein and Cyzen protectively.

A swift movement alerted the beast as Thanis darted in from the shadows, sword drawn. The beast swiped at him, the elf sliding under its claws to slash at the ankles of the creature. The second hand of the beast connected with Thanis' body, a heavy thud sounding as he tumbled backwards.

"Alex, Jera, now!" Thanis commanded, pushing himself up from the ground.

Two more soldiers leapt into the fray, pulling the creature's attention away from Thanis. The human, Alex, was a young man with dark hair and darker eyes against pale white skin, while Jera was a female heron zoa with achromatic feathers in her hair. Jera twisted her body to throw a large spear forward, the weapon lodging into the skin of the monster's chest. It seemed unbothered by the puncture as it turned on Jera, hungry for blood. Approaching, it grabbed the heron's impaled weapon and tossed it aside.

"I've got your spear!" A dark-skinned human cried, dashing out from behind the beast. "Get back, Jera! I'll toss it!"

"Thanks, Nolan!" Jera replied, readying herself.

The Man in Red

The fourth member of the patrol, Nolan, darted underneath the creature, leaping over its foot and tumbling to catch the spear. As the monster lifted a fist, Alex's shield intercepted it before it could reach Jera's skull.

A loud crack sounded as Alex pushed the monster's arm away, his shield groaning under the pressure before snapping in two. Eyes wide, he stared down at his broken shield.

"It broke my shield? This… *thing* is stronger than petrified ironwood?" Alex muttered, astonished.

"Jera, catch!" Nolan's voice snapped Alex to attention as his fellow patrolman prepared to throw Jera's spear into the air.

"Alex, give me a boost, bud!" Jera commanded her human ally. In an instant, Alex locked his hands together. Jera stepped and as he lifted her, the momentum carried her up to catch the thrown spear and drive it into the neck of the beast.

The creature roared, knocking her down to the ground. At the same moment, Tyrus boosted himself up on the same boulder that brought him serenity, to climb the back of the monster and lock himself around its neck, sword pressed against its throat. The creature thrashed as Tyrus tried to sever its head. Tyrus let out a strained yell as the creature threw Tyrus off of its back after only a moment's struggle.

"What the hell *is* this thing?" Nolan asked, glancing at Thanis, who was bleeding heavily from a wound on his head. "It's taking our hits like they're nothing!"

"I have been alive for three hundred years, every single one of which has been spent in this land. I can confirm that I have never, *ever* laid eyes on such a beast," Thanis responded, wiping blood from his forehead. "If it were a native species, we would have felled it by now, so it must be invasive. However, it does not even appear to be from our world at all, much less the Deepwood. That is where my understanding falters."

"I share similar concerns, as well," Edelein added as the patrol turned to her in surprise. "I'm trying to read it so I can come up with a plan that doesn't involve me running out of arrows. Know thy enemy, men."

"We could definitely use a few of those legendary arrows," Thanis replied, ignoring the screaming pain of his wounds as he brandished his blade once more.

"It is not the arrows that are legendary; I am," Edelein retorted, a strong arm grabbing a low-hanging branch as she lifted herself up, vanishing into the foliage above.

"We have the aid of Zenluve's legendary monster hunter and two of the noble Zengarde. Be brave, you three," Thanis instructed his patrol.

Pushing past Thanis to the front of the group, Tyrus bared sharp fangs as he growled his assurance. "This wretched shadow beast does not belong in the Deepwood, that is for certain. You four may be patrolmen, but I am a Zengarde, sworn to protect our people. If a monster such as this made it inside of the walls, we must fight to protect our kingdom until our last breath."

Cyzen and the patrollers fell into formation behind Tyrus. The wolf zoa's sword caught a glimmer of moonlight through a clearing in the trees. Fearless, Tyrus pointed his blade forward towards the unknown creature, his golden eyes cold and determined.

"Stay strong and follow my lead. I will strike at the shadow beast's eyes and create an opening for you while it is blinded," Tyrus commanded, the others nodding silently in agreement.

Bracing his legs, Tyrus dashed forward towards the monster, leaping with every ounce of energy within him.

"Glory to Zenluve!" the Zengarde warrior screamed, twisting his body and slashing across the creature's face with every ounce of strength his body could muster.

10

The Man in Red

Time slowed as metallic shards seemed to hover in the air around Tyrus. Looking down at the hilt of his sword, his eyes were greeted by nothing but a short scrap of metal where his weapon should have been. Fragments of his blade dropped to the ground in slow-motion as the realization hit him.

My sword... broke?

Memories of endless evenings spent honing and caring for the blade flashed before the wolf-man's eyes, from the day he was first gifted it until the exact moment that it shattered into pieces around him.

What is this thing made of...? Tyrus wondered, his eyes slowly turning to meet the mortified gaze of Cyzen, whose face was twisted in the terror of a silent scream as he ran towards his ally, arm outstretched.

A heavy thump connected with Tyrus' midsection, bringing him back to reality for one last fleeting moment as the shadow beast's clawed hand pierced through the Zengarde's armor, smacking him away as if he were an insect. There was a loud snap as he was flung against an ironwood tree, his blood leaving a large stain on the wood where his head had been smashed as he slumped to the ground, lifeless.

"Tyrus…!" Cyzen choked out, turning towards the body of his friend. Sensing the opportunity, the creature moved as quick as lightning, seeming to appear out of nowhere from behind Cyzen with the same wicked grin as its jagged teeth tore into Cyzen's body.

Blood spurted as the unknown monster flung Cyzen's maimed body onto a familiar large stone, the comfort of Tyrus' solitude, stained red with the death of his only friend.

The patrolmen looked on at the scene in icy terror, the sudden realization washing over them that the beast had been toying with their lives the entire time.

"That thing just killed two Zengarde like it was nothing.

Crown of the Alchemist

It's smashing our weapons and tearing through our armor as if it were child's play. We can't win this…!" Jera gasped, tears forming in her eyes.

"Sh-should we fall back?" Nolan turned to look at her, his anxious sweat making his skin feel clammy.

A quick light flashed accompanied by a sharp whistle behind the shattered patrol. An arrow flickered in the moonlight just before landing directly in the center of the eye on the creature's chest. The beast let out a loud roar of agony as it stumbled backwards, searching for the source of the attack.

"That's more like it," Edelein muttered, drawing a second shot. "Look at me, foul beast."

As the monster faltered, Jera turned to Alex, panic flashing in her eyes.

"Alex, now's our chance! We can still escape with our lives if she distracts it long enough. Let's go."

"Are you insane?!" Alex replied, looking at her. "We can *not* just leave her here alone! That's a violation of our duties. We never abandon posts!"

I can't hear what they're squabbling about down there, and I can't afford to focus on that. Edelein thought, lining up her shot. *The monster will likely try to capitalize on their distraction. My best bet is to predict its movement and try to pierce it in the same spot. My first arrow managed to lodge itself, but I will need to hit it the same exact way in order to pierce through and kill this thing. A near-impossible task, or everyone dies. No pressure.*

Cautiously, Edelein lined up her arrow to land right behind the two patrolmen, waiting for the right moment to strike.

It previously utilized Cyzen's hysteria to execute a warp-stepping move behind him, and I theorize that it will be likely to do it again. From my distance, I cannot confirm if the Zengarde are dead or unconscious. If they are alive, they are bleeding out quickly and will not last long without a healer. Either way, nothing will matter if I miss this shot.

The lioness' back muscles screamed as she held her position, bow fully drawn. She counted the seconds in her head as Thanis and Nolan bought time with the beast, her eyes trained on her target.

Shoving the other patrolmen aside, the monster locked eyes on Jera and Alex, grinning as it vanished into the darkness.

"Right… now." Edelein released her arrow as it zipped towards nothing.

In an instant, the beast appeared behind Jera and Alex, poised to strike before stumbling backwards as the second arrow struck the first one, splitting it in half and piercing through the creature's chest.

Black matter spilled out from behind it, the monster throwing its head back with a loud, pained screech as violet cracks began to form across its body. An unfamiliar energy hissed and spilled from it as bright beams of light shot out from each opening, the creature flailing in agony.

In a heartbeat, Edelein's face dropped as she realized the situation in front of her.

"Get away from it!" she screamed down at the others, a moment too late as bright light filled the clearing, radiating from the beast.

The hunter closed her eyes tightly, anticipating the worst as light blinded her vision and a loud whine filled her sensitive ears. The moment lasted only a single second before the burning light faded and the noises subsided. As silence fell over the forest once more, she dared to open her eyes and drink in the scene in front of her.

Everything on the ground in front of Edelein was annihilated, little to nothing remaining. The clearing, once full of wild grasses, was burned into a purplish dust. What was left of the trees were blackened and dead, and nothing remained of the life once there.

"No!" Edelein gasped, dropping down from the tree she stood on. She tossed her bow aside, dashing forward and falling to her knees.

In front of her, six spots of black matter stained the ground where the team had once stood. There were no remains, but the hunter could immediately recognize the position of each lifeless splotch as the location of each of her allies. Her hands shook as she reached towards one of the puddles, before withdrawing and clutching her hands to her chest.

"There's... nothing even left of them." Tears threatened to spill from her distraught eyes as the weight of her sin filled her soul with crippling guilt. "I meant to protect them, yet I... I did this. This is all my fault!"

Edelein cried out into the lifeless night, pouring her fears and agony out against the forest that she called home.

As the young woman wailed, the woods met her cries with silence, the land abandoning the lone survivor to succumb to her shame.

One thought echoed in Edelein's mind as she wiped away the stinging tears, sniffling pathetically as she tried to compose herself.

Everyone is dead because of me.

CHAPTER 1

CORVID ATHENAEUM

A whistling kettle accompanied quiet birdsong as the Keeper of the Athenaeum prepared loose tea leaves for his morning routine. The kitchen was large and open, with arching windows pouring light from the sunrise onto cold marble countertops.

The morning was peaceful and calm, birdsong echoing faintly through the windows of the old, large estate. This building, known as the Corvid Athenaeum, housed a large library dating back generations and served as a school for brilliant young minds seeking a future with alchemical studies.

Steam filled the air as he poured his tea, aromatic and pleasant. The man, silent and gentle, lifted his teacup and continued on his way to the second step of his routine. Stopping in front of a vast expanse of old leather-bound books, his golden eyes scoured each title as he searched for a text that would suit his mood.

Most books within the Athenaeum had already been read by its keeper, but he found comfort in sifting through old stories and re-reading old studies, ever in pursuit of a new perspective.

The keeper stopped as his eyes landed on one book, *The Complete Works of Arvien Marleogne*. His free hand stopped on the book's spine, and he could feel a nostalgic energy as he touched it, even through the black gloves he wore. Picking the book off of the shelf, the man continued on towards his office.

His eyes briefly darted downwards at the book as he walked, a nonfiction dating all of the research of Tevus' most accomplished alchemist.

"Arvien." He breathed quietly, lost in thought. His voice was deep and smooth, a voice befitting of the man's tall, broad frame.

Passing by a large hourglass that had gathered a thick layer of dust, the Corvid Athenaeum's keeper set his tea down on his desk, steam still rising from the cup as he sat in an antique green office chair.

The sun illuminated the edges of his book from the window behind him, reflecting off of tiny dust particles that seemed suspended in space. A gloved hand idly fidgeted with the cover of the book as he opened it to a bookmarked page.

Not a moment had passed before a loud slam alerted the Keeper of the Athenaeum. Identifying the source of the noise as his office door being slammed open, his eyes met one of his students: a sharply dressed twenty-three-year-old human named Luthro Apocathra. Luthro, the Athenaeum's top student, was incredibly intelligent, put-together, and likely to be its eventual successor.

"Master Marleogne!" Luthro bowed, black-and-green hair falling in front of his round glasses as he dipped his head towards the floor, apologetic.

"Luthro. I thought I made it clear that I was not to be disturbed this early in the morning." the Master spoke curtly, slamming his book shut in irritation.

The Man in Red

"My apologies, but this is important. Jana was cleaning up this morning and found a letter that had fallen behind one of the bookshelves. The seal is from the Society of Alchemists, and the date on the envelope is from four months ago."

"Four months?" His eyebrow twitched, the slight movement a signal of the keeper's brief but intense distress. Suppressing his shock, he continued, "Please give it to me. I'll have a look at it."

Luthro nodded, producing the letter from the pocket of his dark green vest. He handed it over to his master, and left with another quick and apologetic bow.

Looking down at the envelope in his hand, all that was written on it was the date and the Master's name: *Gihon Marleogne, Dirigent of Ravencroft.*

Gihon, a thirty-year-old raven zoa, inherited the Corvid Athenaeum upon the death of his master, Arvien Marleogne. Arvien, the woman who created him, served as the former Dirigent of Ravencroft as well as being the Athenaeum's previous keeper. After her death, electing Gihon as the new Dirigent was an easy choice for the Society of Alchemists as Arvien's legacy continued to spread across the continent.

The position of a Dirigent was earned through hard work, devoted research, and tests from the Society. Every city-state housed one Dirigent each all across the continent of Caandemium, with Ravencroft being the one Gihon called home. The Dirigents worked together as the highest level of political status within Caandemium, meeting for summits to discuss global issues.

Caandemium, a primarily meritocratic continent, had established the Society of Alchemists to rule alongside the Church of Prima Luma to further develop their technology and innovation through alchemy, causing a revolution in technological steam-based development. The other continents of Tevus remained traditionalists, prioritizing culture over innovation.

Gihon was well-known throughout the Society as the son of Arvien and a talented alchemist himself. He had an affinity for defense-based alchemy and was built in a way that reflected this preference, with broad shoulders that could easily take hits in battle. He wore black pants and a white dress shirt, with sleeves rolled up to his elbows and the top few buttons left open to reveal his sturdy chest. The outfit was pulled together by a dark green vest and a single feather earring on his left side. Gihon was known to be a stoic man. His only form of creative expression: a single streak of hair dyed teal across his jet-black bangs.

Cutting through the Society's wax seal, Gihon read through the letter silently, eyes growing wide as he began to understand the contents of the message. Standing up abruptly, the Dirigent hurried out of the room, abandoning his book and tea, knowing his peaceful morning was doomed to end early.

Downstairs, two more students chatted together in a lounge. Jana Hearts, the twenty-year-old fellborn who had found the letter, made casual conversation with a human. Spira Vensworth, a tall twenty-three-year-old human with dark skin and star-shaped sunglasses resting low on the bridge of her nose, was a master of alchemical hardlight weaponry, summoning weapons made of tangible light. Her white shirt had no sleeves, and was tucked into bold yellow pants. Jana, a petite girl with light grey-violet skin and small horns, was a fellborn: a race known to be the descendants of the plane-shifting warriors who traveled across realms that were only a fantasy to the average man. The fellborn wore a feminine suit set with a pencil skirt, in the same dark green of the Athenaeum's other members. Jana, ever eager to please her teacher, leaned into a defensive alchemy similar to Gihon's, making her a powerful ally to Spira's heavy striking style.

Footsteps silenced the two girls, both of them turning to

address Gihon as he hurried past them.

"Master Marleogne, good morning!" Jana greeted him with a smile.

"Good morning, Master Gihon," Spira chimed.

"Good morning, you two," Gihon stopped in front of them briefly. "Please go fetch anyone that is currently present in the Athenaeum. Meet me in the lecture hall in five minutes or less."

Without waiting for a response, Gihon turned and continued onwards, lost in thought as his mind raced, worrying about the letter he received.

"This is going to be an issue," Gihon sighed to himself as he walked into the lecture hall.

Four students sat themselves in an otherwise empty classroom, silence weighing heavily in the air around them. Luthro's pocket watch was the only thing audible in the room, ticking quietly in his hand as he stared down at it anxiously.

"Master Gihon seemed upset," Jana whispered, the fellborn nervously playing with her hands. "Do you think it's because I found that letter from the Society?"

"He wouldn't be upset that you found it, but that it was lost," Spira corrected, seeming to be rather unbothered by the situation.

Jana looked at her, and then to Luthro.

"He isn't mad at you, Jana," Luthro assured her, picking up on her facial expressions. "There's probably just something in the letter itself that is bothering him."

"Or he's mad that you bugged him at seven in the

morning," Spira snickered. "You know that Master Gihon prefers to have his early alone time, so he can read."

"He reads all the time, anyway, so what's the difference?" a new voice piped in, coming from a redheaded fox zoa that sat perched on top of a desk. The twenty-four-year-old had a carefree appearance, with a loosened tie and unbuttoned vest, and shaggy ginger hair half-tied up.

"What would you know, Mandus?" Jana retorted, furrowing her eyebrows. "I've never seen you read a book in your life. How are you even in the same class as us?"

"Just a testament to how little reading actually makes a difference. Plus, I have my alchemy textbooks, like the rest of you!"

"You draw in them all day. I've watched you."

"No, I'm with Jana on this one," Luthro sighed. "We work alchemy, which is a very science-and-intellect based system. We use knowledge in combat. I don't know how you're here, either."

"In Mandus' defense, he is phenomenal on the battlefield," Spira nodded, as the fox-boy perked up happily.

"Thank you, great and mighty Spira, warrior of light! Your presence shall be remembered and your life celebrated for all of history."

"Yeah, yeah," Spira waved her hand at him dismissively. "Credit where credit is due, or something. Don't let it go to your head."

"So, what do you think the letter was about?" Jana asked after a beat of silence, mind clearly still elsewhere. "Gihon summoned us here to discuss it, right?"

"Maybe it's about the Dirigent of Velkhamore. He just died, didn't he? Maybe the Society tried to summon Gihon to decide on a new Dirigent," Luthro suggested.

"Do you think he had endorsed anyone, though? Gihon's kind of a recluse. I don't know if any new prospective Dirigents would seek out Gihon's endorsement over some of the more approachable ones," Spira pointed out, leaning back in her chair.

Luthro leaned forward, hand to his chin in thought. "You're right, Spira. Plus, knowing Master Marleogne, I'm sure the trials he would give to a new Dirigent would be particularly challenging."

Mandus raised an eyebrow, looking at Luthro. "You seem excited about the idea of a challenge. Would you try to get Gihon to endorse you for a Dirigent position, one day?"

"Of course," Luthro laughed, "I could handle a trial from Master Marleogne. I would make an excellent Dirigent."

"Remind me when you do, so I can be sure to never visit that city. I don't want to be anywhere that's being governed by the notorious Luthro Apocathra, king of the poindexters."

Luthro glared at the fox-boy, and Mandus laughed, knowing in his mind that he won the diss-battle that he was the only participant of.

"I think you'd be a great Dirigent, Luthro," Jana smiled, "you're so similar to Master Gihon… any city would be lucky to have someone like you."

"Someone like Luthro, or someone like Gihon?" Spira questioned.

"What's the difference?" quipped Mandus, much to Luthro's disdain. "You look and act like a tiny little Gihon."

"Ravencroft became so much better once Gihon took over as Dirigent," Jana continued, oblivious to her peers. "He's smart, kind, and great in battle. The quality of life here is incredible. If Luthro could do that for another city, that city would be better off, too."

Luthro smiled softly, grateful for her words.

Standing up, Mandus peered at Luthro's watch.

"Gihon's taking a while, so I'm going to run out to get a bite from the kitchen." The fox-boy saluted casually, dashing out of the room.

A few seconds after Mandus left and the room returned to a peaceful silence, Gihon entered the room, letter in hand. Luthro snickered under his breath, Jana sighing as Gihon looked at the three of them.

"Where is Mandus?" the teacher asked, exasperated.

"He was here. He'll be back in a second," Spira insisted.

Uncomfortable silence settled over everyone as Gihon eyed the door. Arms crossed, he leaned against his desk at the front of the room while Luthro pulled out his pocket watch again, counting the seconds.

Rapid footsteps drew everyone's attention. Mandus returned, immediately realizing his mistake in leaving.

"You know, for a speed-based alchemist, you are incredibly subpar at time management," Luthro sighed, putting away his pocket watch.

"Oh, come on!" Mandus stomped a foot dramatically as he jumped up to sit on top of a desk by the others. "You know that I can't use my alchemy in the Athenaeum. There's too many turns, and my speed array only works in straight lines. Otherwise, I'd just run into the walls."

"Why don't you just sustain a bulwark array at the same time?" Spira asked, tilting her head. "You'd be able to manage higher speeds and break through a few walls without getting hurt."

Jana gasped at Spira's words, the thought of damaging the Athenaeum making her skin crawl.

"Maintaining two arrays at once is hard! I don't even

have bulwark written into my array, either. Bulwark is better left to sentinels like Gihon and Jana," Mandus fretted with a dejected sigh. "In a battle of mass, I will always be the loser."

"You're already a loser, if that helps," Luthro retorted.

Gihon cleared his throat expectantly, and the boys quieted down as their teacher began to speak.

"Thank you for joining me on such short notice. I have an urgent update from the Society of Alchemists that I must share with you all."

Gihon slammed the letter down on his desk, in a stern manner.

"The phantasm outbreaks have spread beyond Caandemium. There are numerous reports of backlashes occurring in Avalstice, and our allies in the west are horrendously under-equipped to handle the situation."

"Do we... *have* allies in the west?" Spira asked.

"A few. There's the trade port Bethamal, as well as Karribash and Tardonia, but those two have had some tensions lately, and I'm not sure which side we're taking there," Jana recalled pensively.

"Jana is correct," Gihon continued, "but that's for another time. Karribash and Tardonia's territorial spats have to wait for now, because a bigger issue is at hand. The phantasms have reached the Deepwood, and have managed to penetrate the defenses of the Kingdom of Zenluve."

The students clamored amongst themselves, curious. Of the four, Mandus perked up, his fox tail thumping excitedly against the desk he sat on.

"The Kingdom of Zenluve? That's a real place? Master Gihon, tell me right now that this is your attempt at humor, or I'm going to freak out." Mandus grinned, blue eyes sparkling with excitement.

"You've heard of it?" Luthro asked. "It's rare that you'd know something the rest of us don't."

"Yeah, I've never heard of Zenluve." Spira agreed.

"The name sounds familiar, but I don't think our books really talk about Zenluve," Jana nodded, flipping through a textbook as she spoke.

"Zenluve is a legend to zoafolk. My mom used to tell me about it at bedtime as a kid. Honestly, I thought it was a fairytale this whole time. She said it's a secret kingdom run entirely by zoa, being led by generations of these legendary Lion Kings dating back a thousand years. They hide away in the Deepwood and live peacefully in the forest."

"That is… quite accurate, actually." Gihon agreed in surprise, continuing. "Zenluve is a kingdom run by zoa, yes. For a thousand years, they've remained elusive, hidden away in the heart of the most wild, untamed forest in our world. The Deepwood, as you all know, is widely regarded as uninhabitable. It is a gold mine of natural riches, but those who enter with the intention of harvesting it do not make it out alive. No one dares to enter, and the Zenluvians rarely leave. Because of this, they have never made contact with any nation outside of Avalstice, and their relations with the other Avalstan kingdoms are rocky at best. Now, phantasms have shown up within their borders and driven them out of their previous reclusiveness."

"Why don't the Zenluvians just use banishing arrays? Phantasms are tough to fight against, but banishing them isn't too hard." Jana asked, tilting her head with a finger to her chin.

"No one in Avalstice practices modern alchemy the way that we do. Zoa transfiguration is the only recognized use of alchemy in Zenluve, so I theorize that they do not know how to weaponize alchemy in their fight."

"How do you know about all of this, Master Gihon?" Spira

pressed curiously, staring straight ahead.

"The Queen of Zenluve wrote a correspondence to the Society of Alchemists, requesting aid in their quest to rid their land of phantasms."

Luthro pushed up his glasses as he questioned, "If the Zenluvians have never made contact with us before, how are they able to do it now?"

"That part I am unsure of. Alchemists are incredibly rare in Avalstice, so how she knew that the solution to their issue was rooted in alchemy is beyond me. I will have to ask her."

"Wait, you get to talk to her?" Mandus asked, perking up again.

"She's coming to Caandemium. Well, according to this letter from the Society, the Queen said she is sending the Throne's top soldiers to receive alchemical training, and she will personally be overseeing it herself. Because she is a zoa, the Society has asked me to act as an ambassador for her entourage during their stay. They hope that her seeing a zoa in a position of power will ease her nerves about making contact, and establish trade routes with Caandemium. That being said, I must return to Velkhamore at once."

"Wait, you're going right now?" Spira's eyebrows furrowed. "Isn't it all a bit sudden?"

"According to the letter that the Society sent, the Queen and her entourage expect to arrive on the fourth day of the month of Al-Nadi."

"Which is… today." Spira's voice drifted off in realization.

"So you're leaving the Athenaeum? Are we in charge until you get back?" Mandus grinned, tail thumping again.

"Not 'we'," Gihon stared at the fox, his narrow golden eyes stern. "Luthro will be in charge. Resume your studies independently until I return."

"With all due respect, Master Gihon, I would *very* much rather go with you," Mandus pleaded, sighing as Gihon shook his head in denial.

"When will you be returning, then?" Luthro asked, trying to mask his eager excitement to run the Athenaeum in Gihon's absence.

"I cannot say for sure, but teaching a crash-course in alchemy basics to a group of highly trained fighters should not take more than a week. With that being said, I must head out at once. The Society of Alchemists would fall apart entirely if I missed the arrival of the Zenluvians."

Grabbing his cloak from a rack by the door, Gihon continued to speak without looking back.

"Please be more mindful when handling my mail next time. Ignoring a summons of this significance from the Society reflects poorly on all of us. You are dismissed."

Gihon sat alone at the back of a train car, leaning against the window to take in the passing scenery, lost in thought. Velkhamore was a major city, one of the largest in Caandemium, and home to the Society of Alchemists' main headquarters. The train between the city and Gihon's hometown of Ravencroft was a few hours' ride, and a scenic one as the train passed through wide expanses of open farmlands and quaint towns.

Passing through the outskirts of the city, the raven zoa knew his stop would be soon, yet his thoughts continued to race.

The situation in Zenluve must be incredibly dire if they have resorted to seeking foreign aid. It takes a lot to bring a hidden

The Man in Red

society out of hiding.

If my knowledge is correct, the military of Zenluve is known for an elite team of the ten strongest fighters in the Kingdom. These ten are gathered to serve as the Royal Family's personal lap-dogs... Meeting such a team will prove to be insightful for myself as well.

And the Queen... I wonder what she is like. A society run entirely by zoa has probably given her a very different perspective on life. Choosing to personally accompany the entourage shows her willingness to be involved firsthand, or perhaps her lack of trust. I suppose we shall see.

A voice from the announcement system jolted Gihon back into the present as the train screeched to a stop.

"Velkhamore: Grand Bazaar. The train is now stopping." The voice repeated as Gihon rose to his feet, grabbing his trunk.

The Society's Headquarters are a short walk from the Bazaar, so I can stop there to pick up a gift for Her Majesty on my way over. If Torphus really is the one in charge, as had been detailed in his letter, it's likely that the gifts he's chosen for her are going to be alchemical tomes, and we need to ensure that there's something for the Queen that she would actually enjoy.

Stepping off of the train, the Dirigent of Ravencroft was greeted by the sounds, sights, and smells of the familiar city of Velkhamore. Food stalls wafted warm scents of various snacks as people chattered and bustled around him, each one on a sojourn of their own.

As a dirigent, Gihon has spent many days of his life in the city, though he preferred the quiet of his humble hometown. Velkhamore was of second nature to him, shown by how effortlessly he navigated himself through the Bazaar in search of a gift befitting of the Queen.

The Grand Bazaar was Velkhamore's greatest treasure: a pinnacle of tourism, and a major part of the city-state's revenue.

Crown of the Alchemist

Kiosks filled with textiles, jewels, and artisan woodcrafts were lined up in the open-air plaza; with stalls of food, drink, and alchemical trinkets scattered throughout them. Tourists marveled at the sights around them, pointing at items that caught their eyes with delight.

Working his way through the crowd, Gihon found himself stopping in front of a stall filled with a variety of jewelry, ranging from delicate stud earrings to opulent gold necklaces. Stones of every type glimmered in the afternoon sun, rubies and sapphires aglow.

"Finest stones in Tevus!" the seller, a stout dwarven man, hollered as Gihon approached. "Gems and jewels from Avalstice to Shuxing!"

Looking up at Gihon, the dwarf pointed at him, continuing. "You, sir! You look like you've got a good eye, eh?"

"I am looking for a gift. I need something for… a very opulent woman."

"Ohh," the dwarf mused, grinning as he rubbed his beard. "Shopping for yer special lady, are we? Well, I've got just the thing."

Gihon opened his mouth, as if to correct him, but stopped as the dwarf produced an elegant box, opening the lid to reveal a crystal bangle with a bright blue-violet hue.

"This 'un's the elusive leyline crystal, from Avalstice. Said to bring good luck and wealth to anyone who wears it, it does. Surely a good gift for the lovely lady in yer life, eh?" he chuckled, as Gihon peered into the box curiously.

Leyline crystals. How did he get his hands on this? Even I've never seen one before, not in person like this. I have heard rumors about the stone's auspicious nature. Is it… authentic?

"Leyline crystals, is that right?" A new voice caught Gihon's attention as a woman spoke up from behind him.

Turning around, his inquisitive eyes locked onto a zoa girl, ears protruding slightly from underneath the hood of a dark blue cloak. Her face was shadowed and hard to make out, but from what he could tell, she was rather lovely, with soft pale skin and piercing blue eyes peeking out through her sideswept blonde bangs. A light streak embellished the right side of her hair, a single soft highlight against sandy blonde locks.

Brushing past Gihon, the girl continued, addressing the jewelry peddler. "Do you have any real crystals, or just the fake one? I am quite curious."

Turning beet-red, the peddling dwarf pointed a grubby finger at her, looking ready to blow a gasket.

"Don't you go accusin' me of lyin' about my wares, lady! These are as real as they come. Paid a handsome sum for them, I did!"

Instinctively, Gihon stepped between the dwarf and the zoa in an attempt to intervene, but the girl pushed forward to face the dwarf herself.

"No one here knows if leyline crystals are even real, or just an Avalstan myth. If they were, they certainly wouldn't be granting fortune to wearers in the way you describe. It's a rock, for heaven's sake, not a magic artifact."

Sensing the anger from the seller, the girl pivoted as she delicately picked up a necklace adorned with a large sapphire set in gold, a choker made of black felt.

"This sapphire you have is marvelous. Forget the Leyline crystal. A stone of this size and clarity is easily the nicest gem in this entire market. If this gentleman is seeking a gift for his girlfriend, I would gladly recommend this one instead."

"You must have an eye for jewelry, miss," Gihon nodded in agreement, taking the necklace from her hand and passing it to the dwarf. "Admittedly, gemstone appraisal is not my specialty. I have many dwarven friends up north by the mountains, so I have never needed to learn such a skill. I'll take this one, then. Please prepare this for me in your nicest gift box, good sir."

As the seller took the necklace and grumbled under his breath, Gihon turned to address the girl. "Miss, you're a zoa, aren't you? I am too. What is your name?"

"You're a zoa?" she asked, looking him up and down. "You look so... human. You don't have any animal features. No ears, no feathers, and I doubt there's a tail under that cloak, right?"

Gihon laughed, caught off guard by her answer. "No, no tail. Though it seems that *you* do."

"What?" the girl cried out, flustered. "You don't know that. I have a cloak on, too."

"Your tail is... wagging, for lack of a better term," he chuckled, gesturing behind her. She turned over her shoulder to see a slight protrusion from her tail underneath the cloak, moving back-and-forth to betray her eager heart.

Is this the same girl who just stood up so confidently to that peddler a minute ago? She seems so... shy, now. Did I embarrass her? Gihon wondered.

Eyes wide, she forced her tail to still itself, flustered. "O-okay, fine, yeah. I have a tail, because I'm a zoa. But what about you? How am I supposed to believe you're a zoa? All you have is a little feather earring, but something tells me you weren't born with that."

"I wasn't born like this at all. I was hatched many years ago, and transmuted into a zoa. You're a natural-born zoa? Those are somewhat rare around here."

Their eyes locked for a moment, silent.

"Anyways, your name, miss?"

"Oh, it's–"

A cry from the sea of passersby caught her attention.

"EDDIE!" a young man called out, meeting her gaze.

The Man in Red

Her face dropped as the boy ran over to her, taking her arm. He wore a dark green cloak with thick octagonal glasses framing large yellow-orange eyes. His hair was a rusty caramel color, the underside of which was dark brown with streaks of white running through his bangs. Most notably, feathered plumicorns quivered excitedly on top of his head, proudly showcasing his status as an owl zoa. He appeared to be young; no more than eighteen.

"There you are, Eddie. You can't run off like that, you know?" the boy said, grabbing onto the woman's arm.

The girl, Eddie, turned to face Gihon, a look of disappointment on her face. "That's my cue to leave, unfortunately. Best of luck with your special lady, zoa boy. It was a pleasure to meet you, though I doubt our paths will cross again."

Blissfully ignorant of the situation, the owl-boy looked at the dark-haired man with his large and curious eyes. "No way! You're a zoa, too? You don't look like us at all. No furry features, and yet you carry yourself like an avian. Why don't you have feathers?"

"You can't just ask someone why they don't have feathers," the woman reprimanded her young companion. "Come, Alett… let's head back to the carriage before Zander gives us another earful." She turned with an irked flick of her tail.

'Carriage' is a bit of an antiquated word. Is she talking about an autowagon, or is she actually referring to a horse-drawn carriage? They must be tourists from a small town, Gihon thought, glancing down at the gold-plated pocket watch he pulled out from underneath his cloak.

I spent more time talking to the zoa girl than I realized. I need to leave now to arrive at the Society's headquarters before the Zenluvians, the Dirigent realized, centering his mind as he began to focus on his work once more.

"It was a pleasure making your acquaintance, Miss Eddie."

Gihon bid his farewell to the feline, not looking up as he returned his watch to his pocket.

Shock resonated through the zoa girl's body as she whipped around to face him, appalled. Gihon glanced up at her, meeting the zoa's glare with confusion in his golden eyes.

The boy snickered beside her as she stared at Gihon, her expression complex and nuanced beyond the raven's comprehension. Without another word, she turned back around and hustled off, leaving Gihon bewildered by her sudden reaction.

"I told you to stop calling me that," she muttered.

"Oh come on, you liked it," Alett laughed, feathers twittering.

"I did not, do not, and will not."

"That raven guy likes you, I think. I'm going to tell Zander you were flirting with a corvid."

"Do not!" Eddie warned harshly, shooting a glare down at the owl. "You know how he feels about corvidae males!"

Alett laughed, unbothered by his feline friend.

"Oh, you love it, Eddie. You love us, and you love the pretty raven boy."

"Stop speaking at once. I am so tired of being around you, you know." Silencing the boy, she pushed ahead of him.

The boy seemed unbothered by the lioness' quips, though he stopped pushing the subject at her demand. Taking her arm once more, the owl-boy turned around to wave at Gihon one more time before the two vanished into the crowd of passersby without another trace.

CHAPTER 2

THE ZOA ALCHEMIST

"Move it, people!" A loud voice bellowed into the halls of the Society of Alchemists as several employees scurried around, papers and books in hand.

Located deep in the heart of Velkhamore, the Society of Alchemist's main building was large and opulent, serving as the central headquarters for alchemists all across the continent. As a capital of alchemy, dirigents would travel from each corner of Caandemium to meet with each other for semi-annual summits of research and development.

The building itself was tall, made of white stone that boasted detailed columns decorated throughout. Ornate red drapes lined the hallways, matching runners stretching across cold marble flooring.

The Society of Alchemists was a place of pride with halls pristinely kept, a jarring contrast to the frazzled alchemists as they scrambled to make sure everything was in order. As the underlings continued to scramble, the bellowing voice continued.

"Today's the fourth, which means the Zoa Queen and her entourage will be arriving any moment. This is our first time making contact with Zenluve, so make it count!"

The gruff, stern voice belonged to the alchemist Torphus Stonewarden, a well-groomed dwarf with ashy blond hair. His hair was slicked back and kept short on the sides, with a large mustache and expertly-groomed beard. Torphus was one of the four high-ranked alchemists assigned to the Zenluvian entourage by the Society, all four of them being considered for the same promotion into a Dirigent after the death of the previous Dirigent of Velkhamore.

The arrival of the entourage was untimely for the Society, as the power vacuum left by the late Dirigent formed a strong point of contention between the four alchemists. Yet, despite the situation being managed by four people, Torphus found himself to be the one doing most of the work.

The dwarf was pleased knowing that he was more responsible than the others which would make him stand out to the Dirigents, but he also knew that if anything went wrong, he would be the one to take the blame. The pressure welled up inside of him, the anxiety of potential failure weighing on his stout dwarven shoulders.

Checking his pocket watch, Torphus looked towards the door.

"Where exactly is that zoa, Gihon?" Torphus grumbled. "We gave him four months to prepare, and he couldn't even write back to us to confirm he's going to help?"

"I'm sure Dirigent Gihon will be here. Ravencroft is pretty reclusive, and I've heard he's a pretty silent guy, so maybe he didn't feel the urge to respond," Bex, the fire alchemist, pondered.

Bex was the more agreeable of the four, a simple man

with a warm appearance. With tan skin and a bowlcut hairstyle accentuating his kind brown eyes, Bex was often known as the type to see the good in others, and an honorable choice for Dirigent.

"He didn't technically *owe* you a response. He is higher ranked than the rest of us. Although, I do agree that it would look bad for him as Dirigent to not help the Society with such a pressing matter," a new voice chimed, drawing Torphus' attention. Rahzopa spoke confidently, her uniform perfectly pressed, bright orange eyes looking down sternly at Torphus.

Rahzopa was tall and confident, with bronze skin and dark red hair, her many years of competent service to the Society making her a strong contender for the Dirigent position as well.

Looking over at the fourth alchemist, the others fell silent as they waited to hear the opinion of the final contender. With a nonchalant shrug, the final alchemist spoke.

"Gihon probably bailed; cracked under the pressure. There's a lot riding on this, he has no obligation to be here, and he doesn't like Torphus anyway. It sounds like a perfect recipe for abandoning his post," Clotho quipped with an apathetic smirk.

Clotho, the final alchemist, was an entity that claimed to be beyond humanity or gender. The original alchemist by the name of Clotho was a man who lived hundreds of years ago, and developed a practice to transfer his consciousness into body after body. Over his lifetimes, the new bodies created by Clotho were improved and evolved, eventually surpassing human bodily function. Empathy seemed to be one of the things lost through the years, with Clotho becoming a cold and calculating person with little thought or regard for others. However, Clotho was an incredibly intelligent alchemist with hundreds of years of experience, making them another desirable contender for Dirigent if one is willing to overlook their prickly personality.

"Gihon, cracking under pressure? Unlikely," Rahzopa

retorted, the only one other than Torphus who had met Gihon in person years ago. "He's a stoic. I've never seen him so much as break a poker face. He's probably just preening his feathers for his big day as the Queen's escort."

"Enough!" Torphus barked, annoyed, as he faced the others. "You'll have enough time to talk about that featherbrain later. Get a move on!"

Bex, picking up on a sudden change in the air, turned around immediately and hurried off in a flash before Torphus had even finished speaking. Clotho and Rahzopa's faces dropped, staring behind Torphus at the open door behind him. Eyes wide, Rahzopa chuckled nervously, while Clotho's smug expression grew.

"Let's go, Rahzopa," Clotho chuckled, Rahzopa nodding in agreement as both of them turned around to leave at a brisk pace.

Satisfied with their obedience, Torphus nodded to himself, until a deep voice from behind him whose words caused shudders to run up through his spine.

"Is the Society usually this disorderly?" Gihon's cold voice came from above Torphus, the dwarf whipping around anxiously as Gihon towered over him.

A tense moment of silence wavered between the two alchemists, Torphus taking a breath and composing himself into a surprisingly rosy and pleasant demeanor as he greeted Gihon.

"Dirigent Marleogne! Oh, I'm quite relieved to see that you made it. I hope the journey was not too… harsh," Torphus smiled awkwardly.

"Please pardon my silence beforehand, Torphus. One of my students had misplaced the letter you sent, and it was recovered this morning. I departed for Velkhamore the moment I understood the significance of the situation. I would be delighted to help the Zenluvian entourage."

"W-what a relief!" Torphus chuckled anxiously, shaking

The Man in Red

Gihon's hand. "Velkhamore is depending on you, sir. The Society wants to make a good impression on the Zenluvians, as you know... their natural resources are plentiful and incredibly rare. If we could possibly establish trade routes–"

"There will not be trade routes if the Deepwood gets blighted out of existence," Gihon interrupted Torphus. "The priority here is teaching their people about banishment arrays and the basics of alchemy. And Torphus, why are you the head of this project? Where are the other dirigents?"

Torphus felt his blood pressure skyrocket as Gihon spoke in a fully neutral tone, handing his trunk and cloak to a nearby alchemist.

"They refused to aid the Zoa Queen," Torphus admitted after a long moment.

Torphus is a proficient alchemist, but his position was undeniably expedited by dwarven gem money. He's the type to backstab his own people to get ahead, and the Society gave him such a huge responsibility? Gihon thought to himself, before realization hit him. *The higher-ups want Torphus to fail. This entire cultural exchange has been a setup from the other city-states to ruin Velkhamore's reputation. That way, whoever had planned for this can motion to relocate the Society's headquarters to their own city instead.*

"Torphus, I apologize once more that I was unable to provide a response until now. If I had received the letter when you sent it, I could have organized meetings with more dirigents to try to convince them to help," Gihon bowed his head slightly as he spoke.

Taking a moment to compose himself, Torphus gave a forced smile as he replied, "Of course. Right as always, Dirigent Gihon. Regarding trade, I was only thinking about the long-term benefits for our people–"

"Try thinking about the crisis at hand, instead. Their

people are dying, and it is our duty to help them. Trade, if any, is a secondary thought that will not be discussed until the phantasm outbreaks are quelled."

I usually enjoy the company of dwarves, but it seems the one exception is still standing. If this meeting with the Zenluvians is to go well, it seems that I will have my work cut out for me.

The two exchanged glares, a tense silence filling the air. Torphus had only met Gihon one time in the past, briefly, and the exchange had gone rather similarly. The dwarf's blunt attitude and subconscious prejudice against zoafolk often leaked into his desperate attempts to perform well, his nervous nature making him spill out more benevolent ignorance than intended.

Rahzopa, noticing the rising tensions, hurried over to mediate. Shaking Gihon's hand, the Dirigent turned his attention away from Torphus and towards the familiar woman.

"Miss Rahzopa, good to see you," Gihon smiled gently, Rahzopa meeting his gaze warmly.

"Dirigent Gihon, thank you for coming. I am eager to learn about the Zenluvians, as a society that doesn't use alchemy. Do you think they live like the kings of old?" Rahzopa asked, desperate to turn Gihon's attention away from Torphus' temper.

"It is possible. However, their kingdom has survived this way for a thousand years, so there could be elements we are wholly unaware of. The Deepwood may be home to foreign concepts unbeknownst to anyone in Caandemium, though I could imagine they would have some strong traditions and cultural practices, as an isolationist society."

"Don't give them too much credit. It's a society without alchemy, so their technology will certainly be primitive compared to us. They don't interact with the outside world and are run entirely by zoa, so they are likely to be rather... feral, if you will." Torphus sneered.

The Man in Red

"I will not. Zoa aren't *feral*," Gihon shot a cold glare at Torphus, whose attitude was beginning to bubble up again.

"Of the ones I know, they certainly can act like it."

Staring down at him coldly, Gihon's eyes narrowed. "I know the Dirigent that gave you your job, Torphus. Perhaps a lunch with him is in order."

Before the situation could escalate, Bex returned into the main hall, face bright with excitement.

"Everyone, the Zenluvians have arrived! Their autowagons just pulled up outside!" Bex called out, drawing the attention of the other alchemists.

Torphus tensed, eyes wide as he snapped back to reality.

"We will discuss this later," Gihon growled quietly, turning to face the main doors as the others fell in line behind him.

A beat that felt like an eternity dragged on as the alchemists awaited at the entryway. The headquarters of the Society were large and elegant, befitting of the entourage that approached.

Two alchemists standing outside the large, ornate doors pulled them open in unison as the Zenluvians entered.

Eight soldiers filed inside, donning matching green-and-gold uniforms. Each member wore the same fitted sleeveless top, gold trimming around the neck and shoulders. Aside from the top, there was room for individuality between them; with the skirts, pants, and jackets of each warrior further accentuated by a variety of golden accessories.

Of the eight, Gihon noticed two women, one being a pink-haired zoa with downturned ears and the other a platinum blonde elf. The six men included a fellborn, a human, and four zoa. As Gihon's gaze evaluated each soldier that entered, his eyes stopped on the smallest of the group.

In front of him, a teenaged owl zoa with octagonal glasses approached, uniform matching the other warriors. He wore baggy pants with large brown boots, black compression sleeves on his arms with brown gloves, and had a pair of goggles around his neck.

The owl-boy's face lit up as his inquisitive yellow-orange eyes met Gihon's, recognizing the Dirigent immediately.

Wait, I know that kid. Gihon realized. *I saw him earlier at the Grand Bazaar. The owl zoa, the one that Eddie had called 'Alett'.*

Memories flashing from earlier in the day, Gihon remembered the hooded zoa girl that accompanied Alett. Recalling her piercing gaze, a single question popped into his mind as he noticed that she was not among the other guardsmen, like the boy was.

Could this mean... Eddie...

Gihon stopped, unable to finish his thought as the silhouette of a feline woman approached from the bright afternoon light outside. As the zoa stepped inside, Gihon's eyes looked over a tall lioness' beautiful, powerful presence. She appeared to be somewhere in her twenties and wore her honey-blonde hair in a high ponytail which cascaded down to her waist. There was a striking white highlight on her right side, the streak running down through the ringlet curls that framed her face across from familiar side-swept bangs.

Her outfit was well-tailored and refined, with tight white pants and thigh-length black boots. She wore a white blouse with a blue corset resting under her bosom, with a matching blue bolero hanging perfectly off of her shoulders. Gihon's eyes trailed across elegant gold trimming, noting her confidence and bold energy as she passed by the guardsmen, who saluted her as she entered.

"You may bow," she addressed the room bluntly, stopping at the front of the entourage to address the alchemists with a white-gloved hand on her hip.

That woman from the Grand Bazaar is the Queen of

The Man in Red

Zenluve. Gihon realized in dismay.

The young Queen's eyes scanned the room around her, drinking in puzzled looks from the alchemists as they stood in front of her, as if they were trying to decide whether or not she was the Queen they were expecting. Her eyes locked with a familiar golden gaze, the raven-haired man staring with an inquisitive realization back at her.

Gihon returned her stunned look, connecting the dots of the day's events.

As their eyes locked, Gihon could see in her curious blue eyes that she, too, was astounded by the revelation that he was the raven zoa from earlier. After a moment, the lioness regained her composure.

"You may bow," she repeated to the alchemists, who quickly bowed politely in front of her at her second demand.

Gihon could see the faint traces of befuddlement on her face, clearly disgruntled by their lack of courtesy. Behind her, a large, tanned sphynx zoa crossed his muscular arms with a dissatisfied glare, the wrap on his head accentuating the furrow of his eyebrow. The wrap appeared as a blend between a traditional Tozepian head scarf and a hood, the same deep green color as his uniform. Under his glaring bright green eyes, the sphynx had tattoos that Gihon recognized as symbols of ancient Tozepian gods, accompanying another large tattoo on his shoulder. His long and hairless feline ears were pierced several times with gold earrings.

The symbols of 'protector' and 'ward of evil' are tattooed under his eyes. His shoulder is the symbol of life and renewal. How interesting. He clearly takes himself very seriously. With a stature like that, he's more of what I'd expect from the Zenluvian high guard.

Refocusing, Gihon centered himself and approached the Queen. He took her hand and bowed gently, kissing the back of her glove. She looked down at him, pleased by his gesture.

"You must be Her Majesty, Queen Edelein von Luvemann of the Kingdom of Zenluve. It is an honor. My name is Gihon Marleogne, Dirigent of Ravencroft. I am a zoa, like you. The town I govern, however, is much humbler in size than the mighty Zenluve." Gihon kept his head low, hoping she would choose to remember his polite mannerisms now over his actions at the bazaar.

Queen Edelein... that is why Alett called her 'Eddie.' Gihon thought, staring at the ground as he remained bowed. *I called the Queen of Zenluve 'Eddie.' No wonder she looked so displeased with me earlier.*

"The honor is mine, Dirigent Gihon," her voice roused him from his thoughts, and he looked up. Her icy eyes twinkled with amusement at the situation, looking around as he straightened himself upright. "Though, is it perhaps... cultural... for your people to not bow to royals? In my homeland, that is a sign of respect to royalty."

"Ah, no, please, do forgive us," Gihon replied stiffly, feeling a twinge of embarrassment.

This is humiliating, Gihon thought. *How much more unprepared could they have been, with four months to organize everything?*

"If I may, Your Majesty, we were not completely sure that you were the Queen," Clotho added. "We thought that perhaps you might have been an attendant, or emissary of some sort."

Torphus shot a desperate glare at Clotho, seeming to beg the alchemist to silence themselves without making a scene in front of the Queen.

Edelein looked at Clotho, curiously. "If you refer to my attire, it would be foolish for me to spend months on a boat in ceremonial gowns, would it not? The situation calls not for opulence, thus, I assumed that regular trousers would suffice. Would they not?"

"You are... young, for a Queen," Gihon admitted, bowing again in apology. "Please pardon my cohorts."

Her laugh drew Gihon upward, a pleasant sound like wind chimes on a quiet day. He looked up at her, drawn in by her warm and curious presence.

"Hm. I suppose I did leave my age out of my correspondence, as I assumed it would be of no concern to you. I'm twenty-four, if you really must know," her tone was bemused as she crossed her arms.

The same age as Mandus, Gihon thought in surprise.

A beat of silence hung in the air as she looked at Gihon, her authoritative presence searing into him. Torphus, anxious to keep in her favor, stepped forward with several ancient tomes in his calloused dwarven hands. Gihon noticed from the slight tremble in the dwarf's arms and the crease of his forehead that Torphus was nervous about the direction of the conversation and afraid of offending the Queen further.

"Your Majesty, the Society has procured some of our finest texts on the history and tradition of alchemy, to aid with your situation. These are precious artifacts of our people, so please take care of them. Treat this as a symbol of Velkhamore's willingness to help you."

"Yes, thank you for the books. Information is quite valuable at this point." Edelein waved her hand, seeming a bit uninterested as one of her guards stepped forward to take the tomes. The man was a fellborn similar to Jana, with grey-violet skin. His long, straight, jet-black hair was dyed with purple streaks that matched his one visible eye. The other remained hidden beneath his shaggy bangs that gathered around his pointed horns which sat just above his ears. He approached, bowing his head gratefully as he took the tomes from Torphus and stepped back into the formation silently.

Crown of the Alchemist

Noting her disinterest, Gihon stepped forward as he pulled the small gift box out of his pocket and extended it towards her.

Memories flashed in his mind of Edelein helping him pick out the gift, both of them blissfully unaware that she was the one being shopped for. He opened the box, revealing the sapphire choker to her.

Edelein looked into the box, her eyes lighting up in realization. She smiled demurely.

"Without having met," Gihon teased, "I figured that someone such as Your Majesty would prefer fine jewels over old books. I have been informed by a valued and trusted source that this sapphire is one of the highest-quality gemstones we offer in Velkhamore." His gold eyes twinkled in amusement, remembering the words that she had used to describe the gem.

"Your generosity is appreciated. The tomes will service us well, and the necklace certainly is of pristine quality. Your source was quite knowledgeable," the Queen gently smiled as she teased back, before looking over her shoulder and snapping her fingers.

The sound was slightly muffled by her gloves, but the snap still rang out with an assertive force. Behind her, the large sphynx zoa and the owl-boy from the market produced two deep azure boxes, and stepped forward next to Edelein. The Queen took the box from the owl's hands, looking at Gihon with a coy smirk.

"Of course, we also come bearing gifts. In return for your assistance, that is." Opening the box, the alchemists clamored to catch a glimpse of the light from inside of it.

Inside the box, a large crystal about the size of a fist sat nestled within the padding, brilliant blue and violet light shining from within it. The color looked similar to the bangle from the market, but the bangle dulled in comparison to the radiant brightness of the stone in Queen Edelein's box.

"These boxes each hold a leyline crystal... real ones, mind

you. As you may have heard from your legends, the Deepwood sits atop our world's largest leyline, a point of convergence between every plane within reality. We call it the Heart of the Leyline, and it is the fuel source of the Deepwood's powerful presence. Leyline energy is infused into every part of the Deepwood; including the natural springs, flora, fauna, and as you can see, minerals. These stones are incredibly potent with the condensed natural energy of converging planes."

Sparing a glance at Gihon as she recalled a shared memory, she continued, "The crystals do not cause good luck or wealth as your rumors say. However, leyline energy is incredibly grounding to nature and an excellent source of spiritual wellness. We use these crystals to power our technology, provide light, as well as enrich our soil and water purity. Leyline energy restores our material plane back to its purest original forms, restoring nutrients and removing toxins. The charges within them are functionally similar to electricity as well, which is how we have been able to harness it for technology."

"Have you tried using leyline energy in your battle against the phantasms?" Clotho asked.

"No. The Deepwood is guarded by a fae spirit named Nalo. She is our protector, a fearsome warrior affiliated as the fae's warden of the Deepwood. Nalo has gifted us the leyline crystals with the intention of us using them to thrive within nature. The stones must never be used for violence in any way. I trust that once we give these to you, you will hold true to Nalo's wish and use them for research and agriculture, not weaponry. We would prefer to learn your ways instead and remain in the favor of Nalo."

"What happens if you lose Nalo's favor?" Bex asked.

"At best, we are no longer protected from the darkness within the forest; left to fend for ourselves. At worst, we are destroyed, enslaved, and forgotten."

Crown of the Alchemist

Nalo sounds like a Divine Beast. Very few of those remain in the world, if any at all. It would explain how no one has been able to live there other than the Zenluvians. If Nalo can control the forest, she could control the creatures within it, and a Divine Beast would certainly have the ability to see everything within its domain. I would love to ask Queen Edelein more about that, later. Gihon thought, alight with eagerness to learn something that his books could not explain to him.

As Edelein closed the box and returned it to the owl zoa, Gihon caught himself staring curiously at her and averted his gaze politely.

"The crystals are yours, once we are taught effective practices in removing the shadow beasts from our land. Consider them your payment. I will not give them to you until we know that we can trust your people."

"Thank you for your generosity, Your Majesty. Leyline crystals are of legend to us, as is the Kingdom of Zenluve. We will honor your wishes, using them properly." Holding out the necklace box to her, he continued, "Please accept our gifts now as a message of goodwill."

Queen Edelein reached out to take the box from his extended hands. As her hands settled around the sides of the box, the soft satin of her white gloves met the black leather of his. Freezing, she looked up at him with wide doe-like eyes. Soft sunlight bounced from her blonde locks as her eyes twinkled, a peculiar look in her eye that Gihon couldn't identify. The Dirigent felt heat rise to his cheeks as he looked down at her, time seemingly frozen as he imagined the warmth of her hand, wondering for a brief moment as to how her ungloved touch would feel.

Just as quickly as it started, the moment ended, Gihon withdrawing his hands and leaving the gift in hers. Clearing his throat, he looked away from the Queen, his eyes accidentally meeting the piercing green gaze of the sphynx zoa.

The sphynx was staring at him, ears flat and eyes narrow, seeming to have noticed the energy that passed between the Queen and the Dirigent. His lips were pulled back in a small snarl as he growled under his breath.

"Alett, I don't like him." Gihon barely managed to make out the zoa's quiet grumble.

Alett tilted his head as he looked up at the sphynx.

"You don't like anyone, Zander," Alett replied. "What else is new?"

Alett had a light, teasing tone, which the sphynx named Zander clearly did not appreciate.

Queen Edelein had mentioned a man named Zander getting angry at them for leaving. I can see why, now.

Looking back at the Queen, Gihon noticed that she had a warm expression as she nodded politely down at Torphus. Gihon had missed what they were discussing, distracted by the guards, but he could tell from her body language that the Queen looked a bit uneasy, as if eager to move on. The tip of her tail twitched slightly, her gaze briefly darting towards the windows and doors on occasion.

"Your Majesty, I assume you must be weary from your travels. It is a long way from Avalstice, after all. Shall I escort you and your entourage to your prepared quarters for some well-earned rest?" Gihon offered with a kind smile.

Queen Edelein looked over at Gihon, nodding gratefully.

"Yes, I must admit that I am a bit worn out. A royal suite on a ship is still, at the end of the day, on a ship. It would be lovely to sleep in a bed that does not rock each night from waves. I will be much more equipped for a proper meeting tomorrow, if that is alright."

"Please come with me, then. We have prepared a guest

house for you all, often used by visiting nobles and royalty. I do hope it will suit your tastes."

"Anything will be better than the boat. I would be happy to take some time to properly introduce you to my Zengarde, as well."

Gihon nodded, stepping towards the door and looking over his shoulder at the other alchemists.

"We will reconvene tomorrow morning to discuss the Zenluvians' situation, get their account, and figure out how to best help them. Training them in the basics of alchemy will also begin after the meeting. Please prepare yourselves accordingly. Oh, and Bex, please prepare some tea. I have heard from Rahzopa that you dry your own leaves as a hobby, and I would quite like to try it, if you do not mind."

Bex nodded, the other alchemists saluting to Gihon as he turned around. They held the door open for Edelein and the others who exited the building in the same formation they arrived in.

Outside of the Society of Alchemists, the afternoon sun illuminated the cobblestones in front of Edelein, warming the tips of her ears with the joys of summer. Two vehicles were parked ahead of the group, waiting for the Queen to return with her command. Gihon walked silently alongside her, his mind preoccupied with countless thoughts as usual.

The autowagons were high-end models, with one of them being smaller and slightly more opulent than the other. They looked similar to a traditional horse-drawn carriage in style and layout, the only difference being a large front engine where a horse would have stood. The smaller vehicle could seat four guests, the larger one seating six. Steam pumped from the engine as it roared to life, a signature of Velkhamore's modern steam-powered technology. Two drivers bowed as the Zenluvians approached, an older red-skinned fellborn man and a female dwarf.

Both vehicles were the same as the ones the Society had sent to fetch the entourage from the port earlier that day, so the Zenluvians had already had the opportunity to adapt to the change in culture as they began boarding the foreign machines.

Gihon opened the carriage door of the smaller autowagon, motioning to Edelein. Nodding in understanding, the Queen took the hand of the sphynx-cat guard as he helped her lift into the carriage, following closely behind her. The owl-boy, Alett, hopped up unaided and unbothered, vanishing into the cool shade of the autowagon.

As the three entered, Gihon placed a foot onto the step, hoisting himself into the autowagon and sitting next to the owl. The sphynx, who Gihon remembered to be called Zander, crossed his arms and stared disapprovingly, the corner of his lips edging into a quiet snarl.

"The Society has requested for me to accompany you, so I hope you do not mind," Gihon spoke, looking straight ahead at the Queen for approval. She smiled and nodded, not seeming to notice the silent attitude of her guard.

At her agreement, Gihon reached one hand out of the carriage window, knocking on the side of the autowagon. The fellborn driver, understanding the signal, returned to his seat at the front as the autowagon began to move. For a brief moment, Edelein's face twisted uncomfortably as she turned to face the window, forcing herself to return to a neutral expression.

"Do you feel ill, Your Majesty?" Gihon asked. "I know these are a bit different from a horse-drawn carriage in Avalstice, and the motion can lead to some discomfort…"

"I'm alright, thank you," Edelein replied, interrupting him. "I cannot say that I enjoy these mechanical carriages. They feel unnatural. However, I am grateful to the Society for the transportation nonetheless."

Changing the subject, Edelein faced Gihon, peeling her eyes from the window to gaze across the seats at him. They sat directly across from each other, facing each other with nothing more than a few inches to close the distance from their knees in the small autowagon.

"I should introduce you to the Zengarde," she said suddenly, seeming to be eager to avoid the previous conversation.

"Please do, Queen Edelein. I am aware that they are a team of Zenluve's top fighters, sworn exclusively to the Throne, but I would be delighted if you could inform me more about the process and who they are. There is honestly a lot that I would like to ask, if you can indulge my inquisitive nature."

"Of course. I would expect nothing less from your people, and came prepared to share the wonders of my homeland with you. As you said, the Zengarde earn their titles through combat capability. The highest ranked member is the strongest fighter. Once every few years, they compete in a tournament to maintain their places."

"What happens if there is an opening before the tournament?" Gihon asked, curiosity causing him to speak out of turn.

Edelein faltered, a distant look in her eyes. Gihon remembered that in her correspondence, she mentioned two Zengarde being killed, and felt a twinge of embarrassment flush his cheeks as he feared he may have brought up an unpleasant memory.

"The opening stays until the Zengarde Tournament. The Deepwood is inhabited by fae, with links to the fae's Summer Court. The fae are the ones who determine the rankings."

The Man in Red

"Not the royals?"

"No. It's an agreement we have with the fae. It's entertainment for them, and helpful for us. They can see things better than we can through having a deeper connection to the forest than even we do. It's the one time where the fae will enter Zenluve… quite the spectacle for the civilians. The Zengarde Tournament Festival brings in a lot of revenue."

"I see. How interesting. So the rankings are…"

"Determined by the fae through displays of combat capability. Essentially, the Zengarde fight against each other and any other contenders. Zander here is the top rank, he's held that position for twelve years now."

"Zander Khepri," Zander huffed, introducing himself bluntly at the insistence of his Queen. "Ehret of the Zengarde. My fealty is sworn to King Alderis and his direct family alone, so do not expect me to aid you, corvid."

"Twelve years is a while for someone of your age; you must have been young when you first joined. I imagine your prowess must be of high caliber," Gihon noted.

"The small one next to you is only eighteen; the age I was when I first joined the ranks. His name is Alett Strigo, genius extraordinaire."

"High praise from Zander!" Alett beamed as Zander rolled his eyes.

"A genius who is not wise enough to keep crucial details to himself," Zander continued. "This is criticism, not praise. You have a habit of revealing your newest inventions to me on the night before each Zengarde Tournament, and that will continue to be your downfall, Zwitet Alett."

Zwitet must mean the second-rank. It is baffling to think that a kid like him could be the second-strongest fighter in an entire kingdom. Gihon thought, curiously looking over the boy.

Alett was lean, but didn't look like a fighter the way Zander did. The owl's body was thin and he appeared to be more of an intellectual type, reminding Gihon of the Athenaeum's students. As the Dirigent looked over Alett, the boy returned a cheeky grin at Zander's words.

He tells Zander about his inventions because he wants Zander to win, Gihon realized. *He's doing it on purpose to protect Zander's pride.*

"Alett's parents are good friends of mine. They are both members of the Royal Court, and I have worked closely with them in the past," Edelein went on, regaining Gihon's attention. "These two have been loyal to the Throne for years, and I trust them with my life. Anything you teach Alett, he will teach to the others, so please work closely with him when teaching alchemy to my people."

Gihon nodded, his eyes meeting hers gently as he fervently tried to avoid looking at Zander, who was continuing to openly stare daggers at him.

Edelein spared a glance to her left where Zander sat, noticing his behavior. With a sigh, she smiled politely to Gihon.

"Please pardon Zander's temperament, as well. He may look intimidating, but I assure you that he is quite a kindhearted person, and a valiant protector of the Throne. He means well."

Zander's eyes darted towards Edelein for a moment, before returning to Gihon. His face briefly betrayed a complex emotion, a silent look that Edelein seemed to understand immediately.

"Please disregard Her Majesty's statement and continue to be intimidated by me," Zander growled, disgruntled. "It is what keeps her safe."

"You are a noble ally. I do not find you intimidating, Zander," Gihon assured politely.

"Perhaps you should." His eyes narrowed in response, his

slender and hairless ears laid flat against his head.

An uncomfortable silence fell over the group, the only sound being an awkward chuckle from Alett. In front of him, Gihon noticed Edelein lean over to Zander, whispering sternly up at him.

"Zander, behave yourself. We need his help." Gihon could barely make out her whispered warning to the Ehret, their conversation hushed.

"Your Majesty, the proph–"

"It's not him," Edelein interrupted harshly. "He isn't the one we were warned of."

"With all due respect, you cannot be certain. I need to keep you safe. It is what I promised to King Alderis—"

"At least just *try* to get along with him, okay?" Edelein asserted quietly, "End of subject."

As the heated whispers subsided, Gihon found himself small-talking with Alett as the two discussed technology and academics for the remainder of the ride. Edelein had taken to staring out the window to admire the passing scenery of the city, while Zander continued to stare at Gihon warily.

A look of relief crossed the Queen's face as the autowagon slowed to a halt, indicating the group's arrival at their new quarters.

"It seems we have arrived," Gihon said, glancing briefly outside the window. "If you would please come with me, Your Majesty."

Opening the carriage door, Gihon stepped out into the fresh air, grateful for the opportunity to stretch the long legs of his tall figure. Ahead of him, the noble house stood tall and elegant, befitting for the guests it would hold. Tall columns dotted the front entrance, and a large front yard seemed to invite them in.

Turning around, Gihon extended his hand towards the near-empty carriage, awaiting Edelein to step down. Alett stood next to Gihon, bright eyes filled with wonder as he looked over at the noble house excitedly.

Edelein, shrouded by the shade of the carriage roof, stood and stepped towards the door, reaching her hand out to take Gihon's.

"Your Majesty, allow me to–"

Gihon's sentence was cut off abruptly as a tanned hand brushed his own out of the way. Edelein's hand met Zander's instead as he helped her down from the autowagon, the sphinx stopping to throw a glare towards Gihon as he escorted her towards the house.

"Know your place, stranger. She is our Queen. Leave her to us," Zander hissed under his breath as he bumped his shoulder into the Dirigent on his way past.

"I am simply doing my job," Gihon retorted flatly, feeling irritation boil his blood.

"So am I," Zander snapped, leading Edelein inside and leaving Gihon to stand alone with Alett in the entrance.

What did I do to him? Gihon wondered with a sigh.

"Sorry, Gihon," Alett piped up from beside him. "Zander really does mean well… he can just be a bit prickly, is all. He'll warm up to you. I, for one, think you are quite pleasant and I look forward to learning from you."

"Thank you, Alett," Gihon replied, holding the door open for the owl-boy as the two entered the house.

Ahead of them, Zander and Edelein seemed to be in a heated discussion, speaking quietly and sternly to each other. When the others entered the room, they stopped their conversation.

The Man in Red

Edelein approached Gihon.

The lioness looked like she wanted to speak, but before she could say a word, the door opened from behind Gihon, and the other six Zengarde filed in.

"This place is cool," one of the guards, a human with black hair and bright red bangs, laughed happily as he took in his surroundings.

"Zengarde, fall into formation," Edelein spoke with a commanding voice that seemed to be familiar to her.

Their chatter died down as the eight Zengarde lined up silently, holding a hand over their hearts in what appeared to be a Zenluvian salute. Edelein stood in front of them, hands on her hips as she turned to Gihon.

"Dirigent Gihon, these are my Zengarde; fearsome warriors of the Throne. You've already met Zander and Alett, but if you do not mind, I would be delighted to introduce you to the rest of them."

Gihon nodded silently, following Edelein as she walked over to the line of Zengarde warriors. She stopped past Zander and Alett, in front of a third man. He was a wolf zoa, with long, pointed ears, but lacked a tail. His hair was the same pale silvery color as his ears, with messy bangs and spiked-up tufts. His uniform also included a gold armored sleeve and a long white-and-green waist wrap.

"Dritet Jinn Canis." He spoke gruffly, dark blue eyes briefly meeting Gihon before lowering respectfully, one hand resting on the hilt of a sheathed blade.

"Jinn is the second son of the Canis family in Zenluve, the head family of the Canis Clan. His older brother is the current clan head. As you can likely tell, he is a white wolf zoa." Edelein added, "He's an incredible swordsman, but not much of a talker, so please do not take offense if he does not speak to you often. He and I are the same age, so I've known him for most of my life."

"It is an honor to make your acquaintance, Jinn." Gihon smiled politely as Jinn stared silently back at him, offering a small nod in return.

"Next to him is Fiertet Lylia Brightwood," Edelein continued, drawing Gihon's attention towards a tall elven woman with bright green eyes.

Toned and graceful with a surprisingly muscular build, Lylia wore her long platinum hair in a ponytail that was loosely tied halfway down her back. Her uniform had a long skirt, with black leggings showing through the slits on the sides and a golden trim around her hips. She nodded at Gihon politely.

"Lylia has incredible druidic magic. She comes from a tribe of pacifist elves from the Deepwood, so she prefers to heal rather than harm. Although, she will certainly fight if needed, hence her physique."

"It is an honor, Dirigent Gihon," Lylia spoke softly, bowing her head deeply.

Zenluve still has magic users? Gihon wondered in fascination.

Edelein gestured to the two men next in the line: the black-and-red-haired human from earlier and an ox zoa. The human was well-built for a fighter, but looked small compared to the ox, a huge and muscular man that towered over even Gihon. Both of them had large, cheeky grins as Edelein addressed them.

"The human is Fuuntet Thorne Black, a ranger. A fae gifted him the ability to manipulate wind as a child, making him an unparalleled tracker and hunter, second only to myself."

"Second to none, Your Majesty," Thorne replied, hazel eyes burning with mischief.

"Second to myself," Edelein doubled down playfully. "You're three years younger than me. You've still got some catching up to do."

56

The Man in Red

"Are you a hunter as well, Your Majesty?" Gihon asked, curious.

"I am. I'm quite renowned for my archery skills back home, I'll have you know. I do enjoy getting out of the castle and taking out monsters now and then, although I've had less time in the last few years. I would never ask a soldier to do something I am unwilling to do myself, so I prefer to join them on patrols and in battle if I am able to."

"Queen Edelein takes out bigger monsters than any of the rest of us," the ox laughed, triangular gold earrings swinging with his movement. His ears were pointed and downturned, slightly reminiscent of the stubbier point of a dwarven ear, as if a cross between human and bovine ears.

"Everett speaks the truth," Edelein confirmed with a coy smile.

The ox, Everett, took Gihon's hand and shook it firmly, smiling.

"My name is Zextet Everett Smith, sir," Everett said. "I'm twenty, and I'm the group's defender. I'm an ox. Nice to meet you!"

"I can tell, and likewise," Gihon replied.

Everett had reddish-brown hair that was a bit longer on the back, with sweeping middle-parted curtain bangs. Large horns protruded from his skull, indicative of his heritage. His eyes were deep blue and full of energy.

At least they're not all brooding. Everett is a sentinel, like myself, and yet he makes someone of my stature look small, Gihon thought.

Edelein glanced at Gihon briefly before continuing, almost as if she was curiously drinking in his silent thoughts.

"Next to Everett is our resident fellborn, Noentet Nephvir Nyxveil. Another twenty-year-old. The current lineup of Zengarde is surprisingly young, but they remain the most talented Zengarde in history," Edelein pressed on, as Gihon followed to greet the next member.

Lean and compact, Nephvir stood a full head shorter than Gihon, his posture rigid despite the indifference in his eye. Gihon recognized Nephvir as the man who had taken Torphus' tomes, the long-haired fellborn. He stood still as he maintained his salute, but Gihon noticed a slight disinterest in his expression. A violet jacket was tied around his waist, the rest of his outfit appearing rather standard-issue.

"It's nice to meet you, Nephvir," Gihon smiled, thinking.

I wonder what his plane of origin is. He looks like Jana, so it could likely be the Plane of Shadow.

"You too," Nephvir had a quiet voice lilted with a hint of an accent that the Dirigent found himself unable to place.

After a beat of silence, Edelein chimed in again.

"Neph is a shadow-stepper in combat, and outside of combat he loves to write and draw. He's got quite the affinity for the arts."

"Shadow-stepper?"

"I can move from one shadow to the next in the blink of an eye, so long as the shadow is large enough to fit my body." Nephvir explained. "Shadow-stepping."

A fellborn with teleportation, a human with wind manipulation… I am beginning to see how these young fighters are of such high status.

"My turn, Your Majesty. Introduce me to your handsome friend!"

Gihon looked at the source of the voice, curious as his eyes met the rose-pink irises of a young zoa girl.

"Yes, last but not least. Our darling Zentet Cari Beaumont. She's only nineteen, so I expect her to be climbing the ranks past the Zentet position soon. Cari is a zoa transmuted from a beautiful

creature called a Rozufex, native to the Deepwood. It is similar
to a fox, but with a stunning rose-colored fur. Truly one of my
favorite animals, and they make such gorgeous zoa. Cari is another
noblewoman, and has been a close friend of mine since we were
young."

"Oh, you make me blush, Your Majesty," Cari giggled,
winking.

As Gihon looked over Cari, he quickly noticed her sense of
fashion. Her uniform, while still the signature dark green and gold
of the Zengarde, was a high-hipped leotard and a short skirt. She
wore a cropped jacket with large, puffy sleeves, its broad lapel a
light pink color. A matching bow sat on her hip from a sash across
her skirt, along with thigh-high black boots. Her hair was the same
bright color as her eyes, rosy and elegant with two long pigtails
cascading behind her. She had downturned fox-like ears and large,
round glasses that framed her face.

"A pleasure to meet you, miss Cari. What weaponry do you
work with?" Gihon asked warmly, eager to break the ice with the
Zengarde.

"I'm the undefeated whip champion of Zenluve. The
elegance and flow of whip-based combat is like a dance to me,"
Cari chuckled, shaking his hand.

*What a… lively group of people. The next few days will be
quite interesting, indeed*, Gihon thought.

"Dirigent Gihon, do you have any questions?" Edelein
asked.

"Plenty, yes. However, those will be answered in due time.
The Society has requested that I stay at the noble house with you for
the duration of your stay, so that I may see to your every need."

From the corner of Gihon's eye, he saw Zander's face
distort in silent anguish, gritting his teeth while maintaining his
perfectly poised salute.

"There is a master suite at the end of the hall," Gihon continued, ignoring the sphynx. "Please get some rest for now, and make yourselves at home. We will have plenty of time to discuss all these matters tomorrow."

Edelein nodded, waving her hand to the Zengarde. "At ease."

The eight soldiers dropped their salutes, quickly dispersing around the house. Everett and Thorne, as if sharing the same thought, immediately vanished into the kitchen. Lylia, Cari, and Nephvir left to find rooms to claim; Zander and Jinn wordlessly slipped through the back door to spar together. Alett remained in front of Gihon and Edelein.

"Wow, that was fast, huh?" Alett laughed, looking up at Edelein. "Anyways, about our agreement…"

"Once we get home, Alett. Not much I can do about it now," Edelein responded, taking a few steps away from Gihon to go look outside of a window. Her tail was swishing back-and-forth, the tip flicking restlessly.

Alett was silent for a beat as he stared at Edelein's back. He glanced down at her tail and back up to her head, eyes wide in recognition as he interpreted her body language.

"You're gonna have to double it, Eddie," Alett crossed his arms, following her to where she stood.

Edelein paused, considering Alett's words. After a moment, she nodded in agreement.

"Fine, I'll double it. Do we have a deal?"

"Deal," Alett smirked as Edelein sighed, tail still flicking.

Alett can read her. I have no idea what they are referring to, but it is fascinating that they can communicate nonverbally like that.

"One more thing."

Edelein groaned, turning to face Alett.

The Man in Red

"He goes too."

"No!" Edelein exclaimed, stomping her foot.

Who are they talking about? 'Goes' where?

"It's for safety. I'll give you three hours."

Edelein's body froze.

"Three hours? I can't argue against that. I'll agree, but he doesn't go, okay? Alone, only."

"Sure, sure."

I desperately want to ask them for context, but this conversation feels very personal, Gihon thought.

Edelein turned to face Gihon, her tail still swishing.

"Dirigent Gihon, I will be retiring early tonight. My body is still weary from our travels."

"Of course, Your Majesty," Gihon nodded, bowing slightly. "I will prepare dinner for you and the Zengarde."

"Oh, you cook? How lovely. Alett will bring it to my room."

Alett rolled his eyes playfully.

"Mhm, yeah. I'll bring it to her, Gihon, so you just focus on making a delicious meal!" Alett chuckled, a mischievous twinkle in his eye as he nudged Gihon towards the kitchen.

Gihon looked over his shoulder at Edelein, confused as the small owl-boy continued to push him.

"O-oh, goodnight then, Your Majesty."

"Goodnight, Gihon," Edelein laughed warmly, turning and heading down the hall towards the master suite.

CHAPTER 3

✦NIGHTMARE✦

The sound of blades clashing rang from the backyard as the Zengarde honed their ever-perfect skills, the cacophony of metals accompanying the gentle sizzling of the skillet in the kitchen. Gihon stood surrounded by a pleasant aroma, plating a fragrant dish of seared fish and vegetables. The Society had filled the kitchen with goods before their arrival, giving the Dirigent plenty to work with. As a port city, Velkhamore was renowned for its high-quality fresh fish industry, a culinary staple, beloved by many people across Caandemium.

Gihon had always enjoyed cooking as a form of solitude and a way to express gratitude to others, occasionally cooking dinners for his students back at the Corvid Athenaeum, or to welcome esteemed guests.

Taking up the warm plate, Gihon stepped out of the kitchen to where Alett sat, placing the plate down gently on the table. Alett sat at a long, hand-carved wooden table, various tools splayed about as he tinkered with a fine powder in a small petri dish. His backpack was on the table, contents spilling out as he worked, oblivious to the world around him.

"Alett, would you mind bringing Queen Edelein her supper while it's still hot? She asked for you to deliver it to her room."

The owl waved a hand up at Gihon dismissively, not looking away from his work.

"I'm, uh… busy with this right now," Alett admitted, briefly looking up with a sheepish grin. "Would you mind taking it to her?"

Gihon tilted his head slightly, confused. *Is he outright refusing an order from his Queen?* he wondered.

"Are you sure she won't have an issue with that?" Gihon asked.

"Yeah, it's fine. She's not picky about who brings her food. She does this a lot, actually... it's pretty normal."

"Alright," Gihon answered, unsure.

The door to the master suite was closed, with no noise coming from the other side. Gihon raised a fist against the door, hesitating slightly before rapping his knuckles gently on the wood.

"Your Majesty, I've prepared a meal for you. Alett is busy right now, so I hope you do not mind that I brought it to you instead."

Silence greeted the Dirigent, and he paused longer to wait for a response.

"Your Majesty? Are you alright?" Gihon's hand wandered to the door handle, and a light touch indicated to him that the door was unlocked.

She did say she was feeling unwell. I should check on her, in case she's ill.

Gihon pressed on the door handle, twisting it open slowly.

"I'm coming in, Queen Edelein," Gihon cautioned, as to

not alarm her.

Silence.

Poking his head around the door, Gihon's eyes darted around the room, concerned. The large window was open, curtains billowing in the late afternoon breeze. A large bed sat as a centerpiece of the room, perfectly and precisely made up with undisturbed pillows and sheets. The connecting restroom door was open, no sound or movement coming from within.

Panic shot through Gihon's nerves like electricity when he realized that Edelein was nowhere to be found. His eyes locked onto the open window, fearing the worst.

Was she taken? How did no one notice? he thought, eyes wide. *No, there's no sign of a struggle anywhere.*

Realization hit the Dirigent as scenarios began to be ruled out, leaving only a single possibility in his mind.

Did Queen Edelein... sneak out? The Society will kill me if they think I let her run off on her own. Not to mention the Zengarde...

Gihon suddenly remembered her cloaked figure, curiously eyeing the jewelry at the Grand Bazaar. He remembered Alett approaching her, and her swift departure afterwards.

The Bazaar. That's where she is. It's not safe for her to be alone, though. If I hurry, I can find her before anyone notices that she is missing.

Closing the door, Gihon swiftly returned to the kitchen, setting her plate down. Alett looked up at him as he walked past, curious.

Noticing Alett's inquisitive stare, Gihon quickly fabricated an excuse, fidgeting with the cuff of his sleeve that sat rolled atop his elbow.

"The Queen is resting right now, and did not want to be disturbed, so... do not disturb her, please. I remembered that I have some duties to take care of with the Society, so I will be back later tonight. Let her rest peacefully tonight."

Alett chuckled, adjusting his glasses as he looked down at his work again, picking up a tool. "Uh-huh. She needs to rest, so leave it to me! I'll make sure no one disturbs her. Have fun with your Society duties, whatever that means!"

"Thank you, Alett," Gihon nodded, heading for the front door to where the autowagons were parked.

The Grand Bazaar is not too far from here. It seems she went on foot... If I took an autowagon to fetch her, she would likely refuse to come with me, as it seems she prefers to walk. I'll go on foot as well and walk her home.

Setting off at a jog, the Dirigent set off westward in the direction of the Grand Bazaar, his mind racing.

The sun began to hang lower in the sky as the Bazaar approached into view. Lights illuminated the market from street lamps, accompanied by the chatter of hundreds of civilians as they bustled through dozens of stalls.

She likely has not gone too far in, yet. Although... finding her may be more difficult than I thought.

Gihon's golden eyes scanned the throng of bystanders, desperately searching for her signature leonine ears. The seconds seemed to drag on as he weaved through crowds, scouring for any sign of the Queen. The sound of laughter pulled his gaze to the side, a familiar and pleasant sound that reminded the Dirigent of gentle wind chimes.

To the side of him, Edelein's tail swished playfully as she held a small mechanical bird in her hands. It jumped around in her palm, flapping its small wings.

"How precious!" she beamed, setting it down and bowing politely to the kiosk's owner. "Your technology is truly fascinating. I do quite love birds."

Crown of the Alchemist

The man at the stall smiled at her, waving goodbye as she turned to move towards the next shop. As she turned, the Queen bumped into a broad, firm chest. Gihon looked down at her, amused.

A look of horror crossed her face as Edelein's gaze met Gihon's, shocked.

"Gihon! Hello. Do you… frequent this place?"

"I could say the same for you, you know."

As Gihon looked at her, he noticed the shimmering sapphire on her neck, set in gold on a familiar black velvet choker.

She's wearing the necklace I bought for her.

"How did you find me?" she asked.

"Your room was empty, and I was able to deduce a conclusion from remembering the situation in which I found you earlier today. You sneak out often, don't you?"

"Damn it, Alett!" Edelein groaned. "He put you up to this. He sent you to find me."

"No, he doesn't know you're gone…" Gihon trailed off, connecting a new piece of evidence to his theory as he recalled the earlier conversation between the Queen and her Zwitet at the noble house.

She's been negotiating with Alett to let her sneak away. He knew from her body language that she was going to go out tonight, so he planned to keep the Zengarde away from her room for three hours before coming to find her. Is this… some sort of game to them?

One line rang in the Dirigent's mind, calling his attention.

"He goes too" means… they were talking about me. Alett really did send me here, and I failed to even realize it. He came up with an excuse to have me check on Queen Edelein instead of him, so that I would realize that she was missing and go escort her. He wanted me to go with her to keep her safe, against her wishes… that kid really is clever.

The Man in Red

"You're right, I believe. However, Alett did not tell me directly that you were leaving, that part I did discover on my own. I tried to lie to him to cover your tracks."

Edelein laughed in disbelief. "You tried to cover for me? Cute. Though I suppose that now you plan to whisk me back home to the noble house, yes?"

Looking down at her, Gihon noticed the slightest hint of a pout as she puffed her cheeks. The Dirigent laughed heartily, his stoic expression breaking.

"Oh, my. Is the house not to your liking? By the way, the necklace suits you."

Edelein's eyes went wide as she clutched the sapphire on her neck, as if to hide it from view. A faint blush tinted her cheeks as she looked away, a sudden flustered demeanor coming over her as she was caught off guard by his comments.

"N-no, the house is lovely. I truly am grateful... for your hospitality..." Edelein mumbled, tail-tip flicking in embarrassment. "I just thought it would be polite to wear the gift that you got for me, that is all..."

"I jest, Your Majesty, you needn't worry. It is my job to make sure that you are content during your time here, as an ambassador of the Society. I will not force you back to the house, however, I cannot allow you to be alone."

"As expected," Edelein sighed, defeated. "Although... Alett must be in your head. The kid's got no respect for rank, and now he's got you emboldened enough to think that you can compromise with a Queen. Is that right?"

"Yes, that is exactly what I am trying to do. I know you are new to Caandemium, and you will need an escort. I will also have you know that a dirigent is not that far off from an Avalstan king. We do not have monarchy here anymore, and a dirigent is the highest position of power we offer. So a compromise should not be unheard of."

"Oh, pardon my informality, Your Majesty," Edelein quipped. "I like your boldness. I will agree to your request, with one condition."

Gihon nodded, encouraging her to continue.

"I wish for my presence here to be discreet, to not stir up any trouble for my people. I do not want word getting out that my homeland is in trouble, lest prying eyes get too curious. While we are out, please do not refer to me formally."

"Your secret is safe with me, Eddie," Gihon smirked with another light chuckle.

"Suddenly, the Dirigent has become a comedian. Edelein will do just fine, thank you."

Gihon laughed, extending his hand out to her.

"Come now, Miss Edelein. Let me show you the best parts of Velkhamore."

As Edelein took Gihon's outstretched hand, the evening seemed to fly past the two as hours slipped away. Her gentle laugh echoed in Gihon's mind as he recalled her excited looks of wonder and awe at even the smallest things, drinking in the sights and sounds of the city. Gihon felt his chest grow warmer as Edelein indulged in a few different desserts throughout the night, the Dirigent not even stopping to spare a second thought as he bought any treat that he caught her staring longingly at.

Bringing himself back to the present, Gihon found himself sitting on a bench under a street lamp, the lioness by his side as she gazed up into the night sky.

The Man in Red

"You can hardly see any stars from here," she mused, tilting her head to the side.

"The light pollution from the city outshines most stars," Gihon explained as the Queen turned to look at him. "One of the few downsides to living in a place like this."

"Velkhamore is beautiful in its own way, though I do miss the comfort of nature. It feels strange to not see the sky."

"Edelein, why do you run away like this? Does the King find issue with it?" Gihon pried, his own eagerness to know more getting the best of him.

Edelein froze for a moment, icy blue eyes burning into Gihon's curious gaze.

"The King? Why would my father find issue with me going out? He used to sneak out *with* me when I was a kid. Freedom runs in our blood, despite our status."

A twinge of embarrassment tugged at Gihon as he realized that she seemed to have misunderstood his question.

"Ah, no, I meant… the current King, your husband. One of the few things we know here about Zenluve is that your society is a thousand-year-old patriarchy. Every zoa across the continent has heard the stories of the fearsome Zenluvian Lion Kings."

"Husband?!" Edelein exclaimed with a loud laugh, drawing the eyes of passersby. She quieted down quickly, not wanting to draw attention to herself.

"I am not married, no. I reign as the first sovereign Queen of Zenluve. The patriarchy ended with my father, who never produced a son… or any children other than me, admittedly. You see, my mother died when I was very young, and my father refused to remarry. The Court was furious with him, but he was in love. So, regardless of my wishes, I was forced onto the throne after his death."

"Please forgive my misunderstanding, and for meddling."

Crown of the Alchemist

Gihon apologized, noticing Edelein's distant stare as she looked down at the cobblestones in front of her. "I have a habit of being... curious. Zenluve is the one place we don't have books about, and it's been awhile since I've had the opportunity to learn new information from a firsthand account."

It is truly incredible that someone of her age is running an entire kingdom on her own. I'm only a few years older than her, and even I am still rather young for a Dirigent. My situation really only worked because Arvien built Ravencroft herself, and the town is small anyway.

"It's alright. I like that you ask questions. I'm surrounded by those meathead Zengarde all day, so a little intellect is like a breath of fresh air to me. I enjoy your company." Edelein replied softly, still seeming a little distant.

"I am impressed that someone as young as you could run an entire kingdom, Edelein."

"It's a pain, more than anything else. The Royal Court pressures me to marry so that I may produce an heir to the throne. From the day I was old enough to marry, they tried to force it upon me. I have still barely managed to escape that fate to this day."

"Why not?" Gihon asked again, his curiosity overriding his courtesy.

Edelein looked at him, seeming to be surprised that he would ask such a personal question. She hesitated, weighing the choice of how much she was willing to disclose to a Caandemite. After a long moment, she nodded.

"The Zenluvian tradition requires transmuting a lion zoa for the purpose of marriage and breeding. Each Queen before me, including my mother, was transmuted from the wild population. It never sat right with me that we would just pull a free creature from its home, thrust it into society, and make it breed with the King for the sake of preserving the leonine bloodline. My father loved my mother dearly, but I fear he was the exception and not the rule."

Edelein's voice grew soft and lonesome as she continued.

"I want to love the way my father loved, but I fear I could never give my love to an arranged marriage. I need to choose him myself, and that's not really how the transmutation works. Rather, the spouse is hand-selected and groomed into perfection, not preference. It's awful."

"What happened to your father, may I ask? How did he…"

"The Deepwood is a fierce and fickle land, and it— wait!" Edelein cut herself off abruptly, ears twitching as they flicked forward. "They're coming!"

Gihon looked ahead, following her gaze to see the large, muscular figure of Zander weaving his way through the throng of people. Beside him, Alett's plumicorns barely poked over the crowd.

"Zander's going to kill you if he sees that you snuck out with me. He already hates you."

"You're right… you've made me an accomplice to your crimes. This was your plan all along, wasn't it?" Gihon joked, pulling her up to her feet.

She laughed as Gihon pulled her forward, into the crowd. He held tightly onto her hand so she wouldn't get lost in the mob as he crossed to the other side of the street, slipping into an alleyway.

"We can't let them find us, then," Gihon added, pressing her against the brick wall of the alley. "Allow me."

Gihon placed a gloved palm on the wall beside her head, focusing his energy. White lines formed from the center of his palm, glowing a bright teal color as each line connected together to form a small array on the bricks.

A low rumble sounded from the ground as bricks began to form at the opening of the alley, stacking up high until the entryway was closed off entirely, seamless from the buildings on either side as he replicated their materials.

"There. Now, no one will find us," Gihon said, turning his head from his alchemy to look at Edelein.

Her head was close to his hand as he held the array, back against the wall. She looked up and her mind raced with a jumble of thoughts as she met his gaze. Suddenly, Gihon found himself acutely aware of how close his face was to hers, their lips only a few inches apart in the dark privacy of the alley.

Hyper-aware of the warmth of her body close to his, he felt his body lean in ever-so-slightly closer as he felt her hot breath on his lips. Unable to pull himself away, time seemed to freeze; the only sound, his own heartbeat ringing in his ears.

Zander's ears twitched irritably as he pushed through the crowd, drawing annoyed looks from passersby as he bumped into them. Alett followed closely behind, trying not to get lost as he muttered apologies to people while hurrying after Zander's long-legged stride.

"I hate this place. Too many people," Zander grunted, eyes narrowing as they flitted back-and-forth amongst the sea of bodies.

"It is… overstimulating," Alett agreed. "But this is where Eddie's scent led us, and it's where I found her earlier. With any luck, she's bound to be somewhere in this crowd."

"King Alderis gave that kid too much of a taste for adventure when she was young. It's going to get her killed, one day. Especially when one of the Zengarde keeps letting her get away with it."

"Oh come on, don't talk like that. She's got her loyal Ehret to protect her from danger!"

"And it appears the Ehret is the only one doing so," Zander glared down at Alett, who was trailing beside him with a sheepish smile. "If Alderis was still alive…"

"Zander, are you worried that what happened to Alderis will happen to Edelein? That you won't be able to find her, either?"

"Of course I am, Alett. This is exactly how we lost her father nine years ago. I *cannot* let that happen again!" Zander hissed. "These crowds mess with my senses! I can't track her scent here! Do you not realize how serious of an issue that is?"

A few paces away from the two Zengarde, their Queen stood with her back to the wall, one ear turned outwards towards the alley at the muffled sounds of her allies. Gihon held himself close to her, his eyes locked on hers as he pressed a gentle, gloved finger to her lips.

As their voices faded into the cacophony of chatter outside, Gihon pulled away from Edelein. He released his hand from the array, and the bricks crumbled down and opened the entrance of the alleyway once more. Dusting off his pants, the Dirigent spared a quick glance at Edelein, who was looking up at him with a curious light in her eye.

Heat began to rise to the tips of his ears as Gihon realized how close he had allowed himself to stand, remembering the warmth of her body so close to his, the feeling of her breath on his lips. Composing himself, Gihon cleared his throat.

"The plan worked, Your M– Edelein. They've left. If we double back the other way, we should be able to return home before they find us."

"So that way Zander doesn't realize you were with me?"

"So that way Zander does not realize I was with you, yes. His first impression of me has been subpar, to put it nicely."

"Thank you for protecting me, brave warrior," Edelein laughed.

How can she be so casual about this? Gihon thought to himself as he stepped out of the alley, the lioness walking a pace or two behind him.

"Gihon?" Edelein spoke suddenly after a moment of silence between them.

The Dirigent stopped in his tracks, turning to face her with an inquisitive look as he nodded for her to continue. Edelein hesitated for a moment, looking away with a slight blush. It seemed as if she wanted to say something, but shook her head before she spoke.

"Thank you. For everything. For your discretion regarding my… habits… for humoring me, and for the escort. I enjoyed myself tonight."

Maybe she is less casual about this than I realized. Her level-headed demeanor seems to be gone, now. Perhaps it was inappropriate of me to indulge in her fantasies. I need to be more formal with her.

"Of course, the Society of Alchemists has tasked me with overseeing you during your time here. I am just doing my job, that is all. I am glad you enjoyed yourself."

Edelein's ears flattened in response, her eyes darting away as she shifted from foot to foot. "Yes, of course, your job. Excellent work… I will let the Society know."

Too formal. She seems unhappy.

"It is more than… I mean…" Gihon stumbled over his words, trying to find the right thing to say. "I enjoyed spending time with you, as well. I did not mean to imply–"

"There is just… a lot of pressure that comes with being the person I am." Edelein explained, desperate to save the conversation. "Tonight was the first time in ages in which I was allowed to feel free. Tonight, I had the liberty of being myself… of being Edelein. I will cherish this memory, for my duty must resume tomorrow."

Edelein laughed, a hint of bitterness hiding within it. Gihon gazed down at her and saw a faint look of distress in her eyes betraying the deeper thoughts she was holding on to. His eyes softened as he placed a hand on her upper back, the Queen's lonely eyes wavering as they met Gihon's.

"If nothing else, know that you have my support. As Edelein, or anyone else you choose to be. I will stand by your decisions."

"Thank you" she whispered, voice soft as she held his gaze for a long moment.

The noble house was quiet, silence greeting the two as they returned. Edelein's ears swiveled around, mouth slightly open as she drank in the scents inside.

"Everyone is asleep. Zander and Alett aren't back yet. This is perfect."

"You can tell all of that from the scent, outside of the house? Your skills are truly impressive," Gihon mused.

Felines contain an organ on the roof of their mouth that detects scent stronger than a human olfactory system could, which would explain why her mouth was open. It is fascinating to see which traits of a zoa's ancestry end up translated to their humanoid form, Gihon thought.

Edelein opened the door slowly, tail held still and low to the ground as she stepped inside silently. She moved slowly and carefully, reminding Gihon of a stalking lioness in the wild.

"I'm going to bed now, genuinely, this time," Edelein whispered, turning to look up at Gihon as she stopped by her door. "Tomorrow, we insist that we never even left."

Gihon nodded, smiling at her antics. He clasped a hand on her shoulder, silent as to not disturb the others. She nodded back, stepping into the master suite and closing the door behind her.

As the sound of Gihon's footsteps faded into the nighttime quiet, Edelein leaned her back against her closed door, breathing heavily. The Queen let out a shaky sigh, pulling off her white gloves and tossing her bolero on the bed.

Why do I feel like this? Edelein wondered, trying to rub the goosebumps off of her arms. *I feel so cold, and my legs hurt tremendously. I must be truly exhausted, to feel this way.*

Shaking her head, Edelein stepped into the bathroom and turned on the sink. Her mind wandered to thoughts of home, the running stream reminding her of the gentle creeks she used to play in as a child. She splashed the water on her face, trying to rid herself of her mixed-up emotions. As Edelein looked up into the mirror, the hairs on her neck rose as a second face greeted her in the reflection.

Recognizing the face of the shadow beast that ravaged her land and people, she felt the cruel grin of the monster burn itself into her memory once more. Edelein let out a gasp, the fur on her tail bristling as she whipped around to face the creature, her stomach dropping in fear.

As she turned, the bathroom stood quiet, with nothing out of the ordinary. The creature was gone, or perhaps never there to begin with. Edelein clutched her chest, breaths shallow and eyes wide as she trembled.

"It's not real. It's not real. It's not real," she repeated to herself, muttering quietly.

Suddenly, the air around Edelein began to suffocate her, as if the oxygen was drawn out of it. A purple haze surrounded her vision, darkness closing in on her mind and blocking out any of her own thoughts. Terrified, the lioness rushed to turn the lights on, desperate to vanquish the darkness. As her shaking hand pressed the switch, the haze melted away, her thoughts becoming more clear. Edelein took deep breaths, grateful yet afraid.

"I'm fine," Edelein lied to herself, turning towards the shower. "A hot shower and a long rest will do me well... I'll be fine by morning."

As steaming water pasted wet hair to her skin, Edelein looked down at her trembling hands.

I've been on a boat for months. I've likely contracted an illness from the confined spaces, or perhaps sheer exhaustion is catching up to me. There are a lot of potential causes of this, but nothing that some rest cannot fix. Though... I fear that I have never felt an illness quite like this before. She thought as she stepped out of the shower, dressing herself in a soft white robe and laying down to rest.

Edelein stood alone as the cold night air bit her cheeks,

back home in the familiar territory of the Deepwood. The wind billowed out the dark blue cloak she wore, its comforting scent of home only a reminder of everything she had lost. In front of her, the shadow beast loomed with a wicked grin full of sharp teeth.

The loud growling noises of the monster silenced any usual nighttime chatter from the woods, the beast crashing through trees and underbrush as it barreled towards Edelein. The forest held its breath, afraid for its Queen and unable to protect her any longer.

This time, Edelein was alone, without her patrol to aid her. The lioness felt an icy chill in her bones, fear clawing at her body and trying to consume her soul as she stared the beast down. Knuckles white as she gripped tightly onto her bow, she raised her weapon, drawing the string back with all her might.

"Foul beast… your time terrorizing my people is over," she hissed through clenched teeth, lining up her shot against the eye of the creature. "Be gone!"

Edelein loosed her arrow, before a sudden realization overcame her a moment too late.

Why did I shoot at its eye again? My instincts should know better than that. This means that it will—!

Her thoughts were interrupted as her arrow whizzed through the night, piercing into the center of the creature's chest, striking the middle of its eye. The beast cried out, rearing back as it roared in agony.

Instead of the glowing cracks she had expected, Edelein stared at the beast in horror as the inky black skin began to melt away, the beast shrinking down in size as black smoke poured out around it. Once the smoke cleared, the monster was gone, and in its place was a familiar wolf-eared man.

Tyrus stood shakily, Edelein's arrow piercing the armor on his chest. Blood poured out from around the arrowhead, his shaky hands reaching up to his chest to touch the wound gently. The wolf-man looked up at Edelein, golden eyes alight with shock, fear, and pain.

"Your Majesty…" Tyrus coughed, dropping to his knees.

Eyes wide, Edelein dropped her bow as she ran forward towards her old friend, arm extended. She sprinted, but could feel him getting farther away the harder she tried to reach him. Tyrus looked up at her weakly, eyes dull.

"Your Majesty, why did you kill us?" he asked. "We trusted you, we served you…"

"No! I didn't mean to do it! You deserve to live, Tyrus, you'll be alright—!"

"Why did you shoot?!" Tyrus pressed, his voice fierce and firm.

"I didn't know!" Edelein cried out as Tyrus' head slumped backwards, eyes rolling back.

With a sick crack, Tyrus' head snapped forward, his lips twisting into a jagged-toothed grin as he looked up at Edelein.

Terrified, Edelein let out a fearful yelp as the shadow beast reappeared before her from Tyrus' lifeless body, large claws extended towards her as it dashed forward to tear her apart.

Edelein gasped, eyes fluttering open and bolting upright in her bed. A cold sweat chilled her bones as the lioness hyperventilated, clutching her chest. Shaking, Edelein looked down at her pale skin, muttering affirmations to herself as she turned to sit on the edge of her bed.

"It's not real… it's not real," Edelein mumbled, wiping some sweat from her forehead.

Crown of the Alchemist

As she stood, a cold fire began to ache in her legs, knees buckling slightly. Edelein winced, catching herself against the wall as her legs gave out. The burning sensation grew stronger as she forced herself out of her room, afraid of being alone as her body fought against invisible demons.

Normally, Zander would have found me by now… why isn't he here? Why has no one noticed me yet? Edelein thought passively, focusing her energy on putting one foot in front of the other. *Does Seventh Sense not work outside of the Deepwood? Why wouldn't it…?*

Leaning on the wall, Edelein's gaunt eyes landed on Dirigent Gihon, the only person still awake. The Dirigent sat in a large armchair, one leg crossed over the other as he leaned back with an arm behind his head. He appeared to be absorbed in an old book, his soft golden eyes skimming each line as he drank in the words.

"Gihon. Something is wrong with me," she called out weakly, the raven zoa looking up at the sound of his name.

His eyes widened as Gihon noticed the Queen leaning heavily on the wall. She was doubled over in pain, breathing hard and sweating. Without hesitation, Gihon tossed his book aside and ran over to her, grabbing her by the waist as she lost her strength and buckled down against his chest.

"What's going on?" Gihon asked, Edelein shaking her head weakly.

Grabbing a hold of her legs, Gihon swept the Queen up into his arms and walked back into the sitting room.

"I will set you down on the sofa, alright? You seem feverish. Allow me to call for the Zengarde–"

"No!" Edelein hissed quietly. "Don't alert them. I don't know why they haven't noticed my ailment, but if they find out now it will cause an uproar. They will think their Seventh Sense isn't working, and that will make them panic. This is foreign territory to us."

"A doctor, then…"

"No doctors."

"Now is not the time to be stubborn, Edelein, you're ill. At least tell me your symptoms."

"It's… my bones. My bones hurt. They ache and burn, but feel cold."

Gihon's eyebrows furrowed, his mind running through any illness he could think of that would match the description.

Cold burn sounds like a form of neurological damage… Gihon thought.

"And… the shadow beast…"

"What? Did you see a phantasm?" Gihon asked, eyes darting to her bedroom.

"In my mind, in the mirrors, in my nightmares. The creature plagues me."

Gihon set her down and knelt next to her, concerned as he took her wrist. Her skin felt cold to the touch even through his gloves, his fingers running over a small patch of black skin around her fingernails. The color drained from his face as the possibilities narrowed down to a single cause, a cause the Dirigent wished he could be wrong about.

"When you saw the phantasm, everything in front of you was withered, correct? The grass, trees?" he asked gently.

Edelein nodded weakly, shivering.

"Edelein, I have no choice but to be straightforward about this, so please forgive me. I believe you've contracted a rare condition called blight-sickness. You were close enough to the blight to be affected by it, but far enough to not be killed by it right away. Instead, the blight has infected your soul, and it is withering you like it did to the land, but slower."

"Y-you can fix it, can't you? With alchemy?" Edelein asked shakily as Gihon shook his head.

"Blight-sickness is incredibly rare, and fatal. We haven't been able to research it much at all, much less develop a cure for it. If it was a normal physical condition, it would be easier to study, but working with souls can be quite dangerous in alchemy. A lot can go wrong, and—"

"A lot can go wrong?!" Edelein whisper-yelled. "I am going to *die* because your people are too cowardly to study this disease? And I am supposed to trust you to help my people with these outbreaks in my homeland?"

"Edelein, please. I will do everything I can. If you allow me to study you in our downtime together, I may be able to find a cure before it's too late."

"How long do I have?" Edelein asked.

Gihon hesitated, staring down at her with eyes that held a thousand thoughts.

"How long, Gihon?" She repeated.

"It's hard to tell right now, but anywhere from one to five years. It will depend on the rate that this black skin spreads. Once it reaches your heart, it will consume you. For now, you will feel these symptoms in waves of flare-ups. Tomorrow morning you may feel just fine other than some chronic nerve pain. The rest of this... the sweats, chills, loss of breath, that will come and go sporadically. It can be sudden, so be careful. The symptoms will worsen with stress or overexertion, so avoid combat, heated arguments, and so on. You could faint if you overtax yourself."

"You're asking me, a monster hunter, to stay out of combat... and for me, the Queen, to avoid heated debates? You do know what my occupation entails, right?"

Gihon sighed. "As for the Zengarde... your ailment is within your soul, not your body, and I theorize that this Seventh

Sense you mentioned only works physically. They would notice a physical illness in you in a heartbeat, but a soul illness they are not able to see in the same way."

"I can't so much as get the sniffles without Zander running in to fret over me from the other side of the castle. It feels quite unnatural that he hasn't noticed this. However, I stand by not wanting them to know. I cannot afford to cause any unnecessary worry to them right now. We can tell them once the shadow beasts are quelled."

Gihon nodded, understanding. "I will keep this between us, however, please allow me to call for a doctor tomorrow. I am an alchemist, not a medic. I would like a second opinion from a professional. There is a zoa doctor who practices in Velkhamore."

"Meticulousness is just your nature, isn't it?" Edelein mused.

Gihon didn't respond, but looked down at her sympathetically.

"Fine," Edelein relented after a moment. "I'll see a doctor after the meeting tomorrow morning. Do not tell a soul about this otherwise."

"I promise," Gihon affirmed. "I'll also stay here with you until you feel well enough to go to sleep. I won't let you be alone, alright? We can stay up and talk, if you'd like."

Edelein smiled softly, nodding.

"One more thing. I do believe this goes without saying, but I don't want anyone outside of the Society knowing that we are here. Other than the ones we are meeting with for aid, that is. I don't want the world's first impression of my people to be that we are weak or vulnerable. Plus, I would likely be a target for any extremist groups, zoa poachers, or otherwise. We would prefer to remain anonymous."

"No one knows," Gihon assured her. "We take security very

seriously within the Society of Alchemists. The only people who know about you are myself, Torphus, Rahzopa, Clotho, Bex, and a few assistant alchemists. You're safe with us."

Hushed conversation broke the silence of nighttime a ways away from Edelein and Gihon. Two men sat across from each other, little light other than a small candle to illuminate them as it flickered on the small wooden table between them. The first man was obscured, a grey cloak pulled around him with the hood over his eyes so only the lower half of his tan face was visible. Across the table sat a man in a long, bright red coat, boots propped up on the table as he pushed himself back on the chair's rear legs. His face was barely visible in the dim light, so the hooded man could barely make out the piercing golden eyes in front of him. He was a slightly tanned and well-built man in his thirties. Silvery-white hair fell to his waist, shaggy and effortless.

The white-haired man spoke first, breaking the silence.

"So, you're telling me that the Zoa Queen herself is in Velkhamore? I take it she must have received the gift I sent her."

"Yes, she reported about phantasm outbreaks in the Deepwood and has arrived to receive aid from the Society. She has brought eight guardsmen with her to learn some alchemical combat. Honestly, they aren't what the Society expected. All of them are quite young, even the Queen. She's in her mid-twenties, I think."

"Did she bring what I wanted?"

"Yes. Two leyline crystals in return for the Society's help. It's just the thing you need to power up the Gates of Heaven."

The man straightened up, putting his feet back on the

ground as he leaned into his hands eagerly.

"Perfect. She's doing everything as according to plan. Two should be more than enough for the Gates. Killing a few nobles is just a fun bonus for me."

"Aren't you worried about what killing the Queen would do? A war would break out between their land and ours. It would be utter chaos."

The man in red paused, a tense air crackling through the silence. The hooded man shifted in his seat, anxious about stepping out of line. "Oh, darling little Bex. You look nervous. I sense you might still have some ties to the Society," the man sneered.

Bex's face twisted from under his hood, clearly unsettled.

"I-I just think that there's no need for unnecessary bloodshed, that's all…" Bex stammered.

"I'll keep her alive if it benefits me, if she's entertaining, or if she's pretty. Those are my rules. I doubt she'll be any of those, so I'm not bothered by it," the man in red laughed, leaning back again.

"What about our deal? You'll still hold up your end, right?"

"Yeah, yeah," the man waved his hand dismissively. "I'll free you from the Society. You can be like that one girl, the one who ran away to Avalstice after her discoveries were used for the Society's *backwards cruelty*. What's her name again? Eh, I don't care. Yeah, you'll be like her. No one from the Society will ever hear from you again. I'll grant you safe passage to a new life without the pressure and responsibility of a Caandemite alchemist."

"I want to go to Tozepia, in the South. The Society has intentions that I cannot bear to witness at times… I want to be free, live a quiet and kind life in the countryside."

"Genuinely, I could not care less what you do. Wait, didn't you say the Society was trying to promote you to Dirigent? You could have all the power in the world. Why stop here?"

Bex shifted uncomfortably in his chair. "Yes, but I don't

want to be a Dirigent. I just… didn't really know how to say no.
The higher-ups are frightening and I am far too young. I just want to
be free. I'm not made to govern, but for an alchemist of my caliber,
they consider it to be shirking duties to step down. I'm too far along
for them to let me leave peacefully. I'd be shunned, ostracized for
the rest of my life. That is, if they don't find a reason to arrest or kill
me."

"Well, it's good that you realize that now, I guess. You've
got a deal, okay? You've done well giving me all this intel so far. I
just need one more thing from you, and then you're done for good."

"W-what is it?" Bex asked.

"I need you to get one of her guards alone. I'll deliver the
message myself once you do."

Bex paused, surprised.

"Why the guards? You don't want the Queen?" The
alchemist queried.

"Look, kid. I have people on the inside, and it's my job to
know things. How do you think I've been sending phantasms into
their city? One of my associates has been in the Deepwood, setting
up all the backlashes to force the Queen out of hiding so she can
bring me her crystals, and he's been watching Zenluve from the
shadows the entire time. I know about her Zengarde, and I know
that they are driven entirely on instinct. All I need to do is tell one
of them I'm going for the Queen, and all of them will launch into
a panic. If she so much as gets a scratch on her, all eight of them
panic like animals. Their instinct will be to remove her from the
situation. In the disarray, taking the crystals will be pathetically
easy. Targeting her myself poses unnecessary risk, when the much
easier solution is to psychologically damage one of the Zengarde."

The man paused for a moment, thinking. "Their
disorderedly tendencies benefit me more than I first thought,
actually. Go ahead and poison her tea at your meeting tomorrow,

The Man in Red

Bex. The chaos that would ensue from her collapsing or dying would make it laughably easy to take the crystals right then and there while they're fretting over her. It would be so simple that even an imbecile such as yourself could do it, and I won't have to lift a finger."

"W-what if they don't bring the crystals tomorrow?" Bex stuttered, clearly hesitant on the idea of assassinating a royal in front of someone like Zander, the sphynx's tough demeanor haunting Bex's mind.

Unbothered, the man shrugged. "Then go back to the first plan. Get one of the guards alone, and I'll instill a fear so deep in him that he will not find peace for the rest of his life."

"Understood. I'll think of a way to get one of them alone. I-If they don't have the crystals there, that is."

"Good, now get out of here. I'm tired of looking at you," the man gestured, and Bex stood up.

"Oh, a-and one more thing you should know, sir."

"Make it quick."

"Dirigent Gihon is leading the operation with the Zenluvians. I figured you should know about that before you do anything rash."

"Gihon?!" The white-haired man slammed his fist into the table and stood up, face illuminated more clearly in the dim light. His gold eyes felt familiar in a way as they burned with irritation, his sharp features twisted in annoyance. "Why didn't you think to *lead* with that information?"

"I-I…"

"Gihon is, I begrudgingly admit, probably the strongest alchemist in Caandemium other than myself, of course. That bibliophilic hardass is a walking wrench in my plans. Keep him away from—actually, you know what? Frame the poison on him. That'll get him removed long enough for me to do what I need to do," the gold-eyed man laughed, satisfied with his idea.

"What if it doesn't—"

"Enough questions!" the man in red snapped, extending an arm as an array began to glow by his hand, an orb of fire growing brighter as he aimed it at the alchemist. "Go now, before I lose my temper and incinerate you!"

Without another word, Bex scrambled out of the room, slamming the door shut behind him as the man sat back down, grumbling angrily to himself.

CHAPTER 4

A CUP OF TEA

Early in the morning at the Society of Alchemists, Dirigent Gihon stood beside Bex, who was dutifully preparing tea as requested. The two men were standing in a small kitchenette just off of the main hall, often used by alchemists on early shifts for a variety of warm drinks. The cupboards were filled primarily with teas and coffees, and an iron kettle whistled on a single burner as Bex readied his beverage.

The alchemist's hands trembled slightly as he poured hot water into a fine teapot adorned with delicate patterns. Recognizing the brushwork on the porcelain, Gihon nodded approvingly.

The teapot is a Shuxing import. Bex truly does take his tea seriously, not unlike myself, Gihon mused, his attention fixed on the small details.

"Regarding those leyline crystals, Dirigent…" Bex started, breaking the silence.

"Fascinating, is it not?" Gihon replied, a subtle look of

excitement betraying his stoic demeanor. "We've never had the chance to study such a phenomenon."

Bex looked like he wanted to say more, but held his tongue as he closed the jar of dried tea leaves and put his hands in his pockets.

"Rahzopa has spoken fondly of your tea, Bex. I regret not having been able to try it sooner," Gihon continued warmly, a courteous professionalism in his voice as he tried to ease Bex's nerves.

"Y-yes, I grow and dry the leaves myself. I would love to open a tea shop one day, if I'm being honest."

"You should. Why are you trying to become a dirigent, then? You'd never have time for a tea shop. I know I would certainly welcome a diligent man such as yourself any time in Ravencroft, with tea as aromatic as this," Gihon replied, his gaze wandering to the hallway as Edelein passed by.

The Dirigent's eyes remained fixed on the hall ahead, his mind seeming to focus more on Edelein than on the current conversation.

"Right…" Bex trailed off, silence falling between them as he began to pour the steeped tea into small porcelain teacups.

After a moment, Gihon looked back down at the countertop where Bex was preparing tea.

"Is that one for Queen Edelein? Please, allow me to bring it to her," Gihon offered, picking up one of the cups.

I want to check on her before the meeting, to see how her condition is. Gihon thought.

"O-oh, are you sure?" Bex asked, looking a bit restless.

"Of course. There is nothing to be anxious about, Bex. You're an honorable man with a wonderful skill for tea-making. It's quite alright to allow a dirigent to assist you if it is offered, I assure you. Head into the conference room, and I will bring Queen Edelein in so we can start the meeting."

Bex nodded, lips pressed together as he headed into the board room. Gihon walked out into the main hallway, where he saw Edelein standing alone. She was looking out of a large window, seeming grateful for the warm morning sunshine as she allowed herself to get lost in her own silent thoughts.

Alchemists clamored around Gihon as they prepared for the day's work ahead, the Dirigent ignoring them as he approached Edelein, tea in hand.

"Your Majesty? We are ready to begin the meeting. Bex has prepared home-brewed tea that he grew himself, and it's quite lovely. I believe it will help ease your nerves."

"Right... I am here." Edelein turned, fiddling with her gloves as she took the tea from him, staring into the cup idly.

She's definitely thinking about last night. Edelein keeps fidgeting and touching her hands.

"How are you feeling?" Gihon asked, his voice low so as to not be overheard.

"Fine... better... you needn't worry. It is far from how it was yesterday, so I will be alright." Edelein mumbled, seeming like she was trying to convince herself just as much as she was trying to convince the Dirigent.

"Let's go in and start the meeting now, then, if you are ready. There is a lot that we need to explain to you." Gihon put his hand on her back gently, leading her into the conference room.

As Edelein entered the room, the eight Zengarde stood from their seats to salute to her, the alchemists rising to bow politely. The group had all been seated around a long mahogany table, the room's main focal point. Large windows across one wall allowed soft morning light to illuminate the silhouettes of Edelein's allies, and a stone fireplace cast warmth from the far end of the conference area.

Crown of the Alchemist

The Queen sat herself at the head of the table, Gihon taking the seat next to her. Zander's eyes narrowed as he sat on her other side, distrusting as always. His silent stare almost seemed to beg Gihon to try something, to give a reason for a fight. As everyone situated themselves, Torphus began to speak.

"You mentioned appearances of a phantasm within your city walls," Torphus stated. "However, you did not provide any details for us. Care to explain further?"

"Torphus, one would normally begin with a greeting. She is a woman of incredibly high status, so please speak accordingly," Gihon warned, already feeling the exhaustion set in.

"I have omitted details in the best interest of my homeland. We value our privacy, if that was not apparent," Edelein replied simply, leaning back as she set her tea down.

"If you want our help, tell us what happened," Torphus countered, "Your Majesty."

Edelein narrowed her eyes, meeting Torphus' challenging glare as the dwarf continued.

"We are interested in knowing about the symptoms of the event. Your people were exposed to heavy sources of energy. Did that alter anyone near? Are the people suffering from discontentment at the Royal Court's response? You do have a Royal Court, yes?"

Edelein continued to hold her gaze confidently, letting Torphus speak with more and more desperation seeping into his tone.

"Economic hardships? Are trade routes being affected by the phantasm outbreaks? Has the presence of phantasmal beings impacted agriculture in any way, and does that alter what you choose to export?"

Torphus' words met silence, the only sound coming from Clotho as they let out a small chuckle. Edelein's icy blue glare pierced across the table, silencing Clotho with a single look.

"How many of your militia have fallen? Is there a military decline in Zenluve right now?" Torphus pressed desperately.

"Torphus, you're making a fool of yourself right now," Rahzopa whispered. The dwarf stopped, blood rushing to his head as his cheeks flushed. "See how Queen Edelein has been letting you ramble on like this? She's letting you sabotage yourself."

A smirk curled up the corner of Edelein's lip, the Queen letting out a soft huff of amusement as Rahzopa figured out her plan.

"If you are finished, I will disclose precisely the amount of information that I deem necessary to our cause, and that will be sufficient for you. You will not speak to me further unless I ask you a question, Alchemist Torphus," Edelein finally spoke, picking up her teacup and relishing a slow sip to prove her point.

Biting his tongue, Torphus nodded silently.

"Moving on, then," Edelein took command of the meeting, turning to face Gihon. "Dirigent, my people are unversed in the knowledge of alchemy. With your teaching prowess, I assume you would not mind—nay, find enthusiasm in—explaining the basics to us. Speak when you are ready."

She is quite capable of turning on that regal aura of hers at will. Gihon recalled the playful lioness as she wandered around the city the evening before. *Edelein meant it when she said her duties will be resuming. It's like she's a different person now.*

Gihon bowed his head towards Edelein, signaling his respect as he stood up to begin his lecture.

"Absolutely, Your Majesty. Alchemy is the art of transforming matter by accelerating natural reactions, through the use of external energy. We do this by utilizing a system of arrays that allow us to channel energy, giving us access to feats normally not deemed possible," Gihon started, feeling his inner teacher arise as he remembered his first group of students, long ago.

Crown of the Alchemist

"The creature you fought is called a phantasm, and they are created by alchemical backlashes. They are beings from another plane, whisked to ours against their will through poorly-executed alchemy. They are often disoriented, scared even. Our world encases them in what we call a reality shell, which is what keeps them intact until they can return to their plane."

"You saw what happens when reality shells are broken," Clotho added. "Energies of different planes cannot mix, and create an annihilation event when there is nothing separating them."

Rahzopa nodded, turning to look warmly at Edelein. "We can show you how to create banishment arrays. Once you know how to do that, it's only a matter of drawing the weakened phantasm onto the array, and *poof*– it becomes nothing more than a memory, as it gets sent safely into the Sea of Miracles."

Alett looked across the table at Rahzopa, curious. "By the Sea of Miracles, you're referring to the space between planes, right?"

"Yes, Zwitet. It seems you do have some knowledge about all this, then."

"We do possess Tevus' largest leyline. It would be foolish of us to not study the planes at all, especially when–"

"Zwitet Alett," Edelein raised one hand to silence her guard, turning towards Gihon again. "These monsters are created by backlashes, you said. Explain to me what that means."

"You can think of an array as an equation, or code, that helps direct specific chemical reactions," Gihon answered. "Sometimes, there is an imbalance with the equation and the array will attempt to correct itself by drawing material from another plane. When that happens, matter will trade between our plane and another, with a reality shell encasing the newly introduced material."

"Think of it this way," Rahzopa added. "Alchemy is

similar to arithmetic. Writing an array is like writing a math equation. If your equation is wrong, the laws of nature will force new numbers in to correct it for you. For example, if you were to say that one plus one equals three, natural law would draw another digit from a different plane, adding a third 'one' to correct the equation. However, the third digit is not supposed to be here, so it ends up encased in that reality shell, which can be a terrifying and disorienting experience."

"I understand. These reality shells, they are naturally occurring, correct?" Edelein asked.

Gihon nodded. "As far as we know, yes. The Church of Prima Luma believes it is a part of natural law that these shells are created around foreign material. The shells themselves are made of a primordial element that we have not had the pleasure of studying, yet."

"The Church of Prima Luma?" Edelein asked, flicking her tail. "Why would alchemists care about the opinion of a church? Are they that significant to your society?"

You get to ask about our society but we cannot ask about yours? Torphus' face seemed to scream silently, though the dwarf did his best to mask his thoughts as Gihon answered her.

"You have likely heard of the Caandemite Faith Wars of long ago. The Church of Prima Luma was the victor of the war, and now they oversee Caandemium alongside the Society of Alchemists. I will be more than happy to tell you more about our geopolitics, but I fear that now is not the time," Gihon explained, leaning forward slightly as he sat back down.

"Would you mind giving us a detailed account of the phantasm encounter?" Clotho asked, hands folded on the table. "You can leave out details of your kingdom's secrets. It will help us if we know exactly what type of phantasm it was, which you certainly will not be able to tell us directly, so your description of it will have to suffice."

Gihon looked over at Edelein, whose demeanor seemed to have faltered slightly as her eyes got lost in nightmarish memories. Gihon reached from under the table to squeeze her hand gently, assuring her. Edelein looked up, first to Gihon, and then to Clotho as her mind returned to the present. She withdrew her hand from Gihon's to pick up her tea and take a small sip, avoiding eye contact with anyone.

Is she alright...? Gihon thought to himself, concerned.

"Yes," Edelein nodded solemnly, clearing her throat as she tried to ground herself. "I was out on a hunt with two Zengarde. We partnered up with four patrolmen when the attack happened."

"Is it customary for the Queen to do something so lowly as hunting and patrolling?" Clotho asked.

"Not normally, but my father raised me with a love for the forest in my heart. I spent my youth training in archery and tracking, and became known throughout Zenluve as a fearsome monster hunter. I wanted to go out when my Zengarde invited me. Their names were Tyrus and Cyzen. They were good friends of mine."

The faces of the other Zengarde darkened at the mention of their fallen allies.

"Tyrus had wanted to go hunting. It's not unheard of for a Zengarde to hunt monsters every now and then, so I invited him to join me. Cyzen had followed after him and accompanied us as well. We weren't even out of the walls of Zenluve before the shadow beast—ah, excuse me, the phantasm—attacked. There had been rumors of these creatures appearing in Avalstice for some time, and a few patrols had gone missing a little while ago. However, as unfortunate as it sounds... it's not too noteworthy if a patrol is taken out, as the Deepwood can be a brutal place with terrible monsters. It doesn't happen often, but it does happen."

"Was it happening more frequently before the attack?" Bex

asked.

"Yes, I believe so… but again, the instances were not significant enough for us to think it could have been the phantasms we had heard rumors about. We had foolishly thought that no such being would ever dare traverse into the Deepwood."

It is quite unusual that phantasms are in the Deepwood. It would mean that someone is practicing alchemy in Zenluve. Gihon thought, before speaking his next question aloud.

"You don't practice modern alchemy in Zenluve, but you have zoa transfiguration. If someone were to create a zoa, how would they do it? If you don't mind sharing, that is."

Edelein pondered for a moment, seeming to think about whether or not she wanted to disclose the information. After a moment, she shook her head.

"No, Dirigent. Though I will, in good faith, disclose that most of us are descended zoa rather than transmuted zoa."

Gihon nodded, understanding.

"What happened when you saw the phantasm?" Rahzopa asked Edelein. "What did it look like?"

"It was huge, with a horrible grimacing smile. The seven of us tried to fight it, but its skin was incredibly tough. It…" Edelein trailed off, her voice shaking as she bit back tears.

"Please, continue–" Torphus began.

"Torphus, enough!" Gihon snapped, glaring at the far end of the table where the alchemists sat. "This is a hard trauma to make someone relive. Give her time."

"No, it's alright," Edelein mumbled, steeling her nerves as she took another sip of her tea. "The phantasm… destroyed the Zengarde. Tyrus charged in, and it broke his sword. The monster was terribly fast, as well, and went for Cyzen next. They died before they even knew what was happening."

"And the others?" prompted Clotho, indifferent.

"The others are dead because of me. The phantasm had an eye on its chest, which appeared to be a weak spot. I shot at that eye, trying to save them. I didn't know…"

"It's alright, Your Majesty. You are not to blame for this," Gihon reassured her.

"Well, she technically is," Clotho shrugged, Gihon casting a harsh glare at the alchemist.

Edelein clenched her fists, continuing. "When my arrow struck the eye, it began to glow brightly… and when I opened my eyes, nothing was left. The forest was dead, my men disintegrated."

Clotho leaned forward. "This is why it is important to utilize alchemy for the safe removal of a phantasm, rather than shooting them with physical weapons–"

"You think I don't realize that?!" Edelein stood, the impact of her slammed fist knocking over her teacup. "I know. I *know*! I watched six brave soldiers die right in front of my eyes. I, their Queen, the one they swore their lives to protect, could do nothing but sit by and watch them die because I had shot at that horrible thing! I could have had them retreat! I…"

Edelein's eyelids fluttered as she trailed off, swooning as she lost her balance and crumpled to the ground.

Time slowed as Gihon noticed the buckle of Edelein's knees, reaching out and catching her in his arms just before her head hit the floor. The same gaunt look stained her unconscious face as he checked her pulse with two fingers against her pale, clammy neck.

The room erupted into sudden chaos, the Zengarde clamoring amongst themselves as they leaped to their feet in alarm. The alchemists stared ahead at Edelein and Gihon, eyes wide.

"Bex, call for the physician. Rahzopa, fetch me some salt and ammonia immediately from–" Gihon's commands were cut short as Zander let out a loud and catlike yowl, leaping over the table to where Gihon held his Queen.

The Man in Red

"What did you do to her, corvid?!" Zander screeched, ripping Edelein out of Gihon's arms and holding onto her protectively.

Turning, Zander handed Edelein over to the large bovine Zengarde, Everett, who cradled her with a look of concern on his face. The other six Zengarde formed a protective wall between the Queen and the alchemists, bristling with a mix of rage and fear. The sphynx roared in anger, grabbing Gihon's shirt collar and baring his fangs.

"Zander, she needs medical attention. Please let go of me. We can help her."

"You poisoned her, didn't you?!" Zander hissed, knuckles turning white as he pulled Gihon closer. "Lylia, check her tea. You, *corvid*, give me a reason to not tear your throat out right now."

Clotho's laugh sounded from the other side of the table, drawing the attention of the enraged Ehret. Beside him, Bex was tense, face drained of color, frozen in place as he watched the scene unfold. Torphus and Rahzopa turned to face Clotho, shocked by his outburst.

"You want a reason? Here's one. Gihon is the Dirigent of Ravencroft, apprentice and son to the most prominent alchemist of this century, Dirigent Arvien Marleogne. A man of fame like that, and you've got your grimy little paws on him. Strike and he'd kill you first, not to mention the security officers we have posted in the halls. What's your plan, then? Try to kill a dirigent and spend your life rotting in a cell? Or would you rather endanger your team as you all become fugitives in a foreign land, forever unable to return home?"

"Zander..." Lylia, the elf, warned as Zander let go of the Dirigent's collar, claws catching the light as he approached Clotho slowly, seething.

"Every single one of us is prepared to die or kill for our

Queen," Zander spat, looming over Clotho. "I will *gladly* kill a few alchemists to protect or avenge her."

"Zander," Lylia repeated, more sternly.

"You do not understand the weight of your words, cat. I have lived many lives, this body merely one version of myself in a long line of history! You are nothing compared to me, nothing compared to the Dirigent–"

"Clotho," Gihon's deep voice boomed from the other side of the table, commanding everyone's attention. "Do not speak for me."

As Gihon approached, his powerful aura resonated within Zander's instinct, sending chills up his spine. His eyes were cold, burning with frustration as he clenched his fists, dark hair obscuring his face.

Zander's eyes widened, sensing the aura coming from the Dirigent. Black wings folded around him, the dark smoke of his presence filling the room. As he blinked, the vision was gone, Gihon standing over Clotho angrily.

The prophecy… it is him. I knew it. He who will destroy Edelein. Zander thought to himself, muscles tensing as he prepared to spring into action.

Torphus chuckled nervously, desperate to diffuse the situation. "Please, noble Zengarde, have no fear. I can assure you that the Queen is in good hands. We have modern medicine here, and we can take better care of her here than anywhere else. In fact, she'd probably even be better here than in Zenluve, too. Let's not be animals about this, now–"

"Animals?!" Jinn and Cari spat in unison, their fur bristling as Jinn pulled his lips back into a snarl.

"I-I simply mean… our medics here are more practiced than–"

"Our healer is hundreds of years old and has seen, touched,

and healed more than any of your medics would see in their lifetimes, combined!" Zander yelled.

"Zander!" Lylia yelled back, finally getting his attention as the room fell silent. "This hundreds-of-years-old healer has been *trying* to tell you that there's no poison in the Queen's tea, so drop it! Just shut up for one second, please!"

A beat of silence held the room as the elf's words echoed in everyone's minds, the Zengarde stunned and confused.

"There's no sign of any sort of toxin in Eddie's system, either," Alett added, looking up from where Everett held her. "It's almost like she's just… asleep. I can't find anything wrong with her at all."

"Please allow me to explain." Gihon sighed after a moment's hesitation. "I know what happened to Queen Edelein."

The room held its silence, Zander seething with his teeth clenched. Nephvir put a hand on Zander's shoulder, his violet eye bright against black sclera as concern and curiosity reflected in his gaze.

"Let's hear him out, Zander. This will allow us to help her. We have to work with them, not against them. It's in our best interests to be on their side."

Zander nodded coldly to Gihon, indicating for him to speak.

"I met with Her Majesty late last night. I was awake already, and she approached me claiming to feel ill. I evaluated her physical health and symptoms, and while I have an appointment set up for her with a physician later today to confirm it, I believe she has been blighted from the phantasm attack."

The alchemists clamored amongst themselves, appalled. The Zengarde looked around, unsure of the meaning of his words but picking up on the grim nature of it.

"That's not good… at all…" Bex shifted uncomfortably,

eyebrows furrowed as he fidgeted with his hands.

"She is in the early stages of it now, and I hope to find a cure for it before it is too late. She has agreed to let me study her condition. I can assure you all, I would not poison her tea. Bex grew and dried the leaves himself, and I would never sully such a thing. Neither would he, as a man of culture who appreciates such work."

Bex nodded shakily in agreement.

"So she's ill, then," Zander confirmed, the wrap around his hairless head furrowing where his eyebrows would be, "and you expect me to believe that none of us noticed?"

"Queen Edelein expressed the same concern to me last night. Blight-sickness is a disease that affects one's soul, not the body, although it can manifest physical symptoms such as nerve pain and as you have noticed, fainting spells. I believe that your heightened senses work physically, and not spiritually, which is why you cannot notice the blight-sickness in the same way you would for a common illness."

"I notice *everything* about her. Seventh Sense has no limit," Zander denied, defiant.

Alett sighed, adding, "Zander is just upset. You're right, Gihon, our Seventh Sense is in fact physical. It can falter in situations such as big crowds and large-scale unfamiliar territory. Meaning… it works better in Zenluve, because we know the land and thus take in less new stimuli, allowing us to focus better on her."

"I can discern her lies from truths. That isn't physical."

"You notice that because of the subtle changes in her body language and temperature. That is physical, Zander," Alett looked sympathetically up at his ally, understanding his reaction.

Zander growled, flattening his ears angrily. For a moment, Gihon considered asking more, curious about the Seventh Sense.

"Queen Edelein had only mentioned it in passing, and I

would like to know more about your Seventh Sense, as you call it—"

Gihon was interrupted as Everett exclaimed in relief. Looking over, he saw Edelein's eyes flutter open as she picked up her head abruptly, looking around.

"Thank goodness!" Everett smiled down at her as he whispered quietly. "I'm so glad you woke up. Everything is kind of falling apart right now."

"What happened?" Edelein asked as the ox set her down gently.

"You fainted, Your Majesty," Cari stated, still looking concerned.

"Yeah, and then Zander tried to kill Gihon because he thought the Dirigent had poisoned you," Thorne laughed, Lylia elbowing him in warning.

Shut up, Thorne. Lylia's cold green eyes said. *Don't escalate this further.*

Edelein looked around, surprised as she met Gihon's worried gaze.

"I am quite fine, I assure you all," Edelein forced a laugh, looking back at her Zengarde. "I hope I did not cause too much concern. There is nothing amiss."

"Except for the blight-sickness?" Clotho asked flatly, one eyebrow cocked as they called out the Queen's lie.

A shock jolted through the Queen at his words, her head whipping around to stare daggers at Gihon. He looked away, face slightly red as he pursed his lips in embarrassment.

You told them?! Her face screamed silently.

I'm sorry! Gihon's eyes begged in return.

Looking around the room, Torphus stepped up to make the call.

"Dirigent Gihon, please bring Her Majesty back to the

house for some rest. I think we have a good enough record of
the recent events, so I propose we begin basic training now. I do
hope we can all move forward from this, now that the air has been
cleared."

"Some of us need to stay with the Queen," Zander growled.
"I'm not leaving her alone with him."

"Didn't Edelein say that you weren't allowed to talk, little
dwarf?" Cari added, her rose-colored eyes brimming with distrust
behind her round-framed glasses.

"You need to learn how alchemy works for the sake of your
Kingdom. Gihon will be with her, and he could protect her from
anything just as well as the rest of you, so there really is nothing to
worry about," Torphus smiled awkwardly, choosing to ignore Cari's
comment.

"Do not speak of what you do not know, dwarf," Zander's
eyes narrowed. "Actually, do not speak at all. I will enforce Her
Majesty's command from here on."

"Zander, it's really important that we learn from these
guys." Alett looked up at his friend, his large orange eyes
reassuring. "I'm sure she'll be safe with Gihon."

"You did not see what I did, Alett. The pr—"

"It's going to be okay." Alett lowered his voice to a
whisper. "We don't know for sure if it's him. You gotta give him the
benefit of the doubt for now, okay? There's too many variables to
consider… he's not even from Avalstice. It's just a coincidence."

Bex cleared his throat, eyes shifting to flit briefly across
each of the Zengarde, unsure of where to put his gaze.

"There are training grounds outside of the building that we
can use to practice. I know you are here to learn from us, but I think
I could learn from you as well. Perhaps one of you could come spar
with me, outside?"

"I would quite like that," Jinn agreed quickly, the wolf zoa flicking one ear in anticipation. "Studying old texts isn't really my style. I'd learn better from fighting an alchemist."

Gihon nodded in approval. "Zander, Cari, and Nephvir, please go with Rahzopa. Thorne, Everett, and Lylia, please study with Clotho. Torphus, take records of the events and get them filed. Jinn can go outside and spar with Bex. Alett, please accompany me to the noble house. That will give Zander some peace of mind, and I will be able to teach you from my books while Queen Edelein rests."

Splitting them like this will make them the least likely to kill each other while I'm gone, I theorize. Gihon thought to himself. *I also need to apologize to Edelein for using the truth of her condition to get Zander off my back. She seems to be upset by that, reasonably so.*

The Zengarde nodded, saluting Edelein as they broke up into groups. Zander looked incredibly displeased as he approached Alett again, speaking quietly.

"Keep an eye on the corvid, Alett. I still don't trust him around Edelein," Zander hissed under his breath. "Frankly, I hardly trust you alone with them, either. I know you sent him to fetch her after her little stunt last night. His scent was all over her this morning. Do not let them get close, and do not let them be alone at any point. She has yet to produce an heir of First Ancestor Alderich, and–"

"If you want an heir of Alderich, maybe leaving them alone is a good idea," Alett shrugged with a laugh.

Zander clearly did not appreciate the owl's humor, his expression stone-faced.

"A corvid cannot inherit the throne."

"I know, I know. It's fine, I've got it handled!" Alett smiled, giving the sphynx an assuring thumbs-up. "I'll keep an eye on them both. No prophecies, no sneaking off. I'll protect her from the big bad raven boy. It'll be fine!"

"You are making light of a situation that is better handled seriously."

"Counter point, you think every situation should be handled seriously. Crack a joke now and then, Zander," Alett retorted playfully with a dismissive wave as he followed Gihon out of the room.

CHAPTER 5

SPARRING MATCH

A simple triangular array glowed bright orange under Bex's palm, igniting the air surrounding his hand as he pulled his arm backwards, a long whip of flames appearing out of seemingly nowhere. Determination twisted the alchemist's face as he cracked the whip forward towards Jinn, the white wolf waiting until the last moment to sidestep effortlessly.

The sky was overcast, clouds heavy with rain waiting to pour out, almost seeming as if the weather was courteous enough to wait until the fire-wielder finished his training before dousing the area.

As the whip connected with the ground where Jinn's feet had stood, smoke and dust billowed up into the air around him. Bex pulled back his whip and readied himself, expecting the wolf to lunge from his obscured position.

Instead, as the smoke cleared, Bex saw Jinn standing still, one arm reaching towards his sheathed sword silently to just barely touch its hilt.

He's deflecting and dodging everything I've thrown at him so far. Bex thought. *He hasn't even unsheathed his sword yet!*

"How are you so fast?" Bex asked as Jinn easily avoided another attack from his whip.

"I can sense your movements before you make them," Jinn replied calmly, strafing to his right as another blow came in. He ducked low to the ground as Bex cracked the whip towards the wolf's head.

"I can sense your weaknesses just as easily," Jinn continued, lunging up from the ground to kick at Bex's head. "It is known as the Zengarde's *Seventh Sense.*"

The alchemist's eyes widened, dispelling the whip array to block the kick with his arm. The force still sent him skidding backwards, his body weight low to keep himself upright.

Honestly, with a move of that speed and force, I'm just happy I'm still standing. Bex mused silently to himself.

"You are limited by your range." Jinn commented, standing more upright to explain his thoughts, his stance relaxing. "You need to keep your opponent away from your body, or you will lose every time. Your ranged attacks are well-executed, but it is far too easy for me to get in close and defeat you."

At least he thinks they're well-executed. Bex sighed. *Even though not a single one has hit him. His ability to read his enemy is akin to a wizard using foresight, and his speed is dangerous. The only way to win would be to overwhelm him completely, from all directions.*

Bex clenched his teeth, lowering his stance. He held out one arm, pulling a whip of fire back from it with his other hand and holding the position with both hands. A large array began to glow from underneath him, the energy from it rippling upwards across the long grey coat of his alchemist's uniform.

The Man in Red

"Alright, it looks like I'll have to give it my all, then," Bex muttered, feeling the energy course through his veins as flames began to seep upwards from the array.

Flames crawled up behind him, licking the oxygen from the air greedily as the pyre grew taller. With a hiss, the inferno began to take shape, with long fangs forming and clamping down within the mouth of a large viper. The snake took its shape, fully realized as it held its head proud behind its master.

"Try to dodge this!" Bex shouted, the serpent opening its mouth to strike, fangs bared.

The Blazing Basilisk is my ultimate move, with a large radius and incredible speed that engulfs any enemy. It is effectively undodgeable, due to the area of its effect. Bex recalled, as Jinn readied his stance with a soft grunt.

Jinn held his stance, arm close to the hilt of his sword, ready to strike. As the snake lunged down towards him, the wolf zoa stood steady, eyes narrow.

If I strike too early, it will dodge my attack and I will be consumed, Jinn thought, understanding. *I must wait for the opening. Sense it...* Jinn's thoughts raced, his muscles tensing at the last moment. *...Now!*

His eyes widened, gaze intense as his senses triggered an opening. Dashing forward, Jinn pulled his sword from its sheath, leaping up to slice across the mouth of the basilisk. It hissed in pain and pulled backwards, rearing its head up as the flames began to melt and dispel back into the oxygen around it.

Jinn's body twisted as he fell back towards the ground, flipping forwards and landing on his feet, one knee on the ground as he sheathed his sword one more. As the remaining flames fizzled weakly around him like a dying candle, illuminating his physique, Bex's face dropped in astonishment.

Jinn just... destroyed my Blazing Basilisk in one hit, like it was nothing. He... cut through the fire and dispelled it. They said he's only the third-highest rank of the Zengarde? These Zenluvians are monsters.

"You fight well, Alchemist Bex," Jinn affirmed as he stood up straight, extending one hand towards Bex for a handshake.

"You're too kind. I cannot say I feel as if I've fought well, knowing that I couldn't land a single hit on you," Bex replied sheepishly.

"As I mentioned, focus on keeping your range. I would also recommend developing more close-combat techniques to defend yourself from melee attacks."

"You're right about that, close-range was never my specialty. I'm just surprised you could read that on me so quickly," Bex agreed, reaching out to shake Jinn's hand.

"Zenluvian instinct is unmatched by anyone, anywhere. The Zengarde have the strongest instinct of anyone. I read that on you before we even began, and your fighting style only confirmed my suspicions. However, that final move of yours was truly impressive. You should stand proud. Let's go another round, so you may try to use your alchemy in close range."

"Thank you, I do believe I was simply outclassed by the Dritet of the Zengarde. You're a worthy opponent, Jinn, by far the fastest I've met. I'd be happy to go another round and try—"

"Get down!" Bex's statement was cut short by a sudden exclamation from Jinn, who pulled Bex forward towards him, both of them tumbling towards the ground as a pillar of red energy beamed across the exact spot where Bex had stood a moment before.

The beam narrowly missed Bex, barreling past the two and colliding with the trees in the distance with a huge explosion of energy, smoke pouring out from the area it struck.

"What the hell was that?!" Jinn asked, Bex staring at the

smoke as the color drained from his face, not listening to Jinn.

If Jinn didn't pull me out of the way, I would have died, Bex realized in horror.

"Danger. I sense malice," Jinn growled as his Seventh Sense fired off a warning within him, his thumb pressing against the knuckle guard of his hilt, lifting the blade slightly from its sheath.

Both men turned in the direction that the beam of light came from, chills running through Bex's body as a familiar white-haired man greeted them. His bright red coat billowed in the wind, a large and opulent broadsword hoisted over his shoulder as he grinned.

"Thank you for bringing me the Zengarde, Bex. I'll take it from here," he smirked.

Bex's eyes widened as he made the connection in his mind.

"Hang on, d-did you try to hit me?! What about our deal?!" Bex stuttered, trying to stand up for himself against the man he feared so greatly.

"Deal? Bex, who is he? Do you know him?" Jinn asked, his ears flat backwards and the bridge of his nose scrunched up into a snarl.

Bex clenched his teeth, sighing as he glanced sideways at Jinn.

"I'm… sorry, Jinn. I really did enjoy sparring with you. It's just… he's my only way out of this hellhole. He said he could get me out of the prying eyes of the Society, to live a life of peace and quiet. The only thing he wanted was for me to isolate one of you. Listen, he's—"

Bex was cut off as the man ahead of them pressed one hand to the ground, a bright red array glowing under his palm. The assailant's array was chaotic and extravagant, far too many lines connecting into dozens of patterns and shapes. The ground between them began to crack and break, a large pillar of stone rising from beneath Bex to launch him in the air, wind knocked from his lungs.

"Your services are no longer needed. Goodbye," the man snickered, extending his hand to point upwards at Bex.

Red energy began to glow from his fingertips, its core white-hot as he fired another beam towards the alchemist as if he were nothing more than target practice.

"This isn't freedom!" Bex yelled, extending his palm to propel himself out of the way with a blast of flame from his hand. "You lied!"

"I prefer the term half-truth," the white-haired man laughed, looking up at Bex as he tumbled to the ground.

Silently from beside the man, Jinn struck with a powerful leap, similar to the attack he used against Bex's serpent. Without turning to face him, the red-coated man crossed his blade to meet Jinn's casually.

"Not yet, pup. I'll deal with you in a moment," he said, placing his free hand on Jinn's chest as another array began to glow. "Master's busy, so wait your turn like a good dog!"

As the array activated, a strong gust of wind blew Jinn backwards into the air. He dropped his sheath to reinforce his parry with his second hand, breaking the wind current slightly against his blade.

Wind powers? He's like Thorne, then, Jinn thought, holding tightly onto his sword with both hands. *No... this man is far stronger than Thorne, I can sense that much. I should exercise caution in disposing of him.*

"You owe me my freedom!" Bex screamed, leaping into the air as a flurry of fire whips rained down on the ground below.

I already used most of my energy on the Blazing Basilisk. I knew he was coming, but I didn't think he would be targeting me like this...! Bex thought in a panic, mustering all of his remaining strength to focus on his whips.

112

The Man in Red

The man laughed wildly, dodging each strike as they ignited the ground beside him. He dashed and weaved through them with a wicked grin, seeming to enjoy the moment.

He's even faster than Jinn. I thought that if I could get one of the higher-ranked Zengarde to come with me, that maybe they would stand a chance against him. Bex realized in horror. *I was wrong. He's too powerful for any of them.*

"You want freedom?" the man taunted, leaping into the air as his sword began to glow a brilliant white color. "You want to go somewhere the Society of Alchemists cannot find you?"

He's getting too close...! Bex thought as his whips began to dissipate.

"Wish granted!" the man in red yelled in delight, his sword slicing clean through Bex's torso.

For a brief moment, Bex could feel the sword cut through reality itself, a burning fire in the pit of his stomach that put his Basilisk to shame. As the feeling faded, the light in the alchemist's eye did also, the only things reflecting were the particles of light that floated from his midsection as his body began to dissolve.

Landing easily on his feet, the man in red turned to Jinn, completely unbothered by the scene unfolding above him as Bex's body dissipated, motes of light the only thing remaining until they also vanished into nothing.

Jinn looked on in horror, feeling frozen for the first time in his life.

"Bex!" he cried out, trying to understand the situation.

He just... vanished...! Jinn thought. *One strike from that man's blade, and his body dissolved. I've never seen anything like it. I cannot feel Bex's presence any longer, as if he were never here to begin with.*

"What? Why the long face, pup?" the man sneered, the tip of his sword resting in the dirt. "Bex asked me to free him from the clutches of the Society of Alchemists. I'm simply holding up my end of the deal, that's all."

"What kind of monster are you?" Jinn asked quietly, his body yearning to flee though he continued to stand his ground.

"You see this?" the man in red asked as he held up the sword, which glowed slightly in the sunlight but did not seem to carry the same sheen as it did when he struck Bex. "Have you ever heard of the Three Nails of Atzmus, dog?"

What's his plan? Jinn wondered, furrowing his eyebrows.

"The Three Nails of Atzmus. Come on, puppy, the nails that held heaven to the material plane. The first failure of mankind was when the nails were dislodged from the ground, breaking our connection and ability to pass into Ethereus due to humanity's greed and shortcomings. You must know this story, surely."

A subtle confused tilt of Jinn's head made the man in red groan loudly, swinging his sword around in a dramatic fashion.

"The nails that were taken and reforged by the ancient dragon Gabriel and turned into the three Divine Swords! Is none of this familiar to you at all? You really don't know the swords Kether, Chokma, and Baina?"

"The only sword that matters is the one that runs through you," Jinn extended his blade and lowered his stance, eyes narrow.

"Well, the one you're looking at is the Divine Sword, Kether. A single touch from my blade and your fate will be the same as the alchemist's. Do you still want to fight, or are you going to run away to the other Zengarde, you little mutt?"

"Don't call me a mutt," Jinn snapped, the fur on his ears bristling in agitation. "I don't know who you are, but I intend to kill you. I find you to be an incredibly egocentric psychopath, and I have no interest in engaging further with you, scum."

Jinn let out a focused exhale, drawing his fingers along the side of his blade as he lowered his stance.

The Man in Red

"Die," he growled.

"I like your attitude. You'll be much more fun than the crybaby alchemist," the man grinned, clenching his fist around the hilt of his sword.

Before he could finish his thought, Jinn had dashed forward with incredible speed, sword wound up behind him for a powerful strike. He slashed in the blink of an eye, the red-clad man only barely getting his sword in front in time to parry the attack.

"You *are* pretty fast!" the man exclaimed, recalling Bex's earlier comments during their spar. "That strike would have killed most people, I'll admit."

As Jinn's sword recoiled back, the white wolf let the momentum carry him into a second lunge. Anticipating the attack, the gold-eyed swordsman met his blade in another parry.

"Not bad, but it's not going to be enough!" he bellowed gleefully, sliding Jinn's blade away and throwing his guard hand forward for a swift punch.

Jinn's senses fired off as the glove of his opponent reached his jaw, the electrifying feeling of a Seventh Sense welling up inside and moving his limbs on instinct. Letting the momentum of the punch push him, the Dritet dug his heel downwards, pivoting his foot and turning his body as his second hand grabbed the hilt of his sword, using the momentum to carry himself into a strong two-handed strike.

He pivoted at the last second? I could have sworn that I hit him. How did he do that? the man in red wondered, his smug demeanor faltering for a brief moment.

"Did you use the momentum of my fist as kinetic energy for a pivot dodge?" he asked, their swords clashing once more. "Not bad!"

He was able to interpret my movement that quickly? He's deceptively intelligent under that obnoxious facade, Jinn realized.

"It's impressive… for a mutt!"

Jinn tensed, his teeth clenching.

"Do not call me a mutt!" Jinn yelled in frustration, his body moving into a lightning-fast thrust towards the man's head.

Long white hair flowed as the man tilted his head in time to avoid the fatal blow, a deep cut striking his cheek and shaving off a few hairs from his fringe. Jinn tumbled past him as he dodged, catching himself and skidding to a stop.

He's fast, too. A thrust like that should have killed him, yet I've only managed a single scratch. He is a fearsome foe.

"Nice work there, wolf-boy! I guess I should take you a little more seriously, then, yeah?" the man taunted as he wiped the blood from his cheek, echoing Jinn's own thoughts. "I can see why the Queen chose you to be her little lapdog!"

A blood-red array began to glow under the alchemist's palm, red energy swirling in the air around his sword. Another Seventh Sense chilled Jinn's bones, his body leaping on instinct away from his enemy.

The man in red slammed his sword downwards, striking into the ground at his feet. The ground began to groan, opening in a straight line as chunks of dirt and stone began to fly upwards. Gold eyes analyzed silently and as he followed Jinn's movements, the man began to think.

He's headed towards his sheath. Why? Is he trying to flee? he wondered, swinging his sword forwards and unleashing a large slash of red energy that barrelled towards the wolf-man.

Leaping forward to dodge the blast, Jinn tumbled to the ground and grabbed the black sheath of his sword. Pressing whatever energy he could muster, Jinn launched himself upwards, flipping as he threw the scabbard as hard as he could.

A quick blur of black spun towards the attack as Jinn's sheath connected with the pure energy, both men remaining unflinching as the energy exploded around them, detonating as it made contact.

Debris and smoke covered the area as the man in red shivered in ecstasy, a wide grin on his face as he realized that Jinn had figured out his attack once more.

"What incredible battle instincts! Not bad, you little scamp!" he cried out gleefully.

As the smoke cleared, Jinn came through the clouds poised and ready to launch another attack.

Now's my chance…! Jinn thought, arm pulled back and ready to kill.

"This again? I've learned your little tricks," the man mused under his breath. "You may have nicked me with that one last time, but I never make the same mistake twice."

The man in red clutched his sword, spinning it so the hilt faced upwards.

"Unfortunately…" he continued, striking Jinn's stomach with a fierce interception of his attack. "You're still out of your league here, pup."

A pommel strike?! Jinn coughed, winded as he silently realized the reality ahead of him. *He could have killed me easily, but he didn't. Is this… some sort of game to him?*

As the man planted a punch into Jinn's sternum, the realization hit harder as he tumbled backwards to the ground.

I wasn't even close to killing him. He's been toying with me this entire time.

Jinn clutched his midriff, huffing for air as he wiped some blood from his lip. Moaning in pain, the Dritet looked ahead as his opponent held his hand up into the air, energy crackling around him as a large ball of light formed above his palm.

The wolf braced himself for an impact, but just as quickly as the energy formed, it dispersed. The man's hand relaxed and dropped, pointing at Jinn instead.

"No, I'm not going to kill you. Not yet, that is," he sneered, wiping more blood from his cheek. "Let's call it a courtesy for the spar. I almost had fun today, so I think I want to see you again."

Jinn winced, pushing himself up slightly. His muscles trembled as they tried to lift up, the warrior refusing to admit defeat but too damaged from the impact to move.

"I need you to do something for me first. Dogs are good at following orders, are they not? Let's try it. Sit."

At his command, the ground underneath Jinn shifted, stalagmites rising and pushing him onto his knees. Stone held the Dritet firmly in place, arms pinned behind his back. The gold-eyed man chuckled coldly as he approached.

"Good boy. I don't like to repeat myself, so listen closely. There are two important things you need to know." The man's glove glowed red as he knelt down, grabbing Jinn's neck with a scalding grip that burned into his flesh.

Jinn let out a pained cry, struggling weakly against the searing grasp on his throat as the man continued.

"First of all, I'm your master now, pup. Got it? You'll do whatever I say."

As the man let go of Jinn's neck, the smell of burning flesh stung the wolf's sensitive nose. He dropped his head silently, ears flat as he understood his defeat.

"Excellent. Good dogs remain silent. You bark when I tell you to bark, and not a single moment otherwise. Now, the second thing. I'll let my little puppy go because I want to make this more interesting. I need you to deliver a message for me."

Standing back up to his feet, the man placed a black boot on Jinn's chest, looking down at him as he hoisted his sword over his shoulder.

"Tell your Queen she's next. I plan to be a *lot* less gentle with her."

As the shackles of stone loosened around Jinn's wrists, the wolf-man pulled his arms free with a swift tug. Wincing in pain, Jinn pushed himself up onto his feet shakily, his calloused hands gently touching the burn marks on his neck. Jinn looked up in panic as reality set in, his head on a sudden swivel as he realized that the man in red was nowhere to be found.

He vanished as quickly as he appeared and I didn't even notice. There is something off about that man, something I cannot quite place. His presence feels... empty.

A beat passed and Jinn picked up his sword, sheathing it. His eyes widened as he felt his Seventh Sense take over his body, his feet seeming to move of their own accord as they carried him back towards the Society of Alchemists' main headquarters.

That means he'll be able to get to Edelein without any of us noticing. I don't have a lot of time to warn her...!

Weakened, Jinn continued to press forward at the fastest pace he could muster, returning through the back door and pushing past a few alchemists. They looked at him, curious and alarmed, but the Dritet paid no mind as he continued his sprint.

If I can pick up her scent from the entrance of the building, I will be able to make it to the estate on foot. It wasn't too far, and getting everyone gathered into those autowagon machines will take too long.

Jinn approached the front entrance and the warm, familiar scent of the Queen filled his enhanced nostrils. He stopped for a brief moment, drinking in the scent to identify the direction of her movement. Familiar footsteps caused the wolf-man to turn around, his panicked blue eyes meeting the concerned vibrant green of Lylia Brightwood's concerned gaze.

From the expression on Lylia's face, Jinn could tell that she was having the same Seventh Sense reaction as him, her muscles tensed and prepared to spring into action. She was clutching onto her staff, eyebrows furrowed as she read the subtle information from Jinn's body language. Despite her understanding, Lylia's next action was gentle and thought-over.

"Jinn, let me heal you," Lylia instructed, approaching cautiously.

"We don't have time for this, elf!" Jinn snapped, his panic turning into frustration. "I'm going after her and you are following after me in the autowagons once you find the other Zengarde."

"Don't try to pull rank right now, Canis," Lylia's eyes narrowed, placing one hand on his lower back gently as a soft green glow began to radiate. "You won't be of any use to us if you're dead and alone in the street."

Jinn shoved Lylia back, growling.

"Get Zander and the others immediately. I cannot afford to waste a single second when that maniac is on his way to kill Edelein. Meet me at the residence, bring the autowagons and the Zengarde. I'm going on foot to warn her and prepare for relocation. Go!"

Lylia nodded solemnly, sighing to herself as she turned and darted off into the boardrooms. Without another word, Jinn mustered strength into his legs again and took off running down the street.

I hate to have wasted any time, but I think Lylia restored a small fracture in my spine that I had taken from that impact. Running is still a bit difficult, but it's significantly easier now than it was a minute ago. That boost should be enough to get me to the house while remaining upright. Jinn pushed forward through the remaining pain.

As the house began to loom ahead, Jinn's legs continued to burn and grow heavier with each step. Jinn stumbled a bit, gritting his teeth and pushing through as he steadied himself.

The Man in Red

I can sense Alett and Gihon in the main hall and Edelein is in her room with an unknown figure that I assume is the doctor. There's no trace of that man yet, and the house seems to be in order. Jinn slowed to a jog as he reached the doors.

She isn't safe yet, but she's protected now.

In the quiet of the noble house, Edelein sat on her bed as an older gentleman in a white coat pulled off her gloves, holding her fingers against a light. He was a kind-looking owl zoa, with white feathered plumicorns similar to Alett. Straight white hair framed his mature face, along with black rectangular glasses that matched the dark color of his turtleneck. Despite his kind appearance, Edelein looked anxiously at him, uncomfortable as the doctor evaluated her condition. Setting Edelein's hand down on her thigh, he reached for a small notebook and began to jot down his thoughts.

"You mentioned night terrors and a change in your attitude. I'm afraid short tempers and irrational behavior are common symptoms that will likely not be going away soon, either. And… Dirigent Gihon mentioned that you fainted earlier this morning?"

"Yes, sir," Edelein confirmed with a small nod.

The doctor sighed, writing something else down. Edelein shifted uncomfortably on the bed, looking down at the floor as she noticed Gihon approach.

Gihon knocked on the open door politely, noticing that Edelein avoided his gaze as he entered. The doctor looked up at him, forcing a smile as he stood to address the Dirigent with a firm handshake.

"Dirigent Marleogne, hello. Her condition is stable, but…

121

I fear it is in fact blight-sickness, as you suspected. I was hoping to deliver better news to you."

Gihon lowered his voice, leaning closer to the doctor to avoid Edelein's overhearing, oblivious to her tilted ear drinking in every word between them.

"How long does she have?"

"Without a proper cure, I would guess two years. I will give you some stamina potions to help with her fatigue and energy levels which will keep her afoot, but that's all I can do. I'm terribly sorry, Dirigent Marleogne."

Gihon sighed, shutting his eyes tight. The doctor put a comforting hand on his shoulder, his worn-out eyes soft with empathy.

"Losing a loved one can be hard. She seems lovely. Is she your wife?"

Gihon's eyes widened, his ears reddening as Edelein cleared her throat from the bed. The doctor turned to face her, looking back at Gihon's expression. He smiled warmly, affording himself the luxury of a small chuckle.

"Ah, I understand. I remember being young like you two. Pardon me… Dirigent, allow me to leave these with you."

The doctor set his briefcase on the bed, opening it up and rummaging through a variety of bottles and vials. Procuring three small vials filled with a yellow-gold liquid, he handed them to Gihon.

"Stamina potions. Just a small sip is all she needs to restore her energy. Miss, if you feel your symptoms weighing you down, please drink some of this. It's all I have on hand, but you can get more from any standard apothecary. They're expensive, but with the Dirigent by your side I assure you will have no issue with that."

Edelein scoffed under her breath, but nodded as Gihon took the vials from the doctor. Packing up his briefcase, the doctor bowed to Gihon and took his leave. As his footsteps faded, Gihon set the vials down on the dresser gently. He looked at Edelein as if to speak, but she had already laid down with her back to him, tail twitching as it hung off of the bedside.

"Edelein... I am going to resume working on Alett's studies. If you need anything at all, I will be in the main hall. Please call for me."

She huffed in acknowledgement, not speaking. Gihon sighed and closed her door, heading back down the hallway to find the Zwitet.

Alett sat comfortably, a large textbook only inches away from his thick octagonal glasses. Gihon approached and stood over him as the owl pored over the book, drinking in its knowledge.

"Gihon! Welcome back. How is Eddie? Is she okay?"

"She's fine, for now. Resting. Although... she is a bit upset with me. She had asked me not to tell you all about the illness, and I can tell that she's blaming me for betraying her trust."

"It's okay. Zander was genuinely about to rip your throat out. He definitely wasn't bluffing... I know him better than anyone else does, except for Eddie. I met him when Alderis brought him into the Royal Court twelve years ago, but I was just a kid back then, so I only saw him in passing until I joined the Zengarde a few years back."

"I just hope she does not hold it against me for too long. I want the best for her."

"We all do. She'll get over it soon. Let's just focus on the alchemy reading, okay? I'm sure talking about alchemy will cheer you right up."

Gihon sighed. "Why is that? Because I am a dirigent, and I am supposed to live and breathe alchemy? You expect my mere occupation to be the passionate fire that burns within my veins?"

Alett paused in an embarrassed hesitation, fearing he

treaded somewhere he shouldn't have.

"...Yes?"

Gihon stared silently at the owl for a beat, before smiling gently.

"You are correct. Have you been reading while I was meeting with the doctor?"

"Yes, sir. These texts are fascinating. Each of the lines in an array connects it to the material plane, allowing you to draw from its energies. It is almost like writing instructions for the chemical reaction to act a certain way."

"Correct. This is how alchemists manipulate objects. Different alchemists have different techniques that they prefer, which can include manipulating biomass, themselves, or materializing objects out of base elements. You can think of an array as a proclamation of sorts. Or maybe the better way to put it is programming the intended reaction."

"The backlash phantasms... are you really able to use an array to return them safely to their plane, without damaging ours?"

"Yes, utilizing the banishment array. That's this one, here." Gihon flipped the page of the textbook, pointing at a large diagram of an array. "Before we invented this array, we used to have to trace back the origin plane of the phantasm to send it home correctly. It wasn't until we learned that the sea of miracles will send objects and creatures back to their home plane after a while that we simply started banishing phantasms there."

This... is actually doing a great job at taking my mind off of what happened, Gihon realized. *Maybe teaching is more of my forte than I realized. Perhaps Arvien saw in me things that I was not prepared to see in myself.*

Alett's plumicorns twitched suddenly, the owl picking his head up out of the book to turn towards the door. His eyes were wide, body completely still except for the slight twittering of his

The Man in Red

feathers.

"Alett? Is something the matter?" Gihon asked.

Alett didn't respond, shooting up to his feet as the chair tipped over behind him. Leaping over it, the owl pelted down the hallway towards Edelein's room without a word. Before Gihon could react, Jinn flung open the front door, breathing heavily.

Gihon looked over Jinn, eyes widening. The wolf's large shoulders heaved, his hair disheveled. His body was littered with injuries, from burn marks to cut wounds, and he was covered in dirt.

"Are you alright? What happened, Jinn?" Gihon asked, approaching him.

Jinn shoved Gihon out of the way, grabbing the two crystal boxes off of the table.

"Danger. Evacuate the Queen. Everyone else is outside. Go!"

"Slow down, Jinn, and explain the situation to me," Gihon pleaded.

Jinn looked at Gihon briefly, appalled, his eyes wide as if he were expecting the Dirigent to be in motion already. "Move, Gihon! There's no time!"

Alett appeared a moment later, his hand on Edelein's back protectively as he ushered her outside. The Queen was avoiding eye contact with anyone, staring straight ahead as they made their way towards the door. Feeling that he had no other choice, Gihon followed them out.

The two autowagons were parked outside, drivers sharing equally befuddled looks. Gihon caught a glimpse of Jinn handing the crystal boxes to Alett, the owl putting one in his backpack and the second in a smaller satchel on his waist. Alett stood outside of the first vehicle as Jinn vanished into the second. Through the window of the carriage, Gihon could make out Edelein and Zander's silhouettes.

"Gihon, Eddie needs to be relocated immediately. Is there a safehouse here? Somewhere that you—and only you—would know the location to?"

As Gihon paused, Alett pushed further, his eyes desperate.

"We've been compromised. She isn't safe. We need to know that you are on our side right now, or I'll have no choice but to kill you. Please don't make me do that."

Alett looked scared as he spoke, clearly seeming like he did not wish to speak such cruel words to his new friend.

"Gihon, tell me you're on our side. Please."

Gihon's eyebrows furrowed, lost in thought as he tried to understand the situation at hand.

Alett is serious about whatever is going on right now.

"I own a private estate outside of the city. It's in a safe place, hard to locate and unknown to most people. She'll be safe there," Gihon decided after a long moment.

Without taking the time to acknowledge his answer, Alett hopped up wordlessly into the autowagon, motioning for Gihon to follow.

"Well, you get to live another day," Alett laughed nervously as Gihon sat down. "Thanks for that."

CHAPTER 6

TYRANT

As the autowagon began to rock and sway, carrying the Zenluvians out of the city, Gihon pinched between his eyebrows and shut his eyes tightly in frustration.

"Will one of you *please* explain to me what is happening?" he asked, his tone short.

"Tell us where we're going, first," Zander narrowed his eyes in distrust. "Knowing you, it would be of no surprise to learn that you're working with the one that seeks Edelein, and delivering us to him as we speak."

Beside the sphynx zoa, Edelein was shifting uncomfortably in her seat, seeming a bit spooked as her gaze flitted across the passing scenery. The lioness was avoiding eye contact, seeming to still be upset about the events of earlier.

Letting out a tense sigh, Gihon conceded. "I do not disclose this lightly, but it's my personal home. My students use it on occasion as a sanctuary during their travels. Not a soul outside of the Corvid Athenaeum knows of its location, and I would prefer to keep it that way. It will suffice as a safehouse until everything is settled. Now, if you do not mind, what exactly is the situation?"

After a beat of silence, Alett tilted his head curiously.

"You mean… you couldn't tell?" he asked with a genuine tone. "I know you're not a Zengarde, but you're still a zoa. Don't you have senses? Instincts?"

"This is why *we* are Her Majesty's guardsmen, and not you. I knew that I should not have trusted you with her safety," Zander growled under his breath.

"At ease, you two," Edelein spoke, finally addressing Gihon for the first time. "Gihon, I mentioned the Seventh Sense to you before, which stems from zoa heritage. It's a part of our animal roots; being attuned to threats and acting on instinct. What you saw just now is a full-fledged Seventh Sense. My men communicate nonverbally through smell and body language, which allows them to react faster in the face of danger. We believed, until this moment, that every zoa possessed some form of that natural instinct."

"They should. How else will you fight, without instinct?" Zander questioned.

"With logic, Zander. Using your brain; thinking of a solution before acting on anything," Gihon retorted at the sphynx, irritated.

"You sound like Alett," Zander rolled his eyes.

"Why do you say that like it's an insult?" Alett sighed.

"The brain cannot fight, it merely controls the muscle. Act from the muscle instead, and you will be faster," Zander continued.

"If you think that the brain cannot fight, you must not play much chess."

"You expect that your silly games will keep you alive? While you frolic about in your roost, there are zoa fighting to survive in the real world."

128

The Man in Red

Gihon's blood boiled in agitation from Zander's stubborn behavior. Taking a deep breath, Gihon steadied his mind and turned his attention to Edelein, who was seated directly across from him.

"What about your Zengarde that are not zoa?" he asked, eager to ease the tension in the air. "Are they capable of using Seventh Sense as well?"

"Yes, the technique is trained through hard work and discipline. The zoa members just pick up on it faster, but anyone can learn it if they are devoted and have the resources to do so."

"What resources do you mean?"

"Approval from the fae. The Zengarde are chosen by the Summer Court, and the fae's blessing will help them attune to the forest. Being one with your surroundings makes it easier to lean into the instinct."

Alett chimed in, also sensing the uncomfortable air. "Seventh Sense is more about the vibe or energy of something, rather than explicit information. That's the tradeoff... so no, we don't know what exactly attacked Jinn. All I could tell was that he was attacked and defeated in battle by a person who knows of Edelein's location and intends to harm her. He was pretty beat up, meaning his enemy was powerful enough to defeat the Dritet, therefore the only people who might be able to fight such a threat would be myself and Zander. Even then, we don't know the power level of this person, who could surpass both of us, so evacuating is the safer option for now. That way, we can hide her location again and regroup."

"So the Seventh Sense is how you noticed Jinn's panic before he had even entered the room... I understand now," Gihon replied.

"Yeah, I could smell the fear on him long before I saw him. That's why I ran to get Eddie immediately."

"How can you tell that he was attacked by a person and not

a monster, or phantasm?"

"Easy. Firstly, the size and shape of his wounds were of similar size to a humanoid. The burns were likely from magic or alchemy, not a fire-breathing beast. Second, Jinn would expect to defeat a man more than a monster, so losing to a man would alarm him more than if he lost to a beast. His panic was of someone who had been blindsided from a skill difference, which is also why we decided to flee. Jinn is the Dritet, but that doesn't make him exponentially weaker than Zander or me. We're all somewhat close, so him losing that badly means we might not be able to win, either. And finally, his instinct led him to bee-line for our Queen after the fight. That means that the enemy was likely in some way sentient or intelligent, capable of speech, and thus spoke of or implied their intentions to harm her. Finally, he was severely injured, but he didn't suffer any major movement-inhibiting injuries. That means that the enemy likely struck intentionally to avoid breaking his bones, because he wanted Jinn to run away. The man wanted him to deliver a message."

"You picked up on that the moment you saw him?" Gihon asked, impressed. "That is a rather quick form of deductive reasoning."

"Immediately, yes, from his scent and appearance. That's what Seventh Sense is... being able to tell all of that from a moment's glance is much more efficient than sitting down with him to let him explain the situation."

A wave of sudden energy passed through the autowagon, drawing Gihon's attention as he perked up in alarm. The country road ahead stretched between thick expanses of trees on either side, separated only by a grassy shoulder bordering the asphalt. In the center of the road in front of them, a large void was humming with dark energy as the obstruction began to increase in size until the entire path was consumed.

The Man in Red

"Brace yourselves!" Gihon warned, a second too late.

Energy blasted outwards from the dark void, fragments of an unknown material slamming into the autowagons and overturning them harshly. Time seemed to slow as everyone was lifted from their seats, tumbling with the vehicle as it flipped and crashed onto its side. Gihon's eyes met Edelein's, wide and full of fear as she reached for him desperately. Outstretching his hand, Gihon grabbed onto Edelein and pulled her against his chest as they tumbled, a teal array lighting up behind his back as his bulwark reinforced his body.

The autowagon overturned as it careened through the air, Zander's face contorting as he dug his sharp nails into the padded seat, bracing himself across from Alett, who was clutching onto the drapes to remain seated.

A winded gasp expelled between both of them as Gihon's back slammed into the ground and the Queen's body pressed against his.

Gihon winced as the dust settled, clutching tightly around Edelein's waist with one arm, the other supporting her back as she groaned from the impact.

"Edelein, are you hurt?" Gihon asked, forcing one eye open to look at her as he caught his breath.

My bulwark array prevented any injury, but it still knocked the wind out of me.

"I'm alright, I think," Edelein whimpered slightly, her gaze meeting his.

A long moment passed as the two stared at each other, Edelein feeling his firm chest heaving underneath hers as Gihon's face reddened with blush, gripping her waist instinctively. Looking into her eyes, a sudden realization crossed Gihon's mind.

From the day I met her, I had assumed she had slitted pupils, like a cat. Seeing her up close like this… I realize that her pupils are diamond-shaped, not slitted. In hindsight, I should have remembered that her leonine ancestry would not have resulted in slitted pupils; lions have round pupils due to their diurnal nature and larger size. So... why are they shaped like diamonds? What evolutionary trait is that? She is... quite captivating to look at. Gihon thought, before his eyes widened in sudden realization. *W-Why am I thinking about this right now? Should I ask her about her eyes? Is this appropriate? Why does my chest hurt? She's not that heavy...*

A large, tan hand grabbed at the back of Edelein's neck in a swift movement, yanking her upwards by the scruff and pulling her away from the Dirigent. Zander dangled her above the ground, eyes narrow in displeasure as Edelein whined.

"Zander, put me down! I'm not a cub!" Edelein protested. "You cannot *scruff* me like this, I am your Queen. I will not be patronized!"

"If you're not a cub, you are *certainly* acting like one," Zander growled, setting her down. "I told you to stay away from the Dirigent, and yet you're here climbing him like an ironwood tree."

"The autowagon flipped and he caught me! I didn't do anything!" Edelein denied. "You should thank him for catching me, or else I might have been badly injured."

"Yeah, Zander, why didn't you catch *me* like that?" Alett laughed dryly, rubbing his head as he climbed out of the overturned autowagon. "If I get concussed, I'm going to be incredibly useless for the next week."

"I wouldn't mind benching you for a while," Zander snapped, brushing the dirt off of Edelein's clothes as Gihon rose to his feet.

In the autowagon beside them, Jinn was pulling Thorne up, the human looking a bit worse for wear.

"Ow, ow, ow..." Thorne moaned as Jinn hoisted him from

the smoking vehicle.

Jinn looked ahead at the road, ignoring Thorne's complaints.

"We've got company," Jinn stated, brushing debris off of himself.

As everyone's heads turned towards the road ahead, the color drained quickly from Edelein's face, a cold ice chilling her bones as her knees buckled. Zander caught her, supporting her as her legs continued to tremble. Ahead of them, a large inky-black creature let out a deafening roar.

The phantasm was smaller than the one in Zenluve, appearing to be almost mammalian in nature as it stood quadrupedal with a long tail that thrashed about. Huge claws scraped the asphalt below, jaw hanging open as it let out a low growl. Its alien features were illuminated with a violet light from its eyes and mouth, with a large third eye glowing on its chest.

"A phantasm," Gihon muttered, standing up straighter and rolling his wrists in anticipation.

A strong wind emanated from the beast as the backlash cleared, its aura menacing and powerful. Gihon stepped ahead of the others, waving one hand in the air as if to dismiss the others.

"This will be an excellent learning opportunity," Gihon mused, a teal array glowing from his palm.

Gihon's array was clean and articulated, with a heavier visual weight of lines on the lower half that seemed to root the design in a grounded manner.

"Please stand back and allow me to handle this. It appears to be a tyrant shell-type, which will be light work a dirigent."

As Gihon walked forward slowly, his jet-black cloak pulled forward out of thin air through the array in his hand. The cloak seemed to defy gravity as it flowed around his arm, wrapping tightly as it enveloped his left hand and forearm. Lines of turquoise and violet energy highlighted from under the seams as the cloth suddenly took on a metallic sheen.

"This is known as a cloth-to-adamantine transmutation," Gihon explained, not looking back towards the others but remaining fixated on the phantasm ahead.

"Should we be helping him?" Jinn asked, and Thorne shook his head.

"Something tells me we'd only be in his way. This is the thing that killed Tyrus and Cyzen. Even though they were lower rank than us, they were still Zengarde. We're kind of... useless here."

Gihon extended his palm towards the beast, eyes cold.

"Start strong, you wretched thing, for that will be all you'll get."

The phantasm let out a roar, charging a large beam from its mouth and unleashing it towards the Dirigent. Gihon stood strong as the energy approached him, unflinching as he spoke a command into his array.

"Rampart."

As the beam crashed into his space, it was diverted by a sudden shield from the palm of the Dirigent, the phantasm's energy bouncing off and dissipating into the air around him. Both remained drawn out in a stalemate, a battle between an unstoppable force and an immovable object.

"C-can he really deflect an attack like that?" Alett asked, eyes wide in fear.

"I hope not. Is it bad that I want him to get incinerated?" Zander huffed, arms crossed as he watched.

"Gihon..." Edelein whispered anxiously, her eyes wavering as the beam subsided and he released his shield.

Turning around to look at her, Gihon smiled. "Please do not worry about me. I've handled countless phantasms, many of which were far worse. I can handle myself, so please stay back and observe."

Edelein's eyes wavered as they met Gihon's, the shimmering gold hue brimming with confidence against her anxious gaze.

"As we cannot perceive or identify the interior of a phantasm, all we can do is organize them based on the appearance and size of the exterior shell to perceive the estimated threat level. Tyrant-shells are fairly easy to handle, for a seasoned sentinel such as myself," Gihon explained, brandishing the black adamantine sleeve that encased his left arm, leftover fabric from his cloak flowing over his shoulder like a black wing.

The Zengarde murmured amongst themselves, heeding his words while still bristling in anticipation of combat.

"I think he's nerdier than Alett, and that's really saying something," Nephvir commented dryly, brushing long black hair over his shoulders.

"I don't know much about him, but I think Gihon is really passionate about teaching. It's kind of funny," Everett replied to the fellborn, his large bovine body shaking with laughter.

Hearing the sound of the beast's heavy footsteps, the Dirigent returned his focus to the creature ahead of him as it barrelled down the road, growling ferally. The phantasm leapt into the air, claws outstretched as it reached towards Gihon.

"That's more like it," Gihon muttered under his breath, a quiet smirk flitting across his lips as the phantasm closed the distance between them.

As large claws slammed into the ground, dust and debris obscured the phantasm's view. Lifting a claw up from the ground, it peered underneath and found no sign of Gihon, the sentinel having vanished into the cloud of dust. The phantasm looked around, head whipping from side to side as it tried to locate its prey.

A sudden impact drew its attention, a small stone crashing into the beast's face at an unbelievable force. The phantasm stumbled backwards, shaking its head as it located the direction of its attacker. Gihon stood on the side of the road, one hand in his pocket as he chuckled casually. His left hand held another stone, his thumb pressed on it as he prepared for a second strike.

"Have another one," Gihon stated, flicking the rock out of his hand.

The stone careened through the air at an impressive speed, striking the phantasm in the face a second time. The monster stumbled backwards, letting out an irritated grumble as it tried to recenter its balance.

Wasting no time on the opportunity, Gihon darted forward, fist clenched. The phantasm took a blind swipe towards him and the Dirigent easily dodged the blow by using the momentum to launch himself higher into the air. A look of conviction crossed his face as he winded his fist and slammed downwards, the weight of his sturdy frame continuing the momentum. As he landed atop the phantasm, an adamantine-infused punch drove the creature's body down into the asphalt.

More debris kicked up from the impact, a powerful wave of energy reaching the Zenluvians as they watched in eager anticipation.

"Yeah, he doesn't need us," Thorne commented, resting his hands on his hips.

Next to him, Everett nodded in agreement as he studied Gihon's movement, from one defender to the other. Lylia's eyes were wide in fascination as well, the trio drinking in each of Gihon's carefully-executed strikes and dodges.

"This is what alchemy can do...?" Lylia wondered aloud. "It's like magic, but different. It makes more sense seeing it in action as opposed to the textbook teachings."

The Man in Red

"I'd say you should have gone to spar with Jinn and that fire alchemist, but based on how that turned out, I think I'd rather have kept you by my side instead," Thorne snickered. "Wouldn't want a single hair on your pretty head getting hurt."

"If I were there with Jinn, I could have helped. We all could have. He got hurt because he was alone, and we all work better together," Lylia clenched her teeth, frustrated.

"Tell it to the fae, since they always want to make us fight against each other to keep our ranks."

Jinn's eyes followed Gihon's movements, ignoring the familiar banter between Thorne and Lylia. He observed closely as Gihon began to dodge and weave, ducking between the haphazard swipes that the phantasm made and leaping over its ground slams.

"Has he switched to a defensive stance?" Jinn asked, sparing a quick glance at Zander. "He was striking earlier, but now he's just dodging it. Why isn't he attacking?"

"He is evading intentionally," Zander replied curtly, crossing his arms. "The Dirigent tested his foe's strength with a few short blows. Once he confirmed the power level of the enemy, he has now assured himself that it is not a threat. He's letting it attack on the offensive so we can observe it ourselves and gain a stronger comprehension of the beast's style. By dodging, Gihon is showcasing its moveset as a display for us. He is utilizing minimal movement to preserve space, with each step he takes expertly forged through hundreds of battles."

"In other words, he's trying to silently teach us through observation and hands-on experience," Jinn realized.

Behind the broad shoulders of her warriors, Edelein remained frozen in fear as she watched Gihon fight. Glancing briefly over his shoulder, Gihon's eyes met hers again as he let out a quick exhale, smiling gently at her.

"He's... not dead," Edelein whispered to herself, amazed

and horrified as memories flooded her mind, the corpses of her fallen Zengarde plaguing her for another cold moment.

Ahead, Gihon focused once more on the phantasm as it slammed another claw down onto him. A loud clanging noise rang out as Gihon caught the creature's talon against his adamantine sleeve, the monster recoiling backwards like a swordsman whose blade was parried by an impenetrable shield.

Sending the opening from the phantasm's recoil, Gihon lunged forward with his left arm pulled back once more, thrusting forward into a heavy left cross punch that sent the phantasm's large body careening backwards, tumbling weakly as it scraped against the asphalt.

It seems weak enough now, Gihon thought to himself, willing the transmutation on his arm to disband. The Dirigent could feel a familiar energy running up his arm as the adamantine returned to cloth, taking on a long and flexible form that rippled behind him as he ran forward, closing the gap between himself and the beast.

The phantasm steadied itself, digging its claws into the ground as it opened its mouth and began to charge another blast of energy.

Its body seems to have cooled down from its last beam. The time can vary based on the type of phantasm, but their bodies always have to reset before they can attack again. Now that it's ready for another one, it would be wise of me to banish it before it can unleash that blast. It would risk harming the Zenluvians, or further damaging the landscape. We're nearing Ravencroft, so repairing this road might end up being my own problem, anyway.

Gihon launched himself into the air as light gathered in the phantasm's mouth, preparing to strike. Sending forward the long tassels of fabric from his cloak, the strands snaked their way around the beast's neck and tightened as Gihon pulled his arm upwards.

The momentum carried Gihon, the seasoned protector

twisting one leg to torque his body into a feet-first position as he pulled himself downward, the long wisps of his cloak effectively leashing the phantasm. He landed atop the monster's head, the heels of his loafers digging into the beast's shell as it slammed headfirst into the ground. Gihon kept the leash tight with one hand, the other hand summoning an array that looked familiar to the onlookers.

"That's the banishing array," Alett commented. "Gihon showed me that in his book."

"The battle's done, then," Jinn replied, watching Gihon as the array began to glow.

"My apologies for being a bit rough with you, but it's time to go home now," Gihon murmured to the phantasm as it thrashed weakly beneath him.

Silence fell over the group. The phantasm's screeches faded into nothing, the beast dragged to the Sea of Miracles to find its home once more. The wind settled and Gihon let out a soft exhale as he turned to face the others.

Edelein was staring intensely up at him, her eyes swimming in lost memories. Regaining her composure, she cleared her throat and straightened out her clothing.

"Excellent work, Dirigent. It seems we have much to learn from you," she said, looking away awkwardly.

"I hope I have assured you of my protective capabilities. Please feel safe around me."

Edelein nodded, before turning towards the overturned autowagons.

"The danger may have been quelled, but there is still a rather pressing issue at hand. I am no expert at your Caandemite technology, but I do think that these vehicles have been destroyed."

Gesturing behind her towards the autowagon, overturned and smoking, Gihon looked over her shoulder to see Alett giving the vehicle a few swift kicks.

"Percussive maintenance," Alett said, without turning to look at Gihon. "It's... not working."

Gihon nodded solemnly. "I can confirm that they will definitely need a fair bit of work to operate again. My apologies, but I believe we will have to continue on foot."

"Edelein is in no condition to walk," Zander denied. "Can you not use alchemy to fix your machines?"

"I lack the necessary components to do so, and I must admit that mechanical engineering is not exactly my strongest suit as an alchemist. Though I agree, I would rather not have Queen Edelein walk the rest of the way."

"Why is everyone suddenly deciding everything for me? I can walk. I want to walk!" Edelein disagreed, stamping her foot angrily.

"Dirigent Gihon, could you carry her?" Cari suggested.

"No!" Edelein retorted before Gihon could respond. "No one is carrying me! My legs work just fine, thank you!"

"Well, unless someone happens to come by with an autowagon big enough to fit ten people, I don't think there's much of a choice," Everett admitted. "I don't know much about this place either, but I don't think autowagons come in that size."

"Not to mention, Everett counts as at least two people, so we really need eleven seats," Thorne joked.

"Don't forget the drivers of our autowagons," Lylia added as she assessed the older fellborn that had been flung from the driver's seat. "That's two more."

"Right, so... unless someone with thirteen available seats shows up—" Everett started, but stopped abruptly as he felt his Seventh Sense signal within him, turning to look down the road in astonishment.

"This has to be a joke," Everett laughed nervously. "Really?"

The Man in Red

From the direction they had come from, an oversized autowagon pulled over abruptly. The vehicle appeared to be older, with some wear chipping away at its paint. It was large, with a long bed in the back, and appeared to be used for hauling of sorts.

It looks like a farmhand's vehicle. Far from luxurious, but a bed of that size could probably fit most of us, Gihon realized in astonishment.

"Hi! Um, hello!" a petite human woman called out from the autowagon, hopping down and running over to the group. She had curly ginger hair and a round face adorned with freckles. The woman appeared friendly, with a gentle and inviting smile. "Are you guys stranded? Are those your autowagons over there?"

"Our knight in rusting armor," Thorne chuckled. "Yeah, those are ours. How could you tell?"

"Well, you're all standing around here awkwardly. Don't know why else you'd be here. My name's Tessa, I'm a farmer from Ravencroft. Can I help you guys get somewhere?"

"Oh, you're from Ravencroft! You can help us, then. That's your Dirigent, right over there," Thorne snickered, gesturing to Gihon who stared awkwardly, not expecting the sudden recognition.

I... would have preferred to stay anonymous.

"Dirigent Marleogne! Oh, goodness, what happened? Can I help?"

"Miss... Tessa, was it? A pleasure. Yes, we are in fact in need of an escort. My estate is only a few miles from here, but we'd rather avoid going on foot if possible. I will compensate you greatly for the trouble, if you could manage to fit us all into your autowagon."

"Of course, of course! I'm headed that way anyways," Tessa nodded, walking back to her vehicle and gesturing for them to follow. "I can fit two up front, and the rest can pile into the bed. This old thing's carried worse in her day. Does that work?"

Gihon nodded, grateful as he lifted himself into the front

of the autowagon, pulling Edelein up after him. As the Queen sat down at the end, Gihon found the space to be more constricting than anticipated, with his leg and shoulder pressed against hers. She blushed, eyes fixed on the window as she stared out at the gloomy weather.

"Luckily for you two, I'm pretty small. I know otherwise it'd be a tight fit, huh?" Tessa laughed, the engine roaring to life as she resumed her drive.

It's already a tight fit. Gihon thought, trying to take his mind off of the contact he was making with Edelein's warm body.

A long beat of silence passed, the energy in the air feeling a bit stiff and awkward.

"Is there something you two want to talk about?" Tessa blurted out suddenly. "I can feel some sort of tension between you. You can talk, just pretend I'm not here."

Without missing a beat, Gihon began to ramble his pent-up feelings in a manner that surprised everyone in earshot, including himself.

"Edelein, I know you're upset about me revealing your illness to the Zengarde, and I'm sorry. When you fainted… the truth was the only explanation for it. Zander wouldn't have taken anything else from me. He wanted to kill me, and nearly tried to kill Clotho as well. The situation was far from desirable, and telling him the truth was the only way to stop any bloodshed. For someone with the Seventh Sense you mentioned, he doesn't seem to be able to realize that I'm not an enemy."

Tessa's eyes widened as she maintained her silence, wondering if perhaps she had opened up a topic that was better left closed.

"He knows you aren't malicious, for now. Rather, he worries for what is to come. The things you could do, that you may not have intentions of doing."

The Man in Red

"Why?" Gihon asked.

"A foresight from our former High Wizard detailed of a threat to the Throne, and to me. The prophecy mentions what some believe to be a corvid zoa destroying Zenluve."

Gihon nodded in understanding, before freezing up as her words reached him.

"Hold on a moment, Edelein. Your High Wizard? Foresight? Foresight is what caused the disappearance of every wizard around the world. Wizardry has been forgotten and outlawed entirely, not to mention the forbidden art of foresight. I need you to explain this to me immediately."

Edelein looked at him, puzzled.

"When the wizards vanished, we used their remaining artifacts to train new ones. Did you... not do that?" she asked.

"You have remaining artifacts from wizards in Zenluve?" Gihon replied, eyes wide. "Our artifacts were destroyed in the Great Disappearance, anything left was hoarded by dragons and forgotten by mankind. The wizards ensured that no one would be able to follow in their footsteps and doom the world to their foresighted prophecies. Once a foresight occurs, it locks in that reality, with no way to prevent it. They didn't want that to happen anymore. Why is your wizard still using foresight?"

"Our current one is not. Foresight is forbidden in Zenluve as well, as it has caused a great many issues for my family and my people. The prophecy comes from Jax's old master, our previous High Wizard. The wizard's foresight is what killed my father. Needless to say, the wizard was exiled and left to die for his crime."

Gihon's eyes softened, understanding the weight of her words.

"Can you tell me what the prophecy says?" he asked, and she nodded.

Crown of the Alchemist

"In shadows deep, her destiny fulfilled,
The throne is broken as blood is spilled.
Fate entwines with the ruin he brings,
The raven-haired destruction on black wings."

Edelein's face was grim as she continued.

"A broken throne, spilled blood, it's quite on the nose about the oncoming violence it will bring against my family. The High Wizard told my father what he saw, and my father told Zander. He mentioned the Kingdom ablaze, nightmarish creatures, and a raven-haired man with wings as black as night capturing me, dragging me away from the Kingdom, never to be seen again. Zander is one of many who understand that if I were to be killed, my entire bloodline dies with me. Zenluve will no longer have the protection of the Luvemann family, which would be the first of many struggles to come."

Foresights aren't malleable. That future in the prophecy is bound to happen, Gihon realized. *She's going to be taken from Zenluve. No wonder her Court is so uneasy about her future.*

"Do you think I am the raven-haired man your prophecy foretells?" Gihon asked.

"No. Maybe... probably not. Well... I don't think so, at least. Raven-haired doesn't mean it has to be a raven zoa, though the black wings part does heavily imply it. I do hold weight to Zander's concerns, however, that just because you are kind now does not mean you will always be. People can change."

"I am someone who does not change easily. I am a steadfast man, steady in my ways. I promise you, I will not bring harm to you or your Kingdom."

"Not on purpose, you won't," she paused briefly before changing the subject. "Anyways, I appreciate your apology. I would appreciate a cure even more so. I'll be forced to bear as many

144

children as possible as soon as I go home, if you cannot cure me before I return."

Her tone sounded humorous, accompanied by a dry laugh, but Gihon could sense her anxiety.

She sounds like she's joking, but the reality of the situation is that she knows she is going to die. Her duty would fall on producing a viable heir before she dies, which is... quite grim, regardless of how you look at it. Gihon thought to himself.

"Stay here with me, then," Gihon blurted out, before stopping with a wide-eyed blush. "I-I mean, it would be easier to study the cure if you stayed at the Athenaeum—"

Edelein stared at him in surprise. "Gihon, I can't do that. I have to get back to the Kingdom as soon as I can. They need me."

Gihon sighed, understanding. "I will find a cure. I will do everything in my power, both as an alchemist and as a dirigent. And... as your friend, Miss Edelein."

Edelein laughed dryly again. "Yeah, stay in touch with me when we go back to Zenluve. Come visit someday, friend."

A sudden exclamation from the farmer beside them drew their attention, slamming on her brakes.

"There's a man in the middle of the road!" Tessa let out a surprised yelp, slamming on the brakes of her vehicle.

Gihon's arm flung in front of Edelein protectively, keeping her in her seat as the farmhand's truck lurched forward. He dug his heels into the flooring, securing himself as the autowagon screeched to a sudden halt.

"Sorry!" she apologized with a sharp gasp. "There's someone there. Why is he just standing in the road like that? Does he not realize how dangerous that is?! A-and why didn't I see him there until the last moment...?"

Looking ahead, Gihon and Edelein's eyes both widened in unison. The lioness turned to face Gihon fervently, putting one hand on his knee and looking intensely up at him.

"That is the man that hurt Jinn. I can sense it."

"Are you sure?" Gihon asked, uneasy as he recognized the man in red ahead of them. "I have a complicated history with that man, and I can assure you that he is quite possibly the most dangerous—and most wanted—man in Caandemium."

"I care not about his status, for I fear no man," Edelein replied simply. "He wishes for a fight; so be it. We shall fight."

"You are *certain* it was him? And Jinn… survived?"

Edelein nodded, opening the door and stepping down with Gihon following closely behind. "Look at Jinn if you don't believe me."

Glancing over his shoulder, Gihon noticed the Zengarde bristling as they prepared themselves for combat, weapons at the ready. Jinn approached them, sword drawn and extended towards the man in the road. He was pale, though he looked less injured due to Lylia's druidic healing. Knuckles white around the hilt of his sword, he nodded at Edelein, confirming her previous comment.

"The Zengarde can arm themselves within mere seconds. Alett possesses a bag of holding to carry their weapons, and they have coordinated to master the art of quick drawing. We are equipped, and vengeful."

"Shit," Gihon cursed under his breath, his mind racing. "If someone would have told me it was him, I could have better prepared us for this. Admittedly, he has the upper hand right now."

"What do you mean?" Edelein asked. "Have you not listened to a word I said? It's one of him versus all of us."

"Look again, Edelein," Gihon warned.

Turning around, Edelein noticed dozens of hungry eyes gazing from the shadows of the woods on either side of them that were invisible to perception a moment before. Looking up at the white-haired man in the road, she noticed he was now flanked by

The Man in Red

two more people, a man and a woman. The man had wavy silver hair that sat just above his shoulders, donning an open-front violet bodysuit that boasted an incredibly lithe and lean muscular build. The woman wore a sleek orange dress, with an oversized witch-like hat that boasted an open maw, licks of fire sputtering from its pumpkin-like face. Her hair was long and fiery, with coal-black roots that faded into a bright red-orange.

"If he brought this many with him, he knew I was with you, and that gives him the upper hand," Gihon murmured to her. "Stay behind me."

"Your Majesty, it is truly an honor," The man in red bowed deeply, speaking coldly as he raised his head. Looking around at the Zengarde as they bristled anxiously behind her, weapons drawn, his golden eyes assessed each one individually before landing back on Edelein. "What do they feed you Zenluvians? You're all huge. Even for a lady, you're pretty big too."

"Excuse you?" Edelein gasped, baring her fangs.

"Women are *so* dramatic," the man moaned, tilting his head back. "I'm *complimenting* you. You're tall for a girl, and look like a fighter. It's a good thing, so unclench for me, sweetheart."

Gihon's eyes narrowed as he stepped forward to stand in front of Edelein, shielding her from the white-haired man.

"Do not speak to her that way, Solomon," Gihon growled, seething hatred burning in his eyes.

"Dirigent Gihon!" he exclaimed with faux excitement. "What a lovely reunion, seeing you here. Congratulations on the promotion, by the way. The Marleogne nepotism must be nice. I believe it has been a few years since you last interfered with me and my followers, Dirigent."

"Cultists. It's a cult, Solomon," Gihon corrected, but Solomon shrugged nonchalantly.

"I'm a miracle worker. They choose to follow me because

I can help them. What difference is that as opposed to the Church of Prima Luma?"

"The Church of Prima Luma follows a god, not the abomination that faces you in the mirror each morning. Furthermore, they allow their members to leave rather than killing them the moment they are no longer convenient. You're a fraud and a disgrace to alchemical development."

"Enough about me," Solomon continued, his voice dripping with malice. "Speaking of frauds… since when did you decide to frolic with the zoa again? I must say, it's quite surprising to see someone like you intermingling with the complete and utter antithesis of your own morality. The girl will be upset when she finds out the truth, you know."

"What is he talking about, Gihon?" Edelein asked. "How does he know so much about you? Who is he?"

The man laughed. "You'll come to learn this, sweetheart. It's my job to know things, so don't forget that. I know everything about everyone. It's why so many people choose to follow me."

Edelein narrowed her eyes, distrusting.

"What, you don't believe me?" Solomon pouted, followed by another curt laugh. "How about this, then? I know about the phantasms in Zenluve. I know that your dad went missing nine years ago, and that he used to call you Eddie. Now you hate that name, because you're afraid of intimacy. You fear that if someone can love you as Eddie, you will lose them just like you lost your daddy."

That's why she gets so tense when people call her Eddie, it makes sense now, Gihon thought. *Why, then, does Alett still do it? Is he encouraging her to overcome her fears, forcing her into a form of exposure therapy? He seems to show no malice with it.*

Casting a quick glance over his shoulder, Gihon saw the color had drained from Edelein's face. Her body was frozen still, tense and anguished as her ears drooped.

"How did you…" she began, but trailed off as her fighting instincts kicked in, clenching her fists as she began to approach the white-haired man.

Gihon put a hand on Edelein's shoulder to stop her, pulling her back. An array glowed a bright teal on his left palm, illuminating the deep black glove on his hand as his cloak began to free itself from his shoulders. The fabric seemed to move on its own as it was pulled towards the array, twisting and forming into a shortsword in his hand. Grabbing the hilt of the sword, Gihon stared straight ahead at the so-called miracle worker that grinned back at him.

"Stay back, Edelein. He's dangerous," he warned.

Edelein shook her head, taking off her white gloves to expose sharp claw-like nails.

"I told you, I–"

"Stay. Back," Gihon repeated, looking over his shoulder down at her. "I believe in your competence. My job is to protect you from lunatics such as him, and that man is the pinnacle of the exact person I should be shielding you from. I do not doubt you, but I do doubt his ability to perform restraint."

His eyes were burning with a cold fire, their gold glowing with a hatred that dated back even longer than she realized. Edelein felt a chill run up her spine, and she nodded in silence.

"Solomon, if you insist on being a nuisance right now, I will gladly humble you. If you have entered Velkhamore's territory, that means you have become emboldened enough to be overdue for a beating. However, we are traveling with civilians right now. Allow them to leave, and avoid the unnecessary bloodshed," Gihon commanded.

"And if I don't?" Solomon countered, smug.

"I kill you and all of your cultists, right here and now,"

Gihon stated simply.

"Give me the Queen and I'll let the civilians go," Solomon countered as the Divine Sword, Kether, formed from light into his outstretched hand.

Gihon scoffed, eyes narrow. "I'm not giving her to you."

"I'm not anyone's to give," Edelein retorted as she clenched her fists, "and I personally plan on kicking your ass myself for hurting my Dritet."

"Spunky!" Solomon laughed. "You'll be fun to play with, kitty."

"Kitty?!" Edelein hissed with rage, ears flat and fangs bared.

"Edelein, stay out of this," Gihon warned again. "You do not understand the gravity of the situation."

Solomon stretched his arms casually, eyeing them both. "If your little lover's quarrel is finished, I've considered a better counter-offer for your friends' lives."

"What do you want, Solomon?" Gihon asked warily.

Solomon held his sword out, smirking. Opening his hand, the Divine Sword vanished into thin air in front of him, leaving his hand free to point at the Dirigent.

"You and me, Dirigent Gihon. I won't use my Divine Sword, you don't summon Fortress Black. Nothing but alchemy and fists, like we used to. Agree to leave out the Fortress, and I'll let them go."

Gihon paused for a moment, distrusting as he weighed his options. After a few seconds, he turned over his shoulder to look at Tessa, who was cowering slightly by her autowagon.

"Miss Tessa, please take our drivers and escort them back into Velkhamore. I am deeply grateful for your aid until now, and I ask that you take care of yourself. Please send your contact information to the Corvid Athenaeum in Ravencroft and I will have you adequately compensated for your generosity as soon as I finish my business here."

Tessa blinked, hesitating, before nodding silently and climbing back into her autowagon. Both drivers followed quickly after her, the vehicle sputtering to life and slowly turning around to return back towards the north. Solomon watched them leave, eyes narrow, as if contemplating something. Gihon kept his eyes fixed on Solomon, almost daring him to try.

"There, now it's just us. Unfortunately, that's where my benevolence ends," Solomon grinned. "If you won't give me the Queen, I'll have to take her myself."

"No Fortress, no Sword," Gihon confirmed, clenching his fist tightly around his weapon. "You and me. Leave her out of it."

"Ah-ah," Solomon tutted. "I never agreed to leave her out of it. The girl's still mine."

CHAPTER 7

SOLOMON

Sensing the tension in Solomon's legs, Zander called out from his position, hands clasped tightly around the hilts of his curved blades.

"He's attacking, corvid! Strike first!"

Gihon nodded in understanding, his array igniting with a volley of dark energy that coalesced into multiple missiles. As the missiles soared through the air, they took the shape of dark birds, wings spreading proudly as they dove down and pelted Solomon and his two allies. Dust and smoke began to rise up, the debris concealing Gihon's foes.

"Aim, you know what to do," Solomon's cocky voice rang out from the obscurity.

The dust began to disperse as a concentrated beam of flame shot out towards Gihon. As the smoke cleared, Gihon noticed that Solomon had summoned his own rampart array to block the missiles at the last second. Beside him, the silver-haired lancer had vanished, and the woman had extended her arms to release a stream of fire, seeming to control the inferno from the gaping mouth of her pumpkin-like hat.

The woman, Aim, uses her hat to ignite the flames, and then uses her own alchemical array to enhance and control the fire. It serves as fuel for her alchemy, somehow. Is it enchanted? Gihon wondered, activating his rampart array to deflect it as he started to think through potential courses of action.

Behind Gihon, the lancer appeared once more, grinning as he quickly drove his weapon towards the Dirigent. His movements were interrupted suddenly by a powerful knee into his midsection, Edelein letting out a snarl as she spun around to roundhouse kick the silver-haired foe back.

Aim groaned in annoyance. She held her position, eternal flames pouring out to keep Gihon's hands occupied.

"Kimaris, you fool, don't tell me you can't fend off one little girl. This is probably your only chance to take out the Dirigent, so don't go and blow it!"

"Eddie!" Alett called out, throwing a familiar golden warbow into the air.

Looking past the other Zengarde as Solomon's masked army swarmed them, Edelein's eyes locked in on the bow as she caught it effortlessly from midair, quiver following shortly after. Hunting instincts activated, her center of gravity lowered, Edelein pulled an arrow from her quiver.

"Are you actually going to try to fight me with a long-range weapon? I knew royals were stupid, but really–!"

Kimaris' words were cut off as Edelein took a quick sidestep, loosing her arrow a few millimeters from his face.

The heat of Aim's fire subsided for a brief moment, the mage dispelling her fire stream in favor of a localized explosion that barely managed to incinerate Edelein's arrow a mere second before it could pierce her. A second arrow struck in the trail of the first, striking Aim's hat and pinning it to a tree. Behind Gihon, Edelein had crouched down and fired a second shot from below, smirking as her arrow landed as planned.

Solomon reached down, a bright red array illuminating underneath him as he began to scoop a burning blade of magma up from the ground.

I suppose this still upholds the agreement of our duel. Gihon sighed to himself, dropping his rampart array as Aim's fire petered out. *He said no Divine Sword, but his other weapons are still in play. A pyroclastic blade will be a hassle, though.*

Beside Solomon, Kimaris had activated his own violet array, a shadowy black horse rising from the glowing lines and rearing back with a dissonant whinny.

That creature appears to be composed of limbus energy. Has Solomon stooped to the lows of teaching his followers my techniques? How would a man like him be able to figure them out? Gihon wondered as Kimaris hoisted himself up onto the tenebrous mount.

In the shadows of the underbrush beside the road, masked figures began to activate arrays from identical gauntlets, each one crackling with energy as a volley of electric blasts launched at the Zengarde.

"Finally," Everett commented, raising a large shield to block the onslaught of bolts. "I was waiting for these guys to do something interesting."

"Yeah, it's really too bad that we're a whole lot more

interesting than these losers," Nephvir replied, stepping forward and dropping down into Everett's shadow.

Reappearing behind the enemies with a sharp whistle, the cultists whipped around to find Nephvir leaning on a tree behind them, glossy black scythe in hand. The fellborn's long black hair had turned a stark white as the enchanted weapon filled his body with extraplanar energy, seeming to defy gravity as he slashed forward for a low strike. Each swipe of his scythe left a dark afterimage reminiscent of paint strokes, sending a few cultists off-balance as they tried to evade Nephvir's swings.

As the enemies' attention became diverted towards the shadowstepping Noentet Nephvir, the other Zengarde rushed forward to take advantage of Nephvir's distraction. Smoke poured in between the trees, obscuring the cultists' view, isolating them to be picked off individually.

Alett's signature smoke bombs were a familiar tactic to the Zengarde, each of them having years of experience in honing their senses to navigate through the obstruction effortlessly. For the Zengarde's foes, however, these bombs proved time and time again to be a powerful asset in disorienting and separating them from each other.

Pained screams sounded one at a time from several different parts of the smoke, alarming the other cultists as Zander darted from target to target. The sphynx twisted and danced between them, dual blades expertly slicing at each man's major tendons.

Zander gave a single agitated grunt, which the other Zengarde were able to clearly interpret.

We don't have time for lethal combat. Incapacitate as quickly as possible and provide backup to the Queen. We can come back to kill them after ensuring her safety.

Following the Ehret's silent command, the Zengarde began to melt into the smoke, dispatching each cultist before they could realize what was happening. A few soundless slashes and strikes later, each assailant was left on the ground, clutching weakly at severed limbs and sliced muscles.

"I'm heading to Eddie! Finish cleaning up here and come follow me once— whoa!" Alett started, dashing forwards out of the smoke before retreating into a sudden backstep.

The owl's Seventh Sense flared as he stopped in his tracks, narrowly dodging a razor-sharp wind blade. It sliced past him with a sharp wooshing noise, Alett turning his head to see the wind blade had cut clean through a tree on the other side of the road, his face draining of color as he realized how close he had been to ending up with the same fate.

Turning towards the source of the blade, Alett adjusted his goggles as his eyes met a new masked figure, tall and daunting with a longsword in his right hand, and a shortsword in his left. His mask was sharp and angular, only covering half of his face and leaving the bottom half open to reveal a pointed goatee, the same brown color as the long and wavy locks that framed his face.

The cultist wore no shirt, his large torso covered in a thick layer of body hair. Muscles tensed as he drew back his blade for another slash, Alett's bright yellow-orange eyes widening in alarm as a second wind slash barreled towards him.

Gihon let out a sharp exhale as his adamantine shortsword met the scalding blade of Solomon's magma saber. Molten slag was flung in every direction from Solomon's recoil, dripping and sizzling into the asphalt below.

As Solomon swung his arm over his head, Gihon prepared

for a second counter, bracing his arms for the scorching impact. The blade crashed down, missing the Dirigent entirely. Solomon lunged forward for another slash, missing again as more magma was hurled from his sword and into the ground.

The wild grasses that edged the road singed and sputtered, embers sparking into flame on both sides.

Solomon is intentionally avoiding me, Gihon realized. *He's not trying to hit me, he's trying to ignite our surroundings to close us off from the others.*

Sparing a quick glance around the ring of fire, his eyes met Edelein's. She was looking back at him, tail swishing in alarm as she clutched her bow.

"It's for the fire witch," Edelein shouted through the noise of battle as she drank in his pensive expression. "Her hat fed her flames, but now he's providing a new source of energy for her after I removed it. It also gives us less room to dodge the other man and his horse."

Two more excellent reasons to not be trapped in a blazing inferno with Solomon and his lackeys, Gihon thought with a sigh. *Edelein is quite intelligent for picking up on it so quickly.*

"Edelein, I am going to disrupt the ground and delay her access to the flames, and make it exponentially more difficult for the lancer to strike while mounted," Gihon yelled back, a large array activating as he pressed one palm onto the ground. "Please brace yourself immediately!"

Edelein nodded in response, crouching down to lower her center of gravity as the road beneath them fragmented and began to shift. Pillars of stone rose at different heights, the mounted assailant letting out a loud curse as his horse reared back, narrowly avoiding one of the rising columns.

From atop the highest pillar, Aim cackled as she began to wave her arms, magma snaking slowly around each stone shaft as it made its way towards her.

"Your tricks do not inhibit me the way they inhibit my partner, raven!" Aim called out, pulling flames upwards from the slag. "You've simply given me a better view to bear witness as your body melts into the inferno. Well done, Dirigent!"

She's stalling... Aim won't admit it openly, but it did slow her down. The added distance will allow us to dodge her more easily, as well, Gihon noted silently.

"Solomon supports these two better than they support each other," Edelein added. "He's been assisting them, but all these two do is yell at each other. We can use that, somehow."

Looking over her shoulder, Edelein leapt and planted both feet on the stone wall next to her, launching herself out of the way of Kimaris as he barreled through. His charges were sloppy, slowed significantly by the rough terrain.

It's clever of Edelein to use the jagged ground to her own advantage. While it slows the others significantly, this technique seems to speed her up. Does the Deepwood contain a similar topography? Gihon wondered, watching as Edelein darted from pillar to pillar, dodging fire blasts effortlessly.

"She's not distracting the noble and heartless Dirigent, is she?" Solomon laughed heartily, striking at Gihon while his back was turned. "You're getting sloppy, you little stoic."

"I'm not distracted," Gihon countered as he parried Solomon's sword, "I simply enjoy learning, and fighting you is simple enough to where I can manage both simultaneously."

"I would rather eat my own sword than listen to you talk about how much you love to learn and teach. It's painfully embarrassing to witness, the little Arvien-wannabe boy. You're not as impressive as you think."

"I suppose it's a good thing that impressing you is not my priority, then."

The Man in Red

"Is *she* impressed, then?"

Gihon faltered for a brief moment, allowing Solomon to connect a swift punch to the Dirigent's sternum. With a sharp cough, Gihon stepped back and regained his stance. Pressing his attack further, Gihon's newfound aggression set Solomon on a backwards defense.

"Gihon!" Edelein called out, drawing his attention. "Get me up to the top!"

Looking over at her, Gihon realized she was gesturing to the tallest pillar, across from Aim. The Dirigent pressured Solomon to buy some distance before nodding and twisting his wrist into the air.

The groundshift array ignited once more at his command, rotating as stone steps began to jut out one at a time around the tallest pillar. Edelein quickly slung her bow over her shoulder, sprinting up each step as it formed underneath her foot.

"You seemed lonely up here," Edelein called out to Aim, readying her bow once more. "I figured that you would enjoy a bit of company."

"If you're trying to flirt, you're not my type," Aim responded flatly, launching another fire stream towards Edelein.

The lioness sprung up, flipping over the flames and unloading a few more arrows towards Aim. The arrows barely scraped Aim's arms, Edelein's accuracy reduced from her constant movement to avoid being incinerated.

Crouching down, Edelein loosed another low-angled shot, the same one that had struck Aim's hat only a few minutes earlier.

As the arrow whistled through the air, closing the distance between both pillars, a sudden red light stopped the arrow in its tracks. Solomon's rampart shielded Aim, the arrowhead lodging into a translucent glowing red barrier. The array vanished as quickly as it had appeared as Gihon continued to press towards Solomon,

Edelein's arrow dropping to the ground.

Edelein reached for another arrow, gritting her teeth in frustration, when a sudden lurch set her off-balance. Crouching low, the lioness peered over the edge as Kimaris ramped up another charge, ramming his lance directly into the stone.

Underneath her feet, Edelein could feel the pillar veer forward again as it began to topple, having only a moment to react as she ran alongside the collapsing rocks. Summoning her strength to launch herself safely, Edelein leapt from the plummeting tower of stone onto a more steady column.

The Queen took a deep breath, regaining her balance and orienting herself towards her new position. Edelein fumbled for another arrow, pulling her quiver and glancing down into its near-emptied stash of arrows.

"I'm already down to four arrows, and I haven't even taken out a single one of these bastards?" Edelein grumbled under her breath, notching one of her final arrows with caution. "I've lost my touch."

A quick movement from the corner of Gihon's eye caught his attention as Kimaris began to prepare another charge towards Edelein's pillar.

I can't let him destroy all of these groundshifts, or we'll lose our biggest advantage, Gihon thought, turning his focus towards the mounted foe.

Sprinting towards Kimaris and furthering his distance from Solomon, Gihon quickly slammed his palm into the ground again, a familiar teal array illuminating his sharp features. The array

The Man in Red

ignited a second time, now underneath Kimaris and his mount as the shadow horse's hooves began to sink and lodge into the asphalt beneath.

The creature struggled with an alarmed whinny, unable to pull free as Gihon shot another volley of dark ravens. Acting quickly, Kimaris launched himself off of his horse, the beast melting back into shadows and vanishing as the lancer charged on foot towards Gihon.

"Move up, you two!" Solomon commanded in frustration as Edelein continued to weave between fireballs, drawing Aim's focus. "Team up and overwhelm them. All this space between you creates a disadvantage, damn it!"

Kimaris stabbed forward at Gihon, the Dirigent parrying with his adamantine blade. As the impact rang out, Gihon's shortsword began to unfurl, returning to its original cloth form as it wrapped itself around Kimaris' lance. In an instant, the lance quadrupled in weight as the cloth transmuted into adamantine once more. Kimaris dropped his weapon as it grew too heavy to hold, the lance falling and cracking the ground with a loud thud as it hit.

With the distance successfully closed between them, Gihon pulled back for a solid final punch. Kimaris raised his arms to defend himself, but the Dirigent's fist was met by another adamantine surface.

Solomon grinned from behind his adamantine arm as he slid in between to intercept the blow, cocking one eyebrow at the Dirigent as Gihon's face fell in annoyance.

"You must be unable to come up with your own alchemical techniques, if you insist on using mine like this. I let the rampart slide, but this is just pathetic," Gihon sighed.

Solomon pushed Gihon's arm away with his own, before planting a sudden and swift kick into Kimaris' midsection. Kimaris tumbled backwards, an arrow striking through the air where his head was just a moment before.

"You're annoying, you little brat!" Solomon yelled up at Edelein, sidestepping another arrow and swinging a wide arch with his pyroclastic blade to spray molten debris upwards towards the lioness.

Dancing acrobatically between blasts of slag, Edelein slid down a nearby pillar, using the stone as a shield to protect herself from Solomon's attacks as she returned her focus in Aim's direction. The flame witch was looking down at Gihon, drawing fire up from the ground to form a large strike. Her hands clasped together as more energy began to assemble around her, the inferno doubling in size.

"Over here, witch!" Edelein called out.

As Aim turned towards the sudden sound, the angle of her movement was just enough for Edelein's arrow to pierce through her hands. The witch let out an agonizing scream, her hands locked together by the arrow that was pinned through them both.

Nocking her final arrow, Edelein smirked as she lined up her shot. With her eyes expertly fixed on her prey and the bodily posture of a lifelong hunter, the lioness pulled her bowstring back and aimed for the kill.

As her fingers loosened around the string, a sudden pang in her chest resounded as her heart palpitated off-beat for a brief moment. The stutter was just enough to disconnect the expert hunter from her instincts as her arm faltered, the arrow singing through the air and grazing Aim's cheek.

"Interesting," Solomon muttered to himself as he glanced up at Edelein. "She's blighted, isn't she?"

The Man in Red

"You were able to predict the movement of my wind blade? Impressive."

The large cultist spoke with a deep and gruff voice, enunciating his words clearly. Alett hopped in place, keeping his body in motion as he prepared to evade again.

"Yeah, predicting movement is kind of our whole thing, us Zengarde," Alett replied, his hand slowly reaching into a small satchel on his belt as his fellow warriors fell in line behind him.

Zander and Jinn stood on either side of Alett, weapons drawn and fangs bared. The cultist chuckled, adjusting his grip on the hilts of his blades as he dashed forward to initiate the first strike.

Removing his hand from his satchel, Alett tossed a small spherical object forward, the orb colliding with the cultist's body before he could turn to evade it. The bomb exploded into a flurry of thin, razor-sharp wires that entangled the foe's large figure, causing him to stumble to the ground.

"Alett, Zander," Jinn spoke as the cultist attempted to detangle himself from the cables, "I will handle this one. Queen Edelein needs to be removed from the danger immediately. Get her away from the man in red, and the rest of us will catch up with you once this is handled."

"I can hear Edelein ahead," Zander agreed, clutching his swords as he turned his attention towards the smoldering ring of flame that encased his Queen. "She's out of arrows, and fighting hand-to-hand with the fire mage. She is proficient enough in melee combat, but she runs out of energy quickly when up close and will need backup before long."

"Don't die, Jinn! We'll be back for you once she's safe!" Alett encouraged his ally, leaping over the entangled cultist as he finally pulled the wires off of himself.

The cultist straightened himself up, swinging his sword to release a wind blade towards Jinn. As quickly as it appeared, the wind suddenly dispelled a few inches from Jinn's face, the white-haired wolf-man unflinching as he held his ground. Jinn stepped aside, revealing Thorne, who stood with one hand extended outwards as the wind whipped his signature fire-red bangs.

"Didn't anyone ever tell you not to bring wind to a wind fight?" Thorne asked, smirking.

"What the hell is that supposed to mean?" The cultist furrowed his eyebrows under his mask, throwing another wind blade forward.

The second blade dispelled just as the first had, Thorne cocking his head to the side in a mocking manner. Sweeping his leg, Thorne kicked up five small blades from the ground, each dagger hovering in an arc above his head.

"I'll show you what the wind can do," Thorne said as he narrowed his eyes.

"Thorne!" a new voice called out, Thorne's head turning as the blades dropped to the ground again.

Lylia was looking his way, a wall of vines protruding from the ground by her staff. Everett was standing with his back to his elven teammate, his shield raised to protect Cari and Nephvir as they huddled between him and Lylia. Surrounding them, several more cultists had appeared from seemingly nowhere, and lightning barrages were raining down from their gauntlets.

"Take out the newcomers. I can handle this one alone," Jinn said, suddenly appearing behind the large cultist.

Startled, the cultist turned around just in time to avoid a fatal blow, Jinn's sword striking a gash in his side instead.

"Do you have any fun tricks like your human partner?" the large man huffed, raising his weapons.

"I do not," Jinn stated. "I prefer to fight honorably, and I respect those who do the same. A person's true power comes from their pure swordsmanship, would you not agree?"

The Man in Red

The cultist shrugged, swinging both of his weapons in a windmill-like motion as several more gale blades shot forward. Jinn's senses carried him as he avoided each slash and began to slowly close the distance between them.

"I suppose not, then," Jinn sighed, striking forward with his longsword.

The cultist grunted with effort as he parried Jinn's attack, the force skidding him backwards.

His stance is proficient, but not masterful, Jinn thought. *Not to mention that awful wet-dog smell coming from him. It's... offensive, honestly.*

Running forward, the cultist began to close the distance, keeping Jinn in place by sending a cluster of wind blades from both of his swords. Jinn deflected and dodged every slash, preparing for the oncoming parry as his foe closed in.

The cultist let out a flurry of quick swings with his longsword, the shortsword held closer to his chest in a defensive position. Jinn blocked each hit as they came, evaluating the enemy's stance with each swing.

He's taking the shortest route for his blade, which makes all of his attacks predictable.

"You're letting your nerves get the best of you," Jinn cautioned, raising his sword to meet the cultist's double-handed overhead strike.

"Is it your warrior's honor that leads you to give advice to your enemy in battle?" the cultist asked, recoiling from Jinn's parry.

"You won't live long enough to heed my advice, so it is of no conflict to me," Jinn stated simply, eyeing the opening made by his stagger.

Jinn pressed forward with lightning-fast slashes across the cultist's throat, armpits, solar plexus, and midsection. Sliding behind him, Jinn struck the backs of the man's knees, wiping the blood on his waist wrap and sheathing his blade as quickly as he had drawn it.

Standing up, Jinn turned around to assess the situation of his allies. Expecting to gaze upon the corpse of his enemy, Jinn's eyes widened as he realized the cultist was still standing, his blood drying as each of the seven wounds closed.

That didn't kill him?

The cultist let out a low growl, his body hulking and growing hairier as his wounds healed, slowly turning around to face Jinn again. His mask was gone, his humanoid head replaced with that of a mangy brown wolf head, yellow teeth snarling as slimy drool fell from his curled black lips.

As realization hit Jinn, he drew his blade once more, the wolf-man meeting the cold gaze of the man-wolf before him.

A werewolf. That explains the smell, then.

Within the ring of fire, Aim was grappling with Edelein, both fighters exchanging quick and powerful blows. As Gihon's groundshifted pillars began to slowly collapse around them, the women continued to attack each other relentlessly.

Edelein lunged at Aim, swiping at the mage with sharp claws. Aim exhaled, her hands igniting as she deflected the Queen's hits. Edelein winced from the heat but refused to back down, her nails managing to barely reach Aim's face.

Aim grunted as Edelein's claws connected with her cheek, her reaction opening up just enough room for Edelein to follow up with a swift upward kick into her jaw. The mage stumbled and managed to shove Edelein back a step as she wiped the blood from her face, touching her jaw with one hand. Sensing the opportunity, Kimaris charged towards them, still running on foot as he closed the distance. The lancer grabbed at Edelein, but was pushed back by a swift kick to his throat as Edelein retaliated.

"Two on one? Are you really that scared of me?" Edelein taunted, readying her stance for another strike.

Beside them, Solomon began to put distance between himself and Gihon, plunging his sword into one of the remaining pillars. The tower of stone began to buckle and groan, bloating until it exploded outwards into a shower of hot magma. Gihon's eyes widened as he read the attack, summoning another rampart array to protect himself from the blast.

Aim planted a kick against Edelein's braced arms, the force sending her back just enough for Kimaris to grab her firmly.

"You've been so focused on us this whole time. You seem to have forgotten that you're *his* prey, not ours," Kimaris sneered, tossing Edelein aside and into the dirt.

"You—!" Edelein started to stand, before a sudden grip on her hair stopped her in her tracks.

Solomon grabbed Edelein's ponytail, yanking her upwards as she let out a small pained yelp. His face leaned in close to smirk down at the Queen, reveling in the agonized look on her face as he tightened his grip on her hair.

"Edelein!" Gihon exclaimed from underneath his rampart, magma still cascading around him and trapping him in place.

"Your Majesty, I hope my new pet wolfdog delivered my message to—ow!" Solomon began, before being interrupted by the feeling of sharp teeth digging into his throat.

Edelein's nose scrunched as she bit deeply into his neck, fangs piercing his skin as his blood began to seep out and stain her lips.

"You ugly, feral bitch!" Solomon cursed, throwing Edelein

onto the ground, kicking her in the head and grasping at his bleeding neck with a searing hand to close the wound. "You know, I wasn't planning to kill you, but I think you just changed my mind."

Long claws met a sharp blade as Jinn parried the werewolf's attacks, the wolf-man retaliating against the man-wolf with a strong upward slash, slicing clean through his arm. Blood splurted from the werewolf's exposed shoulder, staining the asphalt red as he bent down to pick up his severed limb.

"You're fast, boy," the werewolf growled, holding his arm up into place as it began to quickly reattach.

"I think I liked you more with the mask on," Jinn retorted, standing defensively as he dodged every oncoming attack.

His werewolf form is faster than he was as a human, as expected, Jinn thought. *However, being in a bestial form makes it even easier for my Seventh Sense to predict his movements.*

As Jinn continued to evade the onslaught of attacks, he began to notice the werewolf slowing down as his stamina reached the end of its limit. Sensing the opening, Jinn switched to an offensive stance and began to unleash a fast barrage of slashes all around the werewolf's body. The werewolf stepped back, defensive as he began to divert his energy into healing the wounds created by Jinn's flurry.

The werewolf pulled his arms close to protect his chest, slowing down as he healed each new wound as they came. Retaliating, claws outstretched in one last attempt for his life, the werewolf leapt towards Jinn with a loud roar. The enemy's claws connected with Jinn's still form, until the image vanished from sight and his lupine claws met nothing but air, the werewolf stumbling forward awkwardly as he tried to search for his target.

Chills ran up the werewolf's spine as Jinn appeared behind him, speaking coldly.

"You had a better chance against me in your human form," Jinn stated. "Our Queen is the master of all beastkind, including disgusting creatures such as yourself. The moment you transformed, you had no choice but to succumb to the will of Zenluve."

The weight of Jinn's words hung heavily in the werewolf's mind, his body stiff and unresponsive.

Why can't I move? the werewolf thought as he tried to command his limbs to respond, to flee. *Are his words true? Is this the dominion of the True Queen of Beasts?*

As the werewolf's head began to slowly slide off of its body, Jinn stepped away as if nothing had happened, cleaning the cultist's blood off of his blade for the final time as he returned it to his sheath, the werewolf's corpse finally crumpling to the ground behind him.

"You know, I'm pretty sure dog-fighting is illegal," Thorne snickered as he ripped his knife from the throat of a cultist.

"Dogs. Different from a wolf zoa and a werewolf," Jinn corrected with an annoyed huff, ignoring the human's attempted humor.

Edelein began to struggle to her feet, winded from hitting the ground twice in such a short period of time and feeling the effects of her energy beginning to drain in the exact way that Zander had predicted. Across from her, Solomon stood glowering, one hand on his neck while the other dug his pyroclastic blade into the ground.

"You'll be prettier when you're dead," Solomon spat with murderous intent, swinging his sword forward as another large spatter of magma sprayed towards her.

In an instant, action erupted around the two, as allies began to respond within the blink of an eye. Gihon lunged forward, freed from his molten prison as he grabbed Edelein, holding her close to his chest and turning his back towards Solomon with another rampart array active to block the oncoming attack. An explosion resonated from a small orb at Solomon's feet as Alett's smoke bomb reached its target, enshrouding the Queen from view as the owl arrived, throwing a second bomb that erupted into wires that encased Solomon.

Solomon dropped his weapon, wincing as sharp wires dug into his skin. Alett grabbed Solomon from behind, gloved hands pulling the wires tighter and turning the white-haired foe to face the flames that encased the arena.

"Zander, now!" Alett called out.

Through the flames, a large silhouette appeared, pointed ears laid back in anger as he lurched forward, dual curved blades raised into an offensive stance.

The wires suddenly burst into flames, melting off of Solomon's body as Alett yelped in surprise, dropping the smoldering cables. Solomon shoved a quick elbow backwards into the owl-boy's throat, distancing himself as he began to sprint towards Zander.

As his magma blade vanished into the ground, Solomon lit another array as a new sword appeared in his hand. This second weapon was much thinner, appearing to be significantly lighter and more mobile than the previous one. Each blow made from his new sword pushed Zander back, closer and closer towards the fire.

The Man in Red

"Wind weaponry, again?" Zander muttered, deflecting each hit with a lunge forward to minimize the distance lost. "I see your intentions, and I will not burn."

Close by, Alett and Gihon were fretting over Edelein, the Dirigent keeping her upright as her knees weakened.

"She's exerted too much force. The stress on her body will result in a flare-up of blight symptoms," Gihon noted, one hand on her feverish forehead. "Edelein, you fought well, but it's time for you to rest."

"I'm not backing down," Edelein denied, shaking her head as she tried to steady herself. "I would never—"

"Send your men anywhere that you yourself would not go, we know, Ed," Alett finished her sentence, his large eyes brimming with compassion. "There's a problem ahead, though, that I think you should be far away from."

Past the three allies, Kimaris and Aim were approaching. Aim's hat had been returned to her head, her bloody hands no longer pierced together as Kimaris tossed the broken arrow aside.

"Aim will be unable to use her hands to manipulate the fire due to her injury, but her hat can still spew them loosely," Gihon theorized. "Solomon's wind sword will be an issue, assuming he plans to use it to further oxygenate the air around and enhance the inferno."

"Gihon, can you do the opposite?" Alett asked. "A hypoxic array that removes oxygen?"

"That depends. How is Zenluve's topography? A hypoxic air array is possible, but it will affect everyone within the area, including us. The air will get incredibly thin, like that of a mountaintop. Can you handle fighting without oxygen?"

"Don't worry about us, we're the unstoppable and mighty Zengarde. Plus, I think I've got an idea," Alett grinned, stepping in front of Gihon and Edelein and pulling another bomb out of his satchel. "Zander and I will buy you some time. Take care of Eddie, and ignite that array when you can."

Gihon nodded, turning to face Edelein.

"Do you still have those stamina potions from the doctor?" Gihon asked, looking over her as Edelein struggled to maintain an upright posture.

"They're in Alett's bag." Edelein coughed. "I'm not sure where he left it after the fight started, though. We don't have time for that right now. Can your alchemy make more arrows?"

"Remind me to teach you about hardlight weaponry. I'd have to make each arrow individually, and we don't have the time for that either. I need you to stay back for now so I can focus on the hypoxic air array."

Edelein nodded weakly, giving in to his command.

"Good," Gihon smiled. "It won't take long to finish this fight. Watch closely."

Ahead of them, Zander and Alett were navigating between Aim, Kimaris, and Solomon. Wild spurts of fire were spewing loosely from Aim's hat, amplified by Solomon's wind blade as Kimaris took jabs at Alett, the owl dancing around quickly to avoid his lance.

"Zander, catch!" Alett called out, producing a bomb in each hand.

With one hand, the owl-boy lobbed his first bomb high into the air, the second one being thrown directly at Kimaris' feet. On impact, the second bomb exploded into hot steam, scalding and disorienting the lancer. Zander leaped upwards, catching the first bomb midair and throwing it down in front of Solomon with a swift twist of his feline body.

The bomb detonated into a small cloud, clearing to reveal Alett crouching at Solomon's feet, prepared to strike upwards. Solomon swung loosely down at Alett, whipping his head around in confusion as Alett vanished again.

What is this kid's gimmick? Invisibility? Teleportation? Clones? Solomon wondered, trying to locate Alett through the smog. *What kind of bomb did he just throw at me?*

"Right here, big guy!" Alett called out, appearing through the smoke and landing a firm kick on Solomon's face.

Solomon tumbled backwards, groaning in a mixture of frustration and pain. Lifting his aching body, the red-clad man locked his gaze onto another bomb sailing towards him, this time exploding in midair into a burst of flame.

The embers stopped just before reaching Solomon, seeming to hover suspended in space for a split-second before reversing and being sucked into Aim's wide-brimmed hat, its gaping maw sparking with smoldering energy.

"Enough of you, punk!" Solomon roared, swinging his sword in a wide arc.

A strong galeforce slammed into Alett's lightweight body, the petite owl-boy tumbling backwards through the flames and slamming into a familiar wall of vines on the other side.

Lylia peered down at Alett, helping him up and dusting him off. Alett nodded in appreciation, their looks seeming to communicate nonverbally.

Are you guys doing alright? Alett seemed to ask with inquisitive eyes, adjusting the strap of his goggles.

Lylia was reinforcing Cari, the elegant fox-girl dancing around the cultists as her whip connected with each one of them. Cari leapt and swayed as blasts of fire and lighting missed her lithe body. Lylia's vines sprung up from the ground, entangling a cultist as Cari struck his torso with a harsh crack of her whip, tearing through his clothing and flaying off the outer layer of his skin.

We're fine. More reinforcements keep showing up, but we're holding our own with no issue. Go keep Edelein safe, Lylia responded silently, one hand clasped on Alett's shoulder.

Alett's smoke began to clear out from the impact of Solomon's wind wall, revealing Zander and Kimaris in a heated exchange of blows. Kimaris rammed his lance forward, Zander catching the weapon easily between his swords in a low cross.

Pushing downward to dispel the parry, the sphynx forced Kimaris' lance into the ground as he leapt into the air, planting both feet firmly on the body of the lance. The force of Zander's impact slammed the lance into the ground, Kimaris wincing as he dropped his weapon. Zander leapt forward and dug his knee into Kimaris' sternum, sending his foe stumbling back as the sphynx maintained his stance on top of Kimaris' disarmed weapon.

Kimaris looked quickly down at his lance and back up to Zander, before his eyes darted to an approaching figure. Sensing the energy of Solomon from behind, Zander turned and ducked down, dodging a swift blow from the wind blade. The Ehret kicked upwards, narrowly missing Solomon as the white-haired foe slashed down at him. Zander twisted his body, avoiding the first strike and pushing himself back to his feet in time to catch the second oncoming attack between both blades again.

Disengaging the parry, Zander tossed one of his khopesh blades into the air, shoving his second sword forward to close the distance between himself and his foe. Jutting an elbow into Solomon, Zander extended his palm upwards as his curved weapon dropped down from the air, landing precisely into his supinated hand for a fast swipe. Solomon stepped back to give himself room to swing in retaliation, eyes wide as Zander's sharp blade managed to graze his neck.

Every step backwards that Solomon took was met by a step forward as Zander continued to press the space between them, relentless and fueled by his anger. The sphynx swung his swords with fury, thirsting for the blood of the man that harmed his

The Man in Red

Queen. As Solomon continued to parry and counter him, Zander spared quick and curious glances toward Aim, noticing the fire had decreased.

Aim was standing with one bloodied hand on the brim of her hat, eyebrows furrowed with focus as she tried to prepare a shot.

As I suspected, Zander realized. *The closer I am to her master, the safer. She cannot control her pyre, and she fears striking him.*

Following Zander's gaze, Solomon picked up on the sphynx's epiphany. Igniting a bright red array, Solomon summoned a ball of heavily condensed wind that expanded outwards, flinging both men away from each other. Zander flipped to land on his feet, ducking immediately as a scorching torrent zipped through the air just a millimeter from the tips of his ears.

Solomon let out a smug laugh, his smile fading slowly as his inhales grew shallower. Sparks began to fly from Aim's hat, flames sputtering pathetically and the fuel output increasing as her hat only managed to produce small licks of fire. Zander met Gihon's golden eyes as a large teal array illuminated the arena, winds circling around them as oxygen began to be driven out of the air.

As the flames surrounding the arena began to die out, the remaining Zengarde fell back to join up with Gihon and the others, Alett at the front of the group.

"Thorne, now's a good time to do that thing we talked about!" Alett called out over his shoulder.

"On it, boss!" Thorne confirmed with a grin, gesturing with his hands as a new sphere of air encapsulated himself and his allies.

The Zengarde took deep, grateful breaths as fresh air filled the space surrounding them, Thorne's wind barrier providing proper oxygen to his allies.

"This is surprisingly hard to do," Thorne noted under his breath. "Gihon's array seems to be actively competing against my wind. I don't want to do this again."

"If you shut up, they won't find out that it's hard, and we can bluff our way into never having to do this again," Lylia countered in annoyance.

Agitated, Solomon dug his sword into the ground, creating a wind barrier of his own.

"Fine!" Solomon yelled across the winds at Gihon, eyes narrow. "You win for now, Dirigent, but this isn't over!"

Waving his hand, a large tornado appeared from an array under Solomon's feet, obscuring himself and his allies from view. As the tornado dissipated, the three of them were gone, along with any surviving cultists.

Gihon dispelled his array as the enemies fled, relieved.

On the backline behind Gihon and the Zengarde, Edelein's eyes widened in shock as Solomon appeared in front of her, his lips twisted into a wicked grin as he placed a thumb on her chin, tilting her head up to meet his wild gaze. The Queen's skin crawled at his touch, the inhuman speed of his movement and the unsettling air of his powerful aura freezing her body in fear.

"See you soon, little cub," Solomon whispered into her ear before vanishing out of sight.

CHAPTER 8

FIGHT BACK

"Just like that, the bastard's gone." Thorne sighed, dispelling his wind barrier.

"Edelein, are you okay?" Cari asked gently, the Queen's hollow eyes looking emptily over at her close friend. "You look shaken up."

"It's nothing," Edelein shook her head. "Is anyone hurt?"

"You are, it seems." Lylia replied as approached, gently parting her hair where some dried blood matted her sandy blonde locks.

"Oh, this? It's nothing. I hit my head when Solomon threw me down, it's—"

Before Edelein could finish her protests, a comforting green aura began to emanate from Lylia's gentle fingertips, closing the wound.

"That is incredibly impressive healing magic," Gihon commented, watching in awe as he drank in the scene in front of him. "It rivals top alchemy, I daresay."

"Thank you. It took a few hundred years to master," Lylia responded politely, dipping her head in respect.

"Well, you don't look a day over a hundred," Thorne snickered, winking.

Lylia turned to face him, her face blank and annoyed.

"Your attempts at courtship are not rooted in research, I can see. You are essentially calling me a child. Do you not understand the lifespans of elves, human?"

Thorne paused, thinking.

"You... don't look a day over two hundred?"

"I *am* two hundred."

"Nailed it."

"You nailed... telling me that I look my age?"

Thorne hesitated again, puffing his cheeks.

"Yes," he said, doubling down after a long pause.

"If you two are done with whatever the hell that was, there's a more pressing matter at hand," Zander commented, folding his arms across his chest. "That man, Solomon, vanished entirely in a single heartbeat. Take a whiff. It is as if he were never even here to begin with."

"Zander is right," Alett confirmed with a nod as he removed his goggles, putting his iconic octangular glasses back on. "I can't smell him at all, we're stuck in the middle of a decimated road with no transportation, and I... never mind, we can figure all that out later. Gihon, how far is that house you mentioned?"

"The distance is walkable, even for Edelein in her current state. We should set out now, and I can explain some things along the way," Gihon confirmed, turning and starting southbound down the side of the road.

"Oh, hooray, another alchemy lesson," Thorne groaned as the group followed after Gihon's pace.

The Man in Red

"The man we faced is… an extremely capable and powerful alchemist named Solomon. I have crossed paths with him too many times in my life, and he is a foe that almost rivals my own ability. He is what we call a homunculus: a soulless, artificially-created humanoid. Homunculi lack the basic traits of humanity, such as love or empathy. He is, in every sense, a monster who creates more monsters. The others were the homunculi that he created to serve him and his purpose. Quite insane, the lot of them are. Encountering him in any setting is a nightmare."

"He mentioned being a miracle worker," Edelein stated, her tone urging Gihon to explain further.

"The masked men with him were the cultists who have devoted their lives to his cause. Many years ago, Solomon traveled around Caandemium and utilized high-caliber alchemy to heal and aid people who were particularly lost; be it emotional vulnerability or a desperate situation, he took advantage of each one by offering them a temporary solution in exchange for control of their entire lives. A deal with the devil, if you will. Now they follow him everywhere, metaphorically as soulless as he is. They fight by utilizing artificial gauntlets that Solomon invented himself, which can mimic basic fire and lightning arrays."

"He actually did miracles, then?"

"Not miracles, just alchemy to the uneducated. Solomon is a fraud, and not the messiah those poor people believe him to be. That man has been taking advantage of their vulnerability, and nothing more."

"You said he was created artificially?" Alett asked, and Gihon nodded.

"That's why he doesn't smell," Alett said in unison with Edelein and Zander, the realization hitting the three of them simultaneously.

"What?" Gihon asked, unable to hide his surprise at their

comments.

"Does he have a scent to you, Gihon?" Edelein asked, tilting her head.

"No, I mean… I don't… normally… smell people," Gihon stumbled over his words, unprepared to answer such an unexpected and unorthodox question.

"Everything has a natural fragrance or odor. Plants, animals, humans, everything," Edelein explained. "That man, Solomon, he did not. Neither did the woman or the man with the lance. There was an absence of anything in their presence, almost as if they were not there at all. It was incredibly strange to fight against."

"Why would someone even create an artificial human, anyway?" Alett asked.

"It is a debate of ethics, certainly. In Solomon's case, he creates homunculi as servants. Indentured servitude is seemingly justified when the servant is soulless. Though, when homunculi proved hard to control, many people began to prefer zoa servants instead."

The air grew tense at Gihon's words, the three zoa staring at Gihon in disgust. Behind them, Jinn and Cari were making similar grimacing expressions, while Everett simply winced awkwardly. Thorne, Lylia, and Nephvir exchanged concerned glances, being the only Zengarde that held no zoa heritage.

"Your zoa are *slaves*?" Zander asked, appalled.

"Caandemite tradition places zoa in a lower social caste, stemming from the evolutionary 'superiority' of humans as opposed to animals. Slaves is a strong word that I would not use to refer to the situation, but rather something more akin to servanthood, or a second-class citizenship. Although, there are some that have broken that traditional stigma, such as myself. The idea of zoa being second-class is a bit antiquated these days, though there is still a ways to go before our society reflects anything similar to Zenluve. Admittedly, it's why I don't openly display my feathers. Cohorts of mine on occasion fail to even realize that I am a zoa without prior knowledge of me, which makes my life marginally easier."

The air grew more tense as Edelein and Alett looked up at Gihon, both of their eyes curious and surprised.

"You hide your feathers?" Edelein asked, appalled.

"So you *do* have them!" Alett cried out in excitement, plumicorns twittering. "I knew there was no way you wouldn't have feathers!"

Gihon blinked, realizing for the first time that he had not had this conversation with the Zenluvians yet. Bashfully, the Dirigent lifted his hands to his head, pushing the hair that covered his ears out of the way to reveal a cluster of shiny black raven feathers extending backwards from behind each ear.

"I don't think about it often, so I suppose I forgot to mention it. I don't mind telling people that I am a zoa, and I hold no shame against it. It is simply that when one lives their life in a world of stigma, it becomes easier to hide than it is to be oneself. Displaying my feathers proudly was not worth the headache of prejudice, so I grew my hair out a bit in order to obscure them better."

"You should be proud. You don't seem like the type to change who you are based on the opinions of those around you," Edelein countered.

"You are correct, I am not the type. However, as I said, it was more of a matter of inconvenience than irritation. I was tired of explaining myself all the time. Lately, though, more and more high-caliber alchemists do know about my heritage, so maybe I'm overdue for a haircut."

"I do like your hair as it is, though," Edelein shrugged, turning to stare at the road ahead as Gihon dropped his hands, hair falling to cover his corvid feathers once more. "It just seems like a sad way to live, is all."

"You're right, Edelein. Many of our young zoa have heard your tale and greatly admire your kingdom," Gihon replied solemnly as he added, "I have a zoa student at the Corvid Athenaeum. I wish I could show you the way his eyes lit up when I told him I was meeting you, Your Majesty."

"Your zoa have heard of us, but your scholars have not?" Edelein asked, exasperated.

"We hear tales on the wind of the Zenluvian Lion Kings. Acolytes have passed the stories off as fairytales with no merit, but in the zoa communities, some still believe them to be true. Meeting you does feel a bit like meeting a legend, I must confess. You certainly fight like the noble Lion Kings from the stories," Gihon admitted with a soft smile.

"What does Solomon want with Queen Edelein? Something tells me he's not some zoa fanboy eager to meet his hero," Alett asked.

"I have theories, but I am not certain of anything. Solomon is a long-time enemy of the Society and of Velkhamore, so the most likely outcome is that he seeks to sabotage the budding relationship between our lands."

"He attacked Jinn on the Society's training grounds. For an enemy of Velkhamore, he was allowed access quite easily, it seems," Edelein crossed her arms, pondering.

"That is an oversight on our part, as the representative and ambassador for the Society, I will be personally investigating the cause and I offer the deepest condolences we can, on behalf of any injuries sustained. Solomon must be feeling incredibly emboldened to enter Velkhamore, much less our training grounds. That leads me to believe that he has a plan of some sort."

"Or an insider," Edelein stated.

The Man in Red

Gihon froze up for a moment, uneasy as he considered the idea. Shaking his head in denial, the Dirigent shifted the conversation.

"If he had genuine plans to harm you, I would be surprised that you got out of the situation relatively unscathed. We are here to protect you, but he seemed content to cross blades with me and leave the others to you, which is unusual for him. Solomon was created artificially to have the perfect form, which leads to incredible amounts of narcissism. He wouldn't want a lackey of his to get the final blow on the Queen. Therefore, I do believe that Solomon was not trying to kill you, but perhaps convey a message of sorts. However, it is entirely possible that he plans to return to finish the job, so we should be on alert."

"No such thing will happen," Edelein replied confidently. "He fled with his tail between his legs. He may have caught Jinn off guard, but he is no match for the rest of the Zengarde. My Ehret did an excellent job."

Zander straightened his shoulders, his piercing green eyes sparkling with pride.

"It is a blessing to have such faithful warriors by your side, Your Majesty. They are very strong and fought incredibly well," Gihon smiled, meeting Zander's gaze in a moment of affirmation before the Ehret turned away again.

"How do you know so much about this homunculus, Solomon?" Alett asked suddenly, awakening from the deep thought he found himself in.

Gihon hesitated for a moment, slowing his pace briefly before continuing to walk faster.

"As I mentioned, I have had the absolute displeasure of crossing paths with him on far too many occasions in the past. His cult has lofty goals and frustratingly strong willpower, and I am one of the few alchemists strong enough to thwart his plans."

"He must be pretty strong then, right?" Alett continued.

"The last time he was active, he destroyed an entire city," Gihon scowled, recalling a silent memory. "It seems we are arriving at the house now, so I must save that story for another time. My inability to stop him that day is my most bitter failure as an alchemist, and a terribly unpleasant memory to relive. I do apologize."

Turning off of the road and snaking his way through a narrower path, barely large enough to fit an autowagon, the Dirigent gestured towards the hidden paradise of his private estate.

Gihon's home was large, enshrouded by thick trees. With classic architecture and dark wood, the elegant two-story home stood tall and proud, reminiscent of the man who owned it. The ambiance of a rushing river echoed from a nearby gorge, surrounding his tranquil escape in the comforting sounds of nature.

"A home in the woods, close by to a gorge, unbothered by humankind? Now this is much more my preference than anything that Velkhamore had to offer," Edelein said with a smile.

"I do enjoy solitude, similar to you. The gorge provides more privacy and white noise from the running water below, and the small pathway leading up to the house is often overlooked. I built this home a few years ago, when I took over the Athenaeum. There's an open clearing about two miles from here that my students will use to practice developing their alchemy."

"It's lovely," Edelein replied, turning towards the house. "First and foremost, I would like to change out of these dirty clothes. I'm filthy thanks to that damn homunculus tossing me around."

Edelein looked over her shoulder, sensing an unusual energy from her Zengarde. Everett's large figure fidgeted before admitting his remorseful thoughts.

"We didn't have a chance to fetch your luggage when we

left," the ox said sheepishly with an embarrassed smile.

For a moment, Alett looked like he wanted to speak up, but decided against it as Gihon answered.

Edelein's face dropped, but Gihon chimed in. "My students stay here on occasion, so there will be clothing for you to borrow. I believe that my student Spira is about your size, so feel free to have a look around the house and wear anything that suits you. It will not bother any of them, I assure you."

"Are any of your students here now?" Edelein asked, opening the front door.

The interior of the house had floor-to-ceiling windows, boasting large amounts of natural light in an open floor plan. Through the glass, nothing but forest was beyond them, a sight that Edelein found incredibly pleasing.

A conversation pit sat as the focal piece of the open layout, with long sofas facing a delicate stone fireplace. On one of the sofas, Edelein noticed a pair of grey cat ears poking up from a young figure on the other side. One ear turned backwards at the sound of the Queen's entrance, a teenage girl picking her head up curiously as she turned to look at Edelein. The girl had short silver-grey hair just above her shoulders, with dyed pink highlights accenting her bangs. As the cat-girl sprung to her feet, Edelein noticed her oversized pink sweatshirt and black shorts.

"That answers that question, I suppose. Nora, are you the only one at the house right now?" Gihon asked, addressing the cat zoa.

Nora nodded, looking a bit confused by the situation.

"Just me," she said. "I was on my way back from that mission in Velkhamore that you asked me about. What's going on, Master Marleogne? Who are they?"

"Nora, this is Queen Edelein from the Kingdom of Zenluve. I am overseeing her and her entourage at the request of the Society of Alchemists. We are under a covert operation, so please keep this between us."

Nora's eyes sparkled at the news, and she nodded fervently. Turning to the Queen, Gihon continued.

"Edelein, this is my youngest student, Nora. She is exceptionally talented with volume manipulation alchemy."

"A pleasure, Miss Nora," Edelein dipped her head slightly. "Pardon my attire, and my informality. I must be going now."

"There should be clothes in most of the bedrooms up on the second floor, so please help yourself," Gihon informed her. Edelein waved dismissively as she vanished up the stairs.

"There is a stockpile of necessary travel supplies in a shed I keep at the back of my property," Gihon continued, turning towards the Zengarde. "Nora can show you to it. Help yourselves to any rations or materials you find."

Nora nodded, gesturing for the others to follow as she headed towards the back door.

"I will go with her," Jinn offered.

"Me too, in case you need extra hands to carry anything," Everett added.

"Count me in," chimed Thorne. "I'll be able to sense that weird scentless guy if he shows up again."

Even Thorne couldn't smell Solomon, despite not being a zoa? The Zengarde really do get trained in the ways of their fellow zoa, then. I would love to learn more about their Seventh Senses, Gihon mused.

"Very well. Nora, please retrieve a jar of panax oil for me as well, and a crate labeled 'herbal extracts' located in the back of the shed."

"Yes, sir," Nora bowed her head, opening the back door and leading the three Zengarde outside.

"I plan to send a raven to the Society of Alchemists,

detailing the events and explaining the Queen's predicament. In the meantime, the rest of you are welcome to settle in here. This is my personal home, so please get comfortable and treat it as your own."

As the others began to settle down, Gihon headed up the stairs to check on Edelein, wondering if she was able to find everything she needed. A nagging voice in the back of his mind whispered anxieties about her illness, and Gihon began to overthink as he imagined her alone, victim to another fainting spell.

The first room at the top of the stairs had light spilling from the crack underneath the door, a faint shadow moving around inside to indicate the presence of the Queen.

"Edelein, did you find some fresh clothing? Do you need anything?" Gihon asked, knocking on the door gently.

"Come in," Edelein replied simply.

Gihon stepped inside, closing the door behind him. As he turned to face Edelein, his golden eyes widened slightly as he looked toward her.

Edelein was paying him no mind, looking down as she casually buttoned up a large white dress shirt. The shirt went down to her mid-thigh, and seemed to be the first article of clothing she had found. Her hair was down, hair tie in her mouth.

"Speak, Dirigent," she said, voice muffled around the hair tie as she finished buttoning up the shirt.

"Your Majesty, I…" Gihon trailed off, feeling heat rise to his cheeks, he averted his gaze.

"Is something the matter?" she asked, pulling her hair up and taking the tie out of her mouth.

"N-no, just… perhaps I should look around to find you a pair of trousers. You are a lady, a-and that shirt is a bit masculine, is it not?" Gihon fumbled his words, his mind racing.

"It's alright, Gihon, I appreciate the concern. I looked around a bit, but this one was my favorite. The scent is fresh and calming, with a hint of a pleasant musk to it–"

"It's my shirt," Gihon blurted out, face red.

Edelein's face flushed the same color as his, mouth falling open as realization hit her. A long beat of awkward silence fell between the two as they stared at each other.

"Oh. Would you… like it back?" Edelein asked, trying to compose herself.

"N-no, it's alright," Gihon replied, clearing his throat and turning away politely. "But… you called me inside even though you were not dressed. I am still a man, you know. A gentleman should never see a lady in such a compromising outfit."

Edelein chuckled, the usual chime of her laughter tinted with some lingering embarrassment as she tried to regain her regal aura.

"Gihon, I do believe you understand the responsibility of the Ehret is to *never* leave my side, correct? All of the Zengarde come in and out of my quarters frequently while the Queensmaids are dressing me. No privacy in the castle, I'm afraid. I am used to the… indecency, as you would say. It comes with the territory of having dozens of attendants looking over oneself. I can't remember the last time I got dressed entirely alone, actually."

Zander walks in on her while she is getting dressed? Gihon thought to himself, shocked.

Gihon looked down at the Queen, his ears reddening more as she approached him. Edelein placed one hand on his arm, smiling up at him gently.

"There is nothing to be shy about, Gihon," she reassured him.

Edelein's eyes twinkled with a coy, yet warm, affection as she looked fondly at Gihon. He felt his breath catch in his throat, his heart pounding in his ears as he held her gaze. The moment felt like an eternity before a new voice chimed in.

The Man in Red

"Oh, my. Am I interrupting?" Cari asked as she entered the room, hands on her hips.

Yes, Gihon thought for a brief moment.

"No, not at all," Gihon replied, stepping away.

"I came to fetch Her Majesty's old clothing. I can clean it quickly," Cari chuckled to herself, brushing past Gihon and following Edelein to the bed, where her soiled clothing was laying in a pile.

Leaning into Edelein's ear, Cari whispered, "Ed, does Gihon know that's his shirt yet?"

Edelein flushed red, her ears flattening in embarrassment.

"How did you realize it was his, Cari?" she asked in a hushed voice. "It was an accident. I didn't realize…"

"It smells like him," Cari replied with a simple shrug as she picked up the Queen's garments.

"It… it does carry his scent. I told him it smelled good before I realized it was his. I said that to his face," Edelein sighed, embarrassed. "I told the Dirigent that I enjoy his *musk*. This is humiliating, Cari."

"It's flirting, is what it is," Cari replied. "Something I have *never* seen you do, and I've been your best friend for a decade. You are more charming than you realize, Ed, but I think I need to give you some lessons."

"I'm not…! That's not…" Edelein stammered, her eyes darting towards Gihon as he awkwardly studied a map mounted on the wall and ignored the girls' hushed conversation. "This is a professional environment, and some lunatic just tried to kill me earlier. It's not the time for that. Not to mention that I'm not even permitted to, I would never…"

"Arguably, I would counter that a lunatic trying to kill you is the perfect time to start looking for a man. The Kingdom needs an heir, you know?" Cari ribbed.

Crown of the Alchemist

Edelein's face lost all expression. She may not know how to flirt, but she knew how the conversation was going to end. Grabbing Cari gently by the shoulders, Edelein turned her around.

"Make sure you get these things cleaned quickly," the Queen ordered, shooing her longtime friend out the bedroom door.

"The Zengarde really do walk in on you while you are dressing," Gihon commented, turning from the old map to face Edelein as Cari's footsteps receded.

"Cari is special to me. She was transmuted and gifted to me on my fourteenth birthday, by my father. She was a nine-year-old, a bit younger than they planned for, but I didn't mind. She's been my best friend ever since," Edelein explained. "She has walked in on me long before she ever became a Zengarde."

"Your father gave you... a friend?" Gihon asked.

"I was a bit lonesome as a kid. No siblings, and the only child my age was Jinn; you have seen how socializing with him goes. Joining the Zengarde has opened him up more than you realize. Father wished for me to have a female companion to help explore... femininity, since my mother passed away shortly after my birth, and my father only knew how to show me the outdoors. Grand General Varden, the head of the Zenluvian military, trained me in weapons handling while my father taught me outdoorsmanship. I had no female influence other than the maids, so... he asked the Court Alchemist to transmute my favorite animal into a companion that I could talk to and learn from. She's almost like a little sister to me."

That sounds a bit sad, yet thoughtful. The late King must have been a good man, Gihon commented silently.

"Eddie!" Alett's voice rang out as he hurried up the stairs.

I see that they really do barge in while she is dressing.

"Speak," Edelein affirmed, Alett running in with a panicked look.

190

The Man in Red

"I've been trying to say this but the timing was kind of weird and then you were gone and then it was eating at me and now I think I'm going to explode," Alett rambled in a single panicked breath. "I don't have your stamina potions. I don't have anything. My bag is gone. It wasn't where I left it after the fight, or anywhere nearby."

"What?!" Edelein gasped. "What do you mean it's gone?!"

"I think Solomon and his cult took it. This is awful. A huge problem, really. My satchel isn't big enough to hold everyone's large weapons, and now Solomon has one of our crystals."

"You had the leyline crystals in your bag?!"

"One of them! I'm not stupid enough to carry both crystals in one place, because of things like this! The second one has been in my satchel—"

"You're keeping the second leyline crystal in a bag full of *bombs*?!" Edelein exclaimed in disbelief.

"In my defense, I seem to be everyone's pack-mule, so I didn't have much choice!" Alett retorted.

Edelein sighed in concern, pressing a hand to her furrowed eyebrows.

"Allow me a moment to finish dressing, and I will meet you all downstairs. Gihon, you as well. I need a moment to think about this."

"Yes, Your Majesty," Gihon bowed politely, following Alett downstairs.

"Do you think Solomon took it on purpose?" Alett asked Gihon as they both entered the open common area.

Zander was pacing anxiously around the room, lost in thought. Lylia leaned against a wall, staff in hand as her eyes followed Zander's movement.

"I do, yes," Gihon continued. "I have a more plausible theory, and a second theory that I would quite hope to be untrue, given my previous experiences with the man."

"Your insight is invaluable, Gihon," Alett smiled, looking a bit fatigued. "It seems like that guy is a pain in the rear, and the rest of us are in unfamiliar territory. Thank you for helping us."

Gihon nodded, sitting down in a large armchair with his elbows on his knees, hands folded under his chin in deep thought. Alett sat on a sofa next to him, Zander continuing to pace as rain started to pour outside.

"You let it go unprotected, Alett," Zander scolded.

"We were being ambushed and Eddie was in danger! I know you'd do the same!" Alett argued, Zander huffing and turning away.

Cari entered the room from where she had been washing laundry, wiping damp hands on her skirt as she sat on a loveseat. As Zander paced, Lylia groaned in irritation.

"Zander, will you stop pacing for a moment?" Lylia asked, frustrated. "Why hasn't Nephvir come back yet?"

"You know that Neph doesn't like being involved in high-stress scenarios. He's still outside moping," Alett replied.

"In the rain?" Lylia sighed. The Fiertet thumped her staff on the ground, and a moment later a soaking-wet Nephvir tumbled in from the open back door, dragged in by vines that dropped him off and retreated back outside. At the same moment, Edelein returned from upstairs, the white button-down shirt tucked now into a pair of tight black leather pants.

Gihon looked up at her as she sat down on the couch next to Alett, crossing one leg over the other.

At least the trousers aren't mine. It... looks good on her, Gihon noted, before shaking his head slightly to avoid the distraction.

"Edelein, I have a theory regarding the situation—"

"Solomon took the satchel intentionally, didn't he?"

The Man in Red

Edelein interrupted. "He wasn't after me, he used his threats to me as a distraction for his true intentions. He knew how the Zengarde would react if they thought my life was in danger, and used their emotions as a diversion."

Stunned, Gihon nodded in agreement. "Yes… it was certainly him, and I do believe his threats to you were meant to distract the Zengarde. Now, there's two reasons why he could want the crystal, but one of them is so unbelievably stupid that not even Solomon would attempt it. So I will choose to focus on the plausible answer, which is that he wishes to study it. In Caandemium, we have leylines, but we have not discovered any tangible crystallized leyline energy here. As far as Caandemite researchers are aware, the Deepwood is the only place where that phenomenon occurs. Any alchemist would do just about anything to even see one, much less own one."

"He means to weaponize it?" Edelein asked, a look of offense crossing her face.

"Likely, yes. If not weaponry, he could be looking to utilize its healing properties to convert more cultists and grow his army. Either way, it will be used for evil and not for good, and people will die as a result."

"We need it back, then. Nalo does not allow the crystals to be weaponized."

"What's the less plausible option?" Alett asked.

Gihon hesitated, his face twisting briefly before letting out a soft sigh.

"The Gates of Heaven. Solomon has a history with trying to open a rift between Tevus and the divine plane Ethereus, but it has only ever ended extremely poorly for him. I hate every fiber of that man, but he is astute. Far intelligent enough to know better than to attempt something as dangerous and foolish as that again."

"Do you think he plans to return for the second crystal?"

Crown of the Alchemist

Alett asked.

"Why not just take both while we were distracted? Did he not realize we had a second one?" Nephvir added, wringing water out of his long black hair.

"It is possible he did not know about the second box. Other possibilities would include that he only needed one, or that our forces kept his at bay long enough to only allow him to slip in and take the first one and not both. Alett also had the second crystal on his person during the fight, making it a harder prize to gain without giving away his intentions. If we saw him take it, we would have pursued him."

"You're telling me that either our competence caught him off guard, or that we fell entirely into his trap exactly as he planned it?" Edelein huffed in frustration.

"Unfortunately, that is often how it goes with Solomon," Gihon confirmed.

"There's a chance he will return for the second one, then," Alett pondered, to which Gihon nodded in agreement.

"How did he know about the crystals in the first place?" Edelein asked, uneasy.

"Someone told him," Zander replied curtly, arms crossed.

"I agree," Edelein nodded. "Someone told him about us. It must have been one of the alchemists, since you are the only people who would know."

"What? It wouldn't be an alchemist," Gihon denied, eyebrows furrowed in confusion.

"That is the only possibility, Gihon. There's a rat in the Society."

"The Society of Alchemists is Solomon's biggest enemy. No one in their right mind would help him there. That is a senseless accusation."

"You are too trusting of others, Dirigent Gihon."

The Man in Red

"Perhaps you are not trusting enough," Gihon retorted with a sharp look.

Edelein glared back, the fur on her tail bristling slightly. "Live a day as royalty and you will quickly learn how many of your friends you cannot trust."

"By this logic then, it could have been one of the Zengarde who sold intel," Gihon countered, annoyed.

Zander approached Gihon at this claim, seething as Gihon rose to meet him. They stared coldly at each other as the sphynx spoke with a low and icy tone.

"We have been here for *one* day. We do not even know who that man is. You, on the other hand, seem to know *everything* about him. There is something you are hiding from us, I can sense it on you. You are closer to Solomon than you are telling us. Perhaps it was you that betrayed us, since you're the one bent on destroying our people." Zander growled.

Gihon looked like he wanted to give a cutting response, but Edelein stood up and stepped between them. Placing one hand on each chest, the Queen spoke with an authoritative tone.

"Zander, back off. That is an order. Gihon, do not make the foolish mistake of accusing my men of breaking their oaths to me ever again. The Zengarde would never cross me."

"Do you really not see your own hypocrisy right now?" Gihon snapped, losing his temper.

"It is not hypocrisy if I am correct, which I am. You wish to trust your alchemists, and yet you hold no respect towards your fellow zoakind."

"You have no evidence to prove that you are correct."

"I can sense it. I don't need evidence. I know it was not my men, but yours."

"Sense means nothing here!" Gihon pressed a hand to this temple. "You cannot sense the origin of a betrayal. This is something that is solved with logic, not by simply *sensing* it. Please, I urge you to use your brains for this one."

Offended, Edelein scoffed. "Maybe you cannot perceive what we can, but do not put your shortcomings on us."

"There is no logical reason for an alchemist to work with Solomon," Gihon urged. "Anyone in the Society of Alchemists is smart enough to know that Solomon is a lying snake. We all know about him. We all know that attempting to aid him would only end in one's own demise, in one way or another. No one is foolish enough to do that."

"Perhaps someone was desperate enough to believe in him the way his cultists do," Edelein suggested, eyes narrow.

"Desperate people turn to him, yes. I agree with that. However, no one that high up in the Society would be desperate like that. It's incredibly difficult getting into a high enough position of power through the meritocracy, not to mention how much of an honor it is. Anyone with a high enough rank to meet you would know to not trust Solomon, or be so desperate as to believe his lies. This is not something that instinct can tell you. You are too firmly set on that, and it interferes with your problem-solving."

Edelein approached Gihon, eyes ablaze as she looked up at him. "Perhaps you should learn to trust your instincts, Dirigent. You're a zoa, so act like it. Otherwise, you are no different than a human, though something tells me you don't find that so bad. Why would my people trust yours if this is the best zoa they can offer us? Caandemite zoa are just weak, watered-down versions of their past. You're no zoa, *Dirigent*."

Gihon glared back at her as she spat the last word, frustrated by her stubbornness. After a beat of uncomfortable silence, one of Edelein's ears turned backwards and she cast a sharp glance over her shoulder.

"I can hear you outside. Stop hiding."

The Man in Red

The back door creaked open slowly, all eyes turning towards the sound as Thorne, Everett, and Jinn sheepishly entered the room. Nora entered last, the teenage feline zoa grimacing at the heavy air around the others. The four were all soaked from the rain, arms full of wooden crates.

"Sorry. We didn't want to… interrupt," Everett admitted with a sigh as he set down a few crates. "We… picked up some supplies, Your Majesty."

"So, uh… what's going on?" Thorne asked, his face looking sour. "Actually, no, I don't think I want to know. The air here feels like my childhood. If you're divorcing Gihon, I don't want to know about it. I'm going upstairs."

"Save it, Thorne. Now isn't the time for jokes," Edelein hissed, but Thorne was already ignoring her as he headed up the stairs.

"Your Majesty, I will prepare some of the travel supplies," Everett offered politely. Clearly eager to avoid the situation as well, he picked up the crates and hurried away to the kitchen.

"I'm going to check on Thorne, if that's alright," Lylia spoke quietly to Edelein, who nodded in approval.

"Nora, please accompany Lylia," Gihon requested. "This conversation is a between the Zenluvians and myself."

Nora and Lylia exited the room to find Thorne, leaving only Jinn from the returning group.

"What's going on right now, Queen Edelein?" Jinn asked, a look of concern crossing his normally inexpressive face.

"It seems that our escort does not trust us. Gihon thinks rather lowly of the Zengarde," Edelein crossed her arms, glaring at the Dirigent.

"I do not think lowly of you or your people. I simply disagree with treating your feelings as fact, when all logic dictates otherwise. The facts are right in front of you, and yet you reject them for no reason other than your feelings. Emotions have no place in a discussion such as this."

"Your so-called logic is the one with no ground here. I am certain that my men are innocent. I *know* it was an alchemist that sold us out to Solomon!"

"You know nothing!" Gihon yelled in frustration, clenching his fists as a loud clap of thunder shook the house.

A beat of uncomfortable silence followed as Edelein's eyes widened, flinching. Gihon stopped, taking a pained breath at his uncharacteristic outburst as his chest began to ache.

"I'm sorry, Edelein. Please forgive me. I simply struggle to support using nothing but blind instinct in a situation where logic is so crucial. I should not have raised my voice at you, that was disrespectful of me and in poor taste as the representative of my people. The 'Seventh Sense' your men have has its uses and is quite fascinating to me… though it is rendered useless if allies lack access to the same information," Gihon apologized with a deep and formal bow, bangs falling in front of his eyes.

Jinn took in the situation as it unfolded in front of him, the wolf zoa connecting dots as he caught up. "Gihon, this situation is my fault. I had assumed that you were able to read me the way the Zengarde do, as a zoa. Had I known, I would have explained the situation more clearly to you, and we could have avoided this fate. Allow me."

Taking a deep breath, Jinn continued.

"That man intercepted my spar with the flame alchemist, Bex. They appeared to know each other, but the man toyed with us both. I… failed in my duties. I was unable to protect Bex."

Concerned, Gihon asked, "What happened to Bex?"

"The white-haired one took his life. I was powerless against him… I could only stand by and watch. It all happened so fast."

"Bex is dead?" Gihon pressed, alarmed.

The Man in Red

"He summoned a sword from nothing… a powerful, glowing sword that dissolved everything it touched, including Bex's body. There was nothing left as his body dissipated into light. It was the same weapon he wielded against you earlier before the fight, the one he pointed at you."

"The Divine Sword, Kether."

"Divine?" Edelein scoffed. "That's what Solomon called it earlier. Is he some sort of god? Why does he have a weapon called the Divine Sword?"

"He stole it from the Church of Prima Luma back when he first started his cult. He believed that if he had a divine weapon, he would be equated to a god, and thus worshipped as one. Which unfortunately for us, worked more in his favor than I would have hoped."

"You haven't been able to take it back?"

"Solomon is slippery. He's been hiding from us for years, which is why it was so surprising that he had openly attacked an alchemist in broad daylight in the middle of Velkhamore. He's been exiled from the city, and no one has seen him until now."

"Bex had some sort of deal with Solomon," Jinn continued. "He had been promised a new life, free from the Society of Alchemists, in exchange for isolating one of the Zengarde."

Bex was selling intel to Solomon, then. Gihon thought. *Why?*

"Your Majesty, I was quick to judge, and I was incorrect. I apologize," Gihon admitted. "Bex was in the running for a major promotion, being considered for the new Dirigent of Velkhamore. That is the highest honor a man could receive. Someone of his caliber should have known better."

"Gihon, I feel that we have skipped over something important. Why would Bex have to turn to Solomon just to escape a promotion?" Edelein wondered aloud. "Couldn't he just quit rather than asking a cult leader to fix his problems?"

Gihon hesitated. "It is… not that simple, admittedly. Caandemium is almost exclusively a meritocracy, where competence and intellect can get you anywhere. The consequence of such a society is that if you are naturally gifted in those areas, it can be very hard to live a life where you do not utilize said skills. We do not dwell often on it, because it is rare for an alchemist to want anything other than to be an alchemist. To put it in more familiar terms, Edelein, you have mentioned to me briefly that the Zengarde is Zenluve's highest honor, and very difficult to obtain the status. Imagine someone joining the Zengarde and becoming one of your top elite, only to turn around and leave because they would rather do something else."

"I understand. The Zengarde are paid incredibly well for their service, have the honor of serving the Throne, and are given status as official members of the Royal Court. It is something anyone would yearn for. To work so hard to achieve it, and then to suddenly leave it… there would have to be a deeper corruption within the Throne to push them away."

Surprised at her fast comprehension, Gihon nodded in agreement. "A high-caliber alchemist has only abandoned their post one time in our history. A friend of my mother's, Alina, fled to Avalstice after the Society of Alchemists tried to weaponize her failed research on animal population control. An unforeseen circumstance with her work caused her to accidentally sterilize the village she was working with… her hometown, actually. Disgraced and ashamed, she had no choice but to burn the evidence of her research and flee westward. No one knows where she ended up, and that is probably for the best. I do agree that the Society should not be weaponizing sterilization tactics against our enemies. That whole situation was quite a tragedy, and I believe it to be a smear on the Society's name."

The Man in Red

Alett had a forlorn look on his face, seeming to want to talk, but Edelein shook her head at him with a knowing glance.

"So you have had alchemists flee before, but this does not explain why it must be so drastic. In the example you provided, a Zengarde would be able to leave their post without an issue. Society would perhaps look at them differently, but there would be no harm done. Why does it take burning a lab or turning to a cult in order to leave?"

"In Alina's case, I have heard from others that she was strongarmed by the previous Dirigent into handing over her research. We govern our city-states much like you govern your kingdom, and power corrupts those with impure hearts. Disobeying a power-hungry dirigent could lead to arrest, exile, or silent execution. It is rare, but not impossible that a dirigent could use his power to control alchemists rather than lead them."

"There is no Dirigent of Velkhamore, though. The alchemists we met with, they were being considered for promotion into one, yes? Therefore, who would be forcing Bex's hand like this?"

"That, we may never know. To be recommended for the role, an alchemist must complete three trials from three dirigents; so it was likely one of the three he had spoken to. Once we have dealt with Solomon, I will speak with Rahzopa and the others to find out who had recommended him. I fear a cohort of mine may be out of line."

"Solomon is incredibly cruel, promising him a new life in exchange for intel… only to kill him so mercilessly," Edelein sighed, brows furrowed. "Now that we have a full understanding of the situation, we can move on."

"I was quick to judge you, and I apologize." Gihon admitted.

Alett, who had been listening to the explanation and

observing all the parties involved, rejoined the conversation.

"He used the Queen as a diversion," Alett started, "manipulated and killed an alchemist from the Society, and entered Velkhamore in broad daylight… just to get his hands on a leyline crystal. Solomon is either incredibly intelligent, or incredibly insane."

"He is both, without a doubt," Gihon quickly agreed with a curt nod. "For a man so frivolous, he is more intelligent than he lets on. The insanity, though, is much less subtle."

The Dirigent turned, peering through the window cautiously as he continued. "I will have to explain all of this to the others in Velkhamore. Given the way Jinn alerted Alett and the other Zengarde as well as how quickly we left, the other alchemists are likely confused and concerned. They need to be informed of Bex's death."

"Are you leaving, then?" Edelein asked.

"No, it would be unwise to leave you alone here if Solomon plans to return. You will need me here to guard you, so I will write to them and remain by your side."

Zander growled, displeased as he approached Gihon. "A few minutes ago, you accused us of being on Solomon's side. Now you think you're eligible to guard the Queen? We have no reason to trust you, corvid."

Exasperated, Gihon stepped back to put distance between himself and the enraged sphynx zoa.

"Does your Seventh Sense refuse to tell you that I am not the enemy?" Gihon pleaded, exhausted.

"You said we should use logic," Zander retorted. "You don't trust us, so we don't trust you. Pretty sound logic, if you ask me. Wouldn't you agree, Dirigent?"

"Enough, Ehret!" Edelein snapped, grabbing the leather straps of Zander's sword holsters that crossed his torso and pulling him backwards. "This bickering is getting us nowhere. We have no choice but to trust the Dirigent if we wish to retrieve our leyline crystal."

A soft voice piped up from the couches, everyone turning to look at Nephvir as he spoke. He had his small notebook out, not looking up as he addressed the room.

"Why do we need to fetch the crystal from that psychopath, anyway? We have an endless supply of them at home. Losing one is no big deal."

"I agree," Zander nodded. "Let us just learn what we need to banish the shadow beasts from our land, and return home quickly. Let him keep the crystal."

"We promised two crystals to the Society in exchange for their aid. It would be in poor taste for us to not uphold our end of the deal," Alett offered, to which Edelein nodded.

"Nalo's blessing is not to be misused. More than anything, it is about the principle of our honor and the wellbeing of our people. If Nalo were to find out that a crystal has been used maliciously, Zenluve as a whole could be punished for our negligence," the Queen noted.

"Additionally, when Solomon obtains power, people die. It's quite simple," Gihon adjusted one of his sleeves idly. "I do not know his intentions with the crystal yet, but a very likely outcome of it is that people will get hurt. I will have to pursue him regardless, and although it is a terrible idea diplomatically to bring you along, I will admit that I could use the help."

Jinn folded his arms across his chest with a huff. "Personally, I would like to see Solomon dead. I'd like some revenge."

"Alright, sorry I asked," Nephvir laughed dryly. "We can go get the crystal. I'm always up for a fight."

"Does anyone that isn't named Zander Khepri object to

this?" Edelein asked.

"I do not object, Your Majesty," Zander denied. "I would also like to kill that man."

"Excellent. Well, Everett will do what I command without a second thought, or frankly even a first thought. Lylia will follow orders and she will convince Thorne to as well. That just leaves our young and beautiful darling rosufex. Cari, what do you think?" Edelein asked, turning to her pink-haired friend.

Cari grinned, sitting up straighter. "Your word is my command, Queen. Let's go get that bastard."

Addressing the room, Gihon projected his voice and commanded the attention of the Zengarde.

"Right, thank you for your cooperation. This situation will need to be handled swiftly and discreetly. The Church of Prima Luma tends to run most civil duties; and if they end up getting involved, there would be too much red tape interfering and wasting our precious time. I will inform the Society and request for them to keep everything quiet until we can retrieve the crystal."

The Zengarde remained silent, allowing Gihon to continue his instruction.

"Regarding your original intention for traveling here, I will call upon a few alchemists to join us, if that is alright. They will be able to showcase more alchemy aside from my own and aid you with learning banishment so that I may focus on hunting Solomon. I will send word and have the alchemists join us tomorrow morning. From there, we can meet and discuss a plan. Let us rest now, and reconvene upon their arrival. Any concerns?"

"I have a concern, yes," Zander complained. "I'm tired of alchemists. Let's handle this on our own."

"I think I have had enough with the Society's alchemists, as well," Edelein admitted. "Those two, Torphus and Clotho, were a bit too much for me to handle."

The Man in Red

Gihon nodded, understanding the concern.

"Torphus is not who I would have preferred to oversee your arrival. There has been a bit of a misunderstanding between some of the other dirigents that is not a reflection of the Society of Alchemists. If you will grant us another chance, I have contacts that I can assure will be more to your liking. A zoa, and a few who are much more familiar with our kind."

Edelein remained silent, considering her options.

"We do need to learn. I will allow you to summon a few more allies," Edelein decided.

Alett looked up at Edelein, the Queen looking slightly gaunt as she trembled slightly.

"Are you okay, Eddie?" the owl-boy whispered to her.

Without looking at him, Edelein fixed her eyes forward and ignored the stress that weighed down on her body.

"I am fine. I... just need to rest, I think," The Queen murmured quietly.

Following Alett's gaze, Gihon noticed the unsteadiness in Edelein's posture.

Her face looks a bit paler than usual, Gihon thought. *She needs this conversation to end.*

"Excellent," Gihon agreed. "I can have them here as early as tomorrow morning, as I mentioned. Please, go rest, all of you."

CHAPTER 9

A GAME OF CHESS

Solomon sat with crossed legs, leaning slightly, as he passed a black pawn between his fingers. In the large, empty room, a cold-looking man sat across from him leaning forward to eye the chessboard between them. He had black hair, expertly styled into tousled spikes, dark bangs falling in front of piercing golden eyes. Teal highlights accented his hairstyle, with dark feathers sticking out from behind his ears. He wore an elegant, deep violet suit with a loose red tie, the top buttons of his white shirt open to reveal his firm chest. Picking up the black rook piece, the man spoke with a deep and smooth tenor.

"Rook to D8."

"You know, Naberius, I wasn't expecting you to return from Avalstice so soon," Solomon commented as the man moved the black rook forward. "Bishop to E4."

"What, you really thought I'd sit by and let you have all the fun? I want to watch your plan unfold. It's so deliciously foolish, and Avalstice is devastatingly boring now that little Eddie has left," Naberius mused, picking up the black queen piece.

"Don't you have your own projects to worry about?"

"Queen to C8," Naberius said, ignoring Solomon's question as he set down his queen.

"The Queen is a powerful asset, you know," Solomon chuckled, moving his own white queen piece in response. "E8. Check."

"That is precisely why I want it," Naberius countered, picking up his black rook again to knock over the white queen, freeing himself from the check. "Precisely why I will take it."

Solomon groaned as Naberius seized his queen piece, the black-haired man holding it up to the light in amusement. Meeting Solomon's gaze after a long pause, Naberius smirked.

"I want the Beast, Solomon."

"Not now," Solomon commanded. "That Beast is invaluable to me right now. You'll have to wait. You'll have your turn soon enough."

"I've been waiting for nearly a decade for you to finish your plans so that I can finally have my way. I'm afraid I simply do not see how I cannot act on my own plans without you believing it to be an interference."

"Bishop to D5," Solomon returned his focus to the game, changing the subject. "Check."

"Are you familiar with a creature called the Velstrix? It's a bird of prey, native to the Deepwood," Naberius asked, leaning back in his chair.

Solomon rolled his eyes. "No, Naberius. No one in Caandemium knows anything about the Deepwood. You take one foreign exchange trip there and suddenly you're just the smartest guy in the room, huh?"

Ignoring Solomon's barb, Naberius continued, "The

Crown of the Alchemist

Velstrix is a master hunter. A fascinating and deadly creature that feeds off of anything it can sink its talons into. Rather greedy, those little birds. They'll overhunt their territories, making them a prime target for Zenluvian patrols trying to maintain the forest's balance."

What is he getting at? Solomon wondered silently.

"See, the fascinating part is the extraordinary ability this creature possesses, something that makes it such a powerful foe. The Velstrix gains the intelligence of any creature it consumes. The more powerful prey it hunts, the stronger it gets. If it kills a patrolman, it gains the intelligence of a Zenluvian, causing it to develop strategies that mirror those of the patrols."

"Get to the point, Naberius. You have a habit of talking out of your ass all the time, and I'm really not interested in listening."

"When a Velstrix is cornered, it becomes even more fascinating," Naberius continued, unbothered by Solomon's interjection. "If it feels threatened, it will turn on its own flock. They will eat each other, gaining the intelligence of all of their previously consumed prey. In a way, nothing is more valuable to a Velstrix than killing another Velstrix, even if it's one of its own."

"I see where you're trying to go with this. So, who is the Velstrix? You, or me?" Solomon asked impatiently as he tapped his foot, and Naberius shrugged in reply.

"I believe we both are. Though, which of us would eat the other for power? Whose determination and will to live reigns over the other?"

"Which one of us wants to live at any cost, you mean?"

Naberius smirked, leaning forward as he picked up his rook.

"Rook to E6, blocking your check. Do not underestimate the strength of a fortress. Speaking of… I've caught wind from Kimaris that a certain *rook* is trying to interfere with your plans, like the old days."

208

The Man in Red

"Kimaris, not unlike you, talks too much. Yes, Gihon has been trying to get in my way again. He's getting dangerously close to that Lion Queen, so much so that I theorize his contract with Limbo may be in jeopardy. I'm still several steps ahead of him, though, and I plan to keep it that way. In fact, I've already been working on the perfect foil to slow him down."

"Allocer?"

"Did Kimaris tell you that too, or did you go around reintroducing yourself to everyone in the building before you came up here to play with me?" Solomon pouted and slumped in his chair, his surprise ruined.

"I had the delight of meeting Allocer, yes. I think I'd like to take her with me back to Avalstice, if you don't mind," Naberius chuckled coldly. "I could have fun with a girl like that."

"Slow down, punk. I need her for now. I plan to expedite Gihon's unraveling vulnerability with some delicious mind games first. Also, I made both of you, so you're almost like siblings. Don't be weird."

"You and I both know that homunculi don't work like that. Anyways, I just think you did an excellent job with her creation. Your finest work yet, *Father*."

Solomon paused, considering his words. "You're right, I take back the sibling comment. I don't like you referring to me as your father. You know I'm closer to your god."

"Don't get cocky now, Solomon. Play your turn."

"Fine! Bishop to E6, taking your rook. For such a big game that you spouted, you were willing to lose that precious rook quite unceremoniously."

"Quite frankly, I didn't think you had the nerve to take it."

"You don't think I have the nerve?" Solomon laughed, clenching his fist around the black rook.

"I know how much he means to you, that's all. Without

209

him, what are you?"

"Free."

"Alone."

"Alone!" Solomon scoffed, tightening his grip on the black rook.

"There's a rumor spreading around that you're going soft. Doubts are settling in, from the people that you think trust you."

Solomon gritted his teeth, an orange glow radiating from his palm as the rook in his hand caught fire. Opening his fist, the cinders fluttered to the floor, the rook merely a blazing memory. "I am stronger than ever. I possess the power to finally open the Gates of Heaven and become a true human. I am unstoppable. I am *Solomon*."

"And yet, once more, you have forgotten the significance of a queen in play," Naberius chuckled, moving his queen piece to Solomon's bishop. "Perhaps she is the true foil you overlooked, enthralled by the allure of the rook."

"You know nothing."

"You haven't seen what I've seen. That Queen, she's everything to them. Powerful, magnificent, captivating. Yet, they've been pressuring her into marriage for years now, pathetically desperate for their Queen to produce an heir before she meets the inevitable and untimely end that they all know they cannot stop. My sources informed me that she actually has a nasty little surprise waiting for her at the castle right now, a consequence to her own folly."

Solomon raised his eyebrows, a bored look conveying a silent message.

"I know, you want me to get to the point. You're so focused on Gihon, I fear that the real threat to your plan may be right in front of you without you even realizing it. Don't underestimate Edelein's power and influence. The Zenluvians are so scared of

210

losing their Queen's lineage that they even wrote a cute prophecy about my plan to seize her. They know that I am unstoppable, inevitable. They call me the *destruction on black wings*."

Solomon laughed, the pieces in his mind connecting. "Oh, you're right about that. I've been keeping tabs on the Zenluvians myself. The big scary cat-boy, Zander, thinks the prophecy is about Gihon. It makes *way* more sense that their prophecy is about you."

"You did create me in foul mimicry, so I cannot say that I fault the Ehret for the misunderstanding. I cannot wait to see the look on the cat's face when he meets the real villain to his story," Naberius laughed, familiar golden eyes twinkling in amusement. "The Zenluvians don't know about my… passion project. I've been building it up for years right under their sensitive little zoa noses, and I'm still nothing more than a rumor and a prophecy from some decrepit raisin of a wizard who died to lead King Alderis right into my trap."

"How is that going, anyway? The chimeras?"

"Excellent. I have an army at my command, ready to strike. Ready to conquer the Beast and finally achieve true perfection," Naberius raised his eyebrow expectantly.

"I told you before and I'll tell you again, the Beast is not ready to be conquered. I need to stop Gihon first. You can take my sloppy seconds."

"Are you *that* afraid of Gihon?"

"There is only one way to kill Gihon, and it requires the Beast. He has to be destroyed from within before you can end his life. The Beast is the only way to weaken his contract."

"Limbo's a bitch, huh?" Naberius laughed. "Just don't underestimate her, alright? The Queen, that is."

Looking back down at the board, Solomon picked up a pawn with a coy glance at Naberius. "If you're going for some cryptic symbolism right now, it won't work. Pawn to E6, taking your queen for myself. Now my mere pawn is able to move across the board, becoming a queen, and checkmating your king. My little pawn defeats your queen, and it's game over."

"So the Queen defeats the King. How fitting."

"You lost, Naberius."

"That, I did. It's always a pleasure to challenge you, Solomon. I am glad to see that your skills have not rusted since I left for Avalstice."

"Will you be staying here, then? I wouldn't be opposed to some extra hands in the upcoming battles."

"You have already created the extra hands that you needed." Naberius replied, gesturing towards the door as a pair of icy blue eyes met his gaze from the shadows. "Did you think I wouldn't notice you there, darling?"

"Did I captivate you that much?" Allocer chuckled, her eerily familiar face stepping into the light as she walked towards Naberius' chair.

Allocer was a beautiful blonde, well-endowed in a tight black leather bodysuit. Fishnet leggings met tall black stiletto boots, a token fashion choice for a female homunculus.

"Oh, yes, Solomon's ugly mug is not quite as fun to look at. I'd much prefer the sweet company of a fierce lioness such as yourself."

"You'd better not be thinking anything naughty, little bird."

"You're one to talk, aren't you?"

"Allocer, why are you up here?" Solomon sighed, annoyed at the unfolding interaction. "I'm regretting you already, and you haven't even existed for a full day yet."

"I'm nosy. Is that a crime?"

"Yes, it is. I'm trying to work out some plans, here. Go."

"No," Allocer retorted, sitting down on the arm of Naberius' chair.

212

The Man in Red

Naberius smirked, leaning back and putting his feet on the table, knocking the remaining chess pieces aside.

"Solomon, I do not plan to interfere. I am merely here as a spectator, waiting in the shadows to watch you fail spectacularly, and swoop in to have my way with what remains."

"'Swoop' in? Since when did you develop a sense of humor? Gihon would never make a pun on his avian heritage."

Naberius chuckled as he put one arm around Allocer's waist. "Look, we're on your side. I released the phantasms into Zenluve for you to draw out the Queen and her dogs, and the rest is on you. I gladly offered to help you, and I did my part. Now I intend to watch the rest over a nice drink and another game of chess. How about a rematch?"

Solomon sighed and nodded. "I suppose that I could enjoy defeating you again, Naberius. You need to remember who your master is, you pathetic raven."

Cold light poked through heavy cloud-cover as Gihon and Solomon exchanged blows, the Dirigent's eyes glowing with rage. Solomon dipped and dodged around his fists, laughing as Gihon growled in frustration.

"Too slow!" Solomon yelled out in delight, grabbing Gihon's fist before it could connect with his face.

Gihon froze for a moment, caught off guard by the catch. He tried to pull away with a swift tug, but Solomon held tightly onto his fist.

"Gihon!" Edelein cried out in alarm, running towards the men with fangs bared.

Crown of the Alchemist

The sound of her cry drew the Dirigent's attention, his golden eyes meeting hers for a brief moment.

"Stay back, Edelein!" Gihon warned.

The brief distraction was all Solomon needed to gain the upper hand, striking hard into Gihon's stomach. He stumbled backwards, coughing and winded as his body doubled over in pain. Edelein gasped in fear, running towards Gihon as she called out his name again.

Why is Gihon losing the fight? Edelein wondered as her body carried her over to her ally. *I've seen how capable he is.*

"Ah-ah," Solomon tutted, grabbing Edelein's ponytail and yanking her backwards. "He's mine. I have a better plan for you, little cub."

Edelein yelped in pain as her head was pulled back, Solomon turning her head to stare directly into her eyes.

"Solomon, don't touch her!" Gihon warned, breathing hard as he stood hunched, one hand clutching his midsection.

Solomon glanced over his shoulder at Gihon briefly, before looking back at Edelein.

"You two are gross. I see what's going on between you, and I don't care for it. What I do like, though, is the fear in your eyes. Like a little princess whose valiant knight has been humiliatingly defeated by the big bad dragon. You're cute when you're scared... I can almost see what Gihon likes in you."

Edelein hissed as Solomon placed a gentle finger under her chin, leaning in close.

"Do you want to see a magic trick, kitten?" Solomon asked in a bemused whisper, raising one hand as Gihon ran towards them.

Solomon laughed and snapped his fingers, the world around them burning with a sudden bright white flash. Edelein flinched, shutting her eyes tight to block out the sudden light.

Through her eyelids, Edelein sensed the light fading and

214

cracked open her eyes slightly, confused. The sky around her was dark, heavy rain pouring down and soaking her clothes. The trees were black and dead, a garish purple-and-grey hue consuming the surroundings. Solomon was nowhere to be found, the Queen left standing alone in the muddy road.

"Zander? Alett?" Edelein called out, turning around in concern. "Is anyone here? Gihon?"

"I am here," Gihon's voice drew her attention as she whipped around, the rain-soaked Dirigent's shoulders slumped in defeat as his matted hair covered his face.

"Gihon! Oh, thank goodness…" Edelein ran towards him, painfully slow as her feet dragged through the mud. "The area looks blighted, I was afraid I'd lost you–"

"Blighted," Gihon repeated emptily with a dry laugh, still looking down. "Of course it's blighted. You're here, after all. Infecting the world around you with death."

"W-what?" Edelein stuttered, stopping. "I… I didn't do this! It was Solomon, he was here, don't you remember?"

"You are a curse," Gihon growled.

"I'm not!" Edelein yelled, bolting upright in her bed.

Looking around at the calm and quiet bedroom, Edelein let out a soft sigh.

"Another nightmare. When does it end?" she murmured quietly to herself, wiping cold sweat from her brow.

Standing up shakily, Edelein shifted her weight to support herself along the wall, her legs burning like ice as she forced herself upright. Grunting softly, she hobbled towards the balcony, opening its doors to bring fresh air into her body.

The breeze was cool and welcome as Edelein leaned heavily on the railing, relishing the fresh winds as she took deep breaths and gathered her thoughts.

A cold and hard object pressed suddenly against her arm, startling the lioness. She jumped and looked down, her eyes meeting the curious stare of a raven as it nudged her with its beak. It blinked up at her, letting out a confused *gwah*.

"Oh, um… hello, there," Edelein said. "You seem… as confused as I am. Can I help you, little bird?"

The raven clacked its beak, fluttering its wings and extending one leg towards her. Looking down, Edelein noticed a small scroll on its leg, suddenly understanding the bird's presence.

"Oh! You're one of Gihon's messenger ravens, aren't you? Why are you on my balcony, though?"

The bird looked at her, seeming to understand her question. It peered expectantly into the room, and then back at her.

Edelein paused for a moment, realizing the situation.

I took the master suite out of habit, but Gihon mentioned that this is his personal home. Does that mean… I've been sleeping in Gihon's room? Why wouldn't he tell me?! And the shirt incident earlier… I should have realized this by now when I went through the closet. I'm such a fool. This bird is waiting for Gihon, and has no idea why a woman has walked out onto the balcony. Dammit, why didn't Gihon tell me?! This is so humiliating!

Blush tinted Edelein's cheeks, her embarrassment distracting her from her pain for a moment as she looked down at the raven.

"I will bring this to Gihon, alright? Thank you for delivering it. Good birdie."

The raven let out an affectionate *gwah* as it bumped its head onto her arm, stretching its wings and taking flight into the darkness.

Turning and closing the balcony door behind her, Edelein looked around at the old bookshelves that lined every wall of the room, and then down at the scroll in her hand.

Yes, of course it's Gihon's room. The scent of all of these books, the musk of rich antique wood... how could I not notice? Whatever this scroll is, though, I should probably give it to him immediately. Surely, he's still awake at this hour, right?

A jolt ran through her body as Edelein remembered the heated argument they had gotten into earlier that evening.

Maybe I should wait until the morning, in case he's still angry.

Edelein paused, one hand on the doorknob as she debated going out. After a moment's hesitation, she twisted the knob. Memories of her nightmare seeped back into her brain, consuming her attention, but she vanquished the thoughts as she pushed forward.

I don't want to go back to sleep. It might be nice to share some company for a bit.

As Edelein's thoughts wandered, one hand clutched her nightgown while the other held tight onto the letter. Gihon looked up from his book at the sound of her footsteps, the Dirigent immediately tossing his book aside and standing up abruptly as he began to evaluate her condition.

"Edelein. Are you well? Did you have another nightmare?" Gihon fretted, looking over Edelein's body for signs of distress as he clasped his hands on her shoulders, ready to support her.

Edelein nodded in response to both questions. Gihon stopped as he saw the scroll in her hand, looking at the Queen curiously as he gently took it from her.

"There was a raven on the balcony, um…" Edelein trailed off, Gihon's eyes widening in silent understanding as he realized what she had put together. He blushed, searching for an explanation that eluded him.

Changing the subject, he looked down at the letter. "It's from the Society, likely their reply to the correspondence that I had sent earlier. Thank you for bringing this to me."

"What did you tell them?" Edelein asked, her tone a bit wary.

"Nothing that I was not supposed to tell them, I assure you. I only told them about Solomon."

"You didn't tell them anything that I said in the farmhand's vehicle, correct?"

Gihon paused.

"Correct," Gihon affirmed after a moment.

Were the things she said for my ears only? Edelein knows my position as an alchemist. If this secrecy continues, I will begin to face pressure from my fellow dirigents for omitting details.

"I told you about Zenluve in confidence. Back at the Bazaar, and in the autowagon, I... am not ready for the Society of Alchemists to know about us yet. You'll really keep it to yourself?" Edelein asked, seeming to read Gihon's mind.

"Keeping things to myself is my specialty. Believe it or not, Ravencroft is by far the most elusive city-state in Caandemium. The Society has tried to pressure me about the details of my hometown ever since I took over. Your secrets are safe with me."

Edelein spared an appreciative glance up at him, before looking away. Noticing her demeanor, Gihon took Edelein's hand and walked her over to the sofa.

"I am more concerned for your well-being than whatever the Society has to say. I'll go over it later. You had another nightmare, it seems."

Edelein nodded silently, sitting down.

"Do you want to talk about it?"

The Man in Red

Another nod. Gihon sat beside her, his eyes empathetic.

"It's alright, Edelein. I'm awake, so I will talk with you until you feel safe."

"T-thank you," Edelein choked out, looking down at the ground. "I dreamt about you, and about Solomon. He hurt you, and you blamed the blight on me. Everything was dead around us. I had betrayed you. I…"

Gihon's eyebrows furrowed in concern, placing one hand gently on her cheek.

"Look at me, Edelein. Let me see your face."

He tilted her head up, wiping away a tear with his thumb.

"There is nothing to be afraid of. You are a victim of blight, not a catalyst. Solomon doesn't stand a chance against me, either. Especially with you and the Zengarde by my side. Your mind is being cruel to you," Gihon spoke softly, his gaze gentle and warm.

Edelein didn't respond, trembling slightly at his touch as her wavering eyes met his.

"You have to be strong all the time for everyone," Gihon continued. "I know how hard that is. It is okay to be weak around me. I will hold you upright and I won't tell a soul if you stumble."

Edelein chuckled softly, grateful for his words as he pulled her head onto his chest, holding the back of her head as he embraced her softly.

"I promise that you are safe here. I will protect you. We'll find Solomon and get the crystal back, and then you'll be back home in Zenluve before you know it."

Edelein's shoulders shook as she buried her face in his warm chest, crying silently.

"I miss home," she mumbled.

"I know. Do you want to tell me more about Zenluve? I would love to listen, and help take your mind off of the situation."

"Gihon, I'm sorry for earlier," she said, pulling away from

him and wiping her tears.

The Dirigent blinked, surprised. "N-no, you've no reason to apologize. I lost my temper with you. Additionally, you were right. It was an alchemist that had turned on us. My behavior was inappropriate."

"You'll cure my blight, won't you?" Edelein asked, feeling her mind start to fog up as her thoughts raced.

"I swear to do everything in my power," Gihon replied gently. "These fleeting moments with you give me some ideas to study upon. That's... what I was reading about, actually."

Edelein blinked in surprise as Gihon handed her the book he had set down when she entered the room.

"*The Collected Knowledges of Extraplanar Energies*," Edelein read. "Sounds... boring."

"I am seeking to revisit some old texts about the effects of extraplanar essences on material organisms. I could tell you more about it, if you're interested."

"Is that why you are awake so late every night?" Edelein asked, handing the book back to him.

Gihon shrugged. "I rarely get the peace and quiet that I desire during the day. My head feels the most clear at night, when the world is silent. It is when I am allowed the luxury of thought."

After a beat, Gihon added, "It is also when I am most likely to have some time alone with you. Whether it is out of your necessity or boredom, I enjoy your company. Although, I do wish your nightmares would cease for your own sake. For as long as they continue, however, I shall be awake and ready to listen to your heart."

"I... feel as if I am losing myself. I'm scared," Edelein admitted, her hands idly and unsuccessfully massaging the pain from her legs. "Now that we don't have the potions, either..."

Quickly producing a small vial of golden liquid from his

pocket, Gihon pressed the bottle into her palm.

"I made you more stamina potions. Take this one, and I have a few more ready for when you need them."

Edelein took the vial from his hand, gazing silently into the gold as it sloshed around within its glass prison.

"The panax oil I asked Nora to fetch for me is a key component of stamina elixirs. I wanted to make more for you before we set out, so that's what I was working on after you went upstairs to rest," Gihon explained.

"You asked for the oil before we found out about Alett's bag, though," Edelein pointed out.

"I… was going to make them for you anyway," Gihon admitted, looking away. "I feared that you would run out of them on the road, and I wanted to have extra on hand just in case."

Edelein looked up at him suddenly, her eyes a quivering ocean of mixed emotions as she felt a brief moment of something powerful pass between them. Their eyes locked in an intense beat, the air heavy between them.

After a moment that felt like an eternity, Edelein leaned up slightly, her face inching closer to his. Gihon felt her gentle sigh on his lips, his own breath catching in his throat as his heart began to pound. He leaned in closer, closing the distance between them. His lips a hair's breadth from hers, Gihon hesitated as his mind cleared, his chest throbbing with an unfamiliar pain.

No, this is inappropriate conduct, for a multitude of reasons.

Pulling away, Gihon looked down at the ground, Edelein looking up at him in confusion.

"My apologies, Your Majesty. It is getting late."

"I-I thought you wanted to spend time with me," Edelein stammered, face red as she composed herself.

"I do," Gihon replied, "Edelein, I think rest would benefit

you more right now. I can accompany you until you fall asleep, if you'd like. I believe that books of interest to a man like me would bore you right to sleep rather quickly, so how about I read to you for a bit?"

Edelein nodded, disappointed, leaning on Gihon's shoulder as he picked up his book.

Gihon tensed at her touch, sparing a quick glance towards the exhausted woman on his shoulder before clearing his throat and beginning to read aloud.

CHAPTER 10

REINFORCEMENTS

Dawn light spilled into the main sitting room of Gihon's home, the Dirigent already wide awake. He was occupying a large chair by the window, a cup of tea steaming on the end table beside him as his eyes scanned across the pages of the same book from the night before. A young and chipper voice drew his eyes upward, looking up at Alett as the owl zoa poked his head into the room. His eyes were wide and bright, seeming to have been awake even longer than Gihon.

"Gihon, good morning!" Alett smiled. "Do you know if the Society has any more of those tomes for us to borrow?"

"The tomes we gave you… yesterday?" Gihon asked, as Alett smiled. "Did you… read them all already?"

Alett nodded eagerly, Gihon staring at him in disbelief.

We gave them several very large books. It would have easily been a hundred hours of reading, if not more.

"I told you, the kid's a supergenius," Zander huffed,

brushing past Alett on his way to the kitchen. "He also doesn't sleep. The entire Strigo family is nocturnal by nature, but since Alett's got Zengarde duties, he stays awake all day too."

"This alchemy stuff is fascinating! I can see why my mom is so into it," Alett beamed. "Oh! Gihon, my mom's an alchemist. Did I tell you that?"

"...What?" Gihon responded in disbelief.

How has this not been brought up to me yet? Alett was raised by an alchemist? This means Zenluve does possess some form of alchemy.

"She oversees the zoa transmutations in Zenluve, but that's all she does these days since moving to the Kingdom to be with my dad."

His mother must be a specialized biological alchemist, which is why she hasn't been able to help with the phantasms.

"I grew up more involved with my dad's work than my mom's, though I... wait, I didn't tell you about my dad. My dad is–"

Alett was interrupted by the sound of footsteps, turning his attention as Edelein entered the room. Gihon rose to his feet to greet her, memories of his last interaction with her flooding his mind as he tried to focus on maintaining eye contact.

Relax, Gihon, he thought to himself. *Be a professional. It was simply late, and we were both exhausted, that's all. Nothing happened.*

Gihon's eyes wandered down briefly to her lips, and he felt a blush rise to his cheeks before he quickly banished the thought, looking up at her eyes again.

"Good morning, Your Majesty. I prepared tea not long ago, I believe it should help ease your symptoms a bit. How are you feeling?"

"Tea would be lovely, thank you. I feel better now. Is it in the kitchen?"

224

The Man in Red

"Yes, please, allow me to—"

A loud bang sounded from the front of the house as the door slammed open suddenly. Edelein jumped, her fur bristling as she whipped towards the noise. Zander quickly unsheathed his dual blades, darting in front of Edelein in a flash. A young voice called out from the front, relaxing the Zenluvians as they detected no threat.

"Master Gihon! Your heroes have arrived!" the voice called out, his tone playful and excited.

Please don't make me regret this, Mandus, Gihon thought.

Mandus stood in front of the open door, hands on his hips as his fox-tail swished excitedly. Behind him, Luthro stood with a similar look of regret as Gihon, while Spira and Jana waved politely at their master.

"Mandus! Took you long enough!" Nora replied excitedly, running into the room.

"Nora! What's up, kiddo? Looks like Gihon just lets anyone in here, huh?" Mandus laughed, high-fiving the teenager.

"Welcome, you four," Gihon started. "Thank you for coming on such short notice. I will—"

"Where's the Queen?" Mandus interrupted. "I want to meet her. Is she still asleep?"

Gihon cleared his throat, cocking his head slightly towards Edelein. She was standing directly next to the Dirigent, arms crossed with a bemused expression on her face. Mandus' eyes wandered up to her lion ears, and down to her tail as it swayed. After a brief moment, his face lit up in excitement as he realized who she was.

"Your Majesty, the Lion Queen of Zenluve!" Mandus exclaimed. "No way! You look like you're *my* age! I thought you'd be way older!"

"So did Gihon. You all do fixate on the age thing a lot,

don't you?" Edelein huffed, her tone playfully indignant. "I am Queen Edelein von Luvemann, the sovereign Lion Queen of Zenluve. The Lion King you may know about was my father, Alderis. He passed away about nine years ago, leaving me as the lone heir to the Throne. That about sums it up, yes, Dirigent Gihon?"

Mandus' eyes sparkled with admiration and joy. "Your Majesty, you're a legend to us Caandemite zoa. My mom used to tell me bedtime stories about your ancestors. I cannot believe I get to meet you in person, I can't wait to tell my–"

Luthro interrupted Mandus, stepping in front of him and bowing as he swept her hand up into a gentle kiss.

"Luthro Apocathra, at your service. It is an honor, Your Majesty. Please pardon my cohort. He is easily excitable."

Edelein smiled, chuckling to herself.

He's like a little Gihon. How cute. She thought.

"These four are my top students," Gihon said, Edelein looking over at him expectantly. "I informed them of the situation last night, so they are here to help us locate Solomon and retrieve the crystal. They will also be available to help train the Zengarde in alchemy. Mandus works with speed manipulation, befitting of his personality."

Gihon gestured to Spira and Jana as he continued. "Spira is trained in hardlight weaponry, and Jana prefers sentinel alchemy similar to my own, though her true specialty is potions. They are both incredibly talented young women. Finally, Luthro here works with mass manipulation alchemy, and currently stands as my successor."

Edelein looked at Gihon, and down to the shorter Luthro. She noted the green highlights in his hair and pressed green vest, noticing that Luthro even stood in the same pose as his master. The Queen couldn't help but laugh gently.

The Man in Red

"I can tell."

"What do you mean?" Luthro asked.

"Oh, nothing. I will be grateful for their assistance in returning my crystal. Alett, please fetch the rest of the Zengarde for me."

Alett nodded, leaving the room in a hurry.

Not long after Alett left, all eight Zengarde were gathered around the dining room table. The five alchemy students stood together on one side of the table, with Gihon and Edelein standing together at the head.

Cari looked over Luthro, smiling as she took in his polished appearance.

He's cute, she thought.

Oblivious to her, Luthro began to speak. "I will be happy to teach all of you about my alchemy technique. You see, I utilize what we refer to as mass-manipulation alchemy to alter–"

Less cute when he talks, Cari thought as Luthro rambled on, tuning out his words.

Also ignoring Luthro, Mandus looked at Cari, his head tilted in confusion.

She looks like a fox zoa, but her ears are downturned… and she's pink. Why is she pink? Mandus wondered. *That's way too much hair to dye. I think it's natural… but how? What is she?*

Nora was also looking at Cari, starry-eyed as she gazed in admiration.

She's all pink! That's so cool!

Nephvir approached Jana, extending a hand to her. She

took it, shaking his hand formally.

"Nephvir."

"I'm Jana," she replied. "I didn't realize that Avalstice had fellborn, too. Did Avalstice take part in the Faith Wars, too?"

Nephvir tilted his head curiously. Noticing his confusion, Jana continued.

"Well, I mean… that's when most of us were born, after the plane-shifters returned from the war."

"Oh, I see," Nephvir shook his head. "No, the only plane-shifters in Avalstice are the Red Mantis, which is unfortunately what my old man was."

"Your father is one of the Red Mantis assassins?" Jana asked, intrigued and surprised. "I thought the males were all sterilized."

"Yeah, so did my mother. The bastard lied about it, and didn't tell her he was a shifter, either. He infected her with energy from the Plane of Shadow. Now society hates her for having a fellborn, and she hates me for being a fellborn. Fantastic, is it not?"

"Wow, that's awful. Do Avalstans still believe that fellborn are demon-spawn? That theory was disproved ages ago."

"It has been disproven, but the stigma still remains. It's hard to erase so many years of prejudice. Being a Zengarde helps, though, because now people are too scared to speak up against me."

Nephvir laughed dryly, Jana looking up at him with inquisitive violet eyes. Across the table, Zander was glaring at the students. As his eyes met Spira's, she stared back at him boldly, unfazed.

"You got a problem, kid?" Zander huffed, interrupting Luthro's lecture.

"Are you talking to me?" Spira replied, blinking in surprise.

"Spira is blind, Zander," Gihon corrected with a soft sigh. "Overexposure to the plane of light has impaired her vision. She takes in all light waves that are invisible to the naked eye, which makes it harder for her to see the material plane as we would."

"It's kind of hard to explain, because it's not technically blindness... more that I see *too* much, which makes it harder to see details. Every type of light on the spectrum overlaps, which makes everything way too bright and a bit... glassy, I suppose?"

Pointing towards the wall, Spira continued.

"For example, I can see the heat of the sun coming through the walls, as if the walls were transparent. You, though, are just a vaguely catlike figure. I'm sorry if it seemed that I was staring at you," Spira clarified, continuing to stare straight ahead, almost as if she were looking through Zander entirely.

"One of the advantages to Spira's visual impairment is that it makes her incredibly quick with calculations. Her brain is constantly processing a large amount of visual information at once, so she has developed a skill for sifting through data to find relevant information. Though... it did take a bit of time to get to this point," Gihon added with a soft laugh.

Zander bowed his head slightly towards her, embarrassed. "I apologize for misunderstanding you, alchemist."

Gihon and Edelein both sighed, relieved that Zander had decided to be agreeable for once and drop the subject. The Dirigent crossed his arms, clearing his throat as the room fell silent.

"Thank you for coming out here on such short notice, you four." Gihon addressed his students, who were eagerly stationed on one end of the dining room table.

Edelein stood by his side, tail swishing side-to-side as her eyes swept across the room. Across from the alchemists, the Zengarde were positioned at attention, ready to spring into any action at her command.

"As I disclosed in my correspondence, the situation is urgent. Solomon has shown his face within the city, he killed a high-ranked alchemist on Society grounds, and stole a pure leyline crystal that Queen Edelein brought in exchange for the Society's aid." Gihon continued, his students nodding solemnly in understanding.

"What does he want with the crystal, Master Marleogne?" Jana asked. "What exactly are the crystals capable of?"

"A single leyline crystal contains enough energy to rip a hole in space itself, condensed into a stable crystalline state like carbon to a diamond." Edelein explained. "They hold an electric charge similar to regular crystals, but amplified exponentially. We are unsure as of now what Solomon plans to use it for, but my fear is that he will return for the second one."

"You brought two?!" Mandus exclaimed. "No way, can we see the other one?"

"Not now, Mandus," Gihon and Luthro replied in unison, causing Edelein to chuckle.

"I will be happy to show you all once we have a plan in order. I understand that our leyline crystals are incredibly rare, nothing but a rumor in Caandemium, and thus are valued highly by your alchemists as a potential source of energy and research."

"Making it an incredibly dangerous weapon in the hands of someone like Solomon, and a top priority to retrieve it before he does something irreversible," Gihon finished as Edelein looked up at him in agreement.

"The concerns that Gihon and I share are about the unpredictable variables of the situation. Because we do not know what Solomon intends with my crystal, we cannot be sure if he will return to take the second one or not. Additionally, a group of this size would make it far too easy for Solomon to find us. As grateful as I am for Gihon's students to be joining us, a party of fifteen people out in the wilderness would just be begging Solomon to find us before we can find him. I propose that we split our group into two; a group that will track him down and a group that will stay here in hiding to guard the second stone."

"So, you want trackers to go out, and combatants to stay in?" Thorne asked, running a hand through his bangs casually.

"We have to consider both combat capability and compatibility within these environments," Gihon added. "Those who fight better in open spaces should go out, and close-range or melee fighters should stay here. We should divide those who are able to defend or heal evenly, as well, to utilize our numbers as a great strength rather than a weakness."

"I get it. Since you and Everett both defend, you should be on opposite teams." Thorne nodded in understanding.

"Yes. Miss Lylia is a healer and a druid, which makes her perfect to go out into the wilderness, whereas Jana specializes in potion-making and would be considered a supporter that could stay here where she has access to supplies," Gihon continued. "We essentially need to form two adventure links, leaving one sentinel and one beacon with each group."

"Thorne and I will go out," Edelein stated. "Though I figure that would be obvious."

Thorne chuckled, nudging Lylia. "Nice. It's just you and me, sweet-cheeks."

"It is not. Her Majesty will be accompanying us, and we will likely divide halfway to even out our forces. Also, don't ever call me sweet-cheeks again. Your human ego will get you killed one day," Lylia retorted with an eyeroll.

"Damn, you're right. Smart as ever. That's what I like about you."

"Thorne, watching you fail is physically painful to me," Edelein sighed. "Leave Lylia alone."

Lylia dipped her head slightly. "I can handle Thorne, Your Majesty. Please do not worry. If he gets punched, it will be of his own volition."

Ignoring them, Gihon turned to Edelein as he spoke in a quiet tone. "Is it wise for you to travel right now? Perhaps you should stay here, so we can monitor your condition under safer circumstances."

"I will not sit by and send my men out after a maniac like Solomon. A Queen should never ask her men to do something that she would not be willing to do. I am going."

"Very well, then I shall accompany you to continue studying your blight and to keep you safe should we succeed in finding him."

"I am going," Zander stated curtly, eyes narrow. "Where she goes, I follow. I am not letting her out of my sight again."

"Can I come, too?" Mandus asked Gihon. "Because I'm fast, and my speed arrays work best in open spaces. Not because I want to hang out with the Queen. I mean, I do, but also I am definitely better outside than inside. That's the main reason."

Gihon nodded. "That is true, you do work better in the outdoors. Luthro, you will join us as well. Ladies, please remain here to protect the second crystal in case Solomon returns. In your downtime, please tutor the Zengarde in basic banishment alchemy. Jana, I am putting you in charge of helping them learn their fundamentals."

Jana nodded excitedly, beaming. "Yes, Master Marleogne, I will do my best!"

"I want to join the traveling team," Jinn spoke quietly. "Bex should be avenged."

"You knew him for like, a day, and he's also the one that sold us out. But I like your attitude anyway, Jinn," Thorne cackled.

"He was a good man in a bad situation. I could sense his yearning, his desperation. All he wanted was a new life, and Solomon killed him for it. No one deserves death in pursuit of their own freedom like that."

The Man in Red

"Dangerous thinking, there, bud," Thorne replied.

"Do you not value your freedom? Does it have no weight to you, the boy who ran away? You had the chance to run and survive, Bex didn't. Do not disgrace him when you are no better, human," Jinn retorted.

"Human?! Takes one to know one, Jinn! We all know you're just a tail-less half-breed!" Thorne laughed flippantly as Jinn's ear fur bristled, the wolf-man slamming his hands down on the table in anger.

"Thorne!" Edelein exclaimed in disbelief.

"Has anyone told you that you talk too much?" Jinn retorted with a snarl.

"I do, frequently," Lylia sighed. "I'm so sorry, Jinn. Thorne, that was inappropriate and out of line. Do you need to take another breather? Nobody wants to deal with you right now."

"Let Jinn have his revenge, Thorne," Everett added. "He fights best when he's angry. Which is... most of the time, I think."

"Whose side are you even on?" Jinn sighed, relaxing slightly.

"Are they always like this?" Luthro asked Gihon quietly. "For a team of elite warriors, they act like children."

"Unfortunately, I think the stress of this situation is not helping. Though, they are not entirely unlike you and Mandus," Gihon responded with a quiet chuckle.

Luthro's face dropped, dismayed.

"Anyways, I believe we have our plan," Edelein interrupted. "I will go out with Thorne, Lylia, Jinn, and Zander. Gihon, Luthro, and Mandus will accompany us. That way, half of the Zengarde and alchemists will track Solomon, and the other half will stay here. There will be no objections."

The room fell silent, Edelein huffing in approval. After a beat, Cari raised her hand.

Crown of the Alchemist

"So, let's say Solomon comes back here while your team is out. How do we contact you? I hardly think that writing a letter would be a fast or efficient method of communication when a homunculus has us all by the throat."

"Firstly, I doubt that Solomon is too far away. We should be able to locate him before he finds our location. However, in the event of him reaching the house first, I have some glass around here that we can use to communicate," Gihon explained.

"Oh, quartz! I get it," Alett leaned forward in excitement, immediately understanding the suggestion.

"You really did read everything we gave you. I am impressed with you, Zwitet Alett. Yes, we will be needing pure quartz for this. My students, I assume you are following as well?"

The five students nodded silently.

"You can transmute the glass from the bottles into pure quartz, right?" Alett asked, the Dirigent nodding as Luthro responded by pulling out a golden pocket watch and setting it on the table as he continued Gihon's explanation.

"Easily, yes." Luthro answered. "As I'm sure you're aware, quartz is used to oscillate pocket watches, due to its specific frequency of–"

"Pft, yeah, we all knew this." Mandus interrupted. "Pocket watch oscillation is day one of Gihon's classes. They probably teach the Zengarde about pocket watches in school, too. Spare us the lesson, since we all know so much about it already."

"Queen Edelein, please ignore him. You will learn to tune Mandus out like the rest of us do. We can connect the two quartz pieces by etching parallel connection arrays, which allows them to resonate at the same time when activated."

"By etching amplifier arrays onto the one side of each piece of quartz, the piezoelectricity will magnify to reach the frequency of the other array on the other piece, from a far distance." Gihon added.

A few of the Zengarde looked around blankly at the explanation, confused. Noticing their puzzled expressions, Mandus laughed a little as he waved casually at them.

"Gihon will carve an array onto the quartz so that when someone touches it, the other one will buzz loudly. You caught up?"

Cari nodded. "Thanks, fox-boy. I was getting a little lost there."

"Finally, an alchemist who speaks like a regular person," Thorne sighed. "I'm getting so tired of this. Anyway, we know how to contact each other, but what do you want us to do when we find Solomon?"

"Subdue him by any means necessary and retrieve the crystal. I do not trust whatever he plans to do with that much power," Gihon commanded.

"How far is 'subduing' to an alchemist?" Thorne asked.

"Kill him, if you have to."

"I like the sound of that," Thorne cracked his knuckles with a smirk.

Producing a piece of chalk from his pocket, Gihon began to draw expertly precise lines on the table. As Luthro followed along with his master's work, the young alchemist nodded and left the room to fetch the glass bottles that Gihon had mentioned.

"So why is it that you have to draw this one, but in combat your arrays just appear in the air or on the ground?" Nephvir asked curiously, leaning in.

"Signature arrays, like the one you saw in yesterday's skirmish, are pre-loaded with an alchemist's most frequently used techniques. Since we can only hold so many abilities in one array, we usually reserve them for time-sensitive scenarios such as combat. A basic material purification array such as this one isn't necessary or used too often, so I opt to draw it manually rather than embedding it into my signature." Gihon explained, not looking up to address the fellborn as he finished his linework.

Luthro returned, two glass bottles in hand. Upon inspecting the finished lines, the student nodded in approval and set one bottle down in the center of the array.

Gihon stepped aside, allowing Luthro to lead as he stood at the array, the Zengarde and alchemists surrounding him in anticipation. As he placed one gloved palm against the chalk, the array began to glow a bright green color, light enveloping the bottle. The light faded a few moments later, leaving nothing but a smooth piece of pure quartz where the glass bottle had stood.

Alett pushed up his glasses, leaning in to inspect the quartz as Luthro picked it up.

"How fascinating," Alett murmured under his breath, watching Luthro pass the quartz to Gihon.

"To ensure the accuracy of the amplifier and connecting arrays, I will etch them myself. My etching tools are upstairs, so I will return in a few minutes," Gihon explained, taking the second piece of quartz and leaving the room as Luthro finished his transmutations.

"You're a lot like him, you know," Alett said, turning to Luthro.

Luthro beamed at the praise. "I could only dream of such a thing. Master Marleogne is a true doyen of alchemy, worthy of the title of Dirigent."

"Oh, I meant more in a literal, physical sense."

Luthro stared at Alett in a beat of silent confusion, the Zwitet waving up at his bangs in a clarifying gesture.

"The hair. You both have those cool green streaks."

"Gihon's hair is green?" Luthro asked, eyebrows furrowed as he turned towards the direction the Dirigent had left in.

"I mean, more of a teal, if you ask me," Mandus offered.

The Man in Red

"But yeah, it's technically green. Wait, Luthro, did you really not realize that? I know you're colorblind, but your whole personality revolves around trying to be like Gihon. Are you actually saying the hair is a coincidence?"

"Of course it's unintentional! A-and… my personality is not just trying to be some duplicate of Master Marleogne; I merely admire him, that's all. Is it so, that every man with black and green hair is suddenly a Gihon-wannabe? What about the Zengarde human over there, then?" Luthro denied, pointing at Thorne.

Thorne shook his head with a small sigh. "Nope, my hair is red. Nice try, though. Don't lump me into your mess, nerd."

Luthro clamored awkwardly, fidgeting. "I thought you always compared me to Gihon because you respect my leadership qualities," he said, flustered.

"Well, you see, your first mistake was thinking that we respect you," Mandus laughed.

"Luthro, you are a talented and hardworking alchemist, like Master Marleogne," Jana commented with a smile. "We just… thought that you wanted to look like him too, that's all."

"Wow, you guys really respect Gihon," Alett realized. "I like him a lot, too, though we all did kind of get off on the wrong foot with him thanks to the King of Grumpington over there."

Zander growled under his breath as he faced the window with crossed arms, casting a side glance at Alett with an irritated flick of his ear.

"Everyone wants to be friends with you, Zander!" Alett called out, the sphynx ignoring him and turning away.

"I have no idea what you mean, he seems like a ball of sunshine to me," Mandus laughed.

"Oh, he is. Zander's a big softie, he just doesn't like to show it to anyone," Alett replied fondly, smiling.

Gihon's footsteps signaled his return, the group turning

their attention towards him as he handed one of the quartz stones to Luthro. Holding up the other one, he addressed the room.

"Assuming our alchemy is sound, Luthro's stone should vibrate at a high frequency when I activate the array on the one in my hand, and vice versa."

Gihon pressed his thumb against the array on the quartz stone, Luthro tightening his grip as the stone in his hand began to vibrate and release a high-pitched whine. Cari, Jinn, Mandus, and Nora grimaced, reaching up to cover their ears as Zander clasped his hands over Edelein's.

"Can't you make it... sound better?" Cari asked with a whimper, clutching her soft pink ears.

"It's... so... loud..." Mandus agreed with a scowl.

"My apologies, but it's the best we can do with the time-sensitive situation at hand," Gihon apologized, deactivating the array. "I understand that our mammalian zoa allies have a more acute sense of hearing than the rest of us, but you will have to bear with it for now."

"Now that we have a method of communication, it is imperative that we head out at once. The longer we wait, the further he gets." Edelein demanded, removing Zander's hands from her ears.

Gihon nodded in agreement. "I theorize that it may take us a few days to locate him, considering that we have to follow him on foot. Last night, Everett prepared rations and camp supplies for the journey ahead, so there should be no issue."

"Excellent. I look forward to being out in the wilderness again," Edelein smiled, pleased as she passed by the others to head towards the door. "We can start back to the road where we fought him and track him from there."

"No need, Your Majesty," Thorne interjected, following her out with the rest of the tracking team in tow. "I've got his location."

The Man in Red

How…? Gihon wondered as Thorne took the lead, stopping at the edge of the woods.

"I can feel it in the wind. There's this weird pocket of nothingness south from here, which I assume is him. Watch this."

Thorne snapped his fingers, a headwind picking up and blowing towards the group. Edelein perked up, ears alert and forward as she sniffed the air, mouth slightly ajar as she drank in the scent.

"I smell it too," She confirmed, heading into the woods.

"Did he just… change the direction of the wind with his fingers?" Luthro asked Gihon.

"The fingers were just for show," Thorne quipped. "I actually did it with my mind. Wanna know how? It's a pretty cool story."

Jinn sighed from beside Luthro. "Do not push further with that subject, or Thorne will boast about his fae blessings again. It's rather obnoxious, and not worth your time."

Gihon ignored the others' banter as he suddenly inquired to Edelein, "Your Majesty, you mentioned previously that the homunculi have no scent. How are you able to pick up a trace of him?"

"I've told you that everything has a scent. I'm simply going to where the scent is not."

"Wouldn't the scent of the surrounding area override the emptiness? I'm having trouble comprehending smelling a lack of a scent. Mandus, can you pick it up as a fox zoa?"

"Nope, I'm about as lost as you are. I can almost pick it up a tiny bit, but it's very abstract and vague. On my own, I'd be in the same situation as you. Even now I'm not entirely sure that I get it."

Edelein looked over her shoulder at Gihon, still walking at the head of the group.

"Think of it this way. Imagine a painting where the

environment around the canvas matches the artwork. There's a big hole in the middle of the canvas, but to an untrained eye they don't notice it due to the space behind the canvas matching the paint. We are heavily attuned to scent and hunting, so we can notice that glaring hole while others may not due to the influence of the surrounding environment. Everywhere Solomon goes, there's a faint trace of what feels like a rip in the canvas of scent."

"I see," Gihon responded, "I suppose that makes sense in an abstract sense, like Mandus said."

"Fuuntet Thorne!" Edelein perked up again, turning towards the Zengarde. "Solomon moved. Change the wind to south-southwest."

"Your wish is my command, Your Majesty," Thorne nodded as the wind shifted slightly.

Gihon looked over his shoulder as the border of the woods vanished, the group making their way deeper into the forest.

"I wonder what Solomon is planning," Gihon wondered aloud. "We're getting rather deep into the woods."

"He's trying to throw you off," Edelein answered, "but hasn't taken into account that the Zenluvians are accompanying you, and we work better in nature than in cities."

Gihon remembered hearing the sound of Zander and Alett passing by in Velkhamore when searching for Edelein.

They weren't able to pick out her scent amongst such a large crowd. They were overstimulated by all of the new scents, weakening their Seventh Senses. If Solomon were to truly want to vanish from them, it won't take him long to realize that. The counter is that if he tries to disappear in a city, I'll find him quickly through questioning and connections. Solomon is disadvantaged, and taking his chances.

Edelein winked at Gihon, seeming to notice that he was remembering the moment they shared at the bazaar. Ahead of them,

the forest opened up into a small clearing, the last wisps of fading
daylight catching the ground at their feet.

"We can make camp here tonight," Gihon suggested as
everyone began to set their bags down, relieved. "Rest well, and
we'll be back on the trail at sunrise. Edelein, may I have a word
with you while the others are setting up the camp?"

"Shouldn't I be setting up as well?" She asked.

"Of course not. Not just because you're the Queen, but
you're still ill. My job is to ensure you do not overwork yourself.
Plus, I can make better use of your time if you join me. This way,
please."

Edelein nodded hesitantly, following after Gihon. The
raven zoa looked down at her with a soft smile as he lead her a bit
further outside of the clearing.

"I have something I'd like to show you," Gihon started.
"You need to learn the basics of alchemy, not just the Zengarde. I
cannot guarantee that we will not encounter more phantasms on our
journey, and your skill in battle will be useful to us all. Can I rely on
you?"

Edelein nodded, sitting down on a log.

"Go on then, Master Gihon. Your student is eager to learn,"
she chuckled.

A sudden sharp pain pulled on Gihon's heart, an unfamiliar
stab hitting his chest.

What... what was that? Gihon wondered, touching his chest
briefly. *What just happened to me?*

Sitting down next to her, the Dirigent let his teaching take over his mind, distracting himself from the feeling bubbling within him.

"The basic step one of alchemy is learning to ignite a spark; counterbalancing your potassium and sodium ions to create an internal electricity that you can use to power an array. This won't be hard... young alchemist children can do it, so you can too. That spark serves as the catalyst for a starter array, which can be embedded into larger arrays. Think of it like tinder to a fire. You're the spark, the starter array is the tinder, and the larger array is the wood. You can't just set wood on fire with a little spark," Gihon started.

"I understand."

"Good. Ask me to slow down if you need me to, alright? I don't mind at all. I will also etch an array onto your bow for you that will allow you to strike at phantasms without the blight effect. That way, you can safely weaken them without breaking the reality shell. Without a banishing array, though, you risk killing the creature inside. It's easy to learn the spark, but harder to draw an array without risking a backlash. If I draw your arrays for you, you'll be able to just activate them yourself for the same result."

Standing up from the log, Gihon motioned for her to wait there as he vanished inside of his tent. Returning a moment later with a wool blanket in hand, the Dirigent handed the quilt to Edelein as she stood up. The lioness looked down at the blanket in her hands, confused.

"Rub your hands on it," Gihon instructed.

Edelein nodded obediently, feeling the soft wool between her fingers as she generated friction against it.

"Recognize the feeling you have inside of you right now, and pay attention to how it feels. Feel the fibers of your body reacting to the energy within. That electrifying feeling in your body, the feeling of static electricity that will spark the initialization of your array," Gihon explained, pulling off his glove and touching her neck gently with his bare skin.

As his hand touched her skin, a jolt lifted the fur on her tail, the Queen letting out a small yelp as she jumped. At the sound of her pain, Zander appeared almost instantly, stepping between them and pushing Gihon back with his unsheathed sword.

"What did you do, corvid?" Zander hissed. "Don't touch her!"

"Relax, Zander, please. We are doing some basic alchemy training. Rahzopa should have taught you about the ionic rebalancing for array ignition, surely?"

A sudden hand on Zander's arm caused the sphynx to jump as a static charge startled him, hissing in displeasure as Mandus butted in from behind.

"Don't worry, man, this is a normal part of learning alchemy. Everyone has to get bullied a little bit from ignition static. Let them do their thing and come help me with this tent."

Zander grumbled, but Edelein assured him with a soft touch to his chest. Looking up at him, she smiled.

"It's okay, go help them. I was simply startled, that's all. Gihon's not doing anything he shouldn't be."

The Ehret hesitated, but nodded at her command and returned to the tent where Mandus was struggling against a pole.

"Anyways," Gihon continued, "you'll get used to that little shock. I hardly feel it anymore, honestly. Remember how it felt to have that energy within you and try to summon it again."

Edelein closed her eyes, tail flicking as she focused her energy inwards. After a moment, she opened her eyes and looked up at Gihon, uncharged and defeated.

"That's alright. I'll help you," Gihon smiled gently, clasping her hands in his. "I'm going to give you a little push, and you can do the rest."

Edelein nodded and closed her eyes again, eyebrows furrowed as she focused. After a moment, her eyes snapped open and she smiled brightly as she pulled her hands away from Gihon.

"I did it!" she beamed. "How much energy did you input? How much of that was me?"

"I didn't do anything," Gihon admitted with a soft smile. "It's called a placebo effect. You did that entirely on your own. Great job, Edelein. You should be proud."

Crouching down, Gihon began to draw in the dirt with an expert hand. Edelein squatted down next to him, curious. As his hand withdrew, she looked down at a perfectly-drawn array in the dirt. Picking up an acorn, the Dirigent buried it into the center of the array and looked over at her.

"Do you still have that energy?" Gihon asked.

Edelein nodded.

"Great. Go ahead and touch the array right here. This spot is the starter, and it will trigger the rest of this array," Gihon pointed to a circle near the edge of the array as he gave his instructions.

Edelein reached down, touching the circle and wincing as the static discharged from her body and flowed into the dirt. The array began to glow a mesmerizing royal blue color, the lioness gasping in surprise as a plantlet sprouted from the center of the array.

"A sapling!" Edelein exclaimed. "Is that from the acorn you planted there? Am I growing this little one myself, right now? Is this my doing?"

Gihon nodded warmly, picking her hand up off of the array. The blue glow subsided as her hand was removed, the sapling halting its growth and remaining only a few inches tall.

"This is alchemy. This array draws from our plane's energy and fuels the growth of that acorn, speeding up its life cycle for as long as you continue to pour your energy into it. Some arrays, like this one, require continual contact, while some only need the initial ignition."

"This is amazing. We could help so many people with this. We could regrow the parts of the Deepwood that have been affected by blight." Edelein looked up at him warmly. "You're amazing, Gihon."

Gihon blushed, standing up and helping her to her feet as he picked up her warbow.

"One more thing. I mentioned hardlight weaponry to you before. It's Spira's specialty, but I think you'd benefit from learning it. If I can teach you how to summon hardlight arrows, you'll be able to target phantasms safely."

Edelein nodded as Gihon tapped on the ironwood bow, his thumb resting just above where her grip would sit. The lioness eyed her bow curiously, looking up at Gihon as he instructed further.

"Practice summoning that internal energy tonight, and I will etch a hardlight array right here for you. As long as you have me to draw the linework for you, this will be enough. I'll have your bow done before the morning, and you'll be able to fight off phantasms by yourself as soon as tomorrow."

Edelein nodded again, turning and walking off.

"Oh, and Edelein... one more thing," Gihon added.

The Queen turned around, tilting her head curiously. Gihon paused, doubt suddenly filling his mind as he looked away. An ache pounded in Gihon's chest for a quick moment, before subsiding once more to a comfortable and familiar silence inside of him.

"You won't run out of arrows again, if you use the hardlight array. Work hard on learning it, alright? For your own safety, in case I am not there to protect you for any reason."

"I understand," Edelein assured.

He seemed to have wanted to say something else. What is Gihon hiding from me?

A long moment passed between the two, each expecting the other to speak.

"Goodnight," Gihon said bluntly as he brushed past Edelein, heading off towards his tent.

Edelein blinked, confused.
"Goodnight, Gihon."

CHAPTER 11

TAKE THE SHOT

A day had come and gone since the group had begun their search for Solomon, late afternoon sunshine warming the tips of Edelein's ears as they continued to navigate through the underbrush of the Caandemite woods. Edelein was bringing up the rear, sweat beading on her brow as her breath grew short and staggered.

Noticing the Queen as she fell behind, Gihon slowed to meet her pace, concerned.

"Is it the blight?" Gihon asked, Edelein's tired eyes staring blankly up at him. "Should we stop and rest for a bit?"

"I'm fine," Edelein lied. "I stayed up late practicing those sparks, and my fatigue is catching up to me a bit. That's all."

"There's a small town just a little ways ahead. We can rest there for the night once we arrive," Gihon suggested as he took in his environment, recognizing the area.

A distorted, warbling roar resonated through the air, chills running through the group at the dissonant sound. The familiar cry of a phantasm sent shivers through Edelein's body, the hairs on her tail rising in alarm as her face drained of color.

Memories of her lost allies began to flood back, the Queen remembering Tyrus and Cyzen's lifeless bodies as they buckled underneath the impact of the very same monster. Tremors shook her to her core as an inky black foe busted through the trees, smashing everything in sight.

Drawing their weapons, the Zengarde looked cautiously at the alchemists, as if awaiting an explanation.

"You called the other one a tyrant-shell. What is this one, then?" Zander asked Gihon, lowering his stance.

The phantasm was a bit smaller than the other two, hunched over with a rounder body that was more reminiscent of a horned beetle. It still towered over Gihon by several feet, standing nearly twice as tall as the Dirigent even in its curled-over stance. Six glowing violet eyes decorated its armored insectoid head, and the creature possessed the tell-tale large phantasmal eye on its chest.

"I cannot tell immediately with this one, but it appears defensive in nature. It hasn't attacked yet, and has a thick exoskeleton. It could be a sentinel-shell. We need to stay back and study its movements for a moment first," Gihon responded, summoning his black cloak out of thin air and preparing himself for an attack.

A sudden burst of energy whizzed from behind the group, landing at the feet of the phantasm. The creature reared back, letting out an alarmed squeal as it turned and fled in the opposite direction.

"It's headed towards the town!" Luthro realized. "Mandus, go ahead of us and divert it back this way. We'll follow after you!"

"On it!" Mandus crouched down into a runner's starting position, a red-orange array igniting under his feet.

Mandus' array was messy, with no balance or symmetry whatsoever as jagged lightning-like lines connected from the edges of the outer ring. It almost appeared scribbled-on, a strong reminder

248

of Mandus' haphazard and free spirit.

The fox zoa's head swiveled as he took in his surroundings, his mind racing as he began to program an optimal path for his movement. Bracing himself as he lowered his body, he looked over his shoulder at the others.

"Catch up when you can!" Mandus grinned, a crack of thunder reverberating as he took off in pursuit of the phantasm.

In the blink of an eye, Mandus was gone, the student catching up to the fleeing phantasm instantly. As he approached, the phantasm locked onto Mandus with a hungry gaze, its six violet eyes shifting to a red-orange color.

The phantasm began to speed up, darting deeper into the woods as Mandus continued his pursuit, matching its speed. Lifting a large rock up with its beetle-like horn, the phantasm flung the stone towards Mandus as it continued to flee.

Mandus dispelled his speed array, flipping out of the way of the boulder as it crashed ahead of him. As he slowed down, the phantasm's speed returned to normal, its eyes returning to their usual violet hue.

Realizing the situation, Mandus turned around and hollered back at the others as loud as he could.

"It's not a sentinel-shell!" Mandus yelled, hoping they could still hear him from their far distance. "It's a mirror-shell!"

"What is a mirror-shell?" Edelein asked, turning to Gihon who looked down at her with a puzzled expression.

"A mirror-shell is a phantasm that can copy any ability that it sees. Why?"

"Mandus just said something about a mirror-shell. It was a little hard to hear him, though."

"Oh, alright, great," Gihon gritted his teeth. "My student is going up against a mirror-shell alone. Half of you are still useless against phantasms—no offense—and Mandus is already significantly farther ahead of us. Not to mention the mysterious blast that sent this thing careening in the opposite direction."

"The Zengarde will pursue the origin of the beam," Edelein commanded. "Thorne, use your wind to push Luthro up to assist Mandus."

"Get ready, nerd boy," Thorne snickered, waving his hand as a gust of wind launched Luthro forward, a strong tailwind carrying the student's feet as he sprinted.

"Your Majesty, allow me to stay with the alchemists. I can provide healing against the phantasm if needed," Lylia offered, to which Edelein nodded in approval.

Thorne, Jinn, and Zander turned around at Edelein's demand, drawing their weapons and racing off in the opposite direction to find the source of the blast. As Gihon and Lylia ran forward, Edelein followed behind them for a few steps before stumbling and leaning on her warbow, panting.

"Edelein!" Gihon stopped, turning to look at her.

Lylia grabbed Edelein's shoulders, looking over her in concern.

"She can't run, not like this. It's the blight," Lylia confirmed.

Gihon produced a small vial from his pocket, one of the stamina potions he had made before they left his estate. Popping the cork, Gihon handed the vial to Edelein, who took a small and grateful sip. As the Dirigent returned the potion to his pocket, Edelein attempted to straighten herself up, still leaning on her bow slightly.

"Edelein can make the shot from here," Lylia said, looking ahead and where the small specks of Mandus and Luthro were fighting in the distance. "I've seen my Queen shoot from further out before. We can move up and try to help the others pull our foe back in this direction, as well."

The Man in Red

"Lylia is right. Edelein, I've etched the hardlight array onto your bow," Gihon reminded her, tapping the array above her grip. "Touch it with your thumb and summon that spark we worked on, and the arrow will appear. Can you do it?"

"I-I don't know," Edelein replied shakily. "What if it doesn't work? What if I blight them all again?"

"You won't blight them," Gihon assured her. "Light alchemy doesn't affect phantasms the way physical arrows do. Go ahead and try to summon the arrow."

As Edelein placed one uneasy thumb on the array, a sudden bright light formed into the shape of an arrow, nocked and ready to fly.

I thought she would at least struggle a little bit with it. Light alchemy is a bit complicated. Gihon admitted to himself, looking down at her in surprise. *She made that look easy. Does Edelein hold some sort of affinity towards the plane of light?*

"We don't have time for this, Dirigent," Lylia demanded. "The boys need help. We have to go, now."

"I'll… I'll figure myself out, Edelein assured them, motioning forward with her free hand. "You two go join the others."

Mandus took short bursts of speed, trying to keep out of the phantasm's line of sight. The creature continued to spin around in an attempt to locate Mandus, leaving its defenses open as Luthro prepared his counter.

Drawing two fountain pens from his pocket, Luthro readied his stance as a bright green array began to shine, hovering over his left hand. The array was meticulously designed, with a radial arrangement of circles and lines.

Luthro took both pens in his right hand and tapped them gently against the array, feeling the energy flow into the body of each stylograph as he whipped them forward, throwing them with a sharp exhale.

The pens soared through the air, lodging themselves directly into the two lowest eyes of the beast. The phantasm roared, the force of Luthro's attack sending it tumbling backwards.

The phantasm's eyes began to glow green as it ripped the pens from its eyes, slamming a fist down just an inch away from Mandus' body. The fox yelped, barely managing to leap away in time. The ground erupted underneath the monster's fist, felling trees and kicking up dirt as a large crater formed.

"It saw my mass manipulation technique?" Luthro murmured to himself in realization. "I thought it was focused on Mandus. This will be a bit of an issue, if it's going to use my alchemy to exponentially increase the mass of its fists. A single hit could be fatal."

"It's pretty bad luck going against a phantasm with compound eyes," Mandus complained as he overheard his ally, springing forward to kick the beast. "It's a lot harder to stay in its blind spots!"

"Its eyes aren't compound. Its vision seems to be more arachnid; it has simple eyes on individual axes. I just got unlucky and struck as it looked at me."

"Don't say I never believed in you," Mandus huffed, darting out of view to strike at the creature again.

Touching an elegant black business card reading 'Luthro Apocathra, Alchemist' to his array, Luthro flung the card at the phantasm, striking the two remaining eyes on its left side. The creature squealed in pain again, blinded entirely from the left.

"Gihon and the elf lady are almost here!" Mandus alerted

The Man in Red

Luthro. "Queen Edelein isn't with them. That means she's going to shoot."

"We need to give her an opening," Luthro stated, pulling out his gold-plated pocket watch. "I'm going to hit its blindspot. Mandus, reverse your array from its optic side, and let it see you."

"I can only reverse the array for a few seconds before it drains me, but that should be enough for a legend like her," Mandus agreed with a grin, veering to the creature's right side as Luthro twisted his array and remained on the phantasm's left, touching the pocket watch to his array the same way he had done with the other objects.

Behind them, Gihon evaluated his students' positions and realized their plan. Slowing his pace, he motioned for Lylia to do the same.

"Stay out of the phantasm's sight for now. The boys are going to create an opening for Edelein to strike. I'll head in and banish it as soon as she lands a hit," Gihon explained, the elf giving a slight nod in understanding.

Luthro thrusted his pocket watch upwards, holding tightly onto the chain as it began to lengthen, closing the distance between the body of the watch and the phantasm's head. The watch made contact, a loud crack resonating as the phantasm fell backwards, stumbling and groaning.

As the impact landed, Mandus darted into view on the monster's other side, laughing as he called out, "Mandus is over here, little guy! Look at Mandus!"

The creature's two remaining eyes peered down at the fox, glowing red-orange as Mandus ignited his array. Instead of speeding up, however, the phantasm slowed to a near-standstill. Mandus was frozen as well, both of them moving at a snail's pace as he tried to run back towards the direction where Edelein would be.

The phantasm turned, pursuing Mandus at an equally

decelerated speed. Gihon whipped around in the same direction, calling out to Edelein with all of his strength.

"Take the shot, Edelein!" Gihon yelled.

A ways back, Edelein was standing frozen, hands trembling as she gazed down at the hardlight arrow that was nocked on her bowstring. She looked up at the phantasm, the lioness shaking in fear as she lifted her bow into position.

What if it doesn't work? Edelein wondered, doubts plaguing her mind. *What if I blight them all? What if everyone dies because of me again?*

As the seconds ticked by, Gihon's fervent voice rang out for a second time.

"Edelein! NOW!" he demanded.

Edelein drew her bow back, her unsteady hands having trouble aligning the shot as she tried to aim for the beast's chest. Her eyes wandered to Mandus, his tall fox-eared figure briefly flashing in her mind as she pictured Tyrus, her fallen ally's long zoa ears stained with the blood of her own incompetence.

I... can't do it.

The light arrow dissipated in her hands, vanishing as Edelein dropped her bow to the ground. The Queen sank to her knees, desperately trying to wipe the tears from her eyes as agony began to flow and overwhelm her.

Mandus stumbled, his reverse array dispersing as he began to pant heavily in normal speed, unable to bear the energy output any longer. The phantasm resumed its normal speed as well, lunging at Mandus with outstretched claws.

Edelein didn't shoot...! The thought seemed to echo in everyone's minds at once as the horrors began to unfold in front of them.

Mandus turned as the phantasm launched itself forward, his quick reactions carrying him an extra step away from the monster, but not far enough to avoid the hit as its sharp claws dug into Mandus' chest. Blood spilled out from his torso, staining the grass as the fox zoa collapsed to the ground.

The phantasm let out a low growl, its attention focused on the bleeding fox. A loud smack cracked against its face as Luthro's pocket watch connected with the inky shell, the monster turning around with a pained groan to face the student.

"Mandus!" Gihon cried out in alarm. "Lylia, get to him, now!"

Lylia nodded, peeling off from their dash to head towards Mandus, who was clutching his midsection and groaning weakly in pain as he tried to stop the bleeding.

Wasting no time, Luthro threw another attack from his watch, the chain looping around the phantasm's neck. As the momentum carried the pocket watch around its throat, Luthro activated another array and the watch dropped to the ground, bringing the creature down with it as its mass increased to weigh it down. Immobilized, the phantasm let out a booming roar, shaking the trees.

Four walls of obsidian rose from the ground surrounding the creature, pinning it into place. Gihon twisted his hand as a dark pillar shot up from underneath him, launching the Dirigent into the air and towards the struggling phantasm. He landed on top of the beast, a large banishment array glowing teal as Gihon pressed his hands into the reality shell, his array seeping into it and slowly dissolving the phantasm from underneath him.

The monster squirmed and screeched as the inky surface was pulled into the banishment array, Gihon holding his position with a dark expression until silence finally overcame the woods once more. Gihon dispelled the walls that had once contained the phantasm, turning his attention towards his students. Luthro was running over to Mandus as he shoved his watch back into his pocket, trying to keep his calm demeanor as Gihon followed suit.

Lylia was pressing her hands against Mandus' stomach, deeply focused as a bright green energy encased his wound. The elf didn't seem to acknowledge the alchemists as they arrived, eyebrows furrowed as she began to slowly close the huge gash.

"Why… does your healing… hurt this much?" Mandus complained, wincing in pain.

"Several of your internal organs were torn open. My magic is forcibly regrowing the tissue, expediting a process that would have taken too long for the situation. The other option is dying, would you prefer that instead?" Lylia asked wryly in response.

"N-nope, I'm good. I'll shut up. Bring on the pain, miss elf lady. It makes me feel alive."

"Is he stable?" Gihon pressed. "Will he live?"

"Mandus will make it, but we will both need to rest afterwards. This is using a lot of my magic, and he will need to sleep off the arcane symptoms of regenerating his entire torso."

"Symptoms to healing magic? What does that look like?" Luthro asked.

"His body is going to expend a lot of energy recovering from this and trying to regulate itself into its former stasis, so fatigue will be high for the next day or so. Additionally, an exposure to potent magic energy can cause nausea and vomiting if the body is overworked immediately after. The likelihood of these symptoms increases even more for those who are not commonly exposed to magic."

"So, the more I get injured, the easier it is to be healed?" Mandus connected.

"Correct, but please do not become reckless in order to train yourself to handle magic. Healing takes a lot out of me."

"Yes, ma'am," Mandus smiled weakly as Lylia removed her hands, looking down at the fresh skin that formed over his wound.

Gihon's attention turned towards the sound of slow footsteps, Edelein shakily approaching the group. The Dirigent felt his blood begin to boil, clenching his fists as he confronted her.

"I told you to take the shot. You cannot hesitate like that when your allies are in danger!" Gihon yelled.

Edelein's eyes widened in fear, looking like a lost cub as she trembled before him. "Y-you think I did that on purpose? I was so scared he was going to die. Do you think I wanted Mandus to get hurt?"

"If you didn't, you could have stopped it. This is your fault, Edelein. A mirror-shell like that can go down in one blow from something it cannot see. You were an invaluable asset to us, and you let us all down because of your own insecurities. Worse, you almost killed Mandus! His blood is on your hands!"

Edelein trembled, frustrated and hurt.

"I know, okay? I know! Do you realize how terrifying this is for me? I have lost my friends to these beasts, and I'm scared of losing more of you!" she yelled back, tears welling up in her eyes.

Gihon exhaled, grabbing the lapel of her jacket and pulling her forward angrily. Yanking her face an inch away from his, the Dirigent let out a growl as he asked quietly and sternly, "Edelein, do you think you are the only one who has lost their allies? I cannot let anyone else die under my protection. Not again."

"Master Marleogne, please, put her down," Mandus pleaded politely. "It's not her fault. I was being careless, that's all. Please don't take it out on Queen Edelein."

Gihon looked over at Mandus, eyes cold.

Mandus continued sheepishly at his silence. "It'll take more than some internal bleeding to kill me, anyway. I'm fine, I promise!"

"No, this definitely would have killed you if I wasn't here,"

Lylia whispered.

Gihon felt a sudden sharp pain in his chest, dropping Edelein in surprise and letting out a pained cough. The Dirigent turned around, facing away from the others as one hand touched his chest in alarm, shoulders slumped slightly from the pain.

What's gotten into me? Gihon wondered, taking a deep breath as he faced Edelein again, his tone softer this time.

"Edelein, you're not the only one who is afraid of loss. You have to be brave," he spoke quietly.

"I know. I'm sorry I let you down, Gihon," Edelein replied, looking at the ground.

The underbrush rustled beside the group, everyone turning towards Zander, Thorne, and Jinn as they returned from their chase. They looked disappointed as Thorne spoke.

"We lost whoever shot the blast. I don't know how, I... I've never lost a trail like that. It was there, and then it just ended suddenly."

"The air around was unsettling. We believe it was Solomon," Jinn added.

"Solomon was *behind* us?" Edelein asked, confused.

"Leave him for now," Lylia instructed. "Mandus was hurt quite badly, and I used a lot of my magic healing him. If we ran into Solomon right now, we wouldn't stand a chance."

Luthro turned to face his master, pondering. "I believe that spending the night in the town would be wisest. Master Gihon?"

Gihon was facing away again, one hand clutching the left side of his chest. He nodded solemnly in agreement, falling in line to walk behind the rest of the group as they headed towards the town at a slow pace.

This pain in my chest... I've never felt anything like it before. My emotions feel like they're on fire. Edelein's behavior is drawing something unusual out of me. Gihon admitted to himself silently. *I'm not supposed to feel this way. Why did I lash out like that?*

Gihon gazed ahead at Edelein as she fell in step with Mandus at the front of the group, both of them leading with the group slowly. The fox was looking a bit worse for wear, with a slight hobble to his gait, but otherwise upright. She looked softly at her friend, apologetic.

"Mandus, I'm so sorry. I should have aided you." She spoke with a trembling voice.

"Nah, don't worry about it. Gihon told us about what happened to you guys in Zenluve. It's scary, isn't it? If I hadn't fought off dozens of phantasms already, I would be terrified. My first battle was pretty awful, too, you know," Mandus replied with a weak laugh.

"You admire my people, though. The Kingdom of Zenluve has let you down. Zoa should be looking out for each other," Edelein sighed.

"I admire *you*, Your Majesty. I'm really grateful that you're here, and that I got to meet you. You know, I have a lot of younger siblings back home that I take care of, so I need to be more cautious in battle. For their sake. If I die, no one is left to protect them."

Edelein's ears flattened, drooping in shame. Looking at her, Mandus realized he may have spoken into her anxiety, and perked up.

"W-what I mean is, it's hard to kill me. I've got people that need me, so I'll keep on living whether the bad guys want it or not. You don't need to worry! I'm the unstoppable speedster! A-and I plan to fight for Zenluve, too. I've always told Gihon that I want to move my family to Zenluve one day. My mom and my siblings, you know? They deserve the kind of life that zoa get to have over there."

Edelein smiled gently, hiding her pain. "You are kind, Mandus. Zenluve would welcome you and your family. If you decide to move, send word and I will personally oversee your family's immigration process. However, Gihon is right about me. I need to let go of the trauma that binds me, lest more fall at my hand. My actions were inexcusable. It won't happen again."

Mandus and Edelein fell into a comfortable silence as they pressed onwards.

Jinn was the first to break the silence once the sun began to kiss the treetops, ears forward as he addressed the group behind him.

"The village is up ahead," the wolf huffed, his words seeming to revitalize everyone at the thought of soft beds and warm food.

Ahead of them, the trees parted to reveal the outskirts of a small town, bustling with civilians as they finished their daily routines.

"This is Witsburrow," Gihon commented, searching his mind for familiarities. "We're about a day or two's walk westward from Ravencroft."

"Do you think Solomon is in Ravencroft?" Luthro asked.

"No, he's not that stupid," Gihon replied. "He knows someone from the Athenaeum would find him. Ravencroft is too small for him to hide in. I'm more inclined to believe that his cult has a hidden base in the wilderness, to avoid unwanted attention."

"I need to lay down and rest for a while with Mandus and Lylia," Edelein admitted, hands rubbing her hips as she winced in pain slightly. "I'm exhausted. Anyone who isn't completely drained, please scout around the town for intel or abnormalities."

The Man in Red

Jinn, Thorne, and Zander nodded silently. Luthro looked at them briefly before adding, "I'll go with you. I know this town pretty well."

As the four men made their way into the throng of people, Gihon turned to face the remaining three.

"There's an inn just up the road here. Allow me to get you situated for the night," Gihon offered, leading them down a smaller alleyway and into a humble-looking wooden building.

A halfling sat behind a large desk, scribbling something onto a piece of paper. He looked up at the four, standing up on his chair to greet them as they entered.

"Welcome to the Fullmoon Inn!" he called out to the approaching group.

"Thank you. We have four more meeting us," Gihon informed him, placing a cloth satchel onto the counter. "This should cover it, correct? One night. Keep the change."

The halfling opened the bag, peering inside with wide eyes.

"T-this is enough to rent out the entire building," the halfling murmured, picking up the satchel with both hands.

"Is anyone else currently residing here?" Gihon asked.

The halfling shook his head. "No, sir."

"Good," Gihon affirmed. "Keep it that way, please, and the money's yours. Four men will be in shortly; two zoa in green uniforms and two humans with colored hair. Allow them to enter, but no one else."

"Absolutely, good sir!" the halfling nodded. "Allow us to help you with your bags. Jessie, get in here!"

A door behind the halfling opened quickly, a redheaded human woman rushing out and picking up two of the bags that Gihon had set down on the floor. Edelein and Gihon looked at the petite woman, befuddled as she hurried up the stairs.

"Is it just me, or does she…" Edelein whispered.

"Look exactly like the farmer from the other day, Tessa?" Gihon finished her sentence, sensing the same thing as the Queen.

"Oh!" the woman, Jessie, looked over her shoulder as she set down their bags in front of one of the doors. "Do you folk know Tessa? That's my cousin!"

"For cousins, you look incredibly alike," Gihon commented, picking up the bags as he opened the door.

"We get that a lot," Jessie laughed, waving at them as she started back down the stairs. "If you need anything, let me know. I'm on overnight duty tonight."

"Thank you, miss Tes…Jessie," Gihon corrected himself, holding open the door for Lylia as she entered the room.

"What a friendly family," Lylia commented, setting a bag down on the bed.

Looking down the hallway, Gihon noticed Edelein slinking off towards one of the further rooms and hurried after her.

I need to apologize for raising my voice at her earlier. Gihon thought, jogging to where she was opening the furthest door.

"Edelein, I–" Gihon started.

"Goodnight, Dirigent," Edelein interrupted him, closing the door behind her.

Gihon sighed, pressing his forehead against the door in dismay.

I don't know why I lashed out at her like that. I was worried about Mandus, but I'm not the type of man to raise my voice, especially not at a woman, and even more so not towards a woman I've been tasked with overseeing for work. I was disappointed in myself, and I took it out on her. Edelein didn't deserve that… she was just afraid. I've been in the same position as her before.

Gihon banged his head once gently into the door, regretting his actions silently. After a moment, he heard a crumpling thud from inside the room.

The Man in Red

"Edelein?" Gihon asked, concerned. "Are you alright?"

Silence greeted him, worry beginning to furrow his brow as he knocked on the door.

"Edelein, are you there? Did something happen?"

Silence.

"D-do you need help? May I come in?"

The Dirigent's hand reached towards the door handle, anxiety tugging at his heart as he realized the situation at hand.

If the door is locked, it'll be messy trying to get in. I'm not in the mood to buy a new door for this place. If that thud was her running away again, there's a chance that Zander might sense her in a small town like this, but that's also not an ideal situation to be in. If... wait, the door is unlocked. She didn't lock it behind her when she slammed it in my face. Why... wouldn't she?

Twisting the door handle, Gihon entered the room cautiously, his heart sinking as he took in the situation.

In front of him, the Queen had collapsed onto the floor, unconscious. Gihon ran towards her and dropped to his knees. Picking her head up gently, he noticed her shallow breaths.

She's having a blight flare-up. Gihon realized. *Her symptoms are getting worse.*

Words of advice resonated in his mind as Gihon remembered the instructions that the zoa doctor had given.

The doctor warned me personally about causing undue stress to her. Is this... because of me? Because of what I said to her?

Pulling off her gloves, Gihon gently took her hand in his and looked down at it. The blackened skin that was once only surrounding her fingernails had spread further, reaching down to her knuckles.

The blight is spreading at a faster rate than the doctor predicted. Edelein doesn't have as much time as we were hoping.

Picking up the Queen's frail body, Gihon softly placed her

onto the bed. Drawing the vial from his pocket, the Dirigent picked Edelein's head up and poured a few drops of the stamina elixir into her mouth. Gihon furrowed his eyebrows as he wiped the excess liquid from her lips, touching her forehead gently as he noted her feverish temperature.

This should help stabilize her, but I'm not sure she'll wake up tonight. She just... overworked herself today, is all.

In the distance, the Dirigent could make out the faint sounds of the remaining men as they returned from their patrol of the town, conversing with the innkeeper below.

The Zengarde need to know, but I don't want to interfere with the group's rest. I'll stay with her tonight in case it gets worse, and we can talk about it in the morning.

Gihon heard the sounds of doors closing in the nearby rooms as the others settled in for the night. He noticed a heavy set of footsteps pausing outside of Edelein's door.

Is that one of the Zengarde? Gihon wondered with bated breath, trying to minimize his presence. *Is it Zander? Did he notice an issue with Edelein this time?*

Silence hung heavy in the air for a long moment before the footsteps picked up again and faded into the distance, followed by the quiet sound of a closing door.

The last thing I need is Zander getting the wrong idea about me again, but her safety and the wellbeing of the team comes first. I don't know if she wants me here after what I said to her, but I'll be here the moment she needs me.

Looking down at Edelein's pale face, Gihon sighed.

I've really messed everything up, haven't I?

CHAPTER 12

BARGAINING

Dawn broke through the veil of night as Zander sat cross-legged on the ground, meditating in front of a stream just outside of the town's edge. His eyes were closed, drinking in the sounds and scents of the forest around him as birds sang sweetly to welcome in the coming daylight. The smell of dewdrops on the grass was alluring to the sphynx, the fresh scents of a cool morning bringing him comfort.

Behind him, a single snapping twig echoed, one of the Ehret's hairless ears turning backwards towards the sound. His eyes snapped open and Zander sprung up to his feet, already in a defensive stance and prepared to strike.

Zander growled as Solomon emerged from the bushes, the enemy's tan arms raised and gloved palms outspread.

"I am unarmed," Solomon spoke calmly. "By the looks of it, so are you."

"I'll kill you with my bare hands then!" Zander yowled, leaping towards him.

265

Solomon stepped quickly to the side, light on his feet as he dodged swipes and blows from Zander. He kept his arms raised as he spoke again.

"Slow down there, kittycat. I'm just here to talk. I'm not going to hurt you. At least, not right now, I'm not. I... I have a peace offering to make with you."

Zander growled, his stance low, knowing better than to trust the man in red. He lunged forward, exchanging a few quick blows as Solomon continued to evade and defensively counter. As he grabbed onto Solomon's wrist, he clenched his fist down to snap Solomon's bones. Instead, he backed away unsettled as Solomon's hand crumbled into nothing.

Solomon sighed, "See? Attacking me won't do you any good. I'm not even here, technically. This is a clay-based mimic form."

Solomon scooped the shattered clay from the ground and reformed his hand.

"As I said, I just want to talk. I have an offer to make that I have reason to believe you'll be rather interested in."

"You seek peace, and yet you are so cowardly that you refuse to be here to discuss it?" Zander hissed.

"That's because I'm not an idiot, Zander. If I came to you, you'd try to break my hand off, as we have just seen. I'm far, far away from you right now. I know you're trying to find me to get your little crystal back."

Zander straightened up, alerted.

"How do you know my name?" he asked warily.

"I'll tell you the same thing I told your Queen. It's my job to know things. You'll realize that soon enough," Solomon replied nonchalantly.

"You haven't explained why you suddenly want to make nice with us, homunculus. You really think we'd ever get along with you after you dared to hurt Edelein? You've stolen from our people and injured our Queen. You must be a fool."

Solomon sighed. "Look, I'm sorry about hurting her. She was being a brat and she needed to be punished, but that's not what I'm here about, so let's just move on and forget that it ever happened. I have something that you need, and you have something that I need. Let's call a truce for a moment and talk about it."

"Why should I trust you?"

"You know deep down that I was the one who scared off that phantasm that was attacking you. Mirror-shells are intense to fight against, and you newbies would have all probably died otherwise."

"All you managed was to get Mandus to pursue it and get himself hurt in the process."

"You guys… fought it?" Solomon responded, genuinely surprised for the first time. "I thought you were chasing after me. Who the hell was I running from, then?"

"The rest of us," Zander confirmed with a huff, folding his arms across his chest.

"Ah, I understand now. Well, let's let bygones be bygones. Just hear me out, okay? I'm not going to force you into anything. Just let me explain myself, and you can decide on your own if you want to accept my deal or not. I won't force you, and I won't hurt you. The choice will be entirely yours. How does that sound?"

Zander stared at him silently.

"I know how difficult it is to trust people when you've been through all the hardships that I know you've encountered," Solomon assured him. "I know you're just a poor, lost little sphynx who misses his master. I know you don't trust anyone because you're afraid that if you let people in, you'll lose them again. You and Edelein are similar in that sense."

Zander's face twitched as Solomon stepped closer,

continuing.

"You've always lived for others. After your master died, Eddie's family took you in. Her father was your new master, but he died. Now your current master, Alderis' sweet baby girl, is about to die, too; and you can't stand it. Every time she stumbles, every time you see the gaunt look in her eye, you want to scream and curse God for taking her away from you. You know her time is running out. You know her soul is withering right in front of you, and you are helpless to do anything."

Zander continued to stare at Solomon, his eyes narrow and grieving in silent ways that his lips would never proclaim aloud.

"You love her the way that King Alderis loved you. She's like a sweet little sister, isn't she? Your master's precious daughter, his only child, left in your care. Now she's going to die right in front of you, while all you can do is scream in silence about how unfair and cruel our world is for taking her so soon. She's too young for this fate, and you know it."

For a moment, it almost looked as if Zander's eyes were growing misty, but he chose to clench his fists, his claws pricking his palms to sharpen his focus as Solomon leaned in close.

"She's unmarried, a poor little *nullipara*. Childless. The end of the Great Ancestor Alderich's noble bloodline. You'll have no one left to serve, and the Kingdom will have no one left to worship."

"Gihon will find a cure for her," Zander forced the words out through gritted teeth.

Solomon laughed, stepping back. "Do you really trust Gihon, though? You know the destruction he's capable of. You cannot escape the idea that he could be the one you are waiting for, the one you fear."

Standing still for a moment, Solomon pointed with his thumb towards the town behind him.

The Man in Red

"In fact, Gihon's up in her room right now, and yet
something tells me the two of them are not currently working on
a cure." Solomon gave a knowing wink at Zander, who growled
quietly. "Gihon is alone with her, again, and yet why is she
still sick? Do you wonder if perhaps his masculine urges have
outweighed his diligence towards the future?"

Zander tensed his shoulders, considering Solomon's words,
as the man in red continued.

"For a man who may be destined to destroy your kingdom,
why would he do anything to help? What has he done to cure her
so far, Zander? Nothing. The Dirigent has been too busy trying to
hunt me down instead of devoting his time to saving her like he
promised. Interesting, is it not? You and I both know that if Gihon
had to choose between stopping me and saving her, he would pick
the former without a moment's hesitation. Edelein's a secondhand
plaything to Gihon, an afterthought behind his overwhelming hatred
for me."

"If he doesn't cure her, she will produce heirs before she
passes. She knows her responsibility," Zander said bluntly.

"Oh, but that's such a cruel fate. You know that you would
hate to see her last days carried out in such a way; a breeding
animal, all the while dying slowly and painfully, praying she has
enough strength to produce a healthy child in time so she can die
with the approval of her Royal Court. It's cruel, abusive. You'd do
anything to prevent that fate, wouldn't you? If she's cured, she will
be able to find love the way that you always wanted her to. Slowly,
patiently, and genuinely."

Solomon paused, attempting to read Zander's countenance.
Reaching into his breast pocket, Solomon produced a vial of blue
liquid that shimmered in the early morning light. Zander's eyes
were riveted on the vial.

"Ah, now I have your full attention," Solomon whispered

insidiously, "What if you could be the one who cures the Queen, Zander?"

Acting on instinct, Zander lurched at the vial. Solomon easily evaded him and held the potion high.

"Ah-ah-ah, this isn't free. Try that again and I will shatter the bottle. Or maybe I'll just destroy the town," Solomon's voice grew cold and threatening, "I've done it before. Ask your beloved Dirigent sometime."

The last time he was active, he destroyed an entire city, Gihon's words echoed in Zander's mind, giving weight to Solomon's words.

Zander hesitated before returning to an upright stance.

"Fine. Speak your wishes, quickly."

"The location of your leyline crystal. I know you have a second one, so I recommend not wasting Edelein's precious little time trying to convince me that you don't. Tell me where it is being kept, and the Queen's life is saved."

Zander hesitated again. The only change in his demeanor, his increased respiration. Solomon stepped closer, a look of feigned shock on his face.

"Would you really hesitate to save Alderis' daughter, your Edelein? You'd let her die over a rock?"

At Zander's silence, Solomon continued his temptation.

"Imagine it. You could be the one to grant her a second life, just as her father granted the same to you. It could be *you* that saves her. You could honor your promise to the King. You, not Gihon."

"This isn't about me," Zander hissed through clenched teeth. "I care not for the recognition, only that she lives. The only thing I need is for Edelein to be happy. It is what her father would have wanted."

"An easy choice, then. Hail the savior of the Luvemann bloodline."

The Man in Red

A slight nod by the Ehret was the only sign of agreement. Solomon worked to contain himself as Zander spoke quietly and betrayed his allies.

"There's a private estate, Gihon's personal home. On the road where we first encountered you, continue south down that path and take a right at the fork. Turn at the gorge, and continue straight that way. It's very well hidden, nestled in the forest. That's where we're keeping it."

"Good kitty," Solomon grinned smugly, tossing him the cure.

Zander's eyes widened as he caught the vial, holding it gently in his hands as if it were a delicate baby animal. He looked down at the mysterious liquid, and back up at Solomon.

"Will this really save Edelein?" Zander asked, a quiet desperation in his tone.

"It will revitalize her, as if she were never even sick to begin with. A second chance at life, like I said," Solomon replied. "If for whatever reason you need a second dose of it, come find me and we can work something out. Well… I suppose you're having trouble finding me already, aren't you? Don't worry. If it comes to that, I'll find you first."

"Why are you doing this?" Zander questioned softly.

"I have a few personal reasons to keep Edelein alive. It's got nothing to do with our little game of cat-and-mouse, I assure you. One part is a favor for a friend, one part my selfish curiosities, and one part because I think she and Gihon are going to ruin each other."

"You also think that she shouldn't be around him?" Zander's piercing green eyes met Solomon's gaze as he spoke.

"On the contrary. I have a theory that the closer she gets to him, the easier it will be to undo the bonds that shackle Gihon to his power. If you want Gihon to interfere less with your guardianship over her, it will actually benefit you to let her get close to him."

With that, Solomon turned around to leave, but Zander spoke again.

"Solomon, swear that you will not harm anyone that is in the safehouse."

"You have my word, sphynx. I will not lay a finger on anyone inside the house."

"How much value does your word have?" Zander asked.

"That, my friend, is up for you to decide. I haven't lied to you yet, have I?" Solomon replied as he continued to walk away.

Zander growled and lunged forward, tackling Solomon and smashing his body into fragments of shattered clay. Clutching tightly onto the vial, he stepped over the clay remains and began to walk back towards the town.

"That was for Edelein."

Edelein's eyes opened groggily, the Queen sitting up slowly in her bed as she clutched onto her throbbing skull with one hand. Her hair was disheveled, freed from its usual ponytail, and her gloves were folded neatly on the nightstand beside her.

I... I fainted last night, Edelein recalled slowly. *Did I hit my head? Is that why it hurts so much right now?*

Looking down, Edelein noticed that she was fully dressed other than her hands, and took a moment to assess the growing darkness that had spread from her fingernails to her knuckles.

Dread filled her heart with a sinking sensation, realizing that in only a few days the blight had spread such a distance.

"Two years..." Edelein mumbled quietly. "At this rate, my

life expectancy must be closer to a year or less. I'll be lucky if I even survive the ship back home at all."

Turning to her left, the Queen noticed a familiar figure, slumped in a chair next to her bed. Gihon was fast asleep, leaning back with deep and slow breaths. His vest was draped over the back of the chair, the Dirigent dozing in his white button-up shirt with a few of the top buttons loose, as usual.

Edelein looked at him in surprise, thinking.

Gihon must have found me after I collapsed and brought me to bed. He... stayed here with me all night? I thought he hated me after yesterday's spat. I don't understand men at all.

The lioness stood shakily to her feet, wincing as a stabbing pain shot through the side of her head. Grabbing a blanket from the bed, Edelein approached him with the silent steps of a trained hunter, trying not to wake him.

He must be exhausted. It can't be comfortable sleeping in that chair... poor thing. I'll let him rest. Edelein thought, spreading the blanket gently across his broad shoulders.

Edelein yelped in surprise as Gihon's eyes shot open, the Dirigent grabbing her arms suddenly. The blanket fell to the floor as he leapt to his feet, pinning her down onto the bed in one swift movement.

"Gihon! It's me!" Edelein pleaded as Gihon's grip on her wrists tightened from atop her body, eyes hazy.

Gihon stared down intensely at her for a moment, before his golden eyes cleared. Looking down at her as she squirmed underneath him, Gihon sprung back up, eyes wide.

"Edelein! I-I sincerely apologize. I did not mean to do that. I... I'm not used to waking up with someone standing over me in such a manner," Gihon stuttered, face red in embarrassment as he dusted himself off and took several steps away from her.

"No, I'm sorry that I startled you. I wasn't trying to. I

just… I saw you there, and you looked uncomfortable, so I was bringing you a blanket," Edelein explained, standing up and straightening out her clothing. "Have you been there all night?"

Gihon nodded, "Yes, and I was having a bit of a nightmare myself, which is why I was a bit on edge."

"What did you dream about?"

"Nothing, it's nothing. Just an old memory," Gihon assured her. "I found you on the floor last night, and I believe you hit your head when you fainted. How are you feeling now?"

"I'm alright, I think. Better than I felt yesterday, but a bit sore. It's still quite early, though, if you want to sleep in a bit more. I'm up now, so you can use my bed if you'd like to."

A knock on the door interrupted her thoughts, the Queen's ears perking up in alarm.

"It's Zander. Don't let him see you in here," Edelein instructed quietly, tail flicking as she made her way to the door.

Gihon nodded, slipping around the corner as Edelein opened the door. Zander stood in the doorway as expected, anxiously shifting his weight.

"Your Majesty." Zander greeted her with a deep bow. "I am sorry to disturb your rest so early in the morning, but I have an urgent matter to discuss with you."

"Oh, um, yeah…" Edelein's tail flicked again. "Can you give me a few minutes? I'll meet you outside."

Standing up straight from his bow, Zander eyed her curiously.

"You're already dressed, Your Majesty," he pointed out.

"I… I fell asleep quickly last night, without having time to change. I just woke up, so give me a minute to make myself decent and I shall meet you outside of the inn. Understood?"

"Yes, Your Majesty," Zander bowed his head again before turning to exit down the hallway.

The Man in Red

Edelein closed the door behind her, walking back into the room and facing Gihon. He smiled a bit awkwardly as he joked, "You know, all this sneaking around is going to give people the wrong idea."

"They're going to get the wrong idea regardless. I might as well try to save my dignity in the process," Edelein responded, pulling her hair up into a ponytail. "I'm going to go out and see what Zander wants. Give me a minute or two before you come down. If we enter together, it'll turn heads."

"I thought you said that people would get the wrong idea regardless," Gihon replied with a coy smirk, patting her shoulder reassuringly as she walked out of the room, hoping she wouldn't notice his other hand clutching at his chest again.

Outside, Zander stood next to Jinn, Thorne, and Lylia. Their expressions and whispers were uneasy amongst each other, but they turned and saluted Edelein as she approached. Lylia discreetly plucked a single black hair off of Edelein's lapel, not making eye contact as she swiftly disposed of it behind her back. Edelein blushed at the realization, embarrassed as she straightened herself up.

"Zander, what did you wish to speak with me about?"

"Your Majesty… I believe that I have acquired the cure for your illness," Zander said, holding out the vial to her.

Lylia's kind gaze met Edelein's as she spoke, "I checked it this morning, and it seems safe. No poison or anything. It actually seems to hold a bit of leyline energy in it, too, somehow."

"Wait, safe? Why wouldn't it be safe?" Edelein pressed.

"Where did you get this from?"

"Yeah, Zander, tell her where you got it from," Thorne laughed.

Zander's ears flattened as he looked away.

"I encountered Solomon last night," he admitted under his breath.

"What's going on?" Gihon asked as he approached, Luthro and Mandus in tow.

"Solomon apparently showed up and offered to help us," Edelein explained.

"That's impossible," Gihon refuted. "Solomon wouldn't help us. Surely, this must be some sort of trick."

"It wasn't technically Solomon, but a false form. It looked and sounded like him, but when I broke it, there was clay instead of flesh. He gave me this vial and told me it would cure Edelein's blight," Zander clarified, holding out the vial.

"What? Let me see that, please," Gihon requested as he took the vial and held it up against the sunlight.

"Do you think it's possible that Solomon would have a cure?" Jinn asked Gihon as the Dirigent evaluated the contents of the vial.

"That depends. Did he ask for something in return?" Gihon asked, looking at Zander.

Zander closed his eyes, looking down.

"Zander."

The Ehret looked away, not speaking.

"What did you give him, Zander?" Gihon pressed more sternly.

"He wanted to know the location of the second stone," Zander admitted after a beat.

"You told him where to go?!" Gihon shouted, incredulously.

The Man in Red

"It was for Edelein!" Zander retorted. "Her life is invaluable! We have endless amounts of those crystals at home. One means nothing to me compared to the weight of my Queen's safety. You don't... you don't understand what will become of us if Edelein doesn't survive this."

"Have you considered that it's not the crystal, but what he plans to do with them? Solomon could kill thousands of people if he gets the second one!" Gihon argued. "Did you really not believe that I would be able to cure her myself?"

"Thousands? If anything happens to our Queen, hundreds of thousands of Zenluvians die and a thousand years of culture gets erased as our land, our people, crumble forever!"

Gihon paused, lost in thought as he realized the gravity of Zander's words.

Zander does make a point. Edelein has no heir, and they seem to be pretty hard set on bloodline succession, Gihon processed with a long pause.

"If Edelein dies, why can't Nalo appoint a new ruler?" Gihon asked suddenly.

"Edelein won't die!" Zander yelled, grabbing the collar of Gihon's shirt. "Do not dare speak of such things!"

Edelein sighed, chiming in.

"I do not know what you think Nalo does, but Nalo is an overseer of our people due to an agreement with the First Ancestor Alderich. Without my bloodline, there is no Alderich, giving Nalo no reason to protect us as the contract will have been voided. Nalo has no interest in appointing a successor, and we would likely be left simply to fend for ourselves. Nalo is much more... hands-off than it seems you think," The Queen explained.

"Edelein's life is worth infinitely more to us than a mere few thousand Caandemites. I would wipe your continent off the face of Tevus by my own hand before I let her die under my care,"

Zander hissed as he continued to fume at the Dirigent.

Lylia nodded solemnly, agreeing with Zander. "Ultimately, if we have to choose between our people and yours... we have to choose ours, Gihon. I'm sorry, but I know you would do the same."

Lylia is right. I want the best for the Zenluvians, but if I could only save either their people or mine, I would easily choose to protect mine.

"What have you even done for her, Dirigent? You sneak off with her when no one is looking, but she is no closer to recovery than the day she first met you!" Zander jeered.

"Enough! Gihon is not sneaking around with anyone. I do not appreciate your tone, Ehret," Edelein snapped briefly, before sighing. "Zander does make a point though. Not about the cure, but about the trade. Not only do we have plenty of crystals, but now we know for certain exactly where Solomon is heading. If we head back to the house now, we can intercept him and retrieve our crystal from him. Giving him the location might not be a bad idea, because now we know where he'll be."

"Your Majesty, if I may," Luthro said, "if these crystals are common for you, why go to such lengths to retrieve the one he took?"

"It's like the Dirigent said; I am more concerned with what Solomon plans to do with them. I also educated the other alchemists about our guardian Nalo, and how the crystals are a treasure not meant to be abused. I would prefer to not have Nalo's gift fall into the wrong hands, for the wellbeing of my people."

Gihon sighed, calming himself. "If Solomon asked for something in return, there is a possibility that this is a genuine cure. Nothing is guaranteed, given that Solomon is notoriously untrustworthy, but that does add some legitimacy to the case. If only I could study it, and–"

"Now is no time to be studying. We have no time to waste

if we want to intercept Solomon before he reaches the house, and Queen Edelein needs a cure as quickly as possible," Jinn commented, looking anxiously towards the forest.

"Jinn is right," Zander huffed.

After a moment, Gihon nodded as well.

"I also agree with Jinn," the Dirigent affirmed. "I would love to study whatever is in this vial… but right now, we need Edelein to be healthy, so she can fight. We can't risk her disease worsening and losing out on a valuable member of our team. I also don't love the idea of knowing that Solomon is on his way to ambush Jana and Spira without being able to intercept him. Edelein, the choice is yours. Do you trust the elixir?"

Edelein hesitated for a beat before taking the vial from Gihon's hand, peering into its contents curiously.

"I'll try it," Edelein decided.

"Are you sure?" Gihon pressed, a bit nervous. "It is from Solomon, after all."

"Didn't you just say you'd trust my judgement?" Edelein chuckled, popping the cork off of the vial and holding it up to her lips.

Lylia held her hands up in anticipation, ready to help and heal if needed. Gihon looked down at Edelein in concern as she drank the glowing liquid, one hand raised slightly on instinct to catch her if she swooned.

Everyone looked at the Queen expectantly, silent as she smacked her lips and handled the empty vial to Gihon.

"It tastes vaguely like leyline tea, but more bitter. It's… not great. I think I'd rather just drink leyline tea."

"How do you feel?" Zander quietly asked Edelein as he touched her shoulders, the sphynx's voice surprisingly gentle opposed to his usual brooding demeanor.

Zander's eyes softened, emotion washing over him as

Edelein nodded enthusiastically.

"I feel… great. Like a new fire is burning in my veins, revitalizing my spirit. I feel lighter, as if the weight of my aching bones has been lifted."

Everyone clamored in excitement at the Queen's words. Zander turned around, covering his eyes with one hand as his shoulders shook, relief flooding through his tense muscles. Lylia hugged Edelein, smiling.

"To think that Solomon had a cure for it this whole time…" Luthro murmured.

"Back when we first fought that cult, all they ever did was create backlash after backlash. It's not too surprising that he came up with a cure since tons of his acolytes kept getting blighted and dying off," Mandus replied with a shrug.

"Why would Solomon go through the trouble, though?" Luthro asked. "If I were a cult leader, I would just make something up about the blight being a blessing that guarantees them passage into… whatever made-up cult afterlife they think they have."

"Oh, right. I forgot Solomon doesn't have a heart," Mandus agreed.

Ahead of them, Edelein was already at the edge of the treeline, looking back at the others.

"We don't have time to waste!" Edelein called. "Solomon is well on his way to the safehouse. If we hurry, we can make it there by sundown and intercept him!"

Sundown? Gihon wondered. *It took us two days to get here. Though, I suppose we were going at a slower pace to accommodate for her illness, and had to rest early due to injuries and roadblocks. If we make faster time and nothing goes wrong, I suppose it is possible to be there by the end of today, considering how early it is right now.*

Looking up from his thoughts, Gihon jogged ahead to

catch up with the rest of the group as they headed into the dappled morning light of the forest.

"Gihon, should I be running ahead to warn everyone?" Mandus asked.

"Absolutely not. We have to stick together. If you run into Solomon alone, he'll kill you."

"I'll be fine!" Mandus insisted.

"I know you're as worried about Spira and Jana as I am, but they can hold their own if they need to. I cannot risk a student's life by sending you out alone."

Mandus sighed as Gihon made his way up to Edelein, ending the conversation.

"What is leyline tea?" Gihon asked Edelein as he made his way to the front, matching her quick pace. "You mentioned it earlier, and I wanted to ask you to tell me more."

The leyline under Ravencroft is a point of convergence between several planes of existence. Before Arvien contained the leyline, it was the source of Ravencroft's untamable wilds within the marshes. How did they turn that... into tea?

Edelein was on alert, mouth ajar and ears swiveling. She was trotting at a decent speed, placing each silent step expertly under her to avoid twigs and leaves. One ear turned towards Gihon as he talked, but she continued to fix her gaze on her surroundings as she spoke.

"Oh. You understand that leyline crystals are imbued with leyline energy? Stones weren't the only thing affected by the Deepwood's leyline. I believe I mentioned that our flora and even fauna are affected by the presence of our leyline as well. Simply put, we dry leyline-infused leaves and brew them. I had brought a block of it on the ship over, but I believe it was left behind somewhere on our journey since I haven't seen it in a while. I drink it daily, back at home," Edelein explained.

"Is it common in Zenluve?" Luthro asked from behind them.

"It is, in upper classes. The price is of no issue to me, though. Compared to a tea that is not infused, though, the price tag runs significantly higher. Dirigent Gihon, would you be interested in trying it?"

Gihon nodded eagerly, "Quite. Are you inviting me for a visit?"

"That, or if I can find wherever that tea block went, I'll leave some with you," Edelein chuckled softly.

"I do enjoy tea. That would be lovely," Gihon mused.

"I like when you ask questions," Edelein replied. "You've got a curious heart."

Gihon paused for a moment, thinking. "Do you mind if I ask you more, then?"

Edelein laughed and nodded, "Speak, raven."

She's decided to be more open about her culture. This is my chance to get the answers I've wondered about since we met.

"The other day, when the phantasm attacked the autowagons…" Gihon started, blush creeping up his cheeks as he recalled the event. "When I, ah, broke your fall. I couldn't help but notice that your pupils have a unique shape to them."

"That's not a question," she replied with another laugh. "I do have diamond-shaped pupils. If you're wondering why, I am afraid I cannot answer fully. As far as I am aware, my great ancestor Alderich was a beast with diamond-shaped pupils, and the gene passed down to the firstborn of every king thereafter."

"Only the firstborn?" Gihon wondered aloud before he continued to interview the Queen. "Was Alderich not a lion, then? My understanding has been that your noble ancestry was leonine in heritage. The Lion Kings of Zenluve, are you not?"

"We refer to him as a lion, but Alderich was an ancient

beast far greater than a lion. No one really knows the exact details, but back in the age of unfathomable creatures, he was one of those unfathomable. Our ancient tribe described him as lion-like in appearance, with a tufted tail and glorious mane. We suspect that his species is what today's lions descended from. We marry exclusively lion zoa to preserve the appearance of lionfolk, to honor our heritage."

"Luthro, I think Alderich was a Divine Beast," Mandus whispered.

"There has never been a single case of documented evidence to support the theory of Divine Beasts existing," Luthro denied with a sigh. "Nothing but elven anecdotes."

"There was no documented evidence of Zenluve existing either until they suddenly showed up here. You believe in them now, don't you?"

"I suppose that is true. If any corner of the world was harboring Divine Beasts, it would probably be an esoteric zoa kingdom," Luthro conceded.

Mandus nodded eagerly, turning his attention back towards Edelein as she continued to answer Gihon's questions.

"Luvemann firstborns are another mystery of my family's past, yes. The kings of old had several children with each generation, only the firstborn taking the throne, as expected. It seems genetically impossible, but every firstborn has the signature diamond pupils of Alderich, and not a single other child past that. They usually have thicker hair, and have never once lacked the tufted tail and lion ears. Firstborn ears are usually... a bit pointier, as well. Not significantly, but not as rounded as the transmuted lion zoa wives. Also, until me, every single firstborn was male. Almost as if Alderich himself had reincarnated into each firstborn. Zenluvian texts refer to this phenomenon as the Bestial Spirit, or sometimes the Soul of Alderich."

Gihon took in all of the information in stunned silence, nodding as he listened.

"What happens if a firstborn dies? Have any second children developed these features over time after a death?"

"That's the interesting part," Edelein answered. "Not a single Crown Prince has died prematurely, even a thousand years ago. The King has only ever died after taking the throne and bearing another Crown Prince. Statistically, a miracle, and yet here we are. Some Zenluvians fear not for my premature death, as I have yet to bear the Crown Prince that marks each King. However, because I was the first child to be born as an eldest female, we are unsure if the protections still apply to me or not. I do seem to possess the Bestial Soul, but some wonder if it is possibly a weaker version of it due to the fact that one of the key traits is missing."

Fascinating.

"Excuse me, Your Majesty," Lylia started suddenly. "Should we be using the communication stone to alert the others at the house?"

"I was thinking the same thing, but I didn't want to say it," Thorne admitted.

Luthro answered them, still facing forward. "No. If the relay array goes off, they will think Solomon is attacking us, not the other way around. If that's the case, they would choose to leave the crystal unguarded at the house while they come to find us."

"Luthro is correct," Gihon confirmed as his student beamed confidently. "All we can do with the array is a single noise, which they have been tasked to interpret as us catching up to Solomon ourselves. We didn't exactly prepare for finding Solomon and telling him the location as a part of the plan."

Zander rolled his eyes and snapped, "Edelein is cured. I would do it again in a heartbeat. Do not speak to me that way, corvid."

The Man in Red

"Are you good for a little run, Your Majesty?" Jinn asked, stretching his arms.

"I've been waiting months for a run through the woods like this. I'll race you!" Edelein laughed, launching herself forward into the underbrush.

Jinn and Zander took off after her, Thorne pushing himself forward with a tailwind to keep up. Lylia sighed, looking apologetically at the alchemists.

"If you can use that speed-enhancing alchemy again, now would be a great time for it," Lylia admitted as vines sprung from the ground, propelling her forwards. She grabbed onto a tree branch as it lowered itself, seeming to bend to her will. The branch pulled her, the momentum carrying her off as she chased after her allies.

Mandus grinned widely, looking in eager anticipation at Luthro and Gihon. The two alchemists sighed and nodded.

"Speed is not my preference, but I don't want to lose the others," Gihon confirmed as a large array glowed underneath the feet of all three men.

"Don't worry, I'll start you off easy with an array that goes around the same speed as Edelein and the others. You're not ready for my usual speeds. If you ran into a tree or something, that would be the end of you. We'll play it safe."

Crouching down into a runner's starting pose, Mandus smirked.

"Please keep all arms and legs in standard running movement. Exercise caution around obstacles. And as always, thank you for traveling with Mandus Rail."

As Mandus' speed alchemy began to flow, enhancing the bodies of the three alchemists, they all took off to catch up with Edelein and the others.

"Don't get distracted by the visual stimuli around you, and just focus on the programmed path," Mandus cautioned the other alchemists as their speed increased. "You see that golden trail in the air? Just focus on that."

My body feels automated, as if I have no control. Gihon realized uncomfortably, his eyes locking onto the thin golden strand ahead of him. *When taking in so much visual input, the body does the simplest thing, which is to follow the trail that has been laid out. It's fascinating, but terrible to experience. Speed was never my preference.*

Each step further continued to change the scenery around them, trees blurring into masses of verdant greens. The world seemed to stretch ahead as the group continued on in silence, enhanced speeds making light work of the distance.

As the sun began to set, Edelein slowed her steps and held up one hand to the others. Her movements were perfectly silent, years of her hunting proficiency showing. The Queen looked like a stalking lioness as she crouched low, eyes peering through the underbrush.

"He's up ahead," Edelein whispered, tail hovering just above the ground.

Gesturing forward with a small nod, the group noticed bright white locks of hair catching the dying sunlight as Solomon stood alone, walking calmly through a large open clearing. He was facing away as he walked off in the opposite direction, seeming to not notice the lioness stalking him. The ambient sound of rushing water indicated that they were close to the gorge, the safehouse hidden just beyond.

This is the clearing that my students use to train. Gihon

scanned the area, recognizing where the trees opened up to the edge of the gorge, a steep drop leading to the deep river below.

"Thorne, keep a headwind on me. I'm going to get a bit closer to him and strike from the left. Gihon and Zander, head to the right and go in the moment I lunge, while he's distracted. Mandus and Jinn, be on standby for pursuit in case he tries to flee by guarding the area in front of him. Luthro, you can use your pocket watch to restrain his movement as well. Lylia, stay back here with Thorne and be prepared to go in or stop Solomon if he retreats. He's alone, so we can take him out right now if we are smart about this. We can surround him."

Everyone nodded silently as Edelein peeled off to the western side of the clearing, breaking away into their respective positions. Zander's body was low to the ground in a similar manner to Edelein's as Gihon crouched next to him, trying to conceal their large frames in the shrubs as they kept their eyes fixed on the homunculus ahead.

What a good time to be a feline, Gihon thought, dismayed. *I can't stalk prey in this manner, the way that Edelein and Zander do. I'll be lucky if Solomon doesn't notice me right now.*

As each member found their positions surrounding the man in red, time began to crawl slower.

"Why hasn't Edelein struck him yet?" Zander muttered under his breath after a minute of waiting.

"Is there an issue?" Gihon asked, looking ahead at Solomon, who was still walking by himself, unaware of the predators waiting to attack him.

Zander shook his head briefly, before his ears perked up and he lifted his head up slightly.

"Solomon isn't alone. Edelein is being ambushed!" Zander sprung to his feet in alarm, dashing into the dark foliage.

Gihon jumped up, chasing after Zander anxiously.

Crown of the Alchemist

She's fighting against someone by herself. If it's those homunculi, she needs help. Panic settled into Gihon's chest, tugging at his heart as he poured every ounce of strength into his feet as they pounded into the ground below, begging to reach her in time.

On the other side of the clearing where Edelein was creeping slowly, a sudden movement activated the feline instincts in her muscles as she leapt aside, tumbling out of the way of a man as he threw himself at her.

Edelein tumbled out of the way of her assailant, pressing her feet against the cultist's chest as the momentum catapulted him back. The Queen flipped back onto her feet quickly to lay eyes on three more ambushers cautiously approaching, lurking in the shadows.

"Two in front. One behind. Plus the flipped one… that makes four in total," Edelein muttered to herself as she began to reach for her bow.

The lioness' ears twitched in response to sudden movement behind Edelein, her muscles tensing as she prepared for action. The man behind lunged forward with his alchemical gauntlet sparked, desperate to subdue the Queen. At the same time, one of the men ahead of her ran to rush her from the front. With a swift turn of her shoulders, Edelein allowed the gauntlet to pass by her as she retaliated towards the cultist with an elbow strike to his face. Edelein jutted a single foot out to stumble the assailant forward, shocking the cultist in front as his gauntlet met his ally's chest.

The third enemy cocked his arm back, twisting his hand and sending a lightning charge towards the lioness. Edelein sidestepped, grabbing the second cultist and holding him in the line of fire as the lightning blast hit him instead, electricity coursing through his body and immobilizing him.

Without missing a beat, Edelein dashed forward towards the third foe, leaping at his shoulders. Locking his head between powerful quadriceps, Edelein flipped back and threw him down onto the ground, the cultist landing harshly on his knees with a loud crack. With a combination of a cat's grace and an absorbent amount of torque, Edelein twisted her body to land a powerful kick to the kneeling man's head, his body falling to the ground in a slump.

Whipping around to face her final assailant, Edelein laid eyes on the man who had stumbled from her initial attack. The cultist was silently charging up his gauntlet, the device glowing with a warm orange light as flames began to sputter to life. The relentless warrior Queen quickly removed her bow from over her shoulder, pulling the bow back as her thumb touched its array. A hardlight arrow appeared, just as easily as it did the first time, nocked and ready to strike. Edelein wasted no time in letting it loose at the man's right lung, the cultist stumbling back as his flames shot into the sky.

With the might of pure wilderness in her arms, Edelein slid behind the cultist, wrapping her bow around his neck to keep the air from reaching his punctured lungs. The cultist's arms flailed about, trying desperately to get the lioness off of his neck as he struggled for air. Edelein kicked the back of the man's right knee to get his body lower, smirking to herself as grabbed his head, pushing him until the cultist bowed before the Queen. Edelein quickly turned her bow around while planting her boot on the cultist's back, pulling the bow back as far as it could go before letting it snap straight into the back of the masked man's head.

"Edelein!" Gihon called out as he arrived with Zander, looking down in surprise to see the bodies of four cultists at her feet.

"What are you doing here?" she hissed. "Get in position! I'm going to attack Solomon–"

"You were taking a while, and Zander sensed the ambush. We came to help, but I see that you are fully capable of handling yourself. My apologies."

Edelein looked at both of the men with contempt, rolling her eyes.

"I can handle myself. You of all people, Zander, should know this about me," Edelein scolded.

Zander bowed his head in apology, ears flat.

"I'm sorry, Your Majesty," Zander mumbled.

"You two should apologize for blowing our cover, instead," Edelein moaned, gesturing over Gihon's shoulder to where Solomon was waving at them.

"Hello!" Solomon called out. "Stop skulking about and get out here!"

CHAPTER 13

THE GORGE

Emerging from the bushes, the party surrounded Solomon, the white-haired homunculus laughing mockingly at the heroes' failed attempt to stop him.

Solomon was standing towards the edge of the large clearing with his back towards the drop of the gorge to his right, the forest behind him on his left.

"Goodness, my dear Edelein. Did my cure really work that well? How *ever* did you catch up to me so fast?" he said, slapping a hand to his head with dramatic flair. "I knew I shouldn't have agreed to help you."

"It's 'Your Majesty,' scumbag," Edelein spat.

"Oh, don't be like that. You should be thanking me!" Solomon replied.

"I have no gratitude to offer to a man who steals that which belongs to my people."

Solomon pouted, looking at Zander. "I guess the Luvemann

grace only applies to cat-boys, then. Right, Zander? You got away with stealing from them as a child, but there's nothing left for me."

Zander hissed, ears flat.

"Do not speak to my Ehret again," Edelein warned. "Your attitude is begging for another bite. I went easy on you last time, you know. I would very much like to sink my teeth into you right now, and tear your flesh from your bones."

"Take me out to dinner first, Your Majesty," Solomon winked. "There's no need to be so feral, little wildcat. Let's keep our hands–and teeth–to ourselves this time, alright?"

Gihon narrowed his eyes, speaking in a low tone, "Enough of this. Solomon, give us the crystal and we will make your death swift and merciful. Fight back, and it will hurt a lot more."

"Mmm… all I heard is 'fight back,' which I'm glad to agree with you on. However, as much as I would love to have another charming family reunion with you, I'm having my long-awaited audience with the noble Lion Queen of Zenluve right now. Do you mind waiting your turn?"

"Family reunion?" Edelein asked, turning to Gihon. "What does he mean by that, Gihon?"

"Don't listen to him," Gihon responded curtly.

Solomon gasped dramatically, his hands flying up to cover his mouth as he exclaimed in astonishment.

"Oh, I *cannot* believe this right now. Gihon, you didn't tell them? I'm so wounded."

Edelein looked to Gihon, whose mouth was shut tight, lips pressed together in frustration. Noticing his silence, the Queen looked ahead at Solomon.

"Spit it out, homunculus. How exactly do you know Gihon?" she demanded.

Solomon covered his eyes with one hand, laughing in disbelief. Dropping his hand in an exaggerated motion, Solomon confirmed the fear that Edelein had been hoping she was misunderstanding.

"I suppose I cannot fault you for failing to see any resemblances between my perfect form and that ugly stoic next to you. You see, little cub, Dirigent Gihon is my baby brother."

"Your brother?!" Edelein snapped, whipping around to face the Dirigent. "Gihon, did you not think that this would be *valuable* information for us to know?!"

Silence fell over the large clearing, the sound of the rushing river at the gorge's base resonating louder than ever.

Gihon scowled, clenching his fists as he stared straight ahead at Solomon, avoiding the Queen's judgemental stare, "That man is no brother of mine."

"Don't be like that, Gihon," Solomon pouted mockingly. "I am many things, but a liar is not one of them. I'd rather not be related to you, either, were I to have the choice. Unfortunately, Arvien made me, just as she made you. I may have been incomplete to her, but you and I both know that I am just as much a pathetic excuse of a son to her as you are. You seem to insist so often that Mother Arvien loved each of her children equally, so would she have wanted you to deny our brotherhood? Or am I incomplete to you as well?"

"Incomplete does not begin to describe you. *Abomination* would be my word of choice," Gihon retorted, exhausted by the homunculus' rambling.

"You're so harsh, Gihon. Do you think I deserve to be called such things, simply because my body lacks a soul?"

"I could not care less about the condition of your soul; present or not, cursed, withered, nonexistent. Thousands lay dead at your feet from your self-indulgent hedonism, and I will spare you no more mercy. Your ego has driven you mad, Solomon."

"Would you not be driven to madness as well, if you were

made to love someone who will never return that love in the same way? Someone who died because she loved another more than you, refusing to spare a single glance in your direction?" Solomon looked briefly at Edelein, then back to Gihon. "Losing a love that you were never destined to have?"

"Arvien *did* love you!" Gihon gritted his teeth in frustration, knuckles white under his gloves.

"No, Arvien loved Hiddekel! She loved that stupid baby so much that it killed her. Doesn't that wound you, Gihon? She could have lived for us, but she chose to die to be able to love someone else!"

"Arvien willingly gave her life to have Hidde, but a mother's love does not wane upon the creation of a new child. You sound like a jealous infant. Which is normal for you, I suppose," Gihon replied with a sharp exhale.

I thought Gihon was an only child... just how many siblings does he even have? Edelein wondered, mind racing as she monitored the argument between brothers whose words were growing more heated.

"Maybe Arvien still loved you, her little pet raven. You had a soul. You were complete in your own way. I never asked to be made! I never asked for Arvien to program this unconditional love into me, just to refuse to love me back!" Solomon yelled, burning passionately as he confronted his brother.

Taking a moment, Solomon let out a tense breath. "That's why I'm going to open the Gates of Heaven. I'll force God himself to give me the soul that I deserve, and the world will have no choice but to recognize me as a human, true and complete. I'll finally be undeniably *perfect,* in every way."

Gihon's eyes widened in realization at Solomon's words, before letting out a laugh in disbelief.

"My, you really have finally lost it, haven't you?" Gihon

said. "You still harbor this obsession with the Gates of Heaven? I cannot believe I'm saying such a thing, but I truly, genuinely believed that you were smart enough to resist attempting this little stunt again after what happened in Othalgar. The entire city is a necropolis because of you! You cannot possibly think you can still open the Gates!"

"Oh, but it's different this time. With a little help from a certain someone's leyline crystals, I'll be able to power it properly. Thanks, Eddie." Solomon winked at Edelein, who growled in return.

"I'll kill you," Edelein rasped.

"This is no way to thank your savior. Zander, you would never harm the man who healed your Queen, would you?" Solomon smirked, looking at the Ehret.

"I kill at her command." Zander responded flatly, drawing his blades and lowering his stance.

"So obedient," Solomon laughed. "It's cute, isn't it?"

Gihon spoke up again, the homunculus turning to face him. "Your plan won't work, Solomon. Even if it does, the energy required would still wipe out thousands of people. I won't let anyone else die because of you."

"I deserve to be complete, Gihon!" Solomon raised his voice again, his emotions surprisingly raw. "I deserve a soul, just like you! This world is cruel and unfair anyway, so why not make my mark of justice? Do you not weep for those who were never afforded a real chance at being alive?"

"You *are* alive, Solomon," Gihon reasoned. "Alive enough to kill others on your own selfish whims and eternally disgrace the Marleogne mantle. Perhaps you being alive is the problem, in fact."

"I breathe, I stand, and yet do I truly live? Blood may flow without a soul, but what is the purpose of a heartbeat when the song of a spirit does not sing alongside it?" Solomon lowered his voice to a soft growl as he paused for a moment, taking a deep breath.

As he exhaled, Solomon continued.

"You cannot stop me, Dirigent. I do believe that Aim and Kimaris have brought welcome gifts for you, as well," Solomon grinned, snapping his fingers as the two homunculi stepped out from behind him and into the light of the setting sun.

Gihon's face paled as he noticed the female homunculus, Aim, dragging Mandus behind her by his hair. Luthro was beside him as Kimaris shoved him forward, both students bound by rope around their wrists.

"Mandus! Luthro!" Gihon ran towards his students, taking a few steps forward but stopping as the ground split beneath his feet, encasing his legs in pillars of stone.

Solomon laughed as he held the array, heartless. "You see, little brother, you have one notable weakness. You're easily distracted when someone you care about is in danger. It makes it pathetically easy to get the upper hand on you."

"Where are the Zengarde?" Edelein asked Zander under her breath as the homunculi both threw their captives onto the ground.

"Your wolf is otherwise engaged, if that's what you're wondering," Solomon explained, leaving Edelein unsure if he heard her or if he was simply continuing to prattle on. "He's decided to thin my numbers himself, much like his noble Queen. If you're curious, I can confirm that he is, in fact, heavily outnumbered."

Edelein gnashed her teeth as Solomon continued, gesturing towards a third homunculus as he emerged from the thicket of trees, a draekis male with a body covered in white scales. His draconic features were adorned with shimmering scales and small horns that were angled backwards. He nodded at Solomon, who in turn continued to ramble towards the tense group in front of him.

"I don't believe you've had the pleasure of meeting Agares," Solomon gestured to the drakeling beside him, who bowed his head silently. "He'll be joining us today, so I hope you don't mind being outnumbered."

"Outnumbered?" Gihon scoffed. "Where did you learn to count? There's only four of you."

"Are you sure?" Solomon smirked.

"The draekis smells like the false Solomon that I spoke with," Zander whispered under his breath. "The scent of cold mud."

Agares extended a scaly palm outwards, a white array rumbling the ground beneath as clay figures began to rise from the dirt. They were relatively formless humanoids, solid white with no features other than an unfamiliar sigil on their faces. Dozens of puppets rose to their feet around the clearing, surrounding the group and beginning to close in. Gihon tensed his muscles, breaking himself free from the ground that encased his feet as he drew his cloth shortsword from midair, readying his stance.

"Are you still sure you're not outnumbered?" Solomon repeated, smugly.

As clay golems began to approach Gihon and the others slowly, a volley of daggers suddenly shot out from the underbrush. Every dagger landed squarely in the head of each golem, the figures crumbling from the impact. A single arrow zoomed through the air towards Agares, breaking his concentration on the golem array as the draekis dashed out of the way.

"Is that *my* arrow? I thought I'd lost all of them by now," Edelein asked herself quietly, recognizing the form.

Another dagger sang through the air, the blade lodging directly into the rope binding on Mandus' wrists. The fox let out a surprised yelp, pulling his hands away as the knife sliced through his restraints. Mandus looked down at his now-freed hands, his shock melting into a wide grin.

On the ground by each pile of clay rubble, the daggers began to tremble as they were lifted into the air again, returning to their master as Thorne emerged from the bushes. His hands were extended, commanding the winds as his throwing knives hovered in an arc over his head.

"Didn't anyone tell you not to bring golems to a gale fight?" Thorne smirked.

Solomon let out an annoyed groan, gesturing to Agares as the draekis restarted his array. Golems began to rise from the ground again, slowly returning their shape.

Mandus hurried over to Luthro, holding the remaining dagger as he began to cut through his friend's binding.

"Thorne's making a distraction for us to escape," Mandus commented as the rope snapped underneath his blade.

"I genuinely just think that Thorne's full of himself and wants the attention. The distraction is just an added bonus, not his objective," Luthro replied in a hushed whisper, rubbing his wrists and pulling out his pocket watch. "Better than nothing, though. We can use this."

Tapping his watch to his bright green array, Luthro swung at Aim's hat, knocking it from her head to disarm her. The mage jumped towards it, not missing a beat as she seemed to anticipate the blow. Aim caught her hat in midair, twisting to face Luthro as she fired a quick blast at his feet.

Beside her, shadows began to rise as Kimaris prepared his summon. As his violet array ignited, the creeping darkness began to form a chariot, his shadowy steed eager to race as he mounted up, lance at the ready.

"Go after the ranged strikers. I've got these two," Aim growled, Kimaris nodding in response and charging towards Thorne.

As Kimaris' chariot raced towards Thorne, the fae-blessed Fuuntet tumbled out of the way with a moment to spare. Landing in front of Lylia, his elven ally slammed her staff into the ground as tree roots began to swell and disrupt the ground below, slowing Kimaris' chariot.

Gihon let out a sharp exhale, swinging his shortsword in every direction as golems continued to surround them. Zander remained by his side, his dual blades making light work of the clay figures as they crumbled. Looking around at the piles as they slowly reassembled themselves, the sphynx grumbled to himself as he tried to think of a solution.

"I need to reach the draekis," Edelein noted, taking out another golem with a quick light arrow and turning to Zander. "Can you boost me out of here? We're making no progress like this."

"Cover me, corvid," Zander demanded, sheathing his weapons and locking his hands together as he crouched down.

Gihon nodded, sweeping his sword in a wide arc and knocking a handful of golems down. He kept his back turned on Zander, protecting the sphynx's other side as Edelein ran forward, placing one boot onto his intertwined fingers. Lifting upwards, Zander flung Edelein high into the air, the lioness flipping to correct her angle as she placed both feet onto her bow, pulling it back with her entire body as another hardlight arrow formed.

Good to know that I can activate the array with my boot, Edelein thought, her gambit playing out in her favor as the arrow shot forward, striking Agares' shoulder.

The draekis cried out and turned away quickly, his golems slowing and crumbling slightly. The distraction allowed Gihon and Zander to take out the remaining figures, sighing in relief when they noticed the clay enemies were not regenerating yet.

On the other side of the clearing, Aim was dodging rapid flying daggers as Thorne's blades whizzed past her head, grumbling as she tried to line up a clear shot at him. As Aim threw a fireball forward, Thorne retaliated with a small tunnel of wind, redirecting her attack into the ground.

Crown of the Alchemist

The witch began to conjure a second fireball, running towards Thorne to close the distance and prevent him from using the wind to divert her again. Stepping back, Thorne flicked his wrist and sent his winds to surround Aim, oxygen pouring into the space in front of her as her pyre began to burn brighter and hotter, igniting and exploding in her hand. Aim let out a pained cry as the flames seared her skin, charring her right hand.

"Didn't anyone tell you not to bring fire to—"

"Shut up! Shut up, shut up, shut up!" Aim screeched, superheating her nails and clawing ferociously at Thorne as rage boiled in her veins. "You are *so annoying!*"

Holding tightly onto Thorne's final dagger, Luthro looked around to assess the oncoming enemies. Two cultists were running at him, gauntlets charged and crackling with electricity.

Light work, Luthro thought to himself as he threw the dagger, pelting one of the cultists in the chest.

Thorne's blade wedged itself just under the cultist's collarbone, near his shoulder as he cried out and stumbled. As the second cultist approached Luthro, he threw an amplified hook punch, electricity cracking as it hungered for its target. Luthro dodged the punch, retaliating with a quick jab to his neck before grabbing the gauntlet and increasing its mass. The gauntlet grew impossibly heavy, pulling the cultist to the ground with a loud thunk.

A sudden impact knocked straight into Luthro, wind being driven from the student's chest as Mandus tackled him to the ground. A split second later, Kimaris' chariot raced past, his sharp lance piercing the air where Luthro had stood just a moment before.

"Sorry. I didn't want you to die," Mandus apologized. "I didn't mean to knock you down like that, I was just trying to pull you out of the way. Sometimes I forget that you weigh like eighty pounds."

"Can it, Mandus. Thanks anyway," Luthro sighed, standing up and dusting off his pristinely-kept uniform. "We need to help the others with those golems, so let's finish up these cultists and get a move on."

Mandus nodded in agreement, glancing forward to where Agares stood. A barrage of light arrows rained down on him, deflected by a stone pillar created by Solomon to protect the draconic summoner.

Solomon raised more pillars around Agares as Edelein continued to shoot from a nearby treetop, perched expertly and barely visible.

"Agares, send some golems to the Queen," Solomon commanded, golden eyes fixed on Gihon to gauge the Dirigent's response.

"Come on, Gihon, show us your tricks," Solomon muttered under his breath as the golems began to shift their target, walking towards Edelein's roost. "I'm waiting."

Gihon stood up straighter as the golems changed focus, noticing their new path. Turning to Zander, the Dirigent began to explain.

"We need to relocate Edelein. They're targeting her now."

"What's your suggestion, then?" Zander asked, pelting forward and thinning the enemy's numbers as they ignored him, piling up at the base of Edelein's tree. "Are you telling me this because you have alchemy that will help, or because you want me to tear them apart by hand? I'd prefer the latter."

"I do have something," Gihon admitted, "though I suspect

that Solomon is anticipating it."

As the golems continued to pile on, clamoring over each other and reaching at branches to hoist themselves further up, Edelein looked down in alarm as she fired shot after shot, taking each golem out one at a time.

"There's too many of them!" Edelein cried out, looking around for an escape route, another tree branch within leaping distance that would support her weight.

A quick blade slashed through the mass of clay figures, leaps and dashes cutting them down as they fell back to the ground.

"Jinn!" Edelein breathed a sigh of relief. "You're alright!"

"My apologies for the delay, Your Majesty," Jinn bowed his head. "The woods were swarming with more of those cultists, but I've cleared them out. What... exactly are these things, though?"

"No time to explain. Keep them at bay, please," Edelein requested, turning her focus back to Agares as she tried to pierce through the stone barrier.

Kimaris eyed Gihon and Zander as they fought their way towards Edelein's perch, hoisting his lance as his chariot began to charge forward.

Next to Luthro, Mandus dropped down into a runner's starting position as Luthro continued to fight off cultists.

"You've got this handled over here, right?" Mandus asked, not waiting for an answer as he dashed at lightning speed, pursuing Kimaris.

Mandus caught up to the chariot in an instant, grabbing a loose stick from the ground as he leapt forward. Weighing the branch in his hand, the fox zoa reached out and jammed it in between the chariot's spokes. Kimaris' movement stopped suddenly as his chariot locked up, toppling forward and sending the homunculus tumbling out into the dirt.

Stopping his dash to catch his breath for a quick moment,

The Man in Red

Mandus paused as he noticed a thick blanket of silt and stone hovering around him. Covering his face, the fox glanced around and identified several jagged slivers of stone suspended in space.

Solomon did this to stop me from running. He knows I can't control my movement that well, and I'll hit the stones if I try, Mandus realized, looking over his shoulder as Solomon threw a second handful of dirt into the air.

"Thorne! Switch with me!" Luthro called out, gesturing towards Mandus. "Clear the air for him, and I'll take the pyromaniac."

Thorne nodded, dashing in with Aim in pursuit. Luthro swung his watch chain around his foot, kicking it towards Aim to pull her attention away from the Fuuntet. Aim dodged the kick, Luthro twisting the chain instead to wrap it around her neck. As Luthro's watch increased in mass, it pulled Aim downwards in the same manner as the cultist's gauntlet, her face pressed into the dirt as she pushed and struggled against it to no avail.

Walking up to her, Luthro plucked the hat off of her head, reversing his array as he reduced her fire-spewing hat's mass into near-weightlessness, tossing it into the air and letting the wind carry it away like a dandelion seed.

Solomon ran forward, approaching Gihon and Zander as they continued to fight against golems near the edge of the gorge. The Divine Sword, Kether, appeared in his hand, poised to strike as the homunculus muttered under his breath.

"If nothing else motivated you to show off, maybe you'll be inspired now." Solomon growled, swinging the Divine Sword at

Gihon.

The Dirigent managed a quick parry, stepping back and casting a quick glance at Zander.

"Don't let him activate the Sword. You'll see it start to glow, and it will dissolve you on the spot if it touches you at that point," Gihon warned Zander quietly, the sphynx nodding in silent understanding as he pushed his offense, refusing to give Solomon an opening.

Gihon caught Solomon's leg against his braced arms as he attempted a kick, the homunculus pushing against him and sending his brother back by a few feet, immediately switching his focus for a harsh swing at Zander. The force caught him off guard, the Ehret's position opening up as his balance was lost.

Solomon twisted his blood-red array eagerly as the Divine Sword began to glow white, the same ominous brightness as it had before ending Bex's life. Not allowing Zander any time to recover, Solomon drove his blade forward at the sphynx, a wicked and cruel smile on his face as he imagined sending his foe into oblivion.

Freezing, Solomon's grin faded as his blade stopped a single centimeter before Zander's face. Turning to face Gihon, the homunculus realized that a hastily-created rampart array was the only thing preventing his blade from piercing the throat of the Ehret of the Zengarde.

Gihon's rampart can't block the Divine Sword. Nothing can. Solomon's eyebrows furrowed, before a realization hit him.

Looking closer at the array, and then at Gihon, Solomon noticed an inky black energy seeping up from the ground and into Gihon's array. Gihon was grimacing as his rampart glowed brightly before fading into darkness, his face twisted in pain.

He overflowed the rampart with negative energy, creating an annihilation that he could absorb within the shield's limbus coating when the positive energy of Kether struck, Solomon mused as he realized his brother's strategy.

"You chose to soak up the annihilation into your own body through your array to spare the Ehret."

"Correct. The limbus energy dampened that annihilation event enough to be contained through my array instead of harming others. I'm strong enough to handle something as simple as that," Gihon replied through gritted teeth, feeling the searing pain of mixing energies eating at his body.

"Clever boy," Solomon pushed back, resetting his distance from Zander. "It seems like there's only one thing that will bother you, then. How do you plan to protect the ones you can't reach?"

Solomon smirked, turning his hand outwards as red energy began to glow in his hand. Realization hit Gihon as he launched forward on instinct, the Dirigent kicking Solomon in the chest as his ominous red array shot a blast up at the Queen who was perched above in the treetops.

"Get to Edelein!" Gihon commanded Zander, who was already darting off in her direction.

The kick effectively diverted Solomon's attack and sent Solomon tumbling backwards by a few more steps, one foot slipping on the cliffside as scarlet energy fizzled into the sky above. As the homunculus tried to right himself, Gihon pushed forward on an offensive strike, his blows fueled with searing hatred.

"Careful now, Gihon," Solomon warned with what seemed to be a nervous laugh, trying to step back to a safe distance from the cliffside.

The Dirigent ignored Solomon, his teal array flashing as several small peaks of obsidian disrupted the ground under the homunculus' feet. Solomon's balance was thrown off by his constant evasion, allowing for Gihon to sweep his feet out from under him and plant a firm kick to his brother's face. Solomon stumbled as his body was flung backwards, grasping at the ledge as he tried to prevent himself from falling into the river below.

"You never should have come back," Gihon growled, kicking Solomon's head for a second time and sending the homunculus off the edge in a quick blur of red and white.

Gihon turned around, letting out a frustrated groan as he looked up at Edelein to ensure she was safe. Edelein's face was twisted, obscured in the shadows of the leaves, her arm reaching out towards him.

"Gihon!" Zander warned, running forward.

A whip of water snaked its way around Gihon's ankle, pulling him down sharply. Gihon's head cracked against the ground, grunting in pain from the impact before the whip tugged further, dragging Gihon off of the edge as he weakly clawed at the ground in an attempt to get a grip on anything that could slow his momentum. Zander's blade connected with the ground where the whip was a single heartbeat before, the sphinx letting out an alarmed cry as Gihon's body tumbled down hundreds of feet, joining his brother in the water below.

"Gihon!" Edelein cried out from her perch, leaping to the ground and evading more golems as she sprinted to the edge of the gorge, peering over for any sign of him.

"Edelein, get away from the ledge!" Zander commanded, pulling her back as Jinn raised his sword in between them and the pursuing golems. "It's too risky. We cannot afford to lose both of you!"

Growling and warding off the clay figures with his sword, Jinn cast a quick glance over his shoulder at Zander.

"We need to remove the caster immediately," Jinn commented.

Edelein trembled in Zander's arms as he continued to guide her away from the ledge. "We have to go get him. T-that drop is at least two hundred feet, he won't be able to get back up…" Edelein stuttered, eyes bleary.

"If he had some sort of alchemy to survive a fall like that, I am certain that he will have alchemy that can get him back up," Zander replied flatly. "If not, there's nothing we can do but try to save the ones that are still here. Mandus and Luthro need us. They need you, Edelein. Be strong."

Edelein nodded weakly, shakily wiping her face as she clutched onto her bow. The stone pillars around Agares had dissipated when Solomon fell, leaving the caster open. The lioness drew her bow, eyes empty and expression blank as she lined her arrow to Agares' heart.

A sudden explosion resounded from below, the sound startling Edelein as she released her arrow, soaring past Agares and dissolving into the air.

Beneath them, a black flash shot up from the gorge below, iridescent black feathers catching the dying sunlight as Gihon ascended into the air on dark raven wings. The Dirigent's vest was gone, his remaining clothes soaked with river water. The blood from his head wound had almost fully washed away, with only a few red spots staining his white shirt.

Gihon touched down onto the cliffside next to Edelein, shaking some of the water from his hair, as Solomon sprinted up after him with firm steps on floating arrays. Each array lifted Solomon's feet higher, the homunculus seeming to run along nothing but the air currents as he stood over the ledge, looking down at Gihon and wringing out his own mop of damp white locks.

The large black wings on Gihon's back began to transmorph, returning to a soft fabric cloak wrapped around his shoulders. Reaching into his pocket, Gihon gave Edelein a simple command.

"Stay close to me," he told her quietly, his eyes locked onto Solomon as his hand reached down slowly.

Edelein noticed Gihon withdrawing a small chess piece from his pocket, a black rook. Solomon's eyes widened, his smile beaming at the sight.

"Now!" Solomon commanded, still standing in midair above the others.

A sudden blast of fire struck Gihon in the back, the Dirigent stumbling forward as the rook piece slipped out of his hand. Behind him, Aim was holding her hands out, Luthro's watch reduced to a puddle of gold by her feet.

"She burned through my pocket watch?" Luthro realized, one eyebrow twitching in agitation.

Gihon dove forward, attempting to retrieve the chess piece. Sprinting across the air, Solomon dispelled his arrays and landed on top of Gihon, tackling him to the ground.

"Mandus! The rook!" Gihon commanded.

"I-I'm a little busy!" Mandus admitted, his back to Luthro's as golems surrounded them.

Thorne caught a glimpse of the black rook as it rolled across the battlefield, summoning a gale to push it closer to himself. Just before the windmaster could take hold of it, Thorne was interrupted by Kimaris as the chariot charged directly at him.

Holding his lance close to the ground, Kimaris punted the rook with his weapon. The chess piece soared through the air, landing between Aim and Edelein. The two women looked down at the small object, and back up at each other as they both began to sprint towards it.

"The sea of golems are thicker around the caster's body,"

The Man in Red

Jinn commented, slashing through them.

Zander grunted in agreement, slicing through more of them as the piles of clay rubble increased in his wake. Finally reaching an opening, the sphynx darted forward and sliced clean through Agares' midsection, the draekis' body slumping to the ground before losing its color and dissolving into clay.

"That wasn't the real one?" Jinn asked, looking around for any sign of the caster's actual body.

Lylia touched the ground quickly, a large flower sprouting by her hand. Picking it up and drawing the seeds out of it, the elf whistled at her partner. Thorne looked up towards the sound, understanding her indication as a tailwind picked up behind her. Lylia tossed the seeds into the air, Thorne's winds carrying them forward and into the clay bodies of the figures ahead.

Digging her staff into the ground again, Lylia willed the plants to grow, each one sprouting and growing into twisting flower bushes. The golems struggled against the plants, deeply entangled as their forms slowed down. Each golem froze in place as roots dug themselves deeper into the clay, lifeless figures at the mercy of the elven druid.

As Edelein sprinted towards the rook piece, racing against Aim, she let a few arrows fly in an attempt to slow her enemy down. Aim scorched each arrow with small bursts of flame, lacking the enhancements of her hat to retaliate fully at Edelein. Noticing the two, Kimaris charged forward on his chariot, lance extended to slow the Queen down. Sudden roots began to spring up from the ground, disrupting Kimaris' path as his chariot pulled over quickly. The slow was just enough time to allow Jinn a quick strike with his pommel, knocking the homunculus off of his mount.

A blast of fire narrowly missed Jinn as he dodged quickly to the side, turning to see the homunculus witch surrounded by flame, shards of glass at her feet to indicate that she had thrown an alchemist's fire at the ground, allowing herself a new source of energy to draw from after losing her hat.

Jinn ran towards Aim as Kimaris targeted Edelein, the lancer resorting to his own two feet as he charged at the Queen. Edelein met his crazed eyes, drawing an arrow directly at him until a flick of her ear indicated a second foe's approach. Dispelling the arrow, Edelein tumbled out of the way as Kimaris' steed independently charged at her, the shadowy horse running on a wild rampage as its empty chariot followed after with no master to control it.

A firm impact on Kimaris' lance redirected his momentum as Luthro's pen lodged itself into the black metal, the pen's increased mass redirecting the homunculus away from Edelein. Kimaris swung in retaliation at Luthro as the student approached, ducking out of the way as he laid his hands on the lance.

Recognizing the technique, Kimaris quickly dropped his lance and reached down to pull a small knife from his boot. With a quick slash, he swung at Luthro. The student's eyes widened slightly as he caught the gleam of the blade, maneuvering the lance in his arms and barely managing to block the knife from tearing into him.

How do people fight with such clunky weapons? Luthro wondered, the large lance feeling imbalanced in his hands compared to his pocket watch as he blocked another hit from Kimaris.

Kimaris noted Luthro's imbalance, grinning as he feinted the knife with a jab forward followed by dropping it out of his hand. The homunculus caught the blade in his second hand, driving it into

The Man in Red

Luthro's side.

Luthro gasped in pain as the metal bit into his body, grip loosening. Kimaris pulled his lance from Luthro's arms, hurling it at Edelein as she continued to fire at his steed.

An orange blur interrupted the trajectory of the lance, the weapon seeming to vanish from midair.

This thing is light as a feather, Mandus noticed curiously as he rerouted the lance back in the direction it came.

Mandus saw Luthro as he twisted his body, his friend wincing in pain as he pulled the knife out of his side. Anger began to fill Mandus' lithe body as his eyes locked onto Kimaris, a bestial growl coming from his throat as the fox wound his arm back, the energy of his array flowing into the weapon as he threw it straight at Kimaris.

The lance flew at a near-supersonic speed as it barreled into Kimaris, tearing through the lancer's left arm and several trees behind him. Alchemical energy flowed out from Mandus, the fox realizing he had expended far more than he was intending as he dropped onto one knee and began to pant heavily.

"Dammit... that was... for Luthro..." Mandus wheezed, clutching his chest.

Jinn maintained an offensive stance as he separated Edelein and Aim, his sword raised in a quick flurry of slashes directed at Aim's hands.

The fire witch doesn't have her hat to fuel her flames, but her hands are still capable of creating those wild and untamed arrays, Jinn thought, lunging forward.

Crown of the Alchemist

Aim seemed to ignore Jinn at first, pointing her hand at Edelein as an array began to ignite. Quickly, the homunculus let out a surprised yelp and withdrew her arm as Jinn's blade sliced through the air where her hand had been.

Backing up to create distance between herself and the wolf zoa, Aim began to throw loose sheets of flame in an attempt to thwart her opponent.

Jinn weaved through each wall of fire, slicing at the hungry flames as they roared. Closing his eyes, the Dritet let his senses overtake his body, energy coursing through his spine as his instincts drove him towards the heart of each array that was embedded in the inferno.

I understand. Her fire requires a fuel source, which she outsources to the hat. Without it, she has to manually create them individually, which are harder to maintain, Jinn realized as he disrupted each array.

Aim shot out another wild blast towards Edelein as the lioness dove towards the rook. Jinn diverted the attack with his sword, retaliating with another thrust as he protected his Queen, allowing for her to successfully grab Gihon's artifact.

"Gihon!" Edelein cried out, clutching tightly onto the chess piece.

Gihon and Solomon both looked over from their skirmish, relief washing over Gihon's expression as he noticed Edelein's clenched fist. The Dirigent started towards her, stopping as Solomon grabbed his shirt and tugged him backwards and onto the ground. Gihon fell backwards, tumbling before quickly struggling back to his feet as Solomon closed the distance between himself and the Queen.

Solomon weaved between bodies of friend and foe alike in his sprint towards Edelein, fists clenched in desperation. Emerging from a horde of clay golems, Zander bared his fangs and lowered his stance. He hissed at Solomon, the lone defender protecting Edelein from Solomon's grasp as he stood boldly between them, both swords poised to strike if the man in red dared to step closer to the woman he had sworn himself to protect.

Golems began to close in on Edelein, arms outstretched as they reached for the rook in her hand. Her tail swished anxiously, head on a swivel as she searched for a way to navigate the oncoming attack.

There's too many of them for me to use my bow, Edelein realized, ears flat. *I should avoid melee, because they can outnumber and overwhelm me, and I need to make sure they don't touch Gihon's chess piece. I don't know what this thing is, but I have to trust him.*

Rising to his feet, Gihon watched in horror as the golems approached the Queen, the panicked look in her eye striking a chord in Gihon's chest as a familiar ache welled up inside of him.

There's no time, Gihon thought as his cloak began to unfurl behind him.

Black wings formed on the Dirigent's back as the cloak transmuted, faint violet and green hues shimmering in the evening sunshine as he prepared for flight. With a powerful beat of his wings, Gihon launched himself into the air, diving down over the golems and landing just behind Edelein.

Without wasting a single second, Gihon darted forward and grabbed onto Edelein's waist with one hand, the second curling over her closed fist as a new array ignited under both of them, large and complex. The circle was filled with solid marks as opposed to the usual thin lines of an alchemical pattern, but held the signature teal glow of an array activated by the Dirigent of Ravencroft.

"Fortress Black," Gihon commanded under his breath, his grip tightening around Edelein.

Luthro and Mandus exchanged an uneasy look as Gihon

held onto Edelein's waist. Her face was obscured, buried into the Dirigent's chest as teal light enveloped them both.

"He's..." Mandus started, trailing off in disbelief.

"He connected Edelein's energy into Fortress Black," Luthro realized in horror.

CHAPTER 14

MONSTROSITIES

Jana sat comfortably on the large sofa in the center of Gihon's main sitting room, the setting sun illuminating the pages of her novel through the large windows of his home as she let the words absorb her mind. A sudden knock on the door pulled her out of her story, the fellborn looking over curiously as she set the book down on the antique coffee table beside her.

Spira jogged from upstairs at the sound of the rapping, cautiously slowing her pace as her lightbound eyes focused on the door.

"The others shouldn't be back this soon. Are we expecting anyone? Other students?" Spira asked Jana, conjuring a small hardlight blade to hide behind her wrist.

As Spira's gaze trained on the front entrance, she recognized a familiar feline form as the light wrapped around it. Glassy light waves passed through from the other side, revealing Edelein's casual stance from behind the closed door. A look of surprise crossed her face, quickly transforming to relief as Spira opened the door and dismissed her hidden hardlight blade.

"Queen Edelein! What are you doing here?" Spira asked, adjusting her sunglasses as Edelein brushed past her dismissively.

Edelein was wrapped in a deep blue traveler's cloak as she looked around the room, seeming to drink in her surroundings for a moment before she fervently whipped around to face Spira and Jana.

"We have a problem. Solomon caught wind of your location, and he is heading here immediately for the crystal. Where is it? Is it safe?" Edelein pressed, one of her ears flicking as she peered around anxiously.

"Alett has it, as usual. Did you say Solomon is on his way?" Jana tilted her head, her hand itching to draw her weapon as the tense air sent chills down the fellborn's spine.

"Imminently, yes. I recommend arming yourselves at once," Edelein confirmed.

"Slow down and explain what's going on, Your Majesty," Spira requested, stepping forward as she tried to piece together the situation. "Where are the others?"

"They're buying you all some time, and they sent me ahead to warn you."

They sent the Queen out alone to warn us? Why wouldn't they send Mandus instead? Something isn't adding up, Jana thought doubtfully, a glance at Spira showing that the other student was thinking the same thing.

"Did I hear Eddie?" Alett asked as he came down the stairs, Nephvir following quietly behind him. "Is she back?"

Alett's feathers bristled as he laid eyes on Edelein, a deep unsettling feeling bubbling in the pit of his stomach.

"Alett, are you alright?" Nephvir asked as he noticed the sudden stiffness in his ally.

The Man in Red

As Nephvir spoke, Edelein's eyes seemed to light up for a moment, her gaze flitting down to Alett's satchel for a second before she started to approach him.

"My Zengarde!" Edelein said, smiling. "Could I speak with you privately for a moment?"

Alett nodded slowly as he approached warily, following Edelein into the backyard.

"Alett, our team is having an issue. They're out buying time, but Solomon is coming. You still have the crystal, yes?" Edelein asked, her tone growing desperate.

"Y-yes," Alett confirmed, taking a deep breath.

She smells like our Eddie. This is definitely Ed's cloak, but there's an emptiness to her scent. Is the blight messing with my perception of her smell? Also, didn't we leave our cloaks with our other belongings in Velkhamore? She hasn't worn this since the day we arrived at the Grand Bazaar, Alett pondered, taking a single step away from her.

"Give it to me. Let me verify it myself," Edelein commanded, holding out one hand expectantly.

Alett hesitated, looking down at her hand and back up at her face as he touched his satchel cautiously.

"Hurry, now. You and the others need to prepare for Solomon's arrival. I don't know how much time Gihon and the others will be able to buy you. I'll look after the crystal and–"

"Is it really you, Eddie?" Alett interrupted her, his soft yellow-orange eyes wide and fearful.

Edelein stopped, laughing suddenly.

"What?" she asked. "What's wrong with you, Alett? Of course it's me. I'm Edelein von Luvemann, your Eddie."

Alett let out a surprised yelp, jumping backwards as his hand withdrew from his satchel.

"The Queen would *never* call herself Eddie. You're not

her!" Alett gasped, backing away. "What did you do to her? Is she hurt? Explain yourself, o-or I'll—"

The lioness opened her mouth to retort, but before she could speak, a loud crash echoed from the second floor, drawing Alett's attention.

"That was one of my traps!" Alett called out, starting to run back inside. "Someone go set off the communication stone and alert the—"

The Zwitet was cut off by a sharp pain in his stomach, choking and coughing before he could finish his sentence. In one swift moment, Allocer had produced a dagger from seemingly nowhere and stabbed the owl in his midriff, before quickly pulling it out and slashing the strap of Alett's satchel. The homunculus pulled the bag from off of his belt and took off in a sprint towards the front of the house.

"Alett, what's going on?" Jana asked, alerted by the sudden discord.

"We're under attack!" Allocer cried out as she sprinted towards the door, clutching onto Alett's satchel.

"What the hell?!" Spira exclaimed, two light spears appearing in her hands as Allocer ran past, trying to comprehend the situation.

"That's not Eddie!" Alett screamed, stumbling inside and clutching his heavily bleeding stomach. "She's got my bag!"

"Who are you?!" Nephvir growled, shadow-stepping in front of Allocer and tackling her, pinning her down with an iron-like grip on her wrists. "I don't want to hear you say you're Edelein! I swear, I'll kill you right now. You stabbed your own Zwitet!"

As Nephvir summoned his scythe and pressed it against Allocer, hair now glowing a brilliant white color, the lioness simply laughed.

"Nice scythe," Allocer commented, drawing one finger

across the blade and letting the blood well on her skin. "Will it turn my hair white as well once I take it from you? I fear it may make me look old."

"Its name is Crescent Shadow, and I stole it from the Winter Court. Take it from me, and the fae will hunt you down for the rest of your life. Something tells me a creature like you cannot handle a lifetime of being hunted."

"Quite right, I do prefer the role of the hunter," Allocer smirked, letting the blood run down her arm.

A loud crash sounded overhead, the ceiling caving in as a hulking figure smashed through the second floor.

"Nice to see you, Vepar!" Allocer called out, waving her bloodied hand as much as she could from underneath Nephvir.

A large hand grabbed the back of Nephvir's head, yanking him up into the air and freeing Allocer from beneath him. Nephvir looked at the man who grabbed him, a hulking homunculus with shark-like features. He had sharp teeth, a brackish mohawk, and a large anchor hoisted over his other shoulder as he dangled the fellborn off of the ground. He had no shirt, but his waist was adorned with colorful rags that were tied together into a makeshift wrap over his worn-down trousers. The shark's eyes had darkened at the scent of blood, pupils wide and empty as a blood frenzy consumed him.

Nephvir screamed in agony, his scythe vanishing as he desperately clawed at the hand that squeezed his skull.

Spira lunged forward and sliced at the shark-man's hand, barely managing to break through the surface of his tough skin. Realizing her offensive weaponry would not be enough, a new idea suddenly sparked in her mind.

"Neph!" Spira called out, holding up a shield of light to the shark-man.

As her light illuminated the space, a large shadow of

the shark's hulking figure was cast onto the wall behind, the homunculus wincing slightly from the brightness as his grip tightened and then crushed down onto nothing.

Unclenching his fist, the homunculus swiveled his head around in an attempt to locate Nephvir as the fellborn vanished into darkness, his body melting into the creature's shadow.

Growling, Vepar swung his anchor forward to slam it down onto Spira's light shield, but the loud clang of metal interrupted him as Everett's large axe found itself wedged in the floor between them.

Everett ran in, grabbing the axe and converting it into a shield to deflect another blow from the homunculus.

"Are you all okay? What's going on?!" Everett asked.

"This crazy lady wearing Queen Edelein's cloak just waltzed in here and stabbed Alett!" Nephvir explained in dismay, reappearing from the shadows as his scythe sliced at Vepar's sturdy legs.

"O-okay, um, three things," Everett replied as he deflected a third strike from the anchor. "One, is Alett stable?"

"I'm good!" Alett called from the couch, where Jana had just finished bandaging his stomach. "Jana gave me a healing potion and we're stopping the bleeding now. Kick their asses, guys!"

"Great. Uh, two, Cari and Nora are upstairs alone right now. Some of those cultists came in through the window and they need backup."

"On it!" Jana nodded, taking off towards the stairs.

"What's the third thing?" Nephvir asked, darting through the enemy's legs and sweeping upwards into another strike, still only managing a few scratches against Vepar's tough skin.

"Oh, u-uh, I don't see the crazy lady you mentioned. That's bad, right?"

"Shit!" Nephvir cursed, looking around.

Everett pushed the homunculus away with his shield,

converting it back into an axe. "I've got the big guy. You two go find that lady and punch her for Alett!"

Above the fight against Vepar, Cari and Nora were surrounded in a bedroom on the second floor of the house, five cultists backing them into a wall.

"Are you guys *that* scared of a couple of girls?" Cari asked as Nora stuck out her tongue at their foes from behind Cari. "Is all of this necessary? We're just two regular ladies. Nora here is just a *child*, for crying out loud. You're really going to shoot a kid?"

The cultists ignored Cari's protests, closing in as their gauntlets began to glow. Nora reached into her pocket, pulling out what appeared to be a tiny hammer that fit into the palm of her hand. It had a boxy shape, the handle a light pink color. The feline zoa threw her hammer forward, the petite weapon landing with a quiet thunk against the head of one of the cultists.

"What was that?" the cultist asked with a laugh, looking up in the direction where the small object had ricocheted.

Nora's hammer had bounced off of the cultist's head and was spinning in midair as it flew upwards. With a cheeky grin, a bright pink array illuminated in Nora's palm as she twisted her hand, the hammer suddenly increasing exponentially in size as it crashed down on her enemy's body.

Cari reached behind, unhooking her whip from her belt and lashing out at the cultists. Her whip cracked, a warning signal to the four remaining enemies as they released blasts of fire and lightning from their gauntlets. With another lash, Cari dispelled the alchemical energy, the output from their gauntlets fizzling into nothing.

Steam expelled from the cultists' gauntlets as heat exhaust poured from the devices, the five men rushing at Cari and Nora to fight while their weapons took time to recharge.

"They can't do more of those blasts right away, so keep that in mind," Cari noted quietly to Nora, who nodded as she dashed forward, grabbing the giant hammer and reducing its size slightly to make it more maneuverable as she swung it towards another cultist.

The cultist was flung backwards by the momentum of Nora's hammer, his back slamming into the wall with a harsh thud.

"Behind you, Nora!" Cari warned, her whip ensnaring a cultist and pulling him in for a swift kick to the ribs.

Nora whipped around, lifting her hammer as the final two cultists approached her. Two loud pops sounded from the entrance to the room, both cultists sinking to the ground as their bodies burst into flame. Behind them, Jana stood perfectly poised, gun still smoking as she slowly lowered her arms.

"What the hell did you shoot them with? That was fantastic!" Cari beamed from atop a cultist, her whip wrapped around him as she bashed his head in with its ironwood handle to make him stop struggling.

"Incendiary rounds," Jana explained, popping open the smoking revolver and loading a few more brightly colored bullets in. "I made them myself."

Cari grinned in admiration, dusting the debris off of her jacket. "You are incredibly cool, little fellborn."

Everett locked his axe against Vepar's weapon and

attempted to push him into a wall, buying time for Spira and Nephvir to escape and pursue Allocer.

"You should not have sent your friends away. They were your greatest strength, and without them your death will only be more lonesome."

Vepar spoke with a guttural, daunting voice, his words sending chills through Everett's body.

I'm using every ounce of strength I have just to barely nudge this guy, Everett realized, dread filling his veins.

The shark-man planted a knee into Everett's sternum, the ox barely managing to anticipate and harden his muscles in time to take the blow. Everett wrapped his arm around Vepar's leg and quickly rotated his body to sling Vepar out of the window, glass shattering around both of them as they fell.

A large axe clanged against Vepar's anchor as Everett managed to shove the shark's weapon away enough to give himself an opening. Everett swung his axe to cut Vepar across the chest, blood pouring into the grass from the incision for a single second before the shallow wound began to close itself.

"Your axe is a beautiful weapon. I look forward to taking your head with it," Vepar growled, shoving Everett back.

"I made it myself," Everett boasted. "My father's the greatest blacksmith in all of Zenluve. I was raised well."

"Admirable. I'll take your father's head with it next, then."

The homunculus raised his anchor up to slam it down onto Everett, who blocked it with great strain on his body. Everett let out a loud yell of exertion, pushing back with intense effort as his muscles ached, yearning to let go and succumb. The ground beneath him cracked as Everett continued to push back, teeth clenched in pain and determination. Vepar placed his other hand on the anchor and pushed it down slowly until the sharp pointed fluke began to drive into Everett, the ox grimacing as he tried to hold in a scream.

Vepar's grip loosened as he erupted into flame, Jana's incendiary bullet connecting with thick skin. Letting out a low growl, Vepar threw his anchor at the petite fellborn as he began to break up the ground, kicking up dirt to tame the fire.

Jana summoned a rampart array to block the anchor as it landed heavily by her feet, Everett slicing at the burning shark with his axe. Vepar rammed a smoldering shoulder into Everett, forcing him away as he snuffed out the rest of the blazes.

"Finally, you brought a friend," Vepar grinned widely, sharp teeth glistening.

Spira chased after Allocer, the lioness darting into the woods ahead as a new group of cultists appeared. The three cultists shot fire and lightning from their gauntlets, creating a barrage of attacks to cover Allocer's escape.

The student conjured a hardlight shield to block the incoming attack, her second hand summoning a long spear. As the barrage of flame and electricity subsided, Spira threw the javelin forward beyond the three attackers to where she could still see Allocer's lithe body through her glassy view of the woods. The spear narrowly missed Allocer, the lioness letting out a quick gasp as she twisted her body to the side to evade.

Spira closed her eyes as she detonated her shield into a spray of brilliant light, blinding the cultists that faced her. With her eyes closed, she focused on the infrared heat signatures coming from the gauntlets as she cut down the blinded cultists that were in her way.

Nephvir shadow-stepped behind Allocer to slash at her,

seeming to appear from nothing as he emerged from the trees, white hair flowing like water around him. Allocer ducked, avoiding his attack and retaliating by kicking at Nephvir's knee. Nephvir adjusted the hilt of his scythe to block the kick, stepping backwards. Sensing an opportunity to close the distance, Allocer lunged forward and produced two hidden blades to stab at Nephvir as he backstepped to dodge.

Spira dashed past the incapacitated cultists, sending a wide sweeping swing at Allocer with her spear in an attempt to trip the imposter. Allocer bent her knees, sliding along the ground to dodge the attack. She flipped back to create distance, smirking as she gestured behind the two towards the house.

"Chase me all you want, but your friends back there are going to die if you don't help them," Allocer said casually, tearing Edelein's cloak off and dropping it by her stilettoed feet, revealing a tight black bodysuit and fishnet stockings.

Sensing the truth in her words, Spira and Nephvir took a glance back to see that Vepar had grabbed Everett's axe as it swung and kicked him away, disarming the ox. Vepar brought the axe up to his face, blocking Jana's bullets as she attempted to support her friend. Unbothered by Jana's attacks as they fizzled out against Everett's weapon, Vepar took slow and heavy steps towards the Zengarde with murderous intent.

"Everett!" Cari called out, running from inside and cracking her whip at Vepar.

The whip grazed Vepar's skin, leaving a faint red mark as Cari withdrew her weapon and whipped him again. On the second attack, Vepar grabbed Cari's whip and pulled her in towards his extended arm as it connected with her neck.

Noticing the movement with quick reflexes, Jana reacted in time to bulwark Cari. Jana reinforced Cari's delicate frame just enough to keep her alive. As Nora followed out after, her face dropped as she evaluated the sights in front of her.

In the shade of the woods, Allocer continued to address Nephvir and Spira.

"You see, Vepar is a bit of a special case. Impenetrable skin and regenerative abilities… some of Solomon's finest work, other than myself, of course," Allocer explained with a wide smile. "A true monstrosity. Your sentinel is too weak to stop him, and the little fellborn beacon is running on fumes trying to keep the strikers alive."

Nephvir looked back to find that Allocer had vanished. With no time to waste as Vepar closed in on Everett, Spira and Nephvir started back towards their allies as the chaos continued to unfold.

"Jana!" a voice called from the front of the house.

Jana whipped her head around to see Alett leaning on the doorframe.

"What?!" Jana snapped, firing another shot at Vepar.

"Where is your crafting kit? I have an idea!" Alett asked, projecting his voice to be heard over the cacophony of battle.

"In my bedroom, upstairs!" Jana answered, eyes trained on her enemy. "Second door on the right!"

"Thanks, I'll be back!" Alett assured loudly, disappearing back inside.

Nephvir appeared out of Vepar's shadow to slash at his ankles, which toppled the giant shark momentarily. The injury healed itself in a moment as Vepar kicked the shadow-stepping fellborn. Neph blocked the kick with his scythe, though the force of the attack sent him flying.

"Nora, get his anchor! Make it small!" Cari suggested, her whip cracking through the air as she let out several blows.

"I can't!" Nora denied, clutching onto her hammer as it doubled in size. "My alchemy exclusively manipulates size, not mass like Luthro's. None of us could pick that thing up, no matter how tiny it is. If I shrink it, it essentially becomes a super-bullet for that shark thing to throw at us!"

I tend to fight better against smaller enemies than this thing! Nora thought in dismay, feeling the weight of her youth compared to the experience of the legendary Zengarde.

"It's alright!" Cari reassured her with a smile. "We've got your back. Let's finish him together!"

Nora nodded, running in for a swing of her hammer as Everett jumped up to deliver a powerful punch to Vepar's face. Everett turned around to grab at his axe, pushing down on it and switching it back into a shield. The ox zoa threw two more powerful punches that sent Vepar stumbling, before Vepar struck back and drove the shield into Everett's ribs, cracking them. The shark-man slammed his fist into Everett's collarbone, smashing him into the ground.

Jana unloaded more shots at Vepar, but the bullets didn't seem to slow him down as he raised the shield to block the onslaught of attacks. As Nora struck, Vepar sidestepped before swinging the shield to knock Nora back. Vepar pummeled Everett deeper into the ground, the ox choking and coughing blood as shattered ribs punctured his lungs.

I can't let any of the Zengarde die! Among other things, this would be irreparable for Master Marleogne's reputation within the Society, Jana thought as she began fervently reloading. *Gihon trusted us with their safety.*

Vepar raised the shield, growling as he began to thrust it down onto Everett's neck. Spira slid in to intercept the blow, conjuring two hardlight spears to cross the blade points and catch the shield. The force from the attack continued to drive the spears down as Vepar overpowered her, but Spira remained quick on her feet. The light-wielder planted her spears into the ground, freeing her hands to conjure two more spears to thrust through Vepar's abdomen.

Adrenaline pumped through Spira's veins as she yelled in rage, her light spears piercing straight through the homunculus. Vepar's regeneration kept him upright as he pulled the shield back and slammed it into Spira, who bulwarked herself at the last second. Though her defensive maneuver kept her alive by reducing the damage, Spira let out a pained scream as the shield connected harshly with her body.

Jana ran forward, desperate to draw Vepar's attention away as she fired a round of incendiary bullets at him. As the flames distracted Vepar, Jana took the time to aim and fire an ink round into Vepar's eyes to blind him.

Nora saw the opening and enlarged her hammer further, darting in for another strike. With a powerful swing, she sent Vepar crashing into the perimeter wall of the estate. With a short reprieve, everyone slowly regrouped, helping each other to their feet.

"It's going to take a lot more than this to kill that thing," Nephvir noted. "We've hardly put a dent into him."

"Whatever Alett is doing, he needs to hurry up," Jana replied.

"Alett is a quick thinker and tends to have great ideas, but this is why he relies on making weaponry ahead of time," Cari sighed. "Without his satchel, he's kind of useless."

Jana loaded a bright green bullet into her revolver, firing an emergency healing shot into the air as it exploded into a spray of health-recovering rain over the group. From the crumbled stone wall, Vepar rose again, shaking off the debris.

"I'm here!" Alett ran out from the house, dipping his head apologetically.

"Alright, great Zwitet, what's your genius plan?" Everett asked, still doubled over in pain.

The Man in Red

"This guy… thing… he's a shark, right? There's a chance he's ectothermic. I can't guarantee it will work, but if he's cold-blooded like I'm hoping, these might slow him down."

Alett extended his palm, revealing a handful of small blue orbs.

"Cryo grenades. I couldn't make larger ones because Jana tends to work with smaller objects, but I think they should still work all at once."

Vepar wiped at his eyes, trying to clear the ink before resuming his attack. Spira looked down at the two light spears jutting from his midsection, continuing to stare straight ahead as she spoke.

"Noentet Nephvir, I felt dark energy from your scythe earlier."

Nephvir nodded silently, summoning his scythe as he held it out to her. Spira continued to stare straight ahead, unresponsive.

"Oh, y-yes. This is a fae weapon, from the Winter Court. It's imbued with dark energy."

"Perfect. I have an idea, as well."

Vepar finally cleared the ink out of his eyes, an annoyed huff echoing from his chest as he straightened up. The shark looked at Everett's shield in his hand and adjusted it back to the axe-form before he walked slowly towards the group, ecstatic to kill them.

The group charged Vepar as he smiled gleefully, clutching onto Everett's axe with a toothy grin. Jana opened up the assault with a highly-compressed water bullet, drenching the shark-man.

"This was your plan? What, to give me a bath? This feels *invigorating*, little fellborn."

"Oh, it'll be invigorating, that's for sure," Alett retorted, tossing the grenades forward.

Icy smoke exploded from each pellet, enshrouding the area as temperatures began to drop rapidly. Vepar's jaw clenched as he felt himself slowing down, his skin aching from the cold.

Nephvir dashed in to initiate Spira's plan, his scythe slashing at the protruding light spears instead of hitting Vepar. Nephvir's dark energy connected with the light energy of Spira's weapons, both elements mixing and forming an annihilation event around Vepar's torso.

When dark energy meets light energy, nothing remains, Spira's words echoed in Nephvir's mind as the annihilation blew a large gaping wound into Vepar's midsection. *Use your scythe to hit the spears and the annihilation that follows should destroy him.*

Nora swung down onto Vepar's head, the homunculus catching the hammer with his free hand. The cold slowed down Vepar's movement and healing as Jana began to unload several rounds, each bullet striking the open wound. Spira threw a handful of light daggers into the arm holding Everett's axe as Cari wrapped her whip around Vepar's neck.

Cari flipped over the handle of Nora's enlarged hammer and used her weight to stretch Vepar's neck as Nephvir sliced at the daggers Spira threw to create another annihilation sphere, severing Vepar's arm.

Everett managed to catch his axe as it fell, swinging with all of the remaining energy in his body at the shark's exposed neck. Letting out a loud scream of effort, Everett pushed forward and sliced through Vepar's tough skin, the shark's lifeless head tumbling to the ground.

As Vepar crumpled, the seven fighters collapsed, heaving for air as they finally got to relax their bodies. Silence fell between them all for a long moment, everyone far too exhausted to speak.

"I hate to be the bearer of bad news, but the fake Edelein got away with Alett's satchel," Nephvir admitted after a beat. "She has the crystal, Alett has no more bombs, and we didn't even get to alert the others that this happened."

The Man in Red

"I also… desperately need first aid," Everett coughed, his blood staining the grass beneath him. "Am I the only one injured?"

"Majorly, yes, which is good. I'll take care of you once we go back inside," Jana sighed, falling backwards to lay on the ground.

"Does this mean we still lost, even after all of that?" Nora whined.

Cari sighed, looking out towards the forest.

"Yeah, we lost. Is anyone up to trying to hunt her down?"

"Don't tell Edelein, but no," Everett admitted.

"I think she will understand your case," Cari continued as she rose to her feet, "Ed will give me hell if I don't at least try, though. Anyone whose legs still work, get up. We're going on a little run."

CHAPTER 15

FORTRESS BLACK

"Fortress Black," Gihon growled under his breath, a large teal array enveloping the area underneath his feet in a wide radius that reached all of his allies.

Gihon held tightly onto Edelein's waist as the familiar shock of array ignition electrocuted his veins, an audible crack of energy sounding between them as he activated the array. Her hand was clutching the black rook, face buried into his chest as eight obsidian pillars began to rise from the circle that enveloped them.

"What the hell is that?!" Thorne asked, mouth agape as walls began to form from each pillar, a deep black color that fully absorbed any light that reached it.

"Everyone get to Gihon, now!" Luthro commanded, running towards his master.

Mandus dashed between the closing walls effortlessly, the rest of the Zengarde running after Luthro. With physical prowess that far exceeded the studious alchemist, they passed Luthro easily as Thorne summoned a tailwind that pushed the well-dressed man between the walls just before they enclosed fully.

As the walls completed their formation, large ballistas formed atop each pillar as they fired a dark energy downwards at Solomon and the others.

"Come on, Gihon, we were just playing! There's no need for this!" Solomon whined sarcastically, narrowly dodging blasts. "Put the Fortress away and let's just talk it out, okay?"

Black energy from the ballistas began to rain down on Agares' clay golems, shattering them into pieces around Solomon. Gritting his teeth, the homunculus turned to his allies.

"Keep the Fortress up at all costs, no matter what happens next. Don't let him dispel it. Be careful when you attack it, though, because I'm not in the mood to make more homunculi today," Solomon instructed curtly.

Aim and Kimaris nodded, spreading out to initiate a counterattack.

"Agares," Solomon demanded.

From behind him, a silvery-white drakeling emerged from the shadows of the underbrush as he removed his cloak. The cape was reinforced with alchemically-enhanced lenticular lenses, creating an effective invisibility cloak that shielded him from the Zengarde's keen perception. Agares' true form looked identical to the mimic that had been previously destroyed, his head bowed towards his master.

"Gihon's going to show up and try to take me out. I need you to continue to pressure the ballistas to keep them away from me once I have what I need from him. Give us something grand, alright?"

Agares nodded silently, the few remaining clay figures dissolving around the arena as a large white array opened up the ground, clay trembling and convening as it began to rise up and take the form of a single gigantic golem.

       Inside of the Fortress, Gihon was staring down at the limp body of Queen Edelein in his arms.

"Shit," Gihon muttered.

"Gihon! What happened? What's going on?" Zander demanded, looking around at the new environment that they now found themselves in.

The walls that encased them were a deep and lightless black, resembling an obsidian stone, though the energy that radiated from them felt anything but material. There were sweeping arches overhead that fortified the structure, and violet sconces illuminated the interior with an ominous glow. The Zengarde drank in the setting cautiously as they approached, sensing the ominous otherworldly energy around them. Zander approached Gihon first, Lylia by his side.

"Is it the blight?" Lylia asked, looking down at Edelein.

"Gihon, you touched her while summoning the Fortress, did you not?" Luthro asked cautiously as he joined them.

"I had no choice. Taking the rook from her would have opened up another point of failure, and the potential risk of dropping it again outweighed the benefit. I simply... underestimated how fragile her body actually is right now. I thought she'd be able to handle it."

"You did this to her?" Zander hissed, ears flat as he realized what the Dirigent was saying.

"When Edelein took the rook, she connected her body to the circuit of energy that Fortress Black is composed of. By touching me, the circuit was completed, and the shockwave meant to pass through me and into the Fortress borrowed some energy from Edelein's body as well; reducing the output from myself by taking input from her. Her illness has made her too delicate to handle the massive energy output required for the Fortress."

"The energy output for Gihon's Fortress Black is too much for most people. It's not the Queen's fault that she's too weak for it, really. Gihon's bulwark is what lets him handle it, and he's already a lot larger than her. It's a move that only the most powerful sentinels could pull off alone," Mandus explained.

"I should have been more careful," Gihon sighed as Lylia set a gentle hand on Edelein's cheek. "I should have taken the rook without touching her."

A soft green light emanated from Lylia's palm, Edelein's eyes opening suddenly a moment later. She blinked in confusion as Gihon helped her upright, looking around in curious silence.

"Fortress Black is fully impregnable. This is an ultimate defensive move that will buy us time to regroup and heal while eliminating slower enemies. The ballistas atop my Fortress fire condensed limbus energy at my foes, so it will likely whittle down Solomon's forces while giving us time to figure out a plan. Now that Edelein has been removed from the circuit, I will be able to maintain it for about ten minutes."

"What happens after ten minutes?" Thorne asked.

"Holding the Fortress consumes my life force. After ten minutes, I am forced to drop it due to a loss of energy. If I keep the Fortress active for too long, I will eventually die."

"Fun," Thorne turned to Mandus. "Are all forms of alchemy so weird and bleak?"

"Gihon's alchemy is definitely a special case," Mandus whispered, hand covering his mouth to avoid Gihon noticing.

Jinn perked up suddenly, bristling as he faced the east wall.

Noticing the change in energy, the other three Zengarde began to shift around uneasily, shooting quick glances at each other. Turning towards Gihon, Thorne smiled awkwardly.

"Hey, Gihon, remember when you got all fussy because Jinn wasn't telling you what his Seventh Sense was telling the rest of us?"

Gihon nodded curiously.

"And you said this Fortress Black is impenetrable?"

"No one goes in or out for the next ten minutes," Gihon confirmed.

"Cool, yeah. Allow me to translate for Jinn. What you're telling us is that for the next ten minutes, our allies are alone out there, left to the wolves? No offense, Jinn."

"You know how I feel about that," Jinn growled under his breath, not turning to face him.

"What the wind-idiot means to say is that our allies have arrived," Zander clarified. "They will be fighting Solomon alone, then, if we remain inside."

"The others are here? Did one of you set off the relay stone?" Gihon asked. "I have a way to bring them into the Fortress, if that is the case. Stay put."

The ground under Gihon's feet rumbled as a pillar emerged and began to lift him up, elevating him to the top of the fortress. Exiting to the roof, Gihon placed one hand on a ballista and looked out at the clearing.

A giant golem was standing at Gihon's eye level, winding one arm back to strike at the wall of the Fortress. Ballistas were firing shots at the creature, each one taking a small chunk out of it but not stopping it from moving. Aim and Kimaris were nowhere to be seen, and Solomon was standing in the clearing alone

Did they get hit by the ballistas? Gihon wondered. *No… they likely fled. I cannot imagine that Solomon would tote along a*

homunculus that is unable to outrun Fortress Black.

The golem's fist came down onto the fortress, energy shooting out into the air as its hand bounced off of the wall. Time seemed to freeze for a moment as the energy stilled, before rewinding back into the impact. Energy traveled up the creature's arm in a series of cracks and implosions before the golem suddenly collapsed in on itself, crumbling into shards of white clay on the ground.

"What just happened to my golem?" a silent, invisible voice asked Solomon.

"I told you idiots to be careful. Fortress Black returns any energy that gets put into it at an amplified rate. If you hit it hard, it'll hit you harder. You were supposed to pressure him, not outright physically attack the walls!" Solomon hissed under his breath, careful not to alert Gihon of Agares' presence.

Solomon seems distracted by something. Gihon realized, extending his palm.

Each ballista turned at their master's command, facing the target he marked. Energy welled up from each weapon, electrifying the air around him as Gihon growled the command with a cold and seething hatred in his tone.

"Die."

Black energy shot out from the ballistas, converging to one point as it struck where Solomon was. Smoke and debris clouded the Dirigent's vision as he expended Fortress Black's energy into one drawn-out blast, holding the beams for a few more seconds before releasing them.

As the smoke cleared, Solomon remained standing in the same spot, the Divine Sword raised high in the air. His sword was glowing with a familiar black energy, different from the white energy that the homunculus usually charged his weapon with.

Did he just absorb limbus energy into the Divine Sword?

Gihon thought, eyebrows furrowed in anger as he dropped down outside of the Fortress, running at Solomon.

The Divine Sword quickly vanished from Solomon's hand, his wind blade re-debuting into the fight as its quick parries kept Gihon a few steps back.

Gihon continued to press forward, striking with his fists as his energy continued to be diverted into protecting his allies within the Fortress.

"Release the limbus energy you just absorbed," Gihon demanded.

"Why? What am I going to do with it?" Solomon feigned innocence. "If you get to use Limbo, why can't I?"

"You know damn well why you can't use Limbo, you maniac. You'd destroy the universe with access to limbus energy."

"That's right, I almost forgot that you blindly believe every word Arvien says," Solomon laughed, shoving Gihon back with his sword.

"Master Gihon!" Spira's voice called out.

Turning, the Dirigent laid eyes on five of his allies as they approached, pursuing a leonine woman.

It's Nora, Spira, Alett, Nephvir, Cari… and Edelein?

Shock jolted through Gihon's body as he immediately recognized the situation.

Solomon made a homunculus in Edelein's image!

Jana and Everett were not in pursuit of the Edelein mimic, causing panic to rise in Gihon's eyes as he worked out what must have happened.

They planned to have the mimic infiltrate the house and take the crystal while we were occupied here. I recognize Alett's satchel in her arms. Are the others alive?

Anger replaced the panic, aching and tearing at his heart as he pointed the ballistas down at Allocer with a wave of his hand.

The Man in Red

The lioness effortlessly weaved through the potshots of limbus energy, laughing as she ran to her master.

As the smoke cleared, Solomon and Allocer were gone, the ground where they once stood now charred and glassy.

Damn it… I can tell that they escaped, Gihon cursed under his breath as he returned to the ground, dispelling the Fortress with a pained huff.

As the stones shifted and merged into each other, they began to cascade downwards and seemingly disappear into an unknown pocket of space in the ground itself. Spira and the others were winded as they reconvened with the others, Nora's hands on her knees as she gasped for air. Edelein and the others emerged from the dissipating Fortress, looks of concern on their faces.

"Did you run all the way here?" Gihon asked, surprised. "We're about two miles from the house right now."

"We run more during our morning training back home," Cari laughed, wiping a bit of sweat from her brow. "It's more the speed than the distance. That girl was fast."

"Your Majesty, I'm so sorry," Spira bowed her head. "They ambushed us at the house, and stole your leyline crystal."

"Where is Everett?" Edelein pressed. "As well as the alchemist, Jana? Are they alive?"

"Alive, yes. Worse for wear, a bit," Spira confirmed as Gihon tensed. "Jana is okay, Master Marleogne. She's tending to his wounds."

"Everett took the worst damage of any of us, but we killed the homunculus that hurt him," Nephvir clarified. "He's a big… monster, honestly. No other word to describe what that thing was. Taller and larger than Everett, with a weird shark-like body. Aside from him, there were some cultists, and… well, you just saw the other one, didn't you, Gihon?"

Gihon nodded, "It seems that Solomon has gotten a bit

more bold lately."

The Dirigent spared a quick glance at Edelein, who tilted her head curiously up at him.

"More importantly," Gihon continued. "Solomon planned for all of this to happen. It appears that we were set up. We played right into his hand, and we lost."

Sensing the tension that sparked between Edelein and the Zengarde, Gihon desperately searched for a solution.

"I'm sorry, Edelein, this is my fault," he managed to muster, mind racing. "I should not be outsmarted by someone like Solomon. His methods are increasingly daring, in ways I have come to not expect."

Shooting an irritated glance at him, Edelein snapped, "You should know your own *brother*, shouldn't you?"

Acid dripped from her voice as she spat the word 'brother' at him, and Gihon recognized the root of the behavior. His face betrayed his dejection as he let out a tense sigh.

"I should have told you that Solomon is my brother, I know."

"Did you not think that would be helpful information, Dirigent?" Edelein insisted.

"I am prepared to kill that man with no hesitation. In fact, I tried to do exactly that with the Fortress just a moment ago. Solomon has ended the lives of thousands of people; he is no legacy of Arvien and certainly no brother of mine. Family ties would only get in the way of our objective, so ignoring them would be wise."

The space between the two crackled with an unease noticeable by the others, who were eager for a change in subject. Lylia, noticing the opportunity, approached between them.

"Speaking of that 'Fortress,' can you tell us more about it?" Lylia asked, tilting her head curiously. "Did you create it? It appeared to be incredibly powerful alchemy."

340

The Man in Red

"He isn't the Dirigent of Ravencroft for nothing, you know," interjected Luthro, his chest puffed in pride. "It takes a lot of merit to become someone of such a high status. Gihon's Fortress Black is some of the world's most powerful alchemy."

"Luthro, please," Gihon sighed, noticing a bubbling frustration from Edelein once more. "Allow me to explain it in a way that does not inflate my capabilities quite so much, as we return. I would like to get home quickly to check on Jana and the others."

"Can you walk, Edelein?" Zander asked quietly.

Edelein nodded, starting towards the house. She seemed frustrated by the recent events and eager to see Everett and Alett.

Gihon began to explain his alchemy as the exhausted group pressed forward at the fastest pace they could manage.

"I believe I previously explained alchemy to be rewriting the potential and kinetic energies of our world into other alternative forms, forms that better benefit us, through the destruction and reconstruction of matter. Now, this is not something I intentionally failed to tell you, but rather something that is a heavily-guarded secret of my family, so please forgive my lack of communication until now." Gihon said, eyes fixed on the back of Edelein's head.

"Arvien, my master, was the daughter of a man known as the Mystic King, Bathalzamar Marleogne. In a way, you can consider me to be a form of royalty in the realm of mystics. The Mystic Prince, I supposed I could be called, though I do not identify as anything other than a humble alchemist."

Noticing the silence from the Zenluvians, Gihon allowed himself to continue. "The Mystic King is considered the most powerful wizard of his time, the literal King of Wizardry. Bathalzamar vanished alongside the rest of the wizards nearly twenty-five years ago, in the Great Disappearance. Arvien, while an alchemist at heart, contained a wizard's blood in her veins, which she used in her alchemical developments. I was raised with a combination of both arts, a technique which is now known as mystic alchemy. Mystic alchemy uses magic to enhance the natural capabilities of alchemy, allowing us to manipulate physics itself as seen with my students, or in certain cases, dip into planes outside of our own. Fortress Black is not from any material on our plane, but instead from the limbus plane, the realm more commonly known as Limbo.

Fortress Black is one of many weapons that comprise the Black Armament; a collection of weapons that have been lost through space and time. When the wizards were creating their artifacts, they resulted on occasion in what were similar to alchemical backlashes that absorbed each of these weapons. Limbo is a realm that exists between different planes, separating each plane from the Sea of Miracles. Anything that is lost inevitably finds its way into Limbo."

"So Limbo isn't a plane, technically?" Jinn asked.

"Think of it like the shore on a beach," Mandus clarified. "It's a space that exists between both realms, like a border of sorts. Does that make sense?"

"The limbus plane is guarded by an entity that keeps an inventory of all that is lost. He is known as the Bookkeeper. However, you can make contracts with said guardian, to borrow energies from Limbo… including weapons such as those of the Black Armament," Gihon explained further.

"Have people ever been lost in Limbo?" Edelein queried suddenly, a desperate need to know overcoming her frustrations. "If someone went missing from the material plane, is there a possibility they could have ended up there, too?"

She's thinking about her father, Gihon realized.

"I have only heard about items and artifacts, not people ending up in the limbus plane. It is not entirely impossible, though, as Limbo is a place that I have seldom explored myself. Some people, such as Solomon, are even barred from accessing Limbo entirely."

Edelein looked away, defeated.

"Arvien and I have been there, and she had made many contracts with the bookkeeper I mentioned. During her lifetime, Arvien had obtained a number of powerful artifacts. Several years ago, Arvien made a trade with the Bookkeeper to obtain Fortress Black on my behalf, so I could better protect her in battle after my transmutation."

"Contracts are never one-sided. What are you offering this Bookkeeper fellow in return?" Edelein asked, her pace falling closer to him as she read his uneasy expression.

Gihon paused for a moment, before admitting, "I don't know. Arvien never told me what she traded, only that it was something very important to her. She seemed to not wish to think about it much, so I decided against pressing her for the information. It wasn't my place. Whatever her sacrifice, I'm grateful that she trusted me enough to give up something of her own on my behalf."

Alett's feathers twittered eagerly, drinking in his words. "This contract sounds fascinating. It allows you to draw energy from Limbo instead of Tevus? Due to the fact that Limbo exists outside of physical matter and space, does that mean the energy counts as negative in some way?"

"All energies contain either a positive or negative element to them. For example, Spira's hardlight is positive, but Nephvir's shadow scythe is negative. The Plane of Light and the Plane of Shadow are true opposites, like the positive Plane of Fire and the negative Plane of Water. If they were to work together, they would create annihilation events that could prove to be a risky but effective method of disposing of enemies, as is the natural outcome to mixing positive and negative planes. I would hope that they never have to attempt something so dangerous like that, though it is possible to pull off."

Spira and Nephvir tensed at Gihon's words, sheepishly nodding in agreement.

"You mentioned the planes of fire and water having a similar reaction, but fire and water present on the material plane don't have such a reaction," Lylia pondered aloud.

"Only through the purest forms of their respective planes would they have a violent response. In Spira and Nephvir's example, they directly borrow from the planes for their weaponry. Water on Tevus is different from water on the aquatic plane; material water is closer to neutral in form, which is why water can extinguish a flame without a drastic exothermic reaction," Gihon explained.

Lylia nodded in understanding, Thorne looking a bit lost at the Dirigent's teaching from where he stood beside his elven partner.

"Limbus energy, my specialty, is the one type of energy that is neither positive nor negative. Limbo is the only true neutral that exists, being from a place of eternal in-between." Gihon continued. "It works similarly to a carrier oil. Imbuing Limbo into other types of energy will extend and amplify the positive or negative abilities. It is dangerous when mistreated, and Solomon decided to steal a little bit of my limbus energy before he left just now. That is a move I have never seen him pull before, and I am concerned about what it may result in."

"He could use the limbus energy to amplify whatever it is he's trying to accomplish," Spira realized. "What is he trying to do?"

"He mentioned wanting a soul, and opening the Gates of Heaven," Edelein commented.

Spira's face dropped as she turned towards Gihon. "Like

The Man in Red

Othalgar?"

"Yes, like Othalgar, but now with two leyline crystals and a sword full of limbus energy," Gihon confirmed. "That's enough power to backlash a quarter of the continent, easily. This is the exact reason why Solomon has been barred from entering Limbo."

Edelein looked at Gihon, puzzled by the connection. Sensing her confusion, Gihon elaborated.

"Solomon's obsession with Ethereus. Limbo, serving as a space between life and death, contains what we refer to as the Stairway to Heaven. A direct path to Ethereus itself. If a homunculus were to gain access to Limbo, opening the Stairway could blow a hole in the limbus plane so large that our entire world could fragment as annihilation events spring up across the universe, leading to the untimely demise of all existence as we know it. The Gates of Heaven risk our plane only, but the Stairway risks everything."

"Why did he cure Queen Edelein, if it just means we can hunt him down faster? There's no way we won't find him before he can get to this Gate. His plan isn't going to work," Zander added curiously.

"Solomon wanted Eddie to be cured," Alett realized. "It was a setup from the start. Solomon had fully planned on everything that happened; getting the location from Zander to make him think that Solomon would be the one going there... he *wanted* us to find him. Everything he did was a diversion. The cure meant we would be guaranteed to intercept him before he reached the safehouse, effectively keeping *us* away from the house long enough to allow for a strike team to take on our divided forces. He's brilliant."

"Do not grant Solomon the praise of intelligence. He is insane. Although, I must admit, curing an enemy as a distraction is a powerful move that could have an ulterior motive even beyond this, so we must be cautious going forward." Gihon adjusted his cloak, looking around the forest as the setting sun bathed it in a red glow.

"We need to rest briefly," Gihon concluded. "Tend to your wounds and sleep in warm beds tonight. Tomorrow, we will set out after Solomon. It will be back to camping for us, to remain hidden. Would that be alright, Your Majesty?"

"Approved. I can track his movements quite easily now that the blight does not dull my senses. With Thorne's winds and my hunting, Solomon will be easy to find. In the meantime, let us continue to rotate guard shifts and include patrols in nearby areas," Edelein replied, facing ahead as she led the group forward.

Following after her, Gihon continued, "I will explain more about the Gates of Heaven as well. As I mentioned, Solomon has attempted this once before. I think that is a story you should know, to better illustrate what we are fighting against."

CHAPTER 16

HOME

Gihon's face dropped the moment his home came into view. The front garden was destroyed, stones from the walls littering the ground. An oversized decapitated shark-man stained the grass beneath him with dark blood, a foul odor of decaying fish filling the air.

Strewn about inside were academic papers, bits of broken glass, and wooden splinters from shattered furniture. Blood stained the carpet of both ally and enemy alike, leaving Gihon's once-pristine private estate unrecognizable.

On what remained of a sofa, Everett winced as he sat up, his torso and head bandaged in several places. Jana stood as her master entered the room, bowing politely to him.

"Master Gihon, you're alright!" Jana smiled, relieved. "I'm so sorry about the house, Everett and I were going to clean it up, but he's still… well, Everett took a lot of damage. I've tended his wounds, but he needs rest."

"I don't need to," Everett denied. "I'm feeling way better already, I swear."

"I'm just relieved that you all are alive," Gihon sighed. "Jana is correct. Anyone who is injured, please continue to rest. I will handle the cleanup. Is the thing out there in my garden the creature that did all of this?"

Jana nodded.

"We killed him, but I haven't had the time to remove the body yet. There's five cultists upstairs as well. I'm so sorry, Master Marleogne."

Gihon stepped back outside, Luthro in tow as he approached the homunculus to assess its form. Everett followed behind them, fidgeting slightly but desperate to contribute. From his expression, Gihon could tell that the zoa was being hard on himself for losing the fight.

"Everett, I said you should rest," Gihon reiterated.

"I'm alright. I've been laying down for a bit, and I want to help. That guy is pretty big, so you'll need someone like me to lift him."

Gihon eyed the homunculus' corpse curiously as he squatted down to investigate it.

Touching the colorful rags tied around Vepar's waist, Gihon blinked in surprise as he recognized the patterns.

There have been reports of several maritimers going down in the waters outside of Velkhamore, some even as far as halfway across the ocean from here to Avalstice. These tattered pieces were once flags from those ships. This thing is what's been sinking them, and wearing their colors as a trophy. I should expect nothing less from a creation of Solomon's.

"This creature is massive and far from human, somewhat amphibious in nature. Solomon appears to be experimenting with animal DNA, creating a zoa-homunculus of sorts, with no regard to the regulations against aquatic transmutation. I cannot tell how this beast was even alive. Solomon's trying to play God, it seems." His eyes darted to the large anchor denting the ground next to him. "Was this anchor his weapon?"

Everett nodded. "Yes, sir. That thing weighed a ton, even for me. My weapon's a little worse for wear because of it."

"Honestly, it's impressive you're alive at all after going up alone against something like this. Nephvir was speaking the truth when he called it a monster."

"We've taken down bigger ones back home in the Deepwood. It's just... they usually aren't intelligent. You can't be a meathead and a battle strategist. That's not fair," Everett sighed, wincing in pain.

"We were hoping to remove the body before you returned. I know it's... unsightly." Jana admitted as she caught up to the others in the yard. "Everett could lift it if it wasn't a risk of opening more wounds. My potions are taking a little bit longer to work through his body due to its... density."

"Ha, she called you dense!" Thorne laughed from the doorway as Everett gasped in realization.

"No, I mean that in a literal sense. Everett's mass is incredibly dense, meaning he has a lot of muscle packed into his body. The average humanoid creature has a muscle ratio of around forty percent; but Everett's a bull zoa. Bovines contain a higher density upwards of sixty percent, which is why Everett's body is so thick. It's impressive." Jana spared a quick glance over Everett's shirtless, bandaged torso, eyeing the muscles she spoke of.

"Oh, I'm an ox, not a bull," Everett corrected.

Jana paused, a complex look on her face as she tried to process his words. After a moment, she spoke softly.

"Do you not have... um..." Jana trailed off, blushing and looking away as she realized she was prying too much.

Everett looked down at the tiny fellborn, clearly confused.

"W-Well, I mean… in Caandemium, an ox… wait, Everett, what is the difference between an ox and a bull in Zenluve?" Jana asked sheepishly.

"Oxen are made to work in trade jobs, and bulls aren't. Bull zoa are more aggressive and forward, but ox zoa tend to be harder workers. Normally, a male bovine Zengarde would be a bull, but I actually come from a family of blacksmiths, which is why Smith is my surname. Men in my family have always been oxen and not bulls," Everett explained.

"How do you reproduce if you're all oxen?" Jana blurted out before covering her mouth in shock.

"W-what? Like anyone else does, I guess," Everett laughed nervously, his cheeks turning red.

Luthro sighed loudly, the secondhand embarrassment consuming him as he stepped in to save his classmate.

"In Caandemium, oxen are castrated to dull their hormones and allow them to better focus on their work," Luthro stated bluntly.

Thorne let out a loud guffaw, pointing at Everett.

"She thought you didn't have any stones, man!" Thorne exclaimed, doubling over and clutching his midsection as he laughed.

Everett put together what Thorne and Luthro were saying after a long moment, his face dropping in dismay. Jana turned away in humiliation, silently cursing her curious mind as humiliation burned her ears.

"W-why would you do that to your oxen?" Everett stammered in horror, seeming to have already forgotten Luthro's explanation. "We don't do that in Zenluve. That's awful!"

Gihon cleared his throat, eager to change the subject as he attracted the attention of the others. "If I may ask you all to focus for a moment. Luthro, please come over here and remove the body."

The Man in Red

Luthro nodded, cracking his knuckles as he approached the corpse.

"Luthro? What's Luthro going to do?" Everett countered. "He's the smallest man here. I can take care of it. That's a job for a real man, not a little guy like him."

With an unenthused stare at Everett, Luthro sighed, "Have you forgotten what alchemists do, you big lug?"

Crouching down, Luthro placed his hands on the body with a grimace. An array formed underneath the body at the touch of his hand, glowing with a green light that illuminated Luthro's face through the dim twilight of the evening. Everett watched in awe as Luthro stood up, hoisting the large carcass over his shoulder. "Mass manipulation is my specialty, in case you've forgotten."

Gihon placed one hand down, willing the soil to shift and part as an array opened up the ground into a makeshift grave. Luthro dropped the shark-man into the hole, kicking his head in after like a ball. Twisting his hand the other way, Gihon's array closed the dirt over top of Vepar's lifeless corpse.

"You're just going to bury him in your yard?" Everett asked, a look of disgust on his face.

"Fish make for good fertilizer," Gihon shrugged. "and homunculi don't have souls to haunt with. Overall, it benefits me with little to no consequence."

I fear that the impression of us Caandemites we have left on Everett is subpar at best, Gihon sighed to himself as he stood up.

Luthro faced Everett, wiping his hands on his pants.

"You should be grateful that I used mass manipulation for you here. That thing felt *disgusting*."

As Luthro walked inside, Everett muttered to Thorne under his breath, "I thought that meant he was good at manipulating a lot of people at once, or something. What he just did is way cooler."

Ignoring him, Gihon turned his attention to Edelein, who

was leaning on one of the garden's stone walls behind him. For a moment, it appeared that she was breathing heavily, but she straightened up the moment Gihon turned to face her.

"How are you feeling?" Gihon asked, taking her arm and leading her inside to the broken sofa. She sat down with a huff, the Dirigent taking a seat next to her.

"I'm fine. Just a little winded from the battle, is all. Still upset that you didn't tell us about Solomon being your brother."

"You were connected into Fortress Black, which sapped a huge amount of energy from you. You need rest more than anyone else right now," Gihon's tone was soft and concerned, but Edelein continued to avoid meeting his gaze.

"I'll rest later. You said you had something to say about these Gates of Heaven, and I want to hear the whole story from you. If I find out you're omitting details again, I'll have you executed."

She definitely doesn't have the power to do that here, but I can tell she's upset. And I'd rather not fight all eight Zengarde at once, Gihon thought, tiredly rubbing his temple with one hand.

"Very well. It is important that you know this. All of you."

The Zengarde settled in around the room as Gihon began recalling the details of his past.

"Othalgar was once a very prosperous city, a trade hub in Northern Caandemium. It opened up connections between Caandemium and the far continent of Shuxing, granting access to Eastern medicines and herbs. Their resources were rich, the city teeming with inventors and scholars who dedicated their lives to academics and development. Their alchemy was focused on anti-draconic warfare during the Dragon War, and shifted to publicizing alchemy to the masses, as well as optimizing the quality of livestock experience, which in turn led to a near-perfect practice of zoa transmutation. Needless to say, the city was essentially a utopia of knowledge."

352

The Man in Red

A utopia of knowledge? Sounds like Gihon would have loved that place, then. That seems to be a recurring theme with these Caandemite city-states, Edelein thought to herself as the Dirigent continued.

"A long time ago, Solomon and I used to travel to Othalgar frequently with Arvien. What we failed to realize at the time is that Solomon found himself inspired by alchemical manipulation, and how the Othalgarians had a tendency to play God with their own animals. He thought he could perfect their practice, as a homunculus intentionally created to have a perfect form. This was where he had the idea to open the Gates of Heaven… within the city, so he could force a soul into his body to become truly 'perfect'. I attempted to stop him, telling him it was foolish, but his ego drove him to ignorance. He was missing the ethereal element of humanity itself, and his lack of true divinity is what kept the Gates closed.

His attempt to open the Gates was catastrophic, and the backlash it caused engulfed the entire city. However, the city was not blighted the way you are familiar with, as what happened in Zenluve. The entire city was frozen over as a necropolis, and the citizens were lost within time, neither dead nor alive, almost as if in a limbo of their own. The Society of Alchemists have worked hard to keep the truth of Othalgar under wraps, lest another alchemist get the bright idea to try to repeat his actions. The public simply thinks that Othalgar brought their fate upon themselves by pushing their alchemical research too far."

"You witnessed this happen?" Edelein asked. "You speak as if you were there. Would you not have also become trapped, as the others did?"

"When the backlash started, I only had a moment to react. I managed to grab Solomon and Arvien to protect them with an enhanced rampart shield. However, the others were lost within the backlash."

"Others?"

"We weren't alone. An old adventuring link of ours, we all gathered to try to stop Solomon, but we failed. They perished in the backlash. Somewhere in there, my friends remain. Whatever is left of them, that is."

"You've never returned to find them?" Edelein asked, tilting her head.

Gihon shook his head, eyebrows furrowed. "I want to help them, but getting into Othalgar is effectively impossible with the amount of security the Church has set up. Plus… it's not exactly easy on the heart or mind to waltz back into the place where you watched your own brother decimate thousands of people, including your friends, banishing them to a fate worse than death."

Edelein's gaze softened, and she put a reassuring hand on his arm. "That must have been horrifying. Solomon is attempting to do this again, now? Why would it be any different from the last time?"

"I have a few theories," Gihon said as he met her gaze for a brief moment, before looking back towards the others. "Two things are different about him now. One; he possesses the Divine Sword Kether, which could potentially give him the authority needed as a key to open the Gates."

Jinn's expression lit up in recognition at the words, looking over at Gihon from where he stood on the other side of the room.

"Back in the city, Solomon mentioned Kether to me. He called it one of the three nails that tethered the material plane to the ethereal plane."

"Solomon is correct. The three Divine Swords are heavily guarded by the Church after Ethereus was severed from Tevus. I wish I could tell you how he managed to steal one of them, or how he has been able to activate its full power. Last I had seen Solomon, Kether was nothing but a pristinely-kept blade in his hands. This newfound power of erasure is concerning," Gihon explained. "Solomon is not Kether's chosen hero, so he has found a way to brute force its power. My fear is that he is learning to do the same with the Gates of Heaven."

Edelein listened intently, nodding along.

"You think that Kether's full power can open the Gates, then?" Edelein asked.

"Not by itself, but that is why he wanted the leyline crystals," Gihon theorized. "With enough leyline energy, he could effectively force the Gates of Heaven to open. Think of the sword and the stones like a lockpicking set between us and Ethereus. Solomon can jam the sword in like a key, and then pry open the Gates with the condensed energy of your leyline."

Not to mention that move he pulled that consumed my limbus energy. Solomon is definitely plotting a way to force open the Gates, Gihon thought.

"Between Kether and the crystals, Solomon has dominion over the entire spectrum of the universe, making him as close to a god as a man can be," Alett theorized.

"Dangerous thinking, believing a man could become a god," Zander growled. "It will get him killed."

"It will get a lot more people killed if we let him go through with this. The issue is that the Gates of Heaven do not respond the way he thinks they will," Gihon explained.

"In a lot of ways, the most beneficial thing for us would be if Solomon's plan were to actually work, so it's unfortunate that it won't," Spira commented. "If everything goes the way he hopes for it to, Solomon would get a soul and stop being a chaotic asshole, and there wouldn't be a backlash if he did it right this time around."

"Spoken like an inquisitor of Prima Luma," Mandus chuckled. "You sound like your big sister."

"I suppose I've taken after her a bit," Spira admitted with a dry laugh.

Edelein stood up from the sofa, demanding the attention of both warriors and alchemists alike from their positions scattered around the room.

"Solomon's plan is entirely solid and clearly thought-out, other than the fact that you alchemists hold a different theory on how these Gates of Heaven function. The meticulous attention to detail on the homunculus' part puts us at a natural disadvantage," The Queen said with a tense sigh.

Luthro chimed in, eager as always to contribute.

"Solomon's advantage over people is that he constantly has tricks up his sleeve, utilizing his cunning nature to surprise unsuspecting foes of his. However, I theorize that he has just about played every card he has at this point. We know about the different types of homunculi, and we know his objectives. I believe we should take some time to orient the group and heal our wounds for now, and go at him freshly later on," Luthro explained.

"Luthro is correct," Gihon added, rising from the sofa to stand beside Edelein. "He has five homunculi—four, now—against eight Zengarde, six high-caliber alchemists, and Queen Edelein. We outnumber his main forces three-to-one. The cultists and that draekis man's clay figures are nothing but fodder."

Edelein counted on her fingers for a moment, before looking up at Gihon in confusion.

"Five? There's the mage woman, the lancer male, the summoner draekis, and the now-deceased shark… thing. That's four."

An awkward silence hung over the room as Gihon recalled the lioness zoa darting off with Solomon at the end of the fight. Nephvir and Alett exchanged an uncomfortable look, neither of them seeming to want to speak.

Edelein didn't see the homunculus clone of her. Should I…

The Man in Red

tell her? What if she finds it too unsettling? Gihon wondered.

"No matter, you simply miscounted," Edelein shrugged, breaking the silence. "Anyways, it seems that our journey is far from over. Will everyone be prepared to continue on tomorrow?"

Looking around the crowded room, Edelein's eyes scanned for any signs of disarray. The Zengarde were bristling anxiously, eager to return their crystals out of the hands of evil. The students were all clearly lost in thought, pondering potential courses of action. No one seemed severely injured aside from Everett, but fatigue hung heavy in the air around them all.

"Great, so we move out tomorrow at first light," Edelein finished, standing up. "Dismissed, everyone. Go get some sleep."

"Thank goodness we get to stay here tonight," Cari moaned, slumping into an armchair. "I'm exhausted."

Nora looked at Cari, and then at Gihon.

"Should we help clean up?" Nora asked.

Cari froze, betrayal in her eyes as she glared at the young student.

"Anyone who is able-bodied right now is welcome to help me with restoring order to my house. However, your rest is the top priority," Gihon stated.

Grateful, Cari slumped deeper into her chair. Beside her, Lylia was approaching Jana, taking a seat between her and Everett as she began to assess her ally's injuries.

"Save your magic, Lylia," Jana offered. "My potions will work just as well, it just takes a little longer. You need to preserve your healing for our travels tomorrow."

Lylia glanced down at Jana, and then at Everett. The ox nodded in agreement, putting an assuring hand on the elf's shoulder.

"Alett and I are stable for now. You go relax, Lylia," Everett confirmed.

"You know, I'm glad you didn't die," Thorne chuckled,

sitting on the floor beside the others. "Alett, you too. Getting stabbed probably sucks."

"Yeah, yeah. It'll take more than that to kill me," Alett laughed.

"Jana," Spira called from the other side of the room, "I'm going upstairs with Luthro to get rid of the bodies. Can you come help us clean up?"

Jana nodded, rising to her feet.

"Thank you, Jana," Everett smiled brightly as she got up to leave. "You guys saved my life."

"D-don't mention it," Jana blushed, turning and hurrying up the stairs with the other alchemists.

Mandus leaned on the wall, watching Jana leave. He glanced at Everett and the stairwell where Jana had been, finally looking back at Everett before speaking.

"Jana definitely likes you," Mandus laughed playfully, like a schoolboy teasing his friends. "I've never seen her act like that before."

Thorne gasped, punching Everett's shoulder affectionately as Alett let out a small giggle. The ox zoa furrowed his eyebrows, confused.

"I think she's just being nice. I don't think she likes me like that."

"You are all such children. I'm going to go help the others," Lylia sighed, getting up from her seat and going upstairs. "Yell for me if your pain comes back."

Edelein suppressed a smirk, exhaling sharply.

"I am going to retire for the evening," Edelein announced, her warriors nodding and saluting as their Queen turned away.

As Edelein walked out from the main living room into the battered hallway, broken paintings and shattered glass decorating the floor, a warm hand clasped around her wrist. The lioness stopped, turning around, her gaze met Gihon's.

"I know you're upset about my relationship to Solomon, and I wanted to apologize again," Gihon spoke quietly as he dipped his head in a polite bow. "I can assure you a thousand times over, I have not viewed him as a brother in years. He's a pathetic stain on the Marleogne family tree, better left forgotten. It was not my intention to deceive you."

"I know," Edelein responded, looking away. "I overreacted. I just can't help but feel that time and time again that you are lying to me, and I do not take kindly to liars. I... do know it isn't your intention, though."

"I've had to deal with all of this alone for the last decade, so sharing personal information does not come easily to me. My family has always been very... private, if you will," Gihon revealed with a sigh. "I'll do better."

Edelein nodded, grateful.

"How is your blight, then?" Gihon asked, his voice growing soft. "Will you be able to continue onwards?"

"I would never send my men somewhere that I myself am not willing to go," Edelein huffed, tail flicking. "I thought you would have learned that by now."

"Oh, I've learned that, alright," Gihon chuckled gently. "You're stubborn. I just had to check."

A beat of comfortable silence landed between them as they gazed at each other, a rosy tint on the Queen's cheeks as her piercing blue eyes met Gihon's warm gold ones. After a moment, Edelein spoke her thoughts aloud.

"Have you ever thought about coming to Zenluve?" Edelein asked, averting her gaze again.

Gihon blushed, feeling the tips of his ears redden.

"I... I have, yes," Gihon admitted. "I would love to experience your culture in person. The thought of being the first

Crown of the Alchemist

Caandemite to visit your people, to take account of my experiences to bring home to the Society... it excites me, if I'm being honest."

"You do always think about work before all else, don't you?" Edelein replied dryly. "I never said I wanted you to take account of your experiences. In fact, I thought I made it very clear that I do not want the Society knowing about the inner workings of my kingdom."

"I mean, I would love to visit you and the Zengarde, personally. I suppose I thought that was a given," Gihon replied.

"Ever so studious. Zenluve will always be open for you and your students. I will ensure a royal treatment for any alchemist that visits."

"Even Torphus?"

"No, not him. That dwarf was incredibly prejudiced against our people, though he thought he was hiding it," Edelein huffed, ears flat as Gihon laughed. "I mean you and your students. Though, I will admit in confidence to you that I have been considering the potential future of a relationship between your people and mine. If the crystals are returned and peace is restored, I may consider a culture exchange with a select few alchemists in Zenluve. For you. I know that would improve your reputation with your cohorts at the Society."

"I would be honored. After all of this blows over, I think I would like to take you out for some tea before you return home. It is the least I could do, to thank you for your time."

Edelein froze at Gihon's response, cheeks flushed.

"Are you asking to court me?" Edelein whispered after a long moment.

"Perhaps. I'm... not entirely sure of it myself, to be honest. I just know that I'd like to share a cup of tea with you one day, possibly followed by dessert."

Edelein didn't respond, but her flicking tail betrayed her

eager thoughts to him.

From how she reacted the first night at the Grand Bazaar, I had a theory that she had an affinity for sweets. Her body language confirms it, Gihon thought, looking down at her tail as it swayed back-and-forth.

"Don't you have any tea here?" Edelein spoke up after another long moment.

"Excuse me?"

"This is your house. I mean, I know that it got a bit… destroyed, but you seem like the type of man to have a whole cupboard full of exotic loose-leaf teas."

Damn. She read me like a book.

"I do," Gihon admitted.

"You said you wanted to share tea with me one day. Why not now? Are you worried about the Zengarde being around?" Edelein teased, nudging him.

"I-I suppose it would be of no issue to have them here."

As another sharp pain throbbed in Gihon's chest, his mind began to race.

Why would it be an issue to have the Zengarde present? It's just tea. Tea with the Queen. I'm just furthering the bonds between her people and mine, that's all. This is all a part of the job.

Turning back down the hallway, Gihon paced quickly into the kitchen as Edelein followed closely behind. Opening up a tall cupboard, the Dirigent began to sift through dozens of clear glass jars filled with dried botanicals.

"What type of tea do you prefer, Edelein?" Gihon asked, his face buried in the cabinet to hide his fluster. "I'll make it for you, right now. We can enjoy tea together."

"You're being weird," Edelein commented. "You've made me tea before, the day Mandus and the others arrived. Is this different in some way?"

Gihon froze, thinking.

Is it different? Am I trying to court Edelein? Is this what courting is supposed to be?

"No, it's not different," Gihon replied after a moment's hesitation, straightening himself up as he procured a single jar from the shelf. "My apologies."

Edelein eyed him curiously as Gihon handed her the jar, noting his sudden change in demeanor as he started a kettle of water, his tone and posture stiff.

"This is a delightful red tea, imported straight from Tozepia. It has been my personal favorite for awhile. It has a nutty and full-bodied flavor, quite aromatic, and pairs nicely with sweets. I sometimes serve it with a touch of cream and sugar, similar to Caandemite black tea. It is naturally caffeine-free, like Avalstan teas are," Gihon explained in a flat and instructional manner, though his eyes were still alight with passion.

"You really do know your tea, Dirigent," Edelein sniffed the jar, nodding in approval and handing it back to him. "You are correct about Avalstan teas lacking caffeine, as most brews are considered herbal. You noticed that I do not care for caffeinated drinks?"

"It was a hunch, but I had a feeling. I really do love this tea, though, and I think you will as well," Gihon confirmed, removing his kettle from the stove as it began to whistle and steam.

Pouring the hot water into a teapot filled with the dried red leaves, the Dirigent placed two tea settings outside at a small iron table, in the backyard where Jinn and Zander were sparring. Nephvir was sitting in the grass a stone's throw from the two, nose buried in his notebook.

As Edelein sat down, she looked over at Jinn and Zander with a soft sigh.

"Will you two give it a rest for a bit? You'll need your

energy for tomorrow," Edelein called, both men stopping and turning to face her.

"Our skills must stay honed in the event of the man in red's return," Jinn stated, ears twitching.

"I still have a bit of energy left over. Solomon and his forces are weak when it comes to actual combat. They just use tricks instead of fighting like men," Zander agreed.

Defeated, Edelein sighed again as the Zengarde continued to spar. Gihon sat down next to her, pouring the tea and chuckling at her expression.

"He certainly won't be coming back here. He has what he wants, and now his objective will be to put as much distance between himself and us as possible," Gihon concluded, eyeing Edelein as she took a sip of his recommended beverage.

Edelein's face lit up in delight, tail flicking as she relished in the nuanced hints of cream and sugar that Gihon had promised. The Dirigent had mastered the ratio, only putting enough in to enhance the flavor of the tea without overpowering it.

"So how do we find him, then?" Edelein asked, setting down her cup. "Are we planning to rely on blind tracking again? That did not work out well for us previously, need I remind you."

"That won't be necessary," Gihon looked at her curious expression as he continued, "I know where he's going. Taking the second leyline crystal confirmed my theory, assuming he's planning to use leyline energy to power the array. There's a significant leyline in Caandemium, certainly several times smaller than the one in the Deepwood, but it's the largest one we have. It's protected by a thick swampland south of here. Fortunately for us, it's not too far away."

"Hearing that you have a leyline in Caandemium not unlike ours is quite surprising. A swamp, though? On a list of biomes I would prefer to travel through, I must admit that a swamp would most likely be on the bottom of my list. "

"It's worse than that. The swamp is… well, that should be a story that I share with everyone, not just you. It's incredibly dangerous, and filled with deadly monsters."

"Great. That sounds like a wetter, grosser version of home. We will head there in the morning," Edelein said with a smile, encouraging the Dirigent. "Where is it?"

"Ravencroft. My hometown."

Thank you so much for stepping into the world of Tevus.

The story will resume with book two, so keep in touch via social media for updates and reveals.

Find us everywhere @bluandgihon or on Twitter/X as @BGLyrax. Visit us at bluandgihon.com for more. All links can be found on our website or by checking out bluandgihon.carrd.co.

You can read the webcomic version of Crown of the Alchemist for free by going to cota.bluandgihon.com/read or visiting lyrax.carrd.co.

Join our Discord community to share your thoughts about the story and connect with the Lyrax team! Link to join the fun is at cotawebtoon.carrd.co and/or lyrax.carrd.co.

If you are enjoying the Crown of the Alchemist series, please let us know by leaving a 5-star review and sharing with your friends.

Much love,
B.G. Lyrax

To my mom, who always told everyone I would be a writer
one day.
Thanks for believing in me.

To all my friends who have supported this journey from the
day I first brought up the cool idea I had.

And most importantly, to the other half of the Lyrax team,
my incredible and supportive husband. I love you.

I love all of you.

Finally, a huge thank-you to our Patrons who have supported our journey. There's been a lot of ups and downs from the day we first started to where we are now, and your support means the world to us.

If you'd like to receive exclusive benefits including extra short stories in the COTA world setting, supplementary reading, private AMA events with the creators, digital wallpaper downloads, and more, you can join today at

www.patreon.com/LYRAX